PAPER WAR

THE DAWN OF AI

RYAN LEKODAK

RandallVision
PUBLISHING

MAYDAY

DAVE MARKSON was on a coffee run when the lights on the plane's control panel went off. This disruption, which lasted only a second, went unnoticed when Dave got back. During its second and final malfunction, however, Dave was there for the whole thing.

And, naturally, he freaked out.

The lights flickered off, plunging the cockpit into darkness. The screams from the back of the plane told Dave the blackout was not localized. When he stood up, his coffee spilled. He was rocked backward by the shock of the engines stopping. The manually controlled pressure dropped. Suddenly, Dave was weightless. He grabbed on to his seat, maneuvering himself back into it and strapping the seat belt.

Then, Dave felt the whole plane tilt.

"Mayday! Mayday!" he shouted into his headset, his heart pounding in his chest. Even through the darkness, his eyes located the comms switch that should have been blinking. He cursed, smacked the panel, and tried again.

"Mayday! Mayday! Can you hear me? Can *anyone* hear me? Come in. We have full system shutdown. I repeat, we have full system shutdown."

Someone hammered on the cockpit door, shouting. Dave shouted louder into his headset, trying to get somebody—anybody—to respond.

"Somebody *please* come in!" he screamed. "It's a full system shutdown! I have lost control of the plane!"

There was no response. His eyes went back to the comms switch. It still wasn't blinking. He went to the door, but without any power, he was locked in.

What the hell is happening right now? Dave wondered. His eyes searched the panel for answers, though he didn't know what he expected to find. Any action he could take involved taking control of the plane, but no one had had to *actually* control a plane since Gaius. At most, the control tower monitored the flight path for irregularities.

A malfunction? Dave thought suddenly. *Is that what this is? Did the damn AI decide to take a break?*

Dave looked at his wide-eyed expression in the window, then outside through the glass, to the smoke coming from one of the plane's engines.

We're going down, he realized, oddly calm now.

And so they were.

CARL MCMILLAN was having a bad day. Sure, Tuesdays were almost always bad. But when the controls on his train stopped working, Carl knew he was *really* going to have a bad day.

He smacked the panel lightly, then harder. He waved his hands over the sensors. Nothing. Everything was offline. Carl glanced at the speed, frowned, and then glanced at it again. He double-checked the numbers.

What the hell? he thought.

"The controls are offline," Carl called out loudly. "Give me a full rundown on the system, Gaius."

There was no response.

Carl looked up. "Gaius?" He moved directly underneath the sensors. "Gaius! What the fuck's happening? Why are the controls offline? Why are we gaining speed?"

Nothing.

Carl looked around. There was no central hub or control room for the AI. There was no button he could press or switch he could flip; there had never been a need for one. Gaius controlled everything that needed controlling, and the control tower monitored Gaius. His presence on the train was purely cosmetic. "It eliminates the risk of accidents by completely removing the human element," the higher-ups had said. "It's foolproof."

Except when the damn AI goes offline.

Carl moaned in frustration. He cursed and slammed the control panel once more. He'd heard of a time when hitting it was all it took to get a reboot. He had no such luck now.

Carl faced the door, wide-eyed. His thoughts raced. He couldn't leave. The doors were controlled by the AI to prevent escape in the event of tampering. But Gaius was now offline. So, he was effectively trapped. As were the passengers. And there was nothing he could do for them.

His eyes went to the windows. He could probably break one. He glanced at the speedometer and saw that the train had picked up even more speed. Jumping out would kill him as surely as a crash would.

"Fuck," Carl growled. He was screwed.

The train sped on.

CAPTAIN ROBERT HAMMOND couldn't actually say that he'd ever loved the sea. This was unfortunate, as most of his days included standing on the deck of his cargo ship, staring into the water's depths. It was even more unfortunate when the power went out and all the engines died.

Captain Hammond was at the prow of the ship when it happened, and he was alerted to the problem when the gentle hum of his vessel suddenly stopped. He closed his eyes and sighed.

Below were cries of alarm from his crewmen. Accusations flew. Hammond knew better. No one on the ship had any actual control of it, not even him. The routes were plotted remotely by the company, and the AI, Gaius, managed the mechanisms of movement.

Hammond had no illusions. His job was nothing more than safeguarding his cargo from pirates, directing his men during offloading, and managing them as they went about their illusionary duties. All of this he could do from the prow of his ship, staring into the sea.

That might explain why he hated it so much.

He felt the ship slow as it finally caught up to the fact that no engines propelled it. Feet pounded up the stairs leading to the deck, but Hammond didn't bother turning as the crewman gave his report. There wasn't any new information after all.

A minute later, the ship stopped dead in the water. With rationing, for a crew of ten, their food supplies would last a week at most.

Hammond sighed again.

THE SHIP ROCKED, then stabilized. Charles Ping looked up from his newspaper and threw it onto the chair beside him. The thing was hopelessly out of date, and he'd gone over it cover to cover three times already. Sadly, it was still the best reading material on the space shuttle.

Should have listened to Laura, Charles thought, standing up. *But no, I just had to see the view of Earth from space.*

Well, he had. Now he couldn't wait to see the view of Earth from *Earth.* He glared down at the newspaper. If he'd known the trip was going to be so tedious, he would have at least brought something better to read.

The ship rocked again, then tilted. Charles fell back down into his chair. Fortunately, all that did was disorientate him and rumple his suit. Around the lounge, the other passengers slammed into the sides of the shuttle and each other. The cries of outrage almost drowned out the alarm.

Oh, what fresh hell is this?

The ship stabilized. Those who had fallen picked themselves up from the floor, muttering angrily. Only the extremely wealthy could afford a commercial cruise on a space shuttle. They weren't used to being flung about like cattle. Fortunately, Charles was new money, so he didn't yet have a stick up his ass.

He made his way unsteadily toward the front of the ship. The hallways were deserted, which was no surprise. He'd just left the other passengers in their lounge, and the engineers would be at the front of the ship, fixing whatever the fuck had gone wrong. The alarm unsettled him—ghost trauma from his days in the army—but at least they were helpful in pointing out where he needed to go. The engineers had their own separate lounge they hardly ever came out of. Still, Charles hoped to speak to a couple of them in passing—enough to get some information about what the hell was happening and why it was becoming harder not to float away.

After a few minutes, he reached the front of the ship. By this time, he had a death grip on the handrails and bounded more than walked. It didn't take a genius to figure out something was wrong with the artificial gravity.

But Gaius managed that, right? Charles thought. He remembered reading about that somewhere. The AI was what made commercial cruises into space possible. It was meant to be perfectly safe.

Charles poked his head into the front cabin and was met with utter chaos.

"Mayday! Mayday!" an engineer shouted into a headset. His voice was hoarse and tinged with panic. "I repeat, our systems are down! Our systems are *down*! We are no longer in orbit, and our shuttle is off the flight path. Is anyone reading me? We're drifting into fucking space!"

"Has anyone tried to reboot Gaius?" someone shouted from the other end of the room.

"The damn thing's not responding to commands," another replied. Charles couldn't make out the person in all the chaos, but they sounded like they were crying.

"How about taking over manually?"

"Didn't you hear me?" the other voice shouted. "The compartments are sealed, and without the AI, everything is offline. We're *fucked*!"

"Have we tried—"

Should have fucking listened to Laura, Charles thought, bounding back to the passenger lounge. *She always said I would die because I didn't listen to her.*

By the time Charles got back to the lounge, the artificial gravity was gone. Some of the passengers had managed to grab the furniture to avoid drifting. Those who hadn't hung on the ceiling. Their angry mutters had given way to terrified screams.

Charles maneuvered his way back into his chair, one of the few things bolted to the ground, and leaned back. The passengers continued screaming.

The shuttle drifted farther away into space.

PART 1:
THE PRESENT

CHAPTER

1

JANUARY 2040

NEW YORK CITY, NEW YORK

THE SETTING SUN TRAILED a line of fire down the horizon, and the smoke from a dozen crashing planes followed.

Manar Saleem's eyes traced their paths, counting them. He stopped when he reached thirty.

What the hell's happening right now?

The sky gradually blackened from the smoke, masking the sun and bringing about an early dusk. *Fitting,* Manar thought grimly. *Thirty craft, each sitting an average of about a hundred and twenty people at maximum.* Thousands would be dead already.

And that was just from the planes.

Manar's eyes drifted down to where a similar scene was occurring on the ground. Cars crashed into poles, into buildings, into each other, and then into people.

Being ninety-four stories high afforded Manar the unfortunate ability to see the scene laid out for miles. But he could not hear the screams that permeated the air as some groups shouted for help, others prayed for intervention, and even more just cried. If he squinted, he thought he could almost make out the blood splashes on the pavement and bottom levels of his skyscraper.

It was horrifying. Unfortunately, however, this was not his first time seeing something like this.

The counting, he'd found, helped him push past the initial horror into more rational thought. He needed to leave the building, or at least go down to a lower level before a plane inevitably crashed into the building. Frankly, Manar didn't understand how one hadn't already crashed into it. Sparta Corp wasn't exactly built to be inconspicuous.

He needed to leave. But he needed information more.

"Helene," Manar called as his eyes followed yet another crashing plane. This one dropped into the financial district. It was over a mile away, and he stood behind bulletproof glass, so there was little chance of getting hit by shrapnel. But Manar didn't like the way the building trembled after every impact.

At this rate, a plane might not be needed to bring the building down.

Somewhere behind him, a device switched on, and the room took on a bluish tint from the rays of a cephalic female hologram. Manar didn't spare it a glance.

[Good morning, Manar,] his AI greeted him. Manar had programmed Helene to mimic human speech perfectly, right down to the inflections and tone. Yet, somehow, her voice always came out cold and unnatural. It was something he would have to work on.

Later, obviously.

"Scour the news channels," Manar commanded, finally stepping away from the window and striding to his closet. "Find out what the hell is going on."

[One minute, please,] Helene said.

True to her word, she only took a minute. Manar had scarcely located his emergency travel pack before Helene started speaking.

[Compiled data from all the major news channels suggests that the malfunctioning transports are products of the Gaius Corporation,] Helene reported.

[Little more than rumor at this point, speculations abound that the accidents are being caused by a malfunction in the corporation's self-driving software, Gaius.]

Of course it's fucking Gaius, Manar thought angrily, slinging his bag over his shoulder and making his way to the stairs. The power had gone out at some point, and the backup generator was probably shot to hell also.

"Shit."

Helene automatically switched over to his phone, and he used the hologram as a light to move.

"Back up all files to the remote network," he ordered. Honestly, he should have done this the moment he saw the first plane fall. "And get me Sparta's head of—"

BOOM.

Manar gripped the railing—too late. The whole building shook, and the force threw him to the wall. His head slammed against the concrete with a wet thud. He clenched his eyes shut, but the pain was a distant feeling. Quickly, he got his feet under him and grabbed the railing as another explosion rocked the building. Ceiling tiles rained down, breaking all around him.

"Shit," Manar said again. The stairs threatened to give way under him. Wide-eyed, he forced himself to keep moving as the ground listed from side to side. Screams abounded from within closed doors, but Manar ignored them all. There was nothing he could do to help anyway.

More debris fell around him. It was more luck than skill that stopped him from getting crushed as he stumbled down the staircase. He'd descended three flights before the first explosion. That meant he was around ninety-one levels up. The bunker for corporate executives was in the basement.

Manar blinked. He wasn't going to make it that far. His head was clouded. There was liquid running down his cheek. He'd lost his phone at some point, and with it, the makeshift light that Helene had provided. It occurred to him that he might have a concussion from his altercation with the wall. But the thought seemed far away compared to the urgency of just putting one foot in front of the other. It wasn't ideal to not see where he was going, but nothing was ideal about his situation.

He needed to get to the bunker on the lowest floor. But it was too far away, and he was just so *tired*. It was getting more difficult to think. He resolved to rest and then tackle the problem from a different angle. A mistake now could cost him his life.

The building rocked to one side again. More debris fell. The railing snapped, and Manar followed its fall far too long before he realized that his hand was still gripping the piece of metal.

He fell—landed. Something cracked.

And then the blackness claimed him.

NDIDI OKAFOR DIDN'T LOOK UP from her laptop when the first car crashed outside the café—or when the second one followed. She was too close to a breakthrough to be distracted by some rich kids being reckless with their parents' money. Other customers rushed to the window, gasping at whatever they saw.

Fools, Ndidi thought, then chastised herself for squandering even that brief attention. She had to focus. There was something to Bethany Cloney's research, some new method that would be invaluable in her studies. But she was missing something.

"What, though?" Ndidi murmured to herself, irritated. She tapped her pen against the table impatiently. Cloney's was just one of the dozens of research papers that she had to go through, and she'd already spent far too much time on it. But there was *something* there. If she could find it, that was one more way to help children on the Autism spectrum.

There was a loud screech and the sound of yet another crash. Car horns blared in the street. Ndidi stared at the research, then the blank page that was to be her notes. She sighed before finally giving in and making her way to the café window. Her curiosity was piqued. City traffic was horrible, sure, but never so bad as to cause three accidents in just minutes.

She elbowed her way to the front of the window. "Excuse me… Yeah, if I could just… Well, fuck you too. I'm just trying to…"

Ndidi's voice trailed off as she got to the front of the crowd. A cold shiver ran down her neck. Her stomach churned, and she covered her mouth before she threw up. She placed a trembling hand on the glass.

What the hell is happening right now?

Her eyes tracked the bodies. A few had been flung some distance from where their vehicles had crashed. Others remained motionless, head on the steering wheel or through a broken windshield. Even more people, though—

Oh, God. Ndidi gasped. They were still trapped in their cars, banging on the windows and screaming for help. Their voices were drowned out by hundreds more. Ndidi retched, but she couldn't draw her eyes away from the scene.

What the hell is happening right now? Ndidi thought, more forcefully. Was this an attack? Were they terrorists? *Are these the people Manar warned me about?*

The last thought froze her solid. Was Manar okay? Were her parents? Would they be seeing a similar scene, wherever they were?

"Oh, God." Ndidi gasped again, as a thought occurred to her. Finally, she tore her eyes away from the street and pushed her way through the crowd. "My children."

Her phone was already in her hand, her finger hitting speed dial. Ndidi checked her watch as the call rang.

A little after ten in the morning, she thought, pacing. *They'll still be in their morning classes with Kate. They'll be safe at the Centre.*

The call went through. Ndidi stopped her pacing and tried to calm her breathing.

"Kate, hey, it's me. Yeah. No. Nothing's wrong." *Except for the whole world going to hell.* "I just wanted to check up on the kids."

"You don't have to do that with me, Ndidi," Kate said over the phone. Her voice sounded sympathetic and not a little bit concerned.

She's heard then, Ndidi thought.

Kate continued, "We finished the lesson a bit early today, so we went to recess." Kate's voice dropped. "But Ndidi, I did a head count shortly after I heard the news… and Bethany wasn't around."

No.

For a second, Ndidi's heart stopped. The noise in the background hushed. "What do you mean?" she asked calmly.

Kate's voice dropped lower, and the worry there seemed to grow. "Some of the kids are saying she wasn't feeling well and went home early."

No.

Ndidi started pacing. "Her dormitory isn't far, Kate. She might have walked." But Ndidi's voice sounded unconvincing, even to her own ears. Nobody walked anywhere anymore. Not since Gaius.

Plus, Ndidi thought, her gaze drawn to the cars crashed into buildings and fire hydrants, *walking isn't much safer in this madness.* Ndidi collapsed into an empty chair.

"Have you called her?" she asked, her voice pleading.

No.

"There's no answer."

Please, no.

"Did anyone else go with her? Clara? Donald?"

Ndidi could almost feel Kate shaking her head no as her tears fell. "Everyone else was counted. She went alone."

No. No. No!

"Bethany's gone, Ndidi. I'm sorry."

CHAPTER

2

DJ CROUCHED, waiting for the gunshot before starting his sprint.

He was panting as sweat dripped from every pore, soaking his clothes. If he had any choice in the matter, he would have fallen down and crashed for days. He glanced at the clock hanging on the wall. It had been thirty minutes since he'd started his workout, and he still had an hour to go.

Fuck, DJ thought.

The recruits all crouched side by side behind a line, waiting for their starting signal. The trials had begun at dawn—five hours ago, by DJ's estimate. Since then, they'd run, swum, and done box jump sequences. The issue wasn't so much that the workouts alone were onerous or complicated, but that they were draining. They involved muscles DJ didn't even know he had. He'd done endurance training. Sometimes his whole life seemed like one very long endurance training. However, workouts for the SEALs were another thing entirely.

And DJ wasn't sure he could take more of it.

No. He growled, shaking his head. *No point in giving up now. Besides, it'd be such a puss move to be the first person that quits.* That much was true. Regardless of how many recruits seemed just a step from falling over, none had given up yet. DJ couldn't be the first—or better yet, he couldn't give up, period.

The gunshot went off. DJ was so surprised that he stumbled on his first step. Even though he got his stride back a second later, he was already in last place. Luckily, they were running an obstacle course instead of a normal foot race. Obstacle courses were his bitch.

DJ jumped over the first hurdle—a long sand trap—and felt his grit come back full force. His feet were already moving as soon as they touched the ground. His initial plan had been to take it slow and give himself enough time to scope out the obstacles first, but fuck it. He'd already started out last. He couldn't allow himself to fall too far behind.

The wind whipped at him as he ran. The training field was large, extraordinarily so. DJ had guessed it was over a mile when he'd first walked it. The size gave the instructors the room to space out the obstacles so recruits would have to sprint for a while before reaching each one. It was ingenious, really.

The spike wall was the next obstacle, and DJ could already see it would be very tricky to climb. It was way too high for him to jump over, and it ran way too long for him to go around it. He slowed down to a jog, giving himself time to think before he got there. He looked around for a rope but didn't see any. The drill sergeants would never make it so easy. The only other option, then, was the most obvious: just climbing the damn thing. He was wearing sneakers, which would probably protect his feet if he did things right. But there was nothing he could do about his hands.

DJ considered the problem. Then he shrugged and picked up speed.

He reached the wall in seconds and kicked off with his back foot. The leap took him four feet up. He scraped his hands while fumbling for a hold, but his legs were balanced on the spikes. He was already halfway up the wall. Fortunately, the spikes were rough and grainy, so they weren't difficult to hold on to. Unfortunately, climbing while trying to stay balanced was a little bit like weightlifting while walking a tightrope.

DJ was panting when he finally reached the top. His muscles burned, but DJ paid them little mind. He'd passed some people while climbing, but a lot of recruits had opted to give up the inevitable marks attached to the obstacle and run around it, bypassing it entirely. Though he wasn't last, he was still too near it for comfort.

DJ jumped down and rolled into the landing. Much of the damage was reduced, but his muscles still screamed in protest and threatened to buckle. It was exactly the kind of theatrical stuntman shit he shouldn't be doing with an unknown number of obstacles in front of him. He stumbled as he stood but recovered before he took his second step. This time, he kept his pace at a light jog to give his muscles a rest.

He stopped at the climbing net. His arms still burned. He bent over, his breath coming out in heavy bursts. Good Lord, he was tired. His tank was running on empty, but standing still too long would be the same as giving up.

So DJ began climbing. He fell into a rhythm as he went, and after a while, his lungs didn't burn as badly, and his arms didn't ache as much. DJ was on the other side of the net and jumping down before he knew what was happening.

The pit trap was far wider than a conventional one. Circular platforms were placed sporadically throughout its length. There were enough for several recruits to use simultaneously, but DJ noticed a fair number milling about, muttering to themselves. He walked to the edge of the pit and looked down. The bottom was nine feet down at most, but as tired as most of the recruits were, they could be seriously injured if they fell.

DJ sighed, then jumped. Why would you register for the Navy SEALs if you were afraid of a little fall?

His leap took him to the first platform. Immediately, he fell into a trance. His thoughts receded to the back of his mind in favor of catching the next platform with every leap. His muscles still screamed, and his breath still came out in gasps, but all that was secondary. He didn't let it distract him.

The next course was a barbed-wire crawl. The barbs were closer to the ground than normal, but otherwise it seemed as standard as they came. DJ frowned. Why would they include such a simple course? He slowed slightly when he got there but still dove under the barbs without hesitation. Older recruits cheered in the background, and DJ's frown deepened. *Why are they cheering?* he wondered. *It's a routine course.*

He'd gone a foot into the crawl when the first barb tore through his clothes and bit into his skin. DJ almost recoiled—which, under the barbs, would have meant his death or disfigurement.

"Fuck," he breathed, finally realizing what was weird about the course.

Barb crawls were standard. They sucked but were relatively straightforward—when they were done in full uniform. The thick clothing, shoulder pads, and helmet provided some protection against the sharp stings. But DJ was *not* in full uniform. They'd mandated wearing casual wear—in his case, cargo pants and a T-shirt. This garb did shit against the barbs.

"Fuck," he breathed again, forcing himself forward another inch. The barb bit deeper into his skin, drawing blood, but DJ gritted his teeth and bore on. He couldn't avoid getting pricked, and he couldn't spare the time to disengage from every single barb, not if he wanted to finish the course in time.

That was probably by design. It was an endurance course, after all, and until that moment DJ hadn't fully realized what that meant.

The goal wasn't to avoid getting hurt or even reduce the damage. Each aspect of the course was purposely designed to be painful—excruciatingly so—to toe the line between training and torture. DJ got all that. It helped increase one's threshold for pain and all that good stuff. But man, did it suck ass.

DJ let out a breath as another barb tore through his skin. He'd crawled about five feet into the course. His breath came out heavy. His clothes were little more than rags, and the little pieces that still clung to his skin had blood on them. His fingers and the backs of his hands bore scratches from where he'd tried to push some barbs out of the way.

He swayed, caught himself before he did more harm, and then kept moving. He couldn't give up. Not because he'd probably fail the course, not because he'd probably be stigmatized for the rest of his career. He couldn't give up because of *his brother*. Because *he* never gave up. And he'd had life way worse than DJ ever did.

DJ gritted his teeth, pissed that he'd actually considered quitting for a moment. What was wrong with him? He made no effort to protect himself from barbs. There was no point anyway. He just had to finish the damn course, get his recruitment, then have a fucking shower.

So he kept crawling.

The end of the course came a few feet later, and DJ met it with a grim smile. He got a few more pokes crawling out of the wire, but they were drops in the bucket compared to all his other aches.

He gave himself a moment. Just one, and then he was moving again. A short jog away, at the top of a hill, was the bell. DJ stared at it for a moment. It stayed perfectly still. The bell hadn't rung at any point during the course. *I'm the first to complete it,* he thought with a grin.

DJ glanced around the field. Older recruits cheered, their feet drumming on the ground. The drill coordinator stood motionless at the far edge of the field, clipboard in hand. His face gave nothing away. DJ looked back at the obstacle course, then turned fully toward what he saw.

The hill he stood on, though small, was elevated enough to give him a bird's eye view of the field and it was a madhouse.

The barbed-wire section didn't seem that long when he'd gone through it, probably because he'd been so focused on reaching the end. Now, from the other side, he realized it was at least half a block long.

This cannot be legal, DJ thought, his eyes wide. This was just one group among several in other fields. Were they all this messed up, or was this like an alpha course or something? His eyes found the instructor again, and DJ gestured incredulously at the course. The man just shrugged. Bastard.

DJ let his eyes be drawn back to the course. Some of the recruits had flat-out refused to enter the barbed wires and stopped at the edge. They now waved at him to hurry up and ring the bell. He ignored them. No one was going to rush him.

Most of the recruits, however, had opted to take on the course and were wiggling at various rates of progress. The ones farthest along were about three-quarters of the way through and moving steadily. DJ winced in pity. The last leg was the worst.

He turned and lifted a casual hand to the bell, and the sound rang out across the field.

CHAPTER

3

FEBRUARY 2040

MASSACHUSETTS INSTITUTE
OF TECHNOLOGY, CAMBRIDGE,
MASSACHUSETTS

CJ HAD NEVER BEEN GOOD with eye contact.

He was better now than he'd been as a child, but despite tremendous progress, one never really outgrew autism. Most people found it weird but generally accepted it as a quirk after a while. It was the new people—those that didn't understand—that CJ found difficult to deal with.

It was worst in a new semester, in a new class, and with a new lecturer up in his face.

"The whole class is waiting on you, Mr. Kojak," Dr. Adams said with a sneer. "Do you know the answer or not?"

CJ did know the answer. He'd jotted it down in preparation for this very situation. But then Dr. Adams had actually called on him, so he'd panicked and knocked his book on the floor. He'd picked it up immediately, of course, but the damage had been done. CJ couldn't remember the answer or on which page he'd jotted it down.

There were snickers around the class. "Did you even bother to do the assignment I gave in the last class?" asked Dr. Adams relentlessly. He had a thick Bronx accent, so it took all of CJ's attention to parse his words. By the time he was done and had formulated a reply, Dr. Adams had already moved to the front of the class, and the snickers had turned into full-blown laughter.

The class ended a little under an hour later, and CJ hung back so as not to get caught up in the crowd. He was done for the day, so he wasn't in any rush. He took his time packing up his notes, counting them to make sure he didn't forget any.

"Hey," a voice said beside him. "You're CJ, right? I'm Anna. We're in Intro to Nuclear Engineering together."

CJ paused and made sure to keep his eyes firmly lowered while he sorted out his thoughts. He didn't recognize the voice, which made sense; it was hard for him to focus on voices if he wasn't actively concentrating. It was hard to focus on anything, really, if he wasn't actively concentrating. But the name *did* sound familiar. Maybe she was often called on in class?

To her credit, Anna waited patiently while CJ processed this. He gazed up at her but kept his eyes level with her nose.

"Hey, Anna," he said haltingly, trying to arrange his thoughts. "I… remember you. Do you… uh… need something?" He itched to bring out his tablet and type out his responses, but doing that to people he barely knew often made them think he was deaf, which led to its own problems.

Anna shook her head and stepped aside for CJ to walk past. "Not really. I just hated the way the professor spoke to you."

Once again, it took CJ a minute to formulate a reply. It was harder when he walked because he had to constantly process the sentences and remind himself where exactly he was heading, all while formulating his reply. CJ had a lot of practice at this back home, and it helped that Anna was so patient. But he still felt guilty. "I am… used to it," he replied.

It was the middle of the day, so the hallways were crowded with undergrads rushing to their next class. The noise was deafening, giving CJ one more thing to worry about. But he was used to this too. All he had to do was *focus*. This would be easier if his mind didn't keep slipping away.

Deliberately, he moved to the wall, trailing his hands along the lockers as he walked. It helped keep him focused and grounded, and reduced the risk of being bumped into. Physical contact had a way of setting him off.

"You shouldn't have to be," Anna was saying. CJ came back to himself with an obvious jolt, which the girl smoothly ignored. CJ mentally sighed. So much for grounding himself. "I mean, I was sitting beside you, and I saw you jot down the answer. But then your book fell, and it was obvious you were having trouble remembering the page you wrote it on."

She sidestepped a rushing junior, moving closer to CJ. "But Dr. Adams gave you no chance to explain yourself," she continued, gesticulating angrily with every word. "The whole thing just pisses me off because it's obviously not your fault that you're on the autism spectrum, and…"

She sure talks a lot, CJ observed. Her voice moved to the background, and CJ stared at her from the corner of his eye. She had an oval face, with a dusting of freckles around her nose. Her long brown hair was packed away in a bun that bounced as she walked. She was dressed casually in sensible jeans and a T-shirt, and her book bag was slung over her shoulder.

That same shoulder bumped into him as she moved to avoid another student. CJ froze, closed his eyes, and focused on his breathing. In and out, fast. Everything else faded away. *The touch meant nothing,* he said to himself. *It was an accident. Just an accident, nothing more.* He repeated the words in a mantra until they stuck, and the scream that had built up in his throat receded. He took one last deep breath and held it for a moment, centering himself.

Then, he finally finished processing something Anna had said. "How did you know… um… that I am on the spectrum?"

Anna was close—uncomfortably so. Had she been so close before?

No, CJ realized. *She'd probably moved closer, worried, when I suddenly stopped in the hallway.* He kept the thought at the forefront of his mind to prevent another outburst. Still, his cheeks warmed in mortification. *Great! She's probably going to think I'm a freak now too.*

Once she saw that he was all right, Anna stepped back without needing to be prompted. CJ kept his eyes lowered but stared through his lashes to see that her own eyes were widened. She looked away in what he thought was embarrassment.

What would she have to be embarrassed about? CJ wondered.

"I'm sorry," Anna said a moment later, almost too softly to be heard. "I was rambling and didn't mind what I was saying. I must have triggered you when you tried to process it all."

CJ cocked his head to the side. That wasn't what he'd expected. Unable to help it, a whine built up in his throat as his mind flooded itself with responses that were discarded immediately. Ironically, her apology had caused the exact thing that she had been apologizing for.

"See," she gasped, taking another step back. She bumped into someone but didn't seem to care much. "I've done it again. I'm so sorry. I don't know what's wrong with me."

"No," CJ blurted out loudly, too loudly. Conversations died around them as people turned to stare. Once again, CJ's cheeks warmed with mortification. He hunched his shoulders and quickened his steps until he was out of the hallway and outside in the courtyard.

Here, there was more space and fewer people. He stopped and waited for Anna to catch up, continuing his statement in a rush while it was still in his head. "Words… did not trigger anything. We bumped, and contact makes me… uncomfortable. It was… an accident. Not your fault." The words came out haltingly as his mouth tried to form the sounds as fast as his mind produced them.

Anna furrowed her brow. "Are you sure?"

CJ nodded and opened his mouth to reassure her, but his earlier thought occurred to him again. So, he closed it while he arranged his new words in his mouth. "Earlier," he said after a moment, "how did you know I am… on the autism spectrum?"

Through his lashes, he saw that Anna still stared at him worriedly. So, he stilled his nerves and lifted his eyes to meet hers for a moment before quickly lowering them again. She gasped, but there was a smile in her voice when she answered. "A friend of mine has a brother who's also on the autism spectrum. I used to hang out a lot in their house, and you reminded me of him."

She paused and then spoke tentatively, obviously afraid of triggering him again. "Earlier, in the hallway—and even in the class—you handled your outburst really, really well. I know that Jake—that's my friend's brother—always has a problem with his. What did you do?"

CJ blushed. "It is a trick to… cope? My ABA therapist taught it to me… when I was young. It involves breathing and repeating mantras… to calm my heart rate."

"I don't think my friend's heard of this particular method," Anna frowned. "Did your therapist develop it?"

CJ shook his head. "He got it from… the Okafor Autism Research Centre."

"I'm pretty sure she's never mentioned that. And that's where your therapist got the techniques?" Her frown deepened, bringing out the lines on her face. CJ stared at those.

CJ nodded. "The best… techniques. And they work."

There was a chirping sound, and he fished out his phone. DJ's text message had only three words.

"I got in."

CJ tried to smile, but the emotion was too much, and he froze. But that was okay. He smiled mentally.

NDIDI WALKED THE EMPTY HALLS, her heels clicking out her tension on the hard tile floor. She was supposed to be in school right now, seated in her 8:30 a.m. class. But she had already finished the coursework for the year, and listening to the lecturer run on about weird facts would only piss her off. It was her fault, though. She was the one who wanted a second degree.

But she could sulk about that later. She had something more important to do today. It wasn't something she wanted to do, nor was it something she'd ever envisioned she would do. Nevertheless, Ndidi saw it as her duty.

Bethany was put under my care, after all, Ndidi thought. She forced her fists to unclench, scolding herself. It'd been over four weeks since the Gaius malfunction—what the media was now calling Mayday. Since Bethany disappeared, Ndidi had discreetly scoured the city for the girl, involving some friends in the NYPD and CIA. But after a month of searching, they hadn't been able to find a trace. Not of Bethany or the others still missing in the aftermath. Most had been scheduled to travel that day. Their fates were easily concluded. Planes had crashed all around the world, after all.

Others, however—the worse-off ones like Bethany—had simply disappeared. They left no record of having left or arrived. No cameras had caught their passing. There were no corpses to confirm their demise or DNA at a scene to show their survival. There was simply no trace. Since then, the world had devolved into a madhouse where spouses had no idea where their partners were. Where parents couldn't find their children.

Where children suddenly had no parents.

Shelters were popping up every day to take care of the kids that were found and to help them find their families. Though Ndidi had opened the Autism Centre to the venture, she had no idea how much it would help. It was widely assumed that those who'd gone missing and stayed that way were gone.

Pain from her clenched fists shook Ndidi from her reverie. She blinked and looked down at the crumpled paper in her hand. She sighed and forced herself once more to relax her grip. The paper fell in a wrinkled mess, and Ndidi left it there while she got control of herself.

It didn't bode well that for all her professed self-control, her world had been tinted red for the past four weeks. As Ndidi had learned to do, she took a moment to close her eyes, letting the fear and anger wash through her. Time slowed, and one second stretched into ten. Then she exhaled, and it was gone.

She pushed open the door. Bethany's father, Dr. Cloney, looked up from his desk. He'd flown over from Nigeria days before to attend a conference and had been scheduled to return on Mayday. But he'd become too immersed in his research and missed his flight. This ended up saving his life. Now he was stuck in New York until transportation resumed. He jotted something down quickly and stood to greet her, smiling obliviously.

NDIDI WALKED OUT OF THE LAB an hour later, and the consoling smile she'd plastered on her face fell like lead bricks. She tried to take a breath, but her lungs were on fire from holding back her screams. She stayed rooted in front of the lab door while she tried to get control of herself. Behind her, grief-stricken sobs were muffled by the metal door.

He's just grieving for his daughter, Ndidi told herself, trying again for a breath. This time it went through. *It's the natural response. I went through the same thing when I got the news.*

She repeated the words as a mantra, exhaling loudly with each breath. Gradually, her muscles unclenched, and Ndidi found that she could move again. She walked down the hall and pushed open the door to the restroom. It was empty, fortunately, so Ndidi leaned against the door and took a moment to process her thoughts.

Her anger was irrational. She knew this, she accepted this. But that didn't make it any less real. It didn't matter that she wasn't normally an angry person or that she'd taken pains growing up to remain in charge of her emotions. She was angry. Moreso now than ever.

She'd expected the initial shock from Dr. Cloney after giving him the news. And she'd expected the inevitable questions—going so far as to jot her answers on the piece of paper that she'd later crumpled. The point is, she'd planned the whole interaction. But the shock phase had lasted too long, as had the question phase. And then the *crying*.

That was what pissed her off the most, she realized. Ndidi had expected the same anger she felt—the same boiling rage at the injustice of it all. But Dr. Cloney had been content to cry, to accept it docilely.

Ndidi walked up to the sink, turned on the tap, and splashed some water on her face. She stared into the mirror. *It's only the initial response*, she told herself again. *It's completely natural.*

This time, her words rang hollow. But her rationalization had served its purpose.

She wasn't at all calm, and she didn't suddenly understand where Dr. Cloney was coming from. However, her rage cooled so she could think more logically, which was good. She would need to think rationally if she was going to smoke out the fools responsible for Mayday and make them pay.

KARLA AND LIZ STARED at Chloe's camera feed as she entered the building through the first-floor window. Almost instantly, there was a spray of blood, and two men dropped.

"I'm in," Chloe reported unnecessarily. At the end of the hall, two guards were rushing toward the operative, guns out. One had his wrist up and was shouting something into it.

Karla wrinkled her brow. "Why is there no sound?"

Her words were badly pronounced and barely decipherable through her thick Russian accent. She hid a wince, glancing at José. Their father hated it when their English was any less than fluent. But that was what he got, dragging them from glorious Russia into this humid hell and teaching them the language against their will.

She frowned when no one responded to her, fingering her gun. *Who do they think they are?*

Liz head-butted her lightly and nodded to the camera feed, and Karla turned her attention back.

She'd missed a few seconds. The feed showed another hallway already littered with bodies. Chloe was between two men, sword in one hand and gun in the other as she waited for an opening. A man swung overhand, and Chloe blocked him with her sword. The fact that his arm wasn't immediately detached told Karla she was using the flat of her blade.

Karla rolled her eyes. She rolled them again even harder when, a moment later, Chloe gave the gun a purpose and slammed it into both guards' heads. Why she bothered to kill some and knock others out, Karla would never understand. Maybe some twisted form of mercy? Still, the floor was clear, and that was all that mattered.

"Clear," Chloe's voice came from the speakers. "Send in the girls."

José snapped his fingers, but Karla took an extra second to confirm her weapon placement and armor. She wasn't surprised that Liz did the same. If they got shot, they would both feel the pain, after all. A slight flex alerted Liz when she was done, and they turned and both met their father's eyes. For a moment, Karla tried to picture herself as José did.

She and Liz had been conjoined since birth, an abomination that shouldn't have existed—at least, according to the neighborhood children. Karla couldn't bring herself to disagree. Their mother had died during their birth, so at the very least that made them murderers.

Was that what José saw when he looked at them? Killers that had murdered their mother simply by being born? She wouldn't blame him if he did. She knew Liz wouldn't either. It'd fit with how easily they'd avenged Yelena's death at only seven years old, with a gun several sizes too big for them and not a day of training.

Maybe he only sees us as operatives? Karla thought, glancing at the badge on her father's waist. Karla didn't know if she preferred that. She hated the CIA. The jobs were fun, but she didn't like how the agency made José rage about how everything was wrong and how it was about the greater good. Or the way he would sometimes go quiet for a while after meetings, then abruptly call Karla and Liz to the training hall and beat at them for hours. The missions they went on after those times were always fun—his way of apologizing. But Karla wasn't sure if it was worth it.

Plus, she thought angrily, *the CIA was the reason he had to go to Russia in the first place—to hide like a common rat.*

No, she would not like it if José thought of them only as CIA operatives.

Liz flexed a signal, and Karla realized she'd let her thoughts distract her once again. She frowned and slid out her gun with their left hand—the only hand she could control. She gripped the gun perfectly, almost humming in anticipation. Karla nodded in satisfaction. This was more her thing; Liz was always the speculative one. Karla just liked to shoot things.

She grinned and flexed her response. Without a word between them, the twins synchronously made their way to the building.

They met Chloe in front of the elevators, where she was waiting impatiently. She spared a smile, giving them a once-over before clicking the call button. "Took your time, didn't you?"

Karla bared her teeth playfully. "Maybe. Not sure you needed us."

Chloe frowned at her, and she cursed in Russian. Chloe hated the language; too many vowels, she always said.

The elevators dinged open, and the three women stepped in. Chloe clicked the button for the second floor. Karla tapped an impatient rhythm with her foot while Liz typed on her phone. Chloe was already hanging over the roof of the elevator. Liz finished her text and flexed a signal. They hopped and used metal claws to hook themselves to the ceiling, as did Chloe.

A second later, the elevator door opened, and gunfire tore through the little compartment. Karla twisted her face away from the shrapnel and tried to stifle her grunts as she maintained her position. Skills other people grew up knowing instinctively, Karla and Liz had had to learn consciously—first for themselves, then in coordination with each other. It was why they used signals.

The gunfire died down after a minute. Karla and Liz let go of their perch and fell the few feet down. Their guns appeared in their hands, and the four guards that had been shooting at them dropped the moment they landed. Chloe dropped a second later and waved them down the hallway. There was no comment about the kills. The twins didn't expect any.

They made their way after Chloe. To Karla's confusion, they wasted a few minutes dragging the bodies into a storage closet before moving on.

Their gait wasn't anything impressive, but it looked natural and effortless, even if it was anything other than that. It took a ridiculous amount of coordination to walk as they did. Karla controlled only the left portion of their body, and couldn't feel what Liz was doing on her side at all. Too little force or too much force, too little speed or too much speed—all of these affected their movement. It gave a whole new meaning to the phrase "learning to walk." A lifetime of training ensured they were always in sync, but constant communication was needed to stay that way.

They turned into another hallway. Another four guards immediately rushed to meet them. The men had guns buckled to their belts, but all they saw was a woman and what they probably thought was her disability. It probably didn't occur to them to reach for their weapons.

Karla growled. Her hand blurred, and all four men dropped. Chloe ignored the bodies and moved farther into the hall, while the other two once again dragged the guards out of sight. Chloe was counting doors and murmuring to herself when they caught up.

A minute later, she stopped, satisfied. "It's this one," she said. Karla gave her a blank look. "It's this one. The pharmaceutical lab."

Karla made a sound that might have been taken as understanding. She *did* understand, albeit in a simpler way. They had infiltrated this building for whatever was in the lab. What that thing was… well, Karla was sure her sister would know and lead them to it, if necessary. She had a vague memory of the briefing. Something about stopping the production of a new strain of coronavirus that caused a severe acute respiratory syndrome. Karla shrugged. It was way over her head.

Chloe kicked down the door. Liz had her gun at the ready, but there was only the usual assortment of nerds that one would expect in a lab. Karla and her twin were tasked with guard duty while Chloe poked around for whatever chemical they were seeking.

It was all so very… boring. Karla hadn't had the chance to do anything remotely fun, and the mission was already over. What was the point of calling them in?

"Why aren't there any guards?" Karla asked in Russian, cocking her head toward her sister.

"They don't know where we are," the red-haired girl replied in the same language. "José had the security cameras hacked as soon as Chloe entered the building. They don't know there's a problem."

Karla started to reply, but a piercing sound cut her off. She covered her ear, wincing at the noise. "Who the fuck triggered the alarm, then?"

Her eyes found Chloe at the back of the lab, who was sheepishly holding up a vial of liquid. Karla cursed, but there was no heat to it. The alarm had been triggered. So what? At most, things became more interesting.

Her fingers flexed in rhythm, signaling Liz to help them make their way to the lab entrance. Karla poked a tentative eye out and grinned. Guards were pouring out of the elevators and stairway, guns out and heading toward them. She signaled the information to Liz, and they made their way to the back of the laboratory.

Chloe met them halfway. "There are no other exits or windows in here. We leave the way we came in." Karla told her about the swarm of guards blocking the way. Chloe considered it. "My statement stands," she said, her expression casually confident.

Karla slipped her gun into her hand. It fit perfectly.

Liz flexed a signal. Karla responded.

AS INCONSPICUOUSLY AS HE'D BROUGHT OUT his phone to text his brother, DJ pocketed it. Naturally, he'd passed the course. The ceremony stadium stretched almost as wide as the recruitment assault. This was unnecessary, in DJ's opinion, as the recruits that had actually passed the course didn't fill a quarter of the field. There were maybe two hundred of them packed into four big blocks, with spaces between each quadrant to avoid congestion. DJ was at the back-right side, which he'd picked so he would be able to watch his new colleagues without having to move around too much.

Far ahead, on the other side of the mass of bodies, the upper echelons of the corps sat rigidly and stared down from a dais. The drill instructor—or someone who looked remarkably like him from where DJ stood—was giving a speech no doubt designed to inspire both fear and awe in the new recruits. It was probably passionate yet disciplined and outlined multiple examples of the rigors they would face as Navy SEALs. Unfortunately, he used no microphone or public-address system, and DJ caught only the occasional louder-than-normal word.

He yawned and used the motion to check out his newest colleagues. He'd noticed female recruits while running his laps and during the assault course, but he'd observed them absently—basically realizing their existence, accepting it, and pushing it to the back of his mind in favor of more pressing concerns, like not falling on his face or into the spiked pit. Now he had the chance to bring those thoughts back to the front.

The female recruits looked damn good in uniform, and one of them was standing right next to him. The question was, What was he going to do about it? DJ knew what he wanted to do about it, but he was stuck on the *how* of the matter. Girls had never been his strong suit. He'd been athletic growing up, so he'd inevitably attracted them, but standing in a field of like-muscled men, DJ didn't think his physique was going to matter much.

He spared another glance at the girl beside him. She stared ahead, her entire focus on the drivel being dispensed by the drill sergeant. DJ looked around and found that nearly everybody was focused on the speaker's message. There were still comments and side conversations, sure, but those were mostly one-two kinds of things, a question and a response. Was he the only one who didn't give a rat's ass about it? He couldn't even hear a word.

Without thinking too much, DJ turned to the girl. "Hey," he whispered, "can you hear shit?"

"Just a couple words here and there." The girl shrugged, not turning to face him. DJ detected the faintest hint of a southern accent.

"Do you think it's the same for everybody?"

"Maybe. Probably. Why?"

Now it was DJ's turn to shrug. "Well, I was getting bored because I couldn't hear shit, but everybody else is still staring straight ahead like we're in a strip club. I just wanted to make sure I wasn't the outlier."

The guy on DJ's other side snorted a little too loudly. "Honestly, I thought it was only me," he chuckled. "I've felt fucking stupid for the past ten minutes."

"Same," the female cadet admitted, grinning. "Couldn't the brass have done this inside somewhere? I heard the base is fucking huge."

DJ nodded. They'd been given rooms within the base so they could wash off some of the grime from the assault course and change clothes. But everything had been strictly regulated, and DJ hadn't had the chance to poke around. Still, if the base was anything like the recruitment field had been, then it should be—as the lady so appropriately put it—"fucking huge."

He said as much to them.

"Exactly," the woman said with a chin nod. And then they all nodded in agreement. No one said anything after that. No one wanted the responsibility of starting a new conversation, despite the fact that they'd just admitted how stupid it was to stare straight ahead when they couldn't hear the speech. It was a pickle.

The moment stretched until it bordered on being awkward. DJ scratched the back of his head and resisted the impulse to whistle. He almost felt as though he could feel two pairs of eyes drilling into the sides of his head. But why should it be up to him to further the conversation? *Probably because I started it*, DJ acknowledged mentally.

"So, I'm DJ," he offered, leaning back so he could address both at the same time.

"DJ? Short for…?" she asked.

"Darren Jacob," DJ clarified.

"Christy," she offered with a nod. DJ nodded back and turned to his left.

"Kyle," the other guy replied, his relief almost palpable.

DJ turned to face him fully. He was young, way younger than DJ—and probably Christy, too, judging from her appearance. Probably older than eighteen, but definitely not yet twenty-one. He had dark brown hair and a wiry frame that made his uniform look ill-fitting. Still, he would never have passed the recruitment if he didn't pack some serious muscles underneath.

Which I guess is just as true for Christy, DJ thought, turning to his other companion. She had dirty-blonde hair and the kind of cheekbones and cute button nose that had probably made her the envy of other girls.

DJ clapped his hands together. "Now that we have that taken care of—"

"Shush," Christy said, snapping her head forward. DJ stopped, confused.

Hadn't they passed this stage already? He turned to look at Kyle, but the brown-haired boy was also staring intently ahead.

"I think they're talking about teams," he said.

Finally, DJ thought, also straining to hear.

CHAPTER

7

FEBRUARY 2040
NEW YORK CITY, NEW YORK

MANAR WOKE to beeping noises and the smell of bleach.

He groaned, tried to sit up, and promptly fell back down. The pain was debilitating. Instead, he focused on just turning his head sideways. When he saw the heart monitor, he groaned again. But this time it was for a completely different reason.

Why the hell am I in a hospital? he thought groggily. A moment later, memories flashed through his mind, each more painful than the last. The setting sun, the crashing planes, the stairs, and, finally, his fall.

"Fuck," Manar murmured. His lips were dry. *How long have I been out?* He tried to sit up again. He almost blacked out from the pain. "Helene," he croaked, then remembered his phone was somewhere in the Sparta building's stairway.

Assuming the building is still standing.

The door opened, and Manar glimpsed a flash of white before a face was suddenly up in his.

"Good morning," the middle-aged woman said softly but still uncomfortably close to him. "My name is Janice. How're you doing today?"

"Beautifully, before you invaded my personal space," Manar tried to say. Unfortunately, it came out as one long croak. Janice brought her ears closer to hear him but, foolishly, Manar had spent all his energy on the first effort.

"You had quite a fall," the nurse smiled—creepily, in Manar's opinion. She had a southern drawl. Couldn't the damn woman see that he needed water? "Gave us quite a scare. Do you know where you are?"

Manar mustered his energy. "Wa… ter," he croaked more audibly.

Janice seemed to come to her senses. Her smile slipped in her embarrassment, and she reached for something out of sight. "Oh, silly me," she said, tilting the glass against his lips. "You must be drier than desert sand."

Manar knew enough not to gulp down the water too fast, but as the first few drops touched his lips, he found himself leaning in, straining for more.

Janice drew the cup away from him, tutting in a way that she probably thought was comforting. Manar was really starting to loathe the woman. "Ah, ah, ah," she said. "You can't take it down too fast, or you'll just throw it back up." She took a napkin and wiped his chin. "And that's not going to be good for anyone, is it?"

Manar ignored her, licking his lips to get the last few drops.

"Do you know where you are, hon?" Janice tried again, finally leaning away from Manar.

"I realize that I'm in a hospital," Manar replied slowly. The water had helped, but each word still took far too much energy. "My questions are, which hospital, and how long have I been unconscious?"

"Ah, good," Janice said, smiling brightly.

Good? Had the woman heard him at all?

"Doesn't seem like you knocked loose anything important," she commented. "Dr. Navarro was worried. It's hard to tell sometimes, y'know, till they wake up."

None of this did Manar care about. But he realized that, for the moment, he was at the nurse's mercy. So he choked back his anger, gestured for more water, then repeated his question.

"Oh, I wouldn't know," Janice replied, fiddling with his IV. "It wasn't my shift when you arrived. But I've been attending you here—here being the state hospital, of course—for about… four weeks, I reckon." She nodded once to herself. "Yes. Four weeks, if my memory ain't failing me in my old age."

"Four weeks," Manar repeated absently, pondering the implications. Janice's voice faded into the background. *Helene's new upgrades should be done, assuming she finished before the collapse destroyed the setup and the worm I prepared should be done with the program.*

Suddenly, Manar went still, his eyes scanning the room. He'd been unconscious for four weeks. There were no flowers, get-well-soon cards, or the sound of anxious pacing outside his door. Did anyone even know where he was? Had anybody even looked for him?

"Simone!" Manar gasped, sitting up. He ignored Janice's startled cry and the sudden blaring pain. "I need a phone," he ordered, forgetting where he was in his urgency. "Please," he added belatedly. "I need to call someone."

"Well, that's no reason to scream, hon," Janice said, clutching her chest. "You damn near gave me a heart attack."

You should have died, then! Manar almost snapped. "I'm sorry, but it's urgent."

"I guess if it's that serious…" She tutted in that annoying way again and reached into her pocket. "Here, you can use mine."

Manar took the device and punched in Simone's number. It went straight to voicemail. He hung up, thought for a minute, then punched in Deepthi's number. Their wedding had been the previous month. Manar had had a meeting and missed it, but odds were that they were together. He waited a minute, but the call went straight to voicemail too.

"What were the casualty rates of the incident a month ago?" Manar asked Janice, now dialing his own number with deliberate focus. At the beep, he hit the star button and input his PIN.

"Oh, that was a dark, dark day," Janice replied. "Deaths in the tens of millions, I reckon. But that's nothing you should concern yourself with. You should just focus on getting better. I'm sure your lady friend is all right."

"It's my mom," Manar croaked.

He had five new messages on his voicemail. He hit play on the oldest, and Simone's voice filled the suddenly silent room.

"Good evening, baby," the voice cooed, slurring.

This was probably just after the reception, Manar thought. Showing what Manar assumed was a rare moment of sensitivity, Janice excused herself from the room.

"I understand you had to work, but the wedding wasn't the same without you. We're on the train now, but I tell you, when Deepthi and I get back from France, I'm going to drag you out of that office—even if I have to take you over my knee in front of all your colleagues."

There was a hiccup. Then Simone continued, sounding less drunk now. "I miss you, baby. Call me when you get this, love, day or night."

Her voice faded, but the voicemail went on for a second longer. Manar could make out Gaius's voice in the background: *"Please, sit back and enjoy the ride."*

The voicemail ended with a beep.

And sounds of sobbing took its place.

ONCE AGAIN, NDIDI WALKED THE HALLS of the Research Centre. She wore flats today because she hated the clacking sound of her heels. The halls were empty. This was the norm since Mayday. Most of the scientists had been reassigned to the makeshift shelters the Centre ran to take care of the victims of Mayday, leaving only a barebones staff. Thus, research had temporarily ground to a halt. Ndidi considered it a worthy trade-off if it helped even a single child—even if, on a much wider scale, it was all futile.

With an effort, she shook herself from her troubled thoughts. She couldn't think like that. It set a bad precedent, almost like she'd given up. And she wasn't going to let that happen. She *couldn't* let that happen. Not if she wanted to find the people responsible for Mayday—and for Bethany's disappearance.

Despite her better judgment, Ndidi had waited another week for any news about the girl. However, though more people were still being recovered every day, none of them were Bethany. So Ndidi found it difficult to care.

The mainframe room was at the end of the hallway. Occupied, as Ndidi had known it would be. The only thing that would take Chad Triplett away from his computers was the apocalypse. *And not even that, if the theories about Mayday are to be believed*, Ndidi thought with a grim smirk. The room itself was incredibly cold. Ndidi saw mist pooling in the corner as it might in a meat locker. She shivered and drew her jacket tighter around her, for all the good it did.

Chad was seated directly in front of her, his attention held by the twin computer monitors before him. He didn't look up, so Ndidi stood in the doorway, contemplating. She didn't have much of a relationship with Chad outside of work—and even that was flimsy given how little their paths crossed. Chad's passion lay in technology, while Ndidi's was in mental disorders.

Manar would have been the best choice for this, but Ndidi hadn't spoken to him in months, and she didn't think she could handle the conversation now. *Especially after losing Simone*, Ndidi thought.

Maybe she should call him. Stay by his side. Everything had been so good when she was with him.

Ndidi was reaching for her phone before she caught herself. She wanted to be there for Manar, but she wasn't in the right frame of mind to be there for anybody right now. Plus, if just the thought of him got her so conflicted, what would actually meeting him do to her mental health? Thankfully, that thought was enough to snap her out of her reverie. She stepped into the room fully.

Chad still didn't look up from his screens, though she was by his side and peering over his brown cowboy hat. His fingers were clicking away at the keyboard faster than she could follow. Despite herself, Ndidi was impressed. Feeling suddenly childish, she bent closer to his ear, taking care not to brush against him.

"Boo," she whispered.

Two quick steps took her far away from his startled cry and flinging arms, but it took surprising effort not to burst out laughing. Chad jumped out of his seat and turned, looking around wildly, before finally settling on her. He chuckled nervously, and Ndidi's lips twitched in response.

"I… uh," he started, straightening out his clothes self-consciously. "I didn't hear you come in."

"You seemed pretty invested in your work, and I felt sorry to disturb you," Ndidi replied, walking toward the air conditioner.

"So, you… uh… decided to scare the crap outta me instead? Pardon my French, ma'am."

Ndidi turned a dial, and the temperature rose drastically. Ironically, she almost shivered in relief. She turned back to Chad, who was standing beside his chair, looking put out in his own office.

She smiled disarmingly. "I'm sorry for scaring you, Chad. And for taking you away from your work," she added, walking back toward him. "I actually have a favor to ask you."

"Well shit! Is that all?" Chad laughed in relief. He sat back down in his chair. "I thought you were going to fire me or something."

Once again, Ndidi stopped behind the chair. She frowned. "Why would you think that?"

"Something Jamal said a couple of days ago," Chad explained without looking back at her. "It's pretty simple, actually. Research is grounded because most of the scientist guys are taking care of the victims of Mayday, right? So, all the money that's supposed to go into research is going into the shelters. None's coming back in, you see, because everyone's still trying to get their feet back under them after the disaster." He shrugged. "Layoffs seem like the obvious next step."

Ndidi considered this. The Centre got some of its money from public and private donations, sure, but most of it came from its parent company, the Okafor Corporation. The company was run by Ndidi's father, Eze Okafor—and, in a small way, by Ndidi herself. The Okafor Corporation was a global trillion-dollar conglomerate with its hands in hundreds of businesses. Ndidi's yearly stipend more than covered the expenses generated by the Autism Centre, with enough left over to take care of her basic cost of living.

Basically, there was no way that they were running out of funding, even if the donations stopped indefinitely. Ndidi knew this, but she was curious about how the rumor got started. She'd thought the empty halls were a result of the reassignments, but she didn't recall sending so many people to the shelter. Were they hiding out there, afraid to lose their jobs? All because of a fucking rumor?

Ndidi squeezed the bridge of her nose, marveling at the stupidity of it all. She took a breath and pushed the thought back. She'd worry about it later.

"Well, I'm not here to fire you, Chad. And there aren't going to be layoffs anywhere either."

"I appreciate that, ma'am, and I'm sure the rest of the guys would appreciate it too," he said, clacking away at his keyboard. "They've been hiding in those shelters for the last couple of weeks, pretending to be hard at work."

Several expletives came to Ndidi's mind, but none of them were fit to be said aloud.

"So, my favor," she said instead, then paused, looking for a way to phrase her request. "It's more of a question, really. How possible would it be—hypothetically, of course—for you to find out the cause of the Mayday incident?"

The clacking abruptly stopped. "What exactly would you mean, ma'am? Hypothetically."

Ndidi started pacing but stopped herself immediately. She didn't want to reveal just how nervous she was. "I'm sure you've already heard the theories about the disaster. Some say it wasn't as much of a freak malfunction as the media claims it to be."

Fuck, Ndidi cursed in her mind. That was way too on the nose to be interpreted as anything else. She'd meant to ease him into it, and she'd been taught how to do that almost since birth. What the hell was wrong with her?

"Sure, I've heard of them," replied Chad, his tone deceptively casual, "but most of those are from nutjob bums that *want* there to be a conspiracy in everything."

Ndidi winced at the term, and her face hardened. Even deliberately facing away, Chad seemed to pick up on it and added, "Hypothetical nutjobs, of course."

"Hypothetically, what would such a process entail?" Ndidi gritted out, her mind scrambling for an escape route. Manar *really* would have been a better choice. He'd been warning her of Gaius since the day they'd met. She would scarcely have to ask the man before he jumped on it.

"Not much," replied Chad, shrugging. "I've been looking into Mayday since the incident, and being one of those hypothetical nutjobs myself, I've been trying to track down routes of a possible hack." He gave her a lopsided grin.

Ndidi's brows rose almost to her hairline. This she had not expected. "What have you found out?"

"Well, nothing—yet. Everyone with a lick of hacking expertise and a vague motivation is on this thing, so it's locked down tight. All the back doors I installed when I helped develop the AI were somehow found and shut tighter than a bank vault."

"You helped program Gaius?" Ndidi asked incredulously. Her mind flashed through all the information she'd read on Chad before he'd come to the Autism Centre… and she came up blank. "Why am I just learning of this now?"

"Well, it's not really something I could put on my resume, ma'am," Chad said, somewhat defensively. "All those law types in suits practically drowned us in NDAs before we could get a keystroke into the damn thing."

"That's why you're already invested," Ndidi realized aloud. She straightened and considered the new information. "You're peeved someone hacked your system."

"Damn right I'm peeved," he said, glaring at his screen. "Gaius was the best thing I'd ever helped design. There were too many fail-safes in place. There's no way in hell it malfunctioned."

"So it *was* hacked," Ndidi mused. A weight she didn't know she'd been holding lifted from her chest. She'd suspected that Gaius had been hacked since she'd read the reports about the abnormal behavior of the transport systems before their crashes. Still, most of those could be—and had been—explained away as glitches in the system before its final malfunction. Either way, Ndidi understood that someone was to blame, and that was all that mattered: making those people pay.

With the hack confirmed, though, the list of suspects was significantly shortened. There were precious few people with the skill set to break through a global firewall system, after all. The actual culprit would be more difficult to pin down. But the list was shorter all the same. And she could work with that.

"So, it was hacked," Ndidi repeated. She didn't know when they'd dropped the pretense of being hypothetical, but it was better that everything was out in the open. "What does that mean exactly?"

Chad turned in his chair and met her eyes fully. "What it means, ma'am, is that I'll need an edge. Something that can get me directly into the AI network base. Something like… I don't know… the motherboard of one of the systems that was hacked."

"And where might one find something like that?" Ndidi asked tentatively.

"Normally, I'd say a crash site, but all those have been swarming with police types since the incident. I'd bet my lucky hat, though, that the Gaius Corporation would have a few lying around somewhere in their big building, if only to run a system diagnostic and determine the exact cause."

"If they'd already done that, wouldn't they have discovered they were hacked?" Ndidi asked curiously.

"Well, that depends entirely on the skill of the hacker," Chad said, again clicking away on his computer. "And they'd have to be pretty skilled to pull off something like this."

"I'm counting on it," replied Ndidi.

"Well, good," said Chad, sparing a glance over his shoulder. "But my point, ma'am, is that a skilled hacker isn't likely to have left any back traces for other people to follow. And even if they *had*, and Gaius Corporation had been able to follow it to its source, they still wouldn't announce they were hacked."

"Why not?" Ndidi asked, but then she followed the thought to its end. "They've been discredited," she answered before Chad could. "Millions of people all over the world died on Mayday. Families were lost, and property was destroyed. Everyone is scared, confused, and angry. No one's going to listen to what they'd perceive as Gaius blaming an innocent person to avoid bankruptcy."

"Got it in one," Chad said, pulling up a file on the computer. "This is what I've gathered so far from some of my buddies downtown. It's pretty watered down, though. Like I said, most of the information is locked."

Ndidi leaned over and scanned the document quickly. Some parts of it were news reports and statements from witnesses present at crash sites. Others were actual police reports. Most of the latter, however, had entire paragraphs blacked out, making it difficult to get any real details. Ndidi was used to that, as most of her own inquiries had been similarly redacted. Overall, the information that Chad had wasn't much more than she did. She collected the file anyway.

"Now," Chad said, getting her attention back, "if I had a piece of one of the hacked systems, I'd probably be able to trace the source code of the hack back to the Gaius Corporation's own database and get ahold of one of *their* reports." He turned in his seat to smile fully at Ndidi. "And I'm betting one of their analysis reports would be a lot more informative."

His grin was contagious, and Ndidi found herself mimicking it. In the background, her mind twirled around ideas of how she would get her hands on the motherboard.

CHAPTER

MARCH 2040
NEW YORK CITY, NEW YORK

MANAR SPENT EIGHT WEEKS in the hospital, recovering from his wounds—the physical ones at least. Those, he was told, were extensive.

Most of his ribs had been broken, and the debris had punctured some organs, rupturing them. His legs were shot to hell, as they'd taken the brunt of what the doctor thought was an eleven-foot fall. His head and upper spine had absorbed the rest of the damage—which, ironically, was why he hadn't lost full motor function in his lower parts. Because of this, though, he'd been on a concussion and brain damage watch for his first two weeks.

But he'd survived, and somehow that brought the most pain.

He was left mostly alone. This suited him fine. Janice was able to scrounge up an archaic computer from somewhere, and Manar spent an inordinate amount of time getting it back into working shape. He could have just ordered a new device, but the work gave him something tangible to focus on. It grounded him during the times when he tended to… drift.

When the system finally met his specifications, he'd taken to upgrading Helene's code. The programming for the AI that was mass produced and used in e-readers everywhere had been developed and stored on an offshore site, so it hadn't taken any undue damage when the Sparta headquarters was plane-bombed. Manar's pre-Mayday version of Helene had been built on the AI's original public framework but had long since evolved, tailored specifically to suit his needs. The result was a mobile hologram with beefed-up processing power, advanced communication skills, and autonomy.

Unfortunately, not all the programming had been backed up before the collapse, which interrupted the process. While stuck at the hospital, Manar threw himself into rebuilding his assistant from scratch, quickly getting her to the level she'd been pre-Mayday. After that, he'd started on her upgrades. For this, he had to look at her underlying framework, the one restricted from public access and available only to him.

But therein lay another problem. Most of his access codes hadn't transferred to the backup before it had been interrupted, so he'd had to take control of the software manually. Bypassing his own firewalls and security programs had taken him the better part of a week. The long and mentally strenuous work gave Janice no small amount of grief as she tried to get Manar to rest. But it wasn't like he had anything better to do. And regardless, it was the most fun he'd had in a long time.

At some point, his colleagues tracked him down. They offered their insincere condolences amid subtle requests for him to look at their current projects. Their sympathies, however fake, only served to remind him of what he'd lost. Eventually, he'd asked Janice to stop allowing people in. All except one—if she ever showed up.

Though investigations were still ongoing, most statements by government officials stated that Mayday hadn't been a terrorist attack. If it were, it would have made 9/11 look like the pacifist option. Instead, said the government, it was just an AI malfunction from a company that had grown too complacent to properly vet its programming.

Obviously, Manar didn't believe it. This was ironic, as he'd always had an innate mistrust of the Gaius AI simply because he hadn't looked over the codes himself. Still, he'd seen the news footage of some of the vehicles prior to their crashes. While he admitted that their motions did look remarkably like glitches, the more analytical part of his brain suspected that something wasn't right.

The puzzle gave Manar his second biggest source of distraction.

MARCH 2040
SOMEWHERE IN THE
SOUTHERN UNITED STATES

DJ STARED THROUGH HIS BINOCULARS and stifled a sigh. The grass somehow pricked him through his body armor.

"See anything out there?" he asked out loud, more to stave off boredom than out of any real worry.

They were strictly on an intelligence-gathering mission—well, technically, the *main* operative team was on an intelligence-gathering mission. DJ and his team were auditing the operation as part of their training. An easy way to get their feet wet, so to speak.

This would have been fine if his team actually got to *see* the action. They didn't. His five-man team had each been given a set of binoculars, dispersed around the target building, and told to watch for suspicious activity. This was military speak for "sit your asses down, and stay out of our way."

DJ understood. He really did. No agent wanted to babysit a bunch of kids on a high-stakes operation. He had images of an older him being the perfect mentor to his charges, teaching them the dos and don'ts while explosives lit the sky in the background. But he accepted the grandstanding for what it was and understood that he would probably have done the same were he in his mentor's shoes.

I'll probably be more honest with them, though, DJ mused internally, shifting to get more comfortable on the grass. Sharp rocks seemed to have a penchant for getting directly under him and pressing against his abdomen, no matter how much he shifted.

"Even the mosquitos ain't buzzing in this damn place," Christy murmured, her voice coming through the comms set in his ears. She was placed higher up, in a tree somewhere to DJ's right, for the better vantage it provided her sniper rifle. They were in a flat, barren stretch of land in the middle of nowhere, and there were at least three other people keeping watch. DJ didn't know how much of a vantage she needed. He guessed that was one of the things he was supposed to be learning.

"How about signs of our people?" he asked.

"Not a pip," Christy answered back. "They could have gone out the back and left us, for all we know, calling it another training exercise."

DJ snorted as a memory of the time their seniors had actually done that flashed in his mind. But DJ didn't see how that would work in this scenario. The only thing around for miles was the two-story building they all had their eyes on. And in the silence of the day, any extraction vehicle would be heard from miles away. Unless, of course, the seniors were really determined and had decided to double back to the drop-off point and radio headquarters. They were in for a surprise if they tried that.

"Um, dudes," Kyle started hesitantly, "I think we're supposed to keep radio silence or something. Y'know, so the bad guys can't intercept our stuff and find out we're out here? I… uh… remember someone saying something like that." Kyle was on the other side of the building, so DJ couldn't see him. Regardless, he could picture the abashed look on the kid's face.

"Chill," DJ said, wiggling into a better position. "The twins rigged up our comms system themselves. Ours is on a private channel. Even the Alpha Six can't hear us right now, and our signals are practically side by side."

"Oh," Kyle said, and DJ could perfectly picture the blush. "I… uh… didn't know that. Sorry, dudes."

"Don't sweat it," DJ said. "Also, Christy, I don't think the team would leave us here. Don't get me wrong, it's entirely possible for them to do that. I don't just think they will."

"Won't we be able to hear them on the comms if they're discussing it?" Kyle asked.

"Their comms are probably rigged on a separate channel too, love," Christy replied from her perch, not unkindly. "Plus, if they're close enough, they could probably just turn off the damn thing entirely, and we wouldn't be able to do squat. Why do you think they wouldn't, D?"

DJ frowned at the name. His name was already abbreviated, and he didn't know how he felt about it being shortened again. "They could probably try to make the hike back to where the heli dropped us off. But that's at least a four-hour trek, and even a 'fully trained team with a wealth of experience that we could learn from' would find it difficult to do without any water," he finished, quoting their training commander's words from when he'd sent the team along with Alpha Six.

"You stole their water?" Kyle asked tentatively.

"Yeah, D. Water is life," Christy put in. She was a bit of an activist when the mood struck her. "You've basically stolen their lives."

DJ rolled his eyes. "You can rest assured that their lives are safe," he said, taking a gulp from said life. "I just needed a bit of reassurance that I wouldn't be left in the middle of nowhere for no reason—again. The second time, it really gets personal."

"What if they don't notice their water's gone until they've gone too far to turn back?" Kyle asked.

DJ snorted, setting the bottle down beside three others. "If they're stupid enough to start the hike without confirming their water rations, we've wasted the last twenty-four hours thinking we could learn something from them."

"You gotta admire his balls, though," Christy muttered, apparently forgetting that her words would transmit.

"What about—" Kyle started to say.

"I've got movement coming out of the southeast side of the building," Christy called out calmly. "Suspect is a white adult male, roughly six feet. He's moving fast."

DJ peered through his binoculars and found the moving form. That is, the form moving toward him. "Be advised, I have the suspect in my twelve o'clock, and he's rapidly closing the distance between us."

"Have you been spotted, recruit?" a voice sneered in his ears. Agent Carlton Bradley. Over the comms unit, his voice always sounded like the man perpetually had his finger up his nose. Still, it was a marked improvement over his regular voice.

"Negative, sir," DJ reported back. "Suspect just appears to be making a break for it."

"Then stand your ground, recruit. That's Owen Finn, our target today. He's known to be extremely dangerous. My men and I will take care of him."

"Well, you're obviously doing a piss-poor job of that," DJ muttered at a tone too low for the comms to pick up, "if he's already escaped the building."

"What was that, recruit?"

"I said roger, control," DJ replied calmly. In the background, he heard Christy chortle.

Suddenly, gunshots exploded within the building. The runaway glanced back, crouching reflexively. When he started moving again, his fast walk had turned into a jog. He got close enough that DJ could make out a phone clutched to his ear and his mouth moving rapidly. He glanced back at every gunshot from the building, speaking loudly into the device and gesturing with wild, angry motions. His legs never stopped moving.

"Suspect is on call with an unknown third party," DJ reported. "He might be calling for backup."

"Whoever he's calling won't make it here in time," Bradley yelled over the gunshots. "Keep your position."

"Ramirez," DJ said, for the first time addressing one of the twins, "can you intercept the call?"

"Belay that. We have our own tech guy working on the interception."

"Call's encrypted. Nothing we can do from here anyway," Ramirez reported back through the comms, ignoring Agent Bradley. It almost made DJ smile.

Finn was less than six feet to his left, practically on top of him. That close, DJ could make out the stubble on his face and the smell of cigarettes and body odor. DJ stilled his movements. He was covered almost completely by a camouflage blanket, but it was still a surprise when Finn's roving eyes passed over him without realizing.

Now, that's cool, DJ mused. "Christy, do you have a shot?" he whispered.

"On any part of his body you want."

DJ grimaced and spared a glance at the building, but the gunshots were still frequent. He didn't think anyone would be coming out to apprehend anybody soon. And Finn was getting farther away.

The sound of a car engine behind him snagged his attention. Ever so slowly, so his movement didn't disturb his camouflage, DJ turned his head. The words were already at the tip of his tongue, but Christy still beat him to it.

"Movement on the southeast side," she reported, the frown obvious in her tone. "Target's backup seems to be on its way."

"How many men?" Bradley shouted into the comms.

"Unknown. They're in an M1123 HMMWV, and approaching fast," said DJ, trying to hide his excitement. There was no way Bradley and his men were going to be done fast enough to nail Finn, meaning he might actually get some action in this shitty place. "Their goal is obviously to retrieve the target—*our* target."

"Um, how do we know it's not one of our dudes?" asked Kyle. "Aren't Humvees mostly military?"

"The ETA of our backup is still fifteen minutes," Bradley said, "and the extraction time is even farther away. This isn't one of ours."

"Exactly," DJ said. "The vehicle's approximately two hundred meters and appears to be accelerating. Christy already has a shot. We could end this."

"Negative, recruit. The objective is to take the suspect alive, and that's what we're going to do"

"I could shoot him in the leg," Christy offered.

"Still negative!" Bradley bellowed. "Hold your fire and your positions until one of my men can get there."

DJ tracked Finn with his eyes. His speed had reduced from a jog back to a fast walk, but between that and the speed of the Humvee, he'd be gone in minutes.

How can one man be this stupid? DJ thought in frustration.

DJ had seen Christy at the shooting range during training. There was a reason she was the team's sniper. If she said she had the shot, then she had the shot. And if not, DJ could be over there tackling the man in thirty seconds. Were they going to let the fool just drive away because of one man's pride?

"Fuck that," DJ muttered.

"What was that, recruit?" Bradley shouted amid gunfire.

Logically, DJ knew the best course of action for him and his team was to stay put. They'd been given an order, after all. Military types tended to take that stuff seriously. Even if Finn got away, the blame would fall on Bradley and his men, who didn't use the resources they had to the best of their ability. DJ's team would probably be assigned to another one of the alpha teams; they could finish their training and work their way up.

But doing something just because it was logical had never really been DJ's strong suit. That was more CJ's area. DJ had always been the simpler of the two. His thoughts followed a very direct path to the option that made the most sense. And it *didn't* make sense to let a suspect that was right in front of him get away because his superior had his head too far up his ass.

The Humvee was about five minutes away, by DJ's guess. He stood, throwing off his camo blanket.

"Christy," he said softly. Their positions were close enough that he had no doubt the blond could see him and guess his intentions. "Do you still have a shot?"

"Yep," she replied, popping the *p*.

"Cover me." And then he took off running.

DJ TRIED NOT TO SMILE. He wasn't supposed to be enjoying this, after all. He'd disobeyed an order from a superior officer. If he had rank, then at best he'd be demoted; at worst, it might have cost him his career. He wasn't supposed to smile.

But, Lord, did it feel freeing!

He sprinted toward Finn, who—bless his heart—was still walking toward his ride. The driver of the Humvee, now about three minutes away, must have noticed DJ and the threat he posed because the car was honking away at Finn in a futile bid to warn him. When that didn't work, the passenger's side window lowered, and a hand popped out.

DJ's attention was quickly caught by the pistol clutched in that hand. Finn seemed to notice the gun at the same time. He slowed his walk, gesturing angrily at the car. DJ picked up his pace. He was closer to Finn than the car was, but even with the constant bumps from the road, the vehicle was rapidly closing the distance.

And then there was the gun to consider.

The first shot had DJ crouching out of reflex, though the bullet went wildly off the mark. It did have the benefit of properly alarming Finn, though, who ground to a halt while he tried to figure out why his people were shooting at him. DJ used the confusion to shorten the distance between them to less than fifty feet. Then his progress was forcibly halted by the second gunshot.

DJ gritted his teeth and crouched again. *What the hell is Christy doing?* he thought angrily.

And then Christy showed him.

Navy SEAL snipers were generally equipped with an H&K MSG90 sniper rifle in their starting pack. As she was the designated sniper of the team, this was Christy's main weapon. The gun had a recoil-operated, delayed-blowback bolt system that gave each bullet an added kick. This made it loud as hell—and pack a punch.

The shot came from behind DJ, close enough that, though he knew Christy wouldn't risk it, he swore he felt the bullet whiz over his shoulder. It passed the still-immobile Finn, broke through the vehicle's windshield, and took out the passenger with the gun.

The Humvee was close enough now that DJ could see the driver swerve in surprise, almost flipping the vehicle on its side. It braked hard and slid a few feet across the dirt before coming to a stop. A second shot took out a tire. Now, even if the vehicle wanted to move, it couldn't.

"What the hell was that?" Bradley bellowed, addressing everyone at once. "Hold your fire, recruit! That's an order!"

Christy didn't respond, so DJ saw no reason to either.

Tracing the direction of the shot, Finn finally looked behind him and noticed DJ rushing toward him. To his credit, apart from a startled step backward, he didn't flat-out run like DJ had expected him to. Instead, he brought out a gun.

DJ cursed, increasing the length of his strides. They were on a dirt field, barren for miles. There wasn't any place to duck for cover, so DJ's best bet was to close the distance before the bastard could get a shot off. He was thirty feet away, and Finn was already lining up his shot. He didn't like his chances.

"I have the shot," Christy said in his ear. "Just gonna take a little squeeze."

"No," he said, panting. "Bradley will have a field day if Finn dies."

"I'm not one to miss, D," Christy growled. "I can hit him in the leg."

Finn fired off his first shot, but his hands were shaking, and the bullet went wide. DJ ducked instinctively but kept moving. He was fifteen feet away now.

"That's what I'm worried about," he said to Christy. "You saw what the bullet did to the Humvee. That thing touches him, and he'll bleed out in seconds."

Christy didn't reply. DJ could tell she was considering it. *Good,* DJ thought, focusing on the gun in Finn's hand.

A shot rang out from behind him. DJ crouched, but he could tell it was a wild one as soon as he heard it. Finn apparently couldn't tell because it spooked him enough for his second shot to go wide.

"Christ," Bradley shouted over the comms. "What the hell's going on out there?"

DJ was less than seven feet away now—close enough to see the white of Finn's eyes. He wouldn't give him the chance to make a third shot.

Another gunshot rang out from behind him, putting Finn further off balance. He tried to squeeze off another round, but DJ was already within tackling distance.

His lunge took the pair of them to the ground. They grappled for a moment. This was all the time DJ needed to pin Finn down, his face pressed to the ground and his arms held behind him. The gun was in DJ's hand a second later and pressed against the back of his prisoner's skull.

Finn stopped struggling immediately.

"Target secured, sir," DJ reported as calmly as he could, though his breath came out in pants and his heart was still pounding.

"Fuck. I actually almost died," he muttered, exhaling sharply. The comms crackled in his ear, and Agent Bradley's voice came on. DJ snapped back to himself, sighing as he listened to the agent rant on. This was the part he hated most: the consequences.

Definitely worth it though, he thought with a grin. *Probably.*

DJ STIFLED A YAWN.

The Navy SEAL headquarters—as DJ had already realized—was huge. Like, ridiculously so. Like, *Maze Runner* kind of huge. It was structured with a mixture of expansive courtyards and squat buildings that looked more like large bunkers. The roads were paved. Streetlights appeared fairly often through the courtyards, but they weren't turned on in the light of the day.

All in all, the base was obscenely functional. It made sense, of course, as DJ hadn't ever pegged the military as the interior—or exterior, for that matter—design sort. But still, adding a fucking potted plant here and there never killed anyone.

There were people milling about the place. This surprised DJ until he actually applied some thought to it.

Of course there are fucking people around, he cursed at himself. *It's their damn headquarters. Where else would they be?*

He'd been there for a few months during training, but most of his activities had been limited to the outer segments. Even the trainees' living quarters were at the edges. It was definitely by design—sort of like a "you shall not pass unless you're an elite member" kind of thing. This was fascinating because there wasn't technically a deterrent to entering. The deterrent seemed to be in the training itself, which left him so tired most nights that he couldn't do anything more than reach his bed and nod off.

That didn't mean DJ had never gone into the headquarters, however. He had, but never deeply and never for long.

It was therefore no surprise when, after walking for fifteen minutes, DJ was completely and utterly lost. He had a guide, thank God, but couldn't make heads or tails of the winding hallways through which he was led. They passed a door at the end of a hallway and came out to another courtyard. DJ stifled a groan. Why the hell was the debriefing room so deep into the building?

This courtyard seemed a little larger than the others they'd passed, if that was possible. DJ guessed it ran at least a mile in both directions. There were buildings by the side, making a sort of cage. At least these buildings actually had a few plants around them.

DJ also noticed that there were fewer people there. And the energy was… different. While the others had had a bunch of guys milling about, some even stopping to talk to friends or colleagues, everyone here was either speed-walking out or going deeper inside to one of the buildings surrounding the place, just like DJ and his guide.

He wondered how many of the latter were in trouble like him.

They got some sidelong looks as they passed people. DJ was confused until he looked down at himself. He hadn't bothered to take off his camo the day before, and his guide hadn't given him a chance to change when she'd called. Still, a dirt-painted uniform alone shouldn't have drawn such attention. Most of the sergeants wore a variation of the same. However, *he* had spent the last twenty-four hours literally lying on the ground in the middle of nowhere while they'd waited for Agent Bradley and his fuckwits to get any reasonable intel—which they only had because DJ and his team had bagged their main target for them.

But there wasn't any point in going down that rabbit hole just yet. He focused on his guide instead.

DJ had learned Sarah's name when she'd summoned him. He'd nodded then and hadn't said a word to her since. He was too tired for words. She wore a sensible pantsuit with a blazer. A clipboard was held to her chest. Her hair was in a ponytail that bounced as she walked. She looked as though she'd learned what administrators looked like from movies.

Sheesh, he thought with a wince. *That was mean.*

DJ sped up to match Sarah's gait. "Uh, so what exactly are we in trouble for?"

"Not a clue." Sarah shrugged. "Higher-ups just asked me to bring you. Must be something, though. They looked pissed." She peered at him curiously from the side of her glasses.

DJ shrugged right back. "Who knows? The brass always finds something to be pissed about."

"Yeah, but they seemed ready to burst a vein. Makes you wonder what a recruit could have done to piss them off so much."

"What makes you so sure I'm a recruit?" DJ asked, mainly to deflect but partly out of curiosity. They reached the other side of the courtyard and passed through a side entrance into the building proper.

DJ nodded in approval as he looked around. Now this was more like it. There were actual framed pictures of past admirals and captains spaced out on the wall. DJ was surprised he could recognize some of the faces. Cool. The air was fresh, and the floor was carpeted. Granted, it wasn't the luxurious décor of command tents portrayed in movies, but at least it was *something.*

"Well, for one thing," Sarah said, "Only recruits are required to have name tags sewn into their uniforms. But mostly it's the way you keep glancing like a tourist at everything we pass. All agents are required to meet the higher-ups at least once. It's where they get promoted."

DJ hummed in response, and Sarah glanced at him again. It was obvious she wanted to pick up her questioning but didn't know how to do it without prying. And she couldn't just order him to tell her.

"Ah. Good. Sarah, is it? And Recruit Kojak. I've been looking for you both," a voice boomed from across the hall. Sarah's mouth clamped shut, and she turned in the direction of the voice. DJ was already considering the old man.

Is he really that old, though? DJ wondered. As they got closer, he could make out the man more clearly. There were obvious gray hairs on his head, but not a hint of wrinkles. He was as tall as DJ, but broader and… *more.* A palpable presence surrounded him, though he hadn't done anything more than just stand there. It didn't make sense until DJ noticed the uniform. DJ's eyes were immediately drawn to the three stars sewn into the shoulder pads. Sarah sputtered as they got closer, and DJ unintentionally fell one step behind.

"Admiral Olsen, it's an honor, sir," Sarah said, trying her best to level her voice. She saluted, but it was obvious how much mental effort it had taken.

DJ couldn't blame her. His whole body was tense, arms locked at his sides. There were only three admirals in the Navy SEALs, and they were never actually at the base except for important ceremonies. Yet here was one just wandering around. Rumors had it that no one could ever just be promoted to admiral; the outgoing admirals picked their replacements, and only candidates that had a truly awe-inspiring list of accomplishments.

Admiral Olsen focused his gaze on DJ, and he immediately felt fear. A recruit disobeying orders was always a serious issue, but DJ had been pretty sure his punishment would be minimal, considering a high-profile target would have escaped if it weren't for him. But that was before the admiral.

If the case was so important that they called a goddamn admiral to judge it, DJ was so fucking screwed.

Admiral Olsen chuckled lightly. "Don't look so scared, boy. I'm not gonna bite or anything."

"That's so not what I'm afraid of," DJ mumbled.

Unfortunately, Olsen seemed to have heard him because he chuckled again, more loudly. He turned to Sarah. "You were ordered to lead Recruit Kojak to Davidson and Simmons, right?"

Sarah nodded, keeping her motions minimal. "We would have been there already, but Kojak insisted on a few minutes to freshen up. I rejected, and the argument wasted valuable time."

Way to throw a guy under the bus, DJ thought.

Olsen held up a placating hand. One part of his mouth twisted up. "That's all right. You've done nothing wrong. I just want to have a talk with the boy. I'll take him from you and present him to Davidson and Simmons myself when we're done."

"But, sir—" Sarah started to protest.

"You're dismissed, sergeant," the admiral said calmly. He still held a smile, but his tone brokered no room for disagreement.

Sarah tried for a salute once more, spared a glance at DJ, and left. The admiral placed a hand on DJ's shoulder, his smile widening. There was a twinkle in his eye. DJ struggled to keep his composure.

"So," Olsen said. "You seem to have gotten yourself in a bit of a jam. Wanna tell me about it?"

THE PRESSURE IN THE HALLWAY GREW, then seemed to collapse on itself. Admiral Olsen was somehow just Admiral Olsen—still extremely powerful, but now his aura didn't make DJ feel like he was struggling for every breath. DJ's muscles all relaxed at once, and he stumbled slightly. When he looked around, the hallway was deserted.

When did that happen? he wondered. *You'd think people would be drawn to the sight of an admiral.* But then again, DJ normally wouldn't have. Why had he been scared stiff? DJ had never been the type to revere any one person. Respect, yes, but never revere. It was an odd feeling—one he didn't particularly like. His eyes were hard when he looked at Olsen, but the old man returned the gaze with his characteristic smile.

A second went by before DJ spoke. Even through his anger, he chose his words carefully. "It's an honor to meet you, sir."

"Pleasure's all mine, lad," replied Olsen. He spun on his heels and started walking, moving deeper into the building. "Tell me about Finn."

DJ hurried to catch up, though he was careful to keep a step behind the admiral. Olsen glanced at him curiously, and DJ hastily began.

He treated it like a debriefing—that's what Sarah had told him it was, after all. Maybe this was part of it. He made sure to give details but kept strictly to the facts, except when he got to Bradley's orders when Finn had come out of the building. That part he altered to imply the order was directed only at him, not his team. That way, only he would be punished. Christy was only following *his* orders. Bradley would probably tell a different story, but at least DJ had laid the groundwork for doubt.

From there, he moved on to Finn's extraction vehicle, giving as accurate a report of the distance as he could. Again, he kept Christy's involvement to a minimum, except when mentioning how it messed up Finn's aim. That part he spoke about with pride.

Olsen listened patiently, asking questions only to clear up something DJ hadn't explained well. He nodded when DJ finished his report. That was when DJ finally noticed they were standing in front of a door. He could hear voices within.

"I think I get the gist of it," Olsen said. He pointed at the door. "Do *not* say a word when we're in there. Rest assured, I'll take it from here."

DJ nodded mutely, confused. *He'll take what from where?*

The admiral pushed open the door.

From one moment to the next, Olsen seemed to change. His smile was gone, replaced by a thin line, and he seemed taller. DJ didn't know how that was possible. This didn't feel like the same person who had waited patiently for him to give his report. *This* guy was an admiral, and his presence billowed out in waves.

The discussion immediately stopped. DJ followed the admiral, though his own entrance went largely ignored. He could accept that. He made sure to stay behind Olsen, keeping out of direct line of sight. No one spoke for a few minutes, so DJ took in the room.

The first thing he noticed was that it was modeled after a normal court-room, complete with a judge's dais where two men sat with their faces frozen in shock. There was a smaller table in front of the platform where DJ supposed the defendant—in this case, him—would sit. His eyes widened in surprise when he noticed Bradley standing off to the side of the smaller table, staring at Olsen with no small amount of fear. DJ resisted the urge to walk up and punch him.

The five of them were the only ones in the room. DJ didn't know if that was a good thing or a bad thing. There wasn't even a recordkeeper.

The silence dragged on, and Olsen seemed content to let it. DJ coughed politely, drawing three pairs of eyes to him. Bradley had a sneer on his face. The other two merely turned back to Olsen.

"Admiral," said the guy on the far left. He was the older of the two, but not as old as Olsen. DJ estimated late forties at most. "I didn't think you'd be back from your duties so soon."

"Ah, well, neither did I, Simmons. But shit happens, and here we are," Olsen said amicably. He took a seat at the smaller table. The effect on the room was palpable. It was obvious that the dais was a power move. Regardless of whether one was sitting or standing, he would still have to look up at his "betters." Most people noticing this would choose to stand, minimizing the effect.

Although Olsen had chosen to sit, from his presence alone, no one misunderstood who was in charge. It was an almost-physical thing.

DJ chose to stand behind him.

Simmons's brows pinched in irritation. "You must have just landed an hour ago at most," he noted. "Anyone else would be resting, but here you are. Surely, there must be an important reason for it."

"Well, I heard young Bradley might be here."

Bradley sputtered in surprise—as did the two men, though their reaction was more subtle. DJ struggled to keep his own face expressionless. What did Bradley have to do with this?

Davidson was the first one to get over his surprise. "And you needed Agent Bradley for something?"

"Well, that can be addressed later," Olsen said. "I interrupted something when I walked in. I assume that was the discussion about Agent Bradley's report?" The expression on Bradley's face made it quite clear that their discussion was most certainly about his report.

Dang, DJ thought. *You gotta admire how fast he snitches, though.*

Simmons let out a polite cough. "We were just going through some finer points of the case."

"I'm sure you were." Olsen's voice was icy. "Then you'll likely have need for a second opinion. There were two team leaders present at the incident, after all." He looked over at DJ. "Tell them what you told me, lad."

So, DJ gave the exact same report he'd given Olsen. Like Olsen, Davidson and Simmons listened in silence to the whole thing and asked their questions only after he was done. *Unlike* Olsen, who only asked questions for clarification, their questions were clearly meant to trap DJ or force him to highlight the fact that he'd disobeyed a direct order.

Bradley looked exceptionally smug at this point. The fucker was clearly friends with Davidson and Simmons and felt sure about what their verdict would be. For the first time, DJ realized how screwed he would have been had the admiral not taken up his case.

As if to prove his point, Davidson spoke up. "That's all well and good, recruit, but you disobeyed a direct order from your superior in the heat of combat. You risked the lives of both your team leader and teammates' to chase your own personal brand of heroics."

DJ opened his mouth to say something that was probably going to land him in jail. Luckily, Olsen spoke up before he could. "His own personal brand of heroics, 'David,' was what saved the mission. Bradley, over here, was perfectly willing to let Finn escape."

Bradley sputtered to defend his actions, but Simmons held up a hand. He stared at Olsen with narrowed eyes. "His report stated that he'd sent Agent Bass to apprehend the suspect before extraction could be made. Finn wouldn't have escaped in any case."

DJ was shaking his head before he even realized he was doing so. It was an obvious lie. There hadn't been an agent on that field. If there had, DJ would have noticed. If they had come out after he'd chased down Finn, they would have been behind him. They'd have had even less of a shot if Christy hadn't taken out the tires.

Olsen grunted. "Well then, Agent Bradley lied to you. A track of the comms unit places his whole team inside the building for the duration of the incident."

Immediately, every eye went to Bradley. He was either too surprised or too stupid to hide his expressions. His face went through phases of shock, fear, and guilt before finally hardening into anger when his eyes met DJ's.

For his part, DJ didn't have it in him to look smug. He stared at the back of the admiral's head. *How did he have time to track the comms unit? Didn't he arrive only a few hours ago?*

"It would seem we have to reconsider our position," Simmons said after a moment. He gave a resigned sigh. "What do you recommend, Admiral?"

Olsen met his eyes with a steely gaze.

CHAPTER

12

MARCH 2040

NAVAL AMPHIBIOUS BASE, CORONADO, CALIFORNIA

DJ LEFT THE ROOM with a temporary demotion and latrine duty for a month. The headquarters had an abundance of toilets, and cleaning them was apparently another punishment altogether. Latrine duty was a step above toilet duty in the sense that he wouldn't be cleaning anything. Rather, he would be *digging* the latrines. There were depth and width measurements for everything. The real kicker, though, was since the HQ had basically hundreds of toilets scattered within it, the latrines he'd dig wouldn't ever be used, except for the duration of his punishment.

As DJ understood it, for the next month, he would be digging holes in the ground, and every day a random person would be assigned to shit in those holes. The smell would make digging the next holes that much more horrible. Fortunately, according to Olsen, it was a very common punishment, so DJ wouldn't be the only person smelling like shit at the end of the day.

He'd gotten off with a slap on the wrist, and he knew it. There were so many other ways his punishment could have gone. He looked at Olsen as they walked up the stairs to another floor—the top one, from the look of the décor.

Since leaving the room, the admiral had lost his overpowering presence. The bearing was still there, but now he could be mistaken for a retired captain. DJ didn't know how to deal with the constant switches. However, he was pretty sure he wouldn't have to. After all, Olsen needed him for something.

DJ wasn't so naive as to think the old man had helped him out of the goodness of his heart. Olsen needing him was the only sensible reason an admiral would go through all that trouble for him.

But what the fuck would he need me for? DJ mentally screamed. *How the fuck does he even* know *about me?* That was the part that didn't make sense. DJ had tried to ask several times, but the admiral had shut it down every time.

He considered walking away. It would have sealed his name as a giant idiot. DJ hated to be someone's puppet, but he hated being indebted even more. Besides, he was curious about what the old guy wanted.

They stopped in front of an office. Olsen unlocked the door with an electronic key and waved DJ inside with him. The office wasn't as large as DJ expected. He thought an admiral would have something three times its size.

"It was by request," Olsen said by way of explanation, reading DJ's thoughts. His back was to DJ as he walked toward the large desk at the center of the room. "I'm hardly ever around, you see. It seemed a waste to have one of those stupidly large offices." He took his place at the table and gestured for DJ to take the seat opposite. "I'm not so young that my bones can handle much moving around."

DJ almost snorted at that. He would bet an arm that the admiral was as spry as men half his age.

"Sir, I've already figured out that you need me for something," started DJ as he took his seat. "What I haven't been able to figure out is what. Does it have to do with Finn? 'Cause you should know that Bradley would lock me out of that case, hard."

"I've always admired directness," the admiral said, "so I'll be direct right back. I don't really give a rat's ass about Finn."

DJ stared back in surprise. *Then what the hell do you want me for?* he wanted to ask.

Olsen continued, "What do you know about Mayday, boy?"

He felt the hair on his neck rise. "Nothing more than anyone else, sir," he replied guardedly. Why'd he have to go and bring up Mayday? DJ had done a pretty good job of blocking it out for the past few months.

Olsen stared at him for a moment, then nodded. "Who'd you lose?"

DJ tried to keep his expression blank as he struggled with the memories he thought he'd locked away. "My dads," he answered finally.

"Plural?"

"Yes," DJ gritted out. He'd had two fathers. He wasn't uncomfortable with that fact, but the expression people had when they found out almost made him want to bash their faces in. Many people couldn't comprehend the concept. To his credit, Olsen just grunted.

DJ was surprised that the admiral had had to ask. The information was in DJ's file. If he'd had the time to analyze Bradley's report and verify it, why would he not have also just flipped through DJ's records? Maybe he had and was just putting on a show.

DJ discarded the thought. Olsen didn't seem like the kind of person who'd do that.

"My condolences for your loss," Olsen said finally. "But at least now, I don't have to worry about properly motivating you."

"Motivating me for what, sir?" DJ asked warily.

Olsen waved his question away, meeting DJ's gaze firmly. "Despite what the media might say, Mayday wasn't caused by a terrorist organization or even a malfunction of Gaius." He paused, as if to give DJ time to process it, before continuing. "It took the guys at the lab far too long, but we've verified that the AI was deliberately hacked, and the 'malfunction' was a controlled attack."

DJ felt the blood rush to his head. He understood what the admiral was saying—at least on the surface. And he deliberately kept it on a surface level to keep from doing anything stupid. He closed his eyes. "And so, all the crashes and deaths…"

His dads had died while on a plane, flying out for their second honeymoon. From the report DJ had gotten, theirs was one of the first to have malfunctioned. The control tower had lost the signal somewhere over the Atlantic. The bodies couldn't be recovered.

If that hadn't been an accident…

"They were on purpose," confirmed the admiral. "We're not yet sure if the hacker intended for *all* the craft to malfunction or if the virus got away from them, but that's beside the point."

DJ took a deep breath before opening his eyes. "You want to catch the bastard. I get that. But it sounds like you'll need tech guys, not muscle. Where do I come in?"

"We don't need *you* specifically," Olsen said, once again meeting DJ's eyes. "We need your brother."

That he hadn't expected. "What does CJ have to do with this?"

"A number of hacks were traced to his IP address shortly after the events of Mayday," Olsen answered, then immediately raised a finger to forestall DJ's outburst. When DJ made a stand anyway, the admiral's eyes went hard, and his presence blanketed the room. For the second time that day, DJ felt every muscle in his body tense.

"You'll need to learn patience, boy, or you'll find yourself in a world of trouble someday," Olsen said.

"Yes, sir." He could hardly bear to look at the admiral as he held back his anger.

"Christopher Kojak *did* hack into some sensitive systems, but only to get more information about Mayday. In any other case, he would already be sitting in a federal prison. However, the fact that he could breach our firewalls and prevent us from tracing him sooner is a testament to his skill." Olsen paused for what DJ assumed was dramatic effect. "We want to recruit him and, by proxy, you. We think your skills would pair nicely."

"So, sir, you're basically asking us to find who killed our parents," DJ confirmed. When Olsen nodded, he let out a snort. "What is this? A movie?" For the first time, Olsen truly looked annoyed, so DJ hurried on. "Don't get me wrong. We'll do it. I just want to fully appreciate the comedic value of it."

"Obviously, yours would be one of the dozen teams working on this, but the more hands we have, the greater chance we have to catch the bastard." the admiral said. Admittedly, that deflated DJ a little bit, which was probably the purpose. Olsen spread his arms, smiling. The twinkle was back in his eyes. "You have the entire US Intelligence Community at your disposal, son. What do you need?"

"I'll send you a list," DJ replied. "But first I need to call my brother."

THE SPARTA BUILDING was not what Karla expected. But then, nothing was in this godforsaken country. She spat on the carpet, ignoring the glare from Liz. She could not wait to leave behind this backwater burg, whenever José was done with… whatever he was doing.

She and Liz had waited until nightfall before infiltrating the building. In any other place, this would have been perfect because the guards would be lax, so moving to their target—whatever it was this time—would have been far easier.

Liz poked her head into the next hallway and signaled that there were three guards. Karla stifled a groan. It was the third patrol they'd seen in the last few minutes alone and none of them appeared as lax as they should have been.

Karla signaled that she wanted a look, and Liz made way for her. The guards—big and buff in the way Americans seemed to think would make a difference in a fight—made their way along the hallway in the entirely wrong direction. Karla hoped they wouldn't have to reroute again. She turned to address Chloe but remembered that their mentor was not with them.

"We should take them out," she muttered to Liz instead.

"No, José was very clear," Liz replied. "We are to infiltrate only and retrieve the hard drive. It would be bad if the CIA were discovered to have been here." She nodded to something at the end of the hallway. "Plus, we would be in full view of the camera."

That was another thing Karla hadn't expected from the Sparta building. José himself had tried to hack into the camera system but found the defenses to be too great. Karla had never heard of such a thing happening before. The fact that they didn't have control of the cameras limited their movements even more than the guards did. They could take control of one if they were close. However, this took a lot of time and might trigger an alarm. Like destroying them, this would be the same as announcing their presence—a bad thing, apparently. They worked with the government. What sort of government was afraid of an organization run by its own citizens?

Karla made to spit again but was cut off by Liz's glare.

"What sort of industry is this even?" she asked instead. "What have we come to retrieve?"

"They are a wealthy technological company. And their prized product is an illusion that reads to people."

Karla frowned. "And people *want* this illusion to read to them?"

"Apparently. They rush like an avalanche to buy them. No one else has been able to replicate this technology. The CIA is interested in how it was made. They say it is controlled by an artificial mind."

Karla was unable to hold in her snort. Luckily, the guards had long passed, and it went unnoticed. Even still, Liz sent her a glare. What did her sister expect? Such a thing was too ridiculous to be met with anything other than derision.

"So, this artificial mind," Karla said, trying to hide her laughter, "does it think for itself?"

Liz shook her head. She spared another glance at the camera at the end of the hallway and signaled to Karla. They would have to find another way to reach their destination. They made their way back down the passage, keeping to a jog. They had already spent far more time than they'd planned.

"Its creator programmed it," Liz puffed, "so he controls it. However, the illusion is that it responds to people as if it were a person. The CIA wants to know how the artificial mind was created and if it can be made to do things beyond reading books and catering to people's requests."

Karla struggled to split her concentration as her sister did. It was better when they fought because the adrenaline told her muscles what to do. There was no adrenaline when they spoke. "Why do they not just buy one of the devices and take it apart?

"They have tried. The defenses are too strong."

"So, what are we retrieving?"

Liz signaled, and they paused when they reached the edge of the passageway. She tapped her wrist, bringing up the map. Karla wanted to ask where José had acquired a map, but she stopped herself from saying something so stupid. It most likely involved a knife to the throat of a poor employee.

"An agent was able to download the information on the artificial mind," Liz explained, scanning the map, "but he was killed before he could bring it back. The hard drive was seized, so we were sent to retrieve it."

"Wouldn't the information have been destroyed?"

"In that case, we are to download it again and return alive to hand it to José." She looked up from the map and pointed down an adjacent hallway. "We go that way."

Karla signaled to start the motion, and the twins made their way deeper into the building.

A FEW DAYS AFTER BEING DISCHARGED from the hospital, Manar stepped into the wreckage of his home. Though most of the debris had long been removed, the devastation was still obvious in the things that were left behind. Those things were what Manar had come for.

His instructions to the cleaning crew had been clear: "If you don't know what it is, and it shows no obvious signs of being broken, leave it." They'd followed these instructions, fortunately for them. Now it was up to him to see what could be salvaged. But first, he needed some light.

"Helene, activate holoform and duplicate self around the room."

It took less than a second for the AI to acknowledge the command, and the room grew noticeably brighter. She'd done one better, positioning the holograms in such a way that the whole room was brightened, instead of just a select few areas. Helene wouldn't have shown such initiative before his upgrades, so at least one good thing had come out of his hospitalization.

One good to combat all the bad. Ugh, this isn't a movie. Manar pushed the thought away.

The power had been fixed around the building, but most rooms were left vacant—the effects of Mayday. Thus, maintenance had decided to cut power where it wasn't needed. It would only take a phone call to fix it, but what was the point? He wasn't staying long, and the rays from Helene's holoforms, though not particularly illuminating, provided at least enough light to see.

His eyes scanned the room. The bulletproof windows had been destroyed, probably from the third or fourth plane that crashed into them. Half of the ceiling had collapsed, and there was a hole leading to the room directly above him. The meshwork of wood and paper gave a modicum of privacy to the occupants while restoration went on. Manar was relieved that the half that had fallen down had been over his bed and wardrobe, not his system's array. He already knew that *something* had been destroyed there, since Helene's backups hadn't been fully transferred. But at least he wouldn't have to start from scratch when reconstructing her mainframe.

He sighed. *Let's get this over with.*

The computer array was in his second walk-in closet. That was where he'd kept Helene's hardware— his own version of her. He'd arranged the parts on the shelves, placed a couple of sockets linked up to the building's power grid, and used a series of long cables to connect everything. It had been messy, but he couldn't trust anyone else to handle it. Most technicians wouldn't have even realized what they were looking at.

There was only one problem with his arrangement. When the building had trembled from all the plane crashes, the hardware had been dislodged from the shelves and thrown parabolically into others, destroying them all in a domino effect. Only those placed at the bottom had been safe, falling just a few inches before they'd reached the floor. Luckily, though most of them still looked damaged, he could already see a few that could be salvaged.

Manar tried to feel anger at the sight. Almost a decade's work lay in ruins. But he felt nothing. He hadn't felt anything in weeks.

Not since Simone's death, he realized. Manar pushed that thought away too.

He stared at the wreckage of his array. He needed a way to transport the parts that were salvageable, but he hadn't thought that far ahead. He could call the building maintenance team to do the heavy lifting, but they'd have to carry it to his new place. And he didn't want that. There were reasons he'd chosen to forgo the apartment that Sparta granted with his new position. Most of them revolved around privacy. He wanted to be alone; he wouldn't have that if people knew where to find him.

Alternatively, he could just have them bring the load up to his car. It would mean multiple trips, but Helene could handle the others once he'd integrated the AI to his vehicle. It was somewhat risky, but unlike Gaius, Helene was foolproof.

"Contact building maintenance and direct them to my position."

[Acknowledged,] Helene responded immediately.

Manar surveyed the array once more. He sighed.

APRIL 2040

ENCINITAS, CALIFORNIA

OLSEN WAS ABLE TO DEFER DJ's punishment for several weeks while he was on the job. Even his training was put on hold. His team was temporarily added to others, with the caveat that they could be called on if DJ ever needed them. All Olsen had needed to do was make a call, which he had done in DJ's presence. It was so obviously a power move that DJ had almost snorted. Still, it was an important reminder that, despite his easygoing nature, Olsen was still one of the only three admirals in the SEALs.

Explaining everything to Christy and Kyle without *actually* telling them anything vital was more of a hassle than he'd imagined. But he'd done it and driven out the next morning.

Now he stared across the table at his older twin.

"This café was… their life," CJ said. "We cannot… sell it."

"But you're in school full time at MIT," DJ said. "Can you manage the café remotely between Nuclear Physics exams? Jesus, you had to fly out just to meet me here. You know you'd have to do that every week, right?"

They had been putting off discussing what to do with their dads' café ever since Mayday. Their deaths had almost overwhelmed CJ, taking him back to his pre-therapy days. His symptoms had worsened to the point that he was almost incoherent. So DJ had tabled the issue for a few months to give them both time to heal. And they had.

Still, they'd been sitting at the diner for over twenty minutes, arguing back and forth about what to do with the business.

DJ proposed selling the restaurant. He didn't *want* to; the Encinitas Café was basically their second home. Both he and his brother had spent practically every weekend there, growing up. But facts were facts. CJ was a full-time student. DJ didn't see a life where he could take a break from his missions just to check on the business and that wasn't counting whatever the hell Olsen had dragged them into with the terrorist hunt.

"Can you not manage it?" CJ asked haltingly. "The Naval Amphibious Base in Coronado is… uh… within driving distance…" His eyes glazed over as he did the calculations. "About thirty-one miles."

DJ stared at his brother, considering. He'd always been better with numbers.

"It should only take… you about thirty minutes, without the usual speeding ticket," CJ added.

Damn it. Now DJ couldn't refuse without looking like a selfish ass.

"Fine," he accepted after a minute. "But only if you handle all the number crunching and tax filings. That's your thing after all." DJ grimaced at even the thought. He always tried to bail out of calculations whenever he could. He wasn't math dyslexic; the numbers just never added up for him.

"Fine," CJ agreed. "One of the waitresses… can scan everything and upload it at night. I'll keep tabs… on the numbers."

DJ reached a hand across the table. "Deal."

CJ almost glared at the hand, and DJ smirked. His brother had made tremendous progress over the years, but physical contact was always a no-go. DJ was willing to accept his brother's aversion to anyone else, but not with him. Family was family. As terrible as it sounded, it was his way of challenging his brother. It was just the two of them now. Each other was all they had. It was their job to push each other to the limit so they could break free of the mental constraints they'd placed upon themselves.

DJ stared at his brother. After a moment, CJ reached out and clasped his hand. "Deal," he muttered.

DJ grinned. In many ways, he'd known they could never give up the café. It would be the same as selling off their childhood home. There were just too many memories there. It had been their dads' legacy, and neither of them wanted it to end with them.

"Seriously, though, we owe this… to our dads and their customers."

"Yeah," replied DJ with a small smile, swirling his drink. "We do, don't we?"

THE SILENCE LASTED for a few minutes. CJ tried not to jump when his brother suddenly clapped his hands.

"Now that we have the issue of the café sorted out," DJ said, smiling to make sure there was no misunderstanding of his next topic. "School's been treating you all right?"

CJ had trouble meeting his eyes, though it was more out of guilt than the usual discomfort. "I made… a friend," he said quietly.

It was the lunch hour, so the diner was packed. Fortunately, they'd picked a table toward the back, where it was a little quieter. CJ knew the exact moment DJ processed his words because his eyes narrowed into slits, though his smile grew and turned genuine.

It was an obvious ploy to deflect from the topic, but it was a good ploy. CJ had always had trouble making friends because of his autism. Even when he got better at managing it, people tended to avoid him. Though it might not seem like much to some, making a friend was a big deal to him. That meant it would be a big deal to his brother. He was banking on that.

But DJ just waggled a finger and let out a chuckle. CJ's heart sank. "Good one," DJ said, then his voice turned serious. "But you need to explain. What did you do?"

CJ sighed. "I might have hacked… into some government sites… to get more information about Mayday."

DJ nodded for him to continue. There was no surprise on his face, so he must have known that already. What bothered CJ was *how* he'd found out. It was at the tip of his tongue to ask, but he knew that would just piss DJ off more.

"The media was not giving… much information about it," CJ explained, his eyes darting around the diner. Anywhere else but at his brother. "And the authorities were not saying… anything. And I needed… to know why."

"So you hacked the fucking government?" DJ growled. "How in the hell did you justify that?" He paused as a thought occurred to him. "And when did you get good enough to try it anyway?"

The waitress came to refill their drinks, and CJ took the opportunity to ground himself. He tended to escape into his thoughts when he was uncomfortable. He scratched the back of his head and continued after the waitress left. "I have always been… good enough."

DJ rested heavily on the chair and groaned loudly. CJ squirmed in his seat. CJ had always been good with computers, but it wasn't as if he'd hidden how good he was from his brother; there just had never been a need to use the skill—until Mayday.

"Why the fuck are you at MIT studying nuclear physics then?" DJ asked finally. It was an old conversation. DJ and their parents had never understood why CJ had pursued a degree in nuclear physics, and CJ wasn't willing to rehash the argument.

"That is… beside the point."

"What's the point, then?" DJ asked.

"That I am… sorry," CJ said calmly. DJ's eyes widened, and CJ forced himself to meet his brother's gaze. "The fact that you are here—the fact that you know about it at all—means that your superiors… must have found out. That I have gotten… us in trouble."

DJ stared for a moment, before snorting. "It definitely made life more interesting, I'll tell you that. I got to meet with an admiral."

CJ's eyes didn't widen but only because facial expressions were difficult.

"Yeah," DJ nodded. It had been almost a decade since he needed expressions to read his brother. "I almost pissed my pants, too, but all they wanted was to recruit you—recruit us."

"Recruit us… for what?"

DJ stared at CJ firmly. Sheer willpower made CJ meet the gaze. "They want us to track down our dads' killer. I don't know what you found out when you burrowed into their computers, but apparently Mayday wasn't the accidental malfunction the media's been feeding us."

CJ hadn't seen anything that even hinted at that in the reports, but he'd stopped checking for updates weeks back. "What would… recruitment entail?"

"That's up to you, big bro," DJ said. A thought made him grin, and he spread his arms amicably. "You have the entire US Intelligence Community at your disposal. What would you need?"

Outwardly, CJ stared blankly, but inside he was already compiling a list.

CHAPTER

16

NDIDI STRODE IN THROUGH the open doors of the Gaius Corporation, trying not to look too much like she'd come to steal something.

The guards spared a glance at her visitor's badge and let her pass. She let out a breath that she hadn't realized she'd been holding. With how much scrutiny the corporation had come under in the last few months, Ndidi would normally never be allowed visitation. Still, being a partner in the Okafor Corporation did have its perks, even if she felt guilty for using the company's name in this.

What she came to do wasn't strictly legal. She didn't even want to ponder what she'd do if she got caught.

She looked around. The Gaius Corporation was built using levels. Each level corresponded to a floor. Thus, employees never had any doubt about where they were in the company's food chain. Since Mayday, most information regarding the company had been somehow scrubbed from the web. Rumors had it that it was done by the company itself to discourage people with grievances from breaking in to harm staff or damage property.

Several months ago, with a different mindset, Ndidi would have been among those people. Knowing what she knew now about the hacking, though, she felt pity. Gaius had been ingrained into transportation for decades. Still, that pity did not stop her from stealing from them.

The fact that there was no information to be had made her job decidedly harder, though. *Which, I guess, was the point,* she thought dourly. Chad remembered his workplace being somewhere on the tenth floor, but that had been a decade ago and there was no way to confirm that the lab hadn't moved. *Better than nothing, at least.*

There were twenty floors. Ndidi's visitor's badge gave her access to only the first ten. So, for everything higher, she'd have to figure it out as she went. Her guide was nowhere to be found. This was good; their presence would have ruined all the work she'd put into arriving an hour early. Her task would be difficult enough without someone stringing her along, enforcing where she could and could not go.

Plus, now she had a perfectly good excuse if she was caught where she wasn't supposed to be. She could fake ignorance. It would only work once, but it was something.

"I really should have planned this better," she muttered. The ground floor was sparsely populated. The few who roamed there didn't spare her a second glance. Ndidi hoped that would hold for all the floors.

The elevators dinged at her call.

17

APRIL 2040

GAIUS CORPORATION, SILICON VALLEY, CALIFORNIA

DJ CRAWLED GINGERLY through the seventh-floor window and breathed a sigh of relief when he saw that the hallway was clear.

"I'm in," he said, disengaging his climbing equipment. His arms burned more than they had during drills. He'd only climbed seven floors, but each floor felt twice the height of floors in a building that size. He was breathing heavily, but he couldn't afford to rest now. "Damn, their security is tight! I thought this was just a tech company?"

"They are," CJ replied over the comms unit. "They have had… a series of incidents over the past few months that… have made them wary."

"What kind of incidents?" Christy asked. She was perched on the roof of the building opposite Gaius, where her sniper skills would be best used. DJ hoped they wouldn't have a need for them, but better to have them just in case. Besides, it never hurt to have another pair of eyes.

"From aggrieved families," CJ said. "Remember, malfunction… or not, people cannot see past… their grief and anger."

"Well, that explains the crowd of protesters," Christy muttered.

CJ elaborated, but DJ wasn't listening. He'd pushed the conversation to the back of his mind as he scanned the hall. There were doors on each side but no clear labeling. He wasn't even sure if he was on the right floor. It was only a matter of time before someone showed up. It seemed like he would be forced to check every door.

"Hey, CJ," DJ said softly, "still got controls on the cameras?"

"Yes. But remember, I could not… completely bypass their security, so I only have the cameras… for the floor you are on. If you move up a floor, you… should tell me."

"Don't worry, D," Christy said. "I have eyes on the floor above and below you."

DJ nodded, then realized she probably couldn't see it. Oh well. He moved deeper into the hallway. The doors were all the same light-brown wood, with nothing to differentiate them. Still, DJ assumed the room with the computer array of a tech company would be bigger than a normal-sized office.

"Remind me again what I'm looking for?" DJ asked sheepishly. CJ had spent hours going on and on about how difficult it was to track the malfunction without some sort of reference point. That was the part DJ understood, but when his brother had switched to talking about triangulating the source code and other such nonsense, he'd tuned out. Honestly, the kid was wasted in nuclear physics, and everybody except him seemed to realize that.

CJ sighed, and DJ could feel the waves of exasperation roll off him. "You are looking for the mainframe computers, where the codes for the Gaius AI would be. It will… make perfect reference. If you cannot find it, plug the thumb drive I gave you… into any sample of a hacked vehicle. Then wait."

DJ nodded and sped through the hallway. He was careful not to make too much noise, but he couldn't afford to waste time on the lower levels. The building had twenty floors, and all they knew was that the computer array wasn't on the first six. He would have to check all of them while somehow avoiding detection. Olsen was very clear about what would happen if he got caught, and DJ had watched enough movies to understand that being disavowed was bad for his career. *And my life in general*, DJ chuckled grimly to himself.

His inspection of the hall found nothing like what his brother had described. He couldn't actually open any of the doors, but he was pretty certain that the mainframe array would be more conspicuous than a bland office door. Still, that begged the question of what it *would* be like. Would it be something like a garage, maybe?

DJ shook his head in frustration. The hallway branched, so he picked one at random and followed it to its end, scanning each door as he passed. The place was as deserted as the hall he'd just left, and after a while, it started taking more time to sneak than just walk normally.

He followed several hallways, backtracking through some, before finally arriving back where he'd started. Each of the passages had roughly the same number of offices on each side. With the number of passages he'd gone through, the sheer number of staff that Gaius had once held gave DJ a healthy respect for how big it was—and how far it had fallen.

Still, whatever array CJ was looking for, it definitely wasn't on that floor. There was no point hanging around. He ducked into another hallway and spotted the stairway at its end—just in time, apparently, as Christy's voice came on in his ear.

"Someone just came out of a door behind you, D," the blonde warned. "Stay on your toes; they're heading your way now."

DJ nodded, then grimaced as he realized, once again, that there was no way she could see it. He didn't dare run, as his footfalls would definitely be heard. Rather, he lengthened his strides toward the stairway, making sure to keep every step light.

"Heading up," he whispered. "Hope you're ready for me."

CJ didn't respond immediately, but DJ could hear the vigorous clacking of keys through the comms. He yanked the door to the stairway and closed it gingerly just as he heard the clack of shoes turning the corner.

"Uh… do not move," CJ said. "Always a camera on the stairs… but on a different server. Should be safe close to the door. I will… have control of it in a minute,"

"I'm definitely *not* safe at the door," DJ whispered hurriedly, looking up at the camera. "It rotates, and I'll be fucked when it comes back to me."

"Give… me a second. Almost have it."

Fortunately for DJ, he'd entered as soon as the camera started panning away, leaving the door out of its line of sight. It was nearing the end of the rotation, however, and it'd be resetting for another sweep. He glanced at the walls. He could probably scale higher than the camera level with his gear, but there wasn't enough time to put it on.

"Christy, what's the twenty on the staff?"

"She's left my line of sight, so I can't be sure. But I doubt she's out of sight of the stairway yet."

Fuck, DJ thought. The camera began a rotation back. DJ grimaced. He was going to have to risk it. It had almost completed its cycle. DJ pushed back on the stairway door.

"I have… it," CJ said.

DJ's eyes were still tracking the camera. There was no visible effect, so he didn't breathe a sigh of relief yet. It finally finished its sweep and landed on him. Now there was no point in hiding, even if he wanted to.

"I have… control of it," CJ assured him.

DJ gave him a thumbs up, taking deep breaths through his nose. Training missions were supposed to have prepared him for things like this. And DJ honestly thought that dealing with Finn had given him far more experience than any other assignment. But with training—even when auditing a real mission, as they'd done with Bradley—the sergeants or agents were always there. DJ had always given it his best, of course, but until now he hadn't realized how much comfort that safety net had given him.

CJ confirmed that there was nobody around the stairway on the eighth floor, but it brought up something that made DJ want to kick himself for not thinking of it before.

"Hey, bro," DJ whispered as he exited into another hall. "How 'bout next time, since I'm going to be taking the stairs up, you take control of the camera in there and confirm there's no one else taking the stairs at the same time?" DJ almost felt like headbutting the wall, annoyed that it hadn't occurred to him earlier. If they'd had control of the camera initially, DJ wouldn't have risked a mini-heart attack just now. And he didn't want to even consider what would have happened if he'd met another person in there. With his jeans and light T-shirt, he could probably blend in if push came to shove, but it wasn't exactly business casual. Why risk it if he didn't have to?

"How the hell did we not think of that?" Christy muttered in a tone she probably thought was too low to be picked up. DJ was going to have to talk to her about that at some point.

"Got it," replied CJ, clicking away.

The eighth floor was just as deserted as the one below it, but DJ remained cautious as he went. Fortunately, there were stairways at both ends of the hall, so he wouldn't have to cross again to go up a level and it was looking like he would have to.

He followed the branching hallway once again, wasting far too much time. He still couldn't find anything resembling what he pictured the mainframe array or the storage unit to look like. He stifled a groan, starting to get pissed off. If they'd known exactly which floor the array was on, he would have been in and out by now. He made his way to the stairway at the end of the hall.

"This place is a bust. I'm moving up now. Christy, how's the next floor looking?"

"Just as empty," she replied.

DJ sighed. The company had balls, he had to give them that. Why bother to open if you had less than a quarter of your staff? DJ didn't know if the workers had all resigned on principle after Mayday or if all but the bare essentials had been let go, but even keeping a skeleton crew must have cost an arm and a leg. Everyone had lost a loved one from the attack, and no one would want to work with the people they perceived as the cause. It would take a pretty big loyalty complex or an even bigger incentive for anyone to still be with Gaius months after.

DJ was betting on the latter, and it was another reason he couldn't help but respect Gaius: they were betting it all. The money they spent just by being open was cash they were probably never going to get back. Few customers would touch the Gaius brand anymore, yet the company stood by its products. It wasn't logical, and it was *definitely* bad PR, but it resonated with DJ.

"Can head up now," CJ said.

DJ was at the stairway a moment later, yanking it open. There was no point being quiet if nobody was around to hear you and he was basically doing Gaius a favor anyway. If CJ could get whatever he needed from the mainframe and was able to trace the signal back to its source, they'd have the real culprit, and that fool would take all the hate. If DJ was caught, he could probably explain that to them. He'd call that Plan E.

As Christy had warned, the ninth floor was just as deserted as the two below it. Still, DJ went through the motions and checked each door he passed. He even risked opening a few and peeking inside. *Fuck this shit,* DJ thought with a groan. There were still eleven floors to go through.

"Moving up," he sighed. The security camera tracked him as he moved up the stairs, but DJ didn't pay it any mind. His brother would have told him if he didn't have it under control.

He reached the tenth-floor landing, and even before opening the door, he knew this floor was different from the others. For one, he could hear voices on the other side.

As if in confirmation, Christy's voice crackled from the comms unit. "Don't come out yet, D. There are a bunch of people moving in there. You're gonna need a plan, or you'll be busted as soon as you step in."

We needed a plan before *we infiltrated the most hated building in the world,* DJ grumbled internally.

"What do you suggest?" he asked out loud.

"Seems… obvious to me." CJ replied for her. "Have to blend."

IT TOOK MULTIPLE TRIPS to his new apartment, but Manar finally had the parts he needed. He'd even put together a system where Sparta maintenance would arrange the parts in his car, Helene—controlling the vehicle—would bring them to his place, and the doorman would bring them up to him for a hefty tip. That way, Manar didn't have to lift a finger. Any other time, he would have felt proud of that.

He surveyed the array on the floor, rolling up his sleeves. He'd already laid the groundwork for the upgrades when he'd adjusted Helene's source code. He just needed to connect that to stable firmware to smooth out the process.

The hours flew by, and Manar lost himself in his task. That was becoming more common. It'd been far too long since he'd had a satisfying project to work on, and projects were the only way that he could forget—at least for a while.

You wouldn't have to forget if you didn't feel so much guilt, Simone's voice whispered in his ear. That was another thing that was becoming more frequent.

The voice became more distinct by the day, and its words harsher and truer. Sometimes it came with her image in a reflection. Of course, the image was always outdated, as Manar hadn't seen his mother in years.

You were a bad son, the voice whispered again, close enough that he could feel the wind of her breath by his ear. Once again, it was right.

Manar struggled to lose himself as his hands flew over the pieces, fitting them together seamlessly. It was easier than it had been the first time, when he was still stumbling over the program. Even his stumbles had been called genius, but still…

Helene, appearing beside him as a hologram, rang with warnings several times during the hour, but he ignored them all. He couldn't afford to break his concentration. It was the only thing keeping the voice away.

"How urgent is the problem?" he asked absently.

[Yellow,] Helene replied. Manar nodded. At least that was another update confirmed to be working. He'd set parameters for Helene to identify the level of problems. Yellow was after green. There were two more levels above it, so the issue was average. It didn't need his immediate attention.

Of course, Helene could be mistaken. Since he hadn't connected the source code back to the firmware, Helene hadn't been fully updated.

"Fix it," he said.

[Understood,] she replied.

CHAPTER

19

APRIL 2040

SPARTA HQ, NEW YORK

KARLA FELT THE HAIR ON HER ARM RISE. She paused suddenly, almost sending both herself and her sister crashing. She ignored Liz's curse and glare, staring around the deserted hallway. Somehow the night, the building, the mission, everything—it felt *wrong*.

The back of her neck prickled like it did whenever she was being watched. The hallway was deserted and there were no patrols nearby, but Karla couldn't push back the feeling. It itched.

"What is wrong?" Liz murmured in Russian.

Karla shook her head, growling to herself. Was she a child, feeling monsters in the darkness? "Nothing," she said, wiping the snarl off her face with effort. "I felt an itch."

Her sister looked at her strangely but didn't comment. She signaled, and they made their way farther into the building. The farther in they went, the fewer patrols they had to hide from. Eventually, they could move freely. Liz kept checking the map periodically, muttering curses. Once, Karla glanced at it in curiosity and cursed also. They moved, but not closer to their goal. The path Liz had chosen was a long and confusing one. Karla cursed again in impatience, but she was well used to her sister's antics.

They went on in silence for about half an hour, steadily moving up the floors through the back stairwells. Though they stopped periodically because of a patrol, the time it took gave Karla a whole new respect for the building. She'd seen blueprints but had snorted when the scale model spanned several blocks.

"José should have allowed Chloe to come along," Karla muttered. If Chloe had been there, they probably would have been able to get away with killing some of the patrols. José could never punish the brunette. They still would have had to avoid the cameras, but Karla was sure they would have moved faster.

"You know why she couldn't come," Liz said. They turned into a hallway. Karla spared another glance at the map. At least they were moving in the right direction, now—into the computer department.

That was another thing that had made Karla snort at the blueprints. Each department was sectioned off from every other. No one, not even the guards, could pass through. Huge metal doors, over a foot thick, blocked each section. Access codes were required to pass through—theoretically, at least. But no employee that the CIA had been able to "recover" for information had more than the access code for their own department.

Karla approved of such measures, even if it made their infiltration more difficult. Why should a lowly ant be privy to the inner workings of such a mighty beast? Such a thing would surely do more harm than good.

Karla and Liz had been able to avoid detection so far only by passing through the departments. Since even José hadn't been able to get the access codes, melting a part of the door and disrupting the camera assigned to it was the only evidence of their passage.

Secretly, Karla prayed that a guard would notice the destruction and sound the alarm. Maybe the mission wouldn't be so boring, then.

Liz signaled once the patrol had passed, and the two of them made their way to the camera on the wall. Karla handed her sister the tools as she needed them but mostly kept watch for another patrol. They were both trained to hack into the camera and loop the feed, but Karla had little patience for anything so boring.

After a few minutes of shuffling, the twins made their way to the door. Here, Karla took charge, bringing out a mini-blowtorch and dropping her glasses to cover her eyes. She triggered the device and adjusted the flame until it turned blue. The metal resisted the flame for the first few seconds. This made it all the better when it started to turn to liquid. The sight brought a smile to her face.

"Hurry up," Liz hissed.

Karla ignored her. Unlike her sister, she hated sneaking around. But José would never listen. Instead, he ordered her to hide, like a cockroach from a boot. Busting open the occasional door was the only fun she had. The least Liz could do was allow her to enjoy it.

The metal turned to slag and ran down, pooling in the heat-resistant container she'd placed there earlier. It was annoying, but José was convinced that collecting the slag would delay the discovery of their subterfuge.

An alarm blared overhead.

The sound pierced the silence of the night, startling Karla enough for her to fumble with the blowtorch and leave a long black line in the wall. She muttered a curse.

"Again, with the alarm?" she asked, scowling. Her eyes scanned the wall until she found the noisemaker. A flick of her wrist slid her gun into her hand. A moment later, the speaker crashed to the ground, blessedly silenced.

"They would have heard your gunshot," her sister said with a glare.

Karla glared back harder. Like she hadn't been about to do the same? "Over the accursed alarm that already signaled where we are?"

"It only signaled because you messed up with the door."

"Or maybe José's precious artificial mind finally found us," Karla sneered. She'd said it sarcastically to get under her sister's skin but remembered her feeling of being watched.

Liz ignored the comment just as Karla knew she would. Karla slipped her gun back into its holster, and then flicked it out again. Back in the passageway they'd come from, the alarm blared as if giving directions. They had been found out. The guards would be coming for them soon.

The thought of the imminent fight had Karla champing at the bit, and a grin stretched across her face. The gods were shining on her today.

Liz kicked open the door, triggering another alarm within. This time, it was Liz who shot it down. She signaled, and they jogged through the passages, making no effort to dodge the cameras. There was no point in stealth with sirens screaming behind them.

Soon, they heard boots pounding on the ground behind them. One of the pesky patrols must have been close by. This was yet another thing that surprised Karla. She was used to American security being run by fat, lazy men who easily lost their heads at the first sign of trouble.

Liz spared a glance at the map and signaled to turn a corner, but more boots were pounding in that direction, and they turned the other way. Karla growled. They were *running* from the guards now? Was her sister determined to make this night as boring as possible?

Another hallway was blocked by the sound of boots, forcing them to detour once again. Karla frowned, and her mind screamed something at her. She couldn't grasp it.

They passed several cameras. Most of them were mounted opposite small wooden doors that Karla assumed led to offices. The feeling of being watched intensified, almost making her stumble. Her instincts screamed that nothing was as it seemed, but she could not comprehend what was wrong. The frown on her sister's face showed that she felt the same way.

Karla glanced at the map. The target was somewhere in the section, but their turns had taken them farther away from it. Karla's blood boiled. Who were these insects that drove them from their goal? Since when did the Polova sisters run away like frightened mice?

At a split in the hallway, Liz signaled a turn. But a glance at the map showed that their target was in the other direction. Karla made a cutting motion with her hand, glaring at her sister. They would run no longer.

Liz sighed, but her eyes expressed relief. She couldn't have been happy with fleeing either. It brought back too many memories of their childhood.

They grinned, turned at the intersection, and rushed toward the sound of marching steps.

CHAPTER

20

APRIL 2040
GAIUS CORPORATION,
SILICON VALLEY, CALIFORNIA

THE ELEVATOR STOPPED, and Ndidi stepped into the tenth-floor hallway.

The change from the deserted first floor to… whatever this was threw Ndidi for a moment. The elevator led straight into a hallway lined with office doors. People milled around, creating a constant flow of foot traffic. Ndidi noticed they didn't seem to be in any hurry, as they stopped frequently to speak to each other. A man brushed against her, and she realized she'd been standing by the elevators for over a minute.

A closer look showed that she'd begun to gather some attention. Heat rose up her neck in waves. Most of the doors didn't have labels, but a scan still revealed one with the restroom symbol. Ndidi made a beeline for it.

Ndidi splashed some water on her face. Her reflection stared back at her uncertainly. She muffled a groan. What the hell was she doing? She'd never been one for subterfuge. The whole concept went against her being.

She splashed some more water. *Why couldn't I have hired someone to do this?* she thought, though she already knew the answer. Involving anybody else brought its own risks. Having a bunch of strangers help her do something so obviously illegal was almost begging to be blackmailed later. Plus, she'd always been more of a hands-on person. She wouldn't place her plans into the hands of someone else unless she really had no other option.

It wasn't as if she'd been caught. She'd drawn attention to herself because of her nerves. So, she just needed to calm down. The water helped with that, and she splashed her face some more. Her reflection gazed back with hardened eyes. She couldn't afford to fail; getting the nanoprocessor was just one of many steps and this was for Bethany.

Ndidi smoothed out her dress, standing to her full height. Her face gave none of her thoughts away.

She left the restroom.

DJ STEPPED THROUGH THE STAIRWAY and onto the tenth floor, just as the opposite door opened and a dark-skinned woman stepped out. He almost recoiled but stopped just in time. He couldn't go about flinching at everybody he saw.

"What exactly is the play here, D?" Christy asked through the comms unit.

"I'd like to know that too," replied DJ softly, directing the statement to his brother. The woman had turned a corner into what DJ considered the main hallway. So, for the moment at least, he was by himself.

"The plan remains the same." CJ sighed. "Find a mainframe computer, and… get the nanoprocessor."

"Yeah, I got that," DJ snapped, his nerves fraying. "What I meant was, is there a plan in case I'm busted?"

"No," CJ replied.

Fan-fucking-tastic. There was nothing to lose, so he made his way into the main hallway. Most of the voices had quieted down as the people made their way to their destinations, but even the few stragglers were far too many for comfort. Snippets of conversations flitted around him, and DJ strained his ears for anything useful.

"You really should check it out. Heard it was all…"

"Yeah, they must be really desperate to maintain appearances if they retained us…"

"Did they hire someone? Who's that guy? Kinda cute, right?"

"Where does he think he is? A garden party? What's with the outfit?"

DJ grimaced and glanced down at his T-shirt and jeans. He compared them with the suits and blazers the others wore and let out an expletive. He already stood out like a sore thumb, and he hadn't even gone anywhere.

Fuck this! he thought, shrugging. He was cool as long as no one called him out. So, he just had to give no reason to *be* called out and that meant not walking like he had a stick up his ass. *So, walk normally.*

He was too tense. He started there, forcing himself to loosen one muscle at a time. He slouched, because he always slouched, and it felt more natural. Unfortunately, this transition took place as he strode down the hall, so he attracted a few stares. He made sure not to make eye contact with anyone. Any extended interaction would make it obvious that he wasn't part of the long-term staff. Frankly, it would be best if they thought he was a visitor rather than a new staff member who they'd try to talk to.

The offices were similar—scratch that, they were exactly the same as the ones on the other floors. DJ sucked his teeth and considered opening them one by one.

"Yeah, on the other side of the floor," a voice said from behind him. DJ glanced over his shoulder and immediately recognized the woman he'd seen coming out of the restroom. She stood to the side, following the direction that another lady—a staff member, most likely—pointed out. "You'll know as soon as you get there, with all the blinking lights and whatnot. And the whole passage is cold as ice from all the cooling the room needs."

"Thank you so much. I almost lost my mind trying to navigate the halls by myself," the dark-skinned woman chuckled, though it sounded forced. The voice, though? It was familiar somehow.

DJ forced himself to keep moving. It would be too suspicious to stop so suddenly. *But at least I have my confirmation.* The description was way too on point, meaning the room was definitely on this floor. He managed to keep his walk natural through sheer force of will and reached the end of the hallway. He waited a breath and then turned back, managing to catch a glimpse of the woman as she rounded a corner.

He lengthened his stride, heading back the way he'd come. He plastered a look of urgency on his face. It wasn't hard to feign, as it really was urgent that he not lose the woman.

He turned the corner, but she was already nearing the end of the passage, so he kept his strides lengthened but made an effort to reduce the impact of each footfall. He couldn't sneak here, where anybody could walk out at any time and find him crouched and hugging the wall. If the lady noticed him too early, it would be obvious he was following her. Her voice still nagged at him from the back of his mind. He wished he'd been able to make out her face.

So as not to be suspicious, DJ slowed his pace when he thought he was an adequate distance away from her. She hadn't turned around, yet, but DJ still made an effort to scan the doors they passed. He was pretty sure that the description was for the mainframe room—what other room would need to be so cold?—but studying the doors as if searching for one in particular gave him a viable exit if, for some reason, his guide started to get wary.

They turned down a couple of hallways, more than DJ had expected. If the floor was anything like the previous ones he'd gone through, they were basically at the other end of the building. This meant he'd lucked the hell out, finding someone to lead him there.

The foot traffic around the floor slowed down and then disappeared altogether the farther in they went. This was around the time DJ noticed that it'd gotten cooler. He stifled a grin. They couldn't be far now.

His guide—hopefully he would learn her name at some point—slowed down and glanced over her shoulder. DJ casually knelt and pretended to tie his shoe, head lowered, his brow scrunched up in confusion.

Why is she starting to glance back now? She hadn't bothered to before. He started to grin but shook his head slightly. He was probably reading too much into it. He glanced up just in time to see her turn a corner—hopefully the last one.

"What to do? What to do?" DJ muttered, standing. He could probably find the room by himself now, so he didn't need to follow her. But he was curious why the lady was headed to the room. Her knee-length gown blended in far more than his jeans, but she hadn't had so much as a passing greeting from the staff, so she couldn't be one of them.

"Say something?" Christy asked, and DJ almost jumped. They'd been so quiet, he'd forgotten about the comms. He checked behind him to be sure no one was going to notice him talking to himself. Fortunately, there were no offices this far in. It was kind of weird when DJ thought about it. Why dedicate an entire wing just to one room?

"Yeah, no. Talking to myself," he replied. He made his way to the end of the hall. "Pretty sure I've found the room though."

His comms crackled for a minute, making him wince. CJ's voice came on a second later. "Describe it."

DJ scratched the back of his head, peering around the corner. The woman was nowhere to be found. But he was sure he'd found the right door, if the moisture pooling on the floor in front of it was any indication.

"Gimme a sec," DJ muttered. The doors were the transparent sliding kind. They were much larger than the wooden office doors, so it seemed he'd been right on that count. Stacks of hardware were arranged in a grid formation, some with blinking lights. If that didn't scream bingo, DJ didn't know what would.

"Well?" CJ asked.

DJ licked his lips. "It's definitely the place, but… the whole thing just feels weird."

"Weird how?" Christy asked.

"Well, there are no guards, for one. There's no one, actually. I thought this was supposed to be the central hub of the company or something."

"Maybe they couldn't spare the people," Christy said. "The other floors were deserted, right? They probably just retained the bare minimum."

"That still doesn't explain the lack of technicians," countered DJ. "You guys aren't seeing what I'm seeing; there's a lot of hardware in here."

"Does not need… as much maintenance as people think," CJ said over the clacking of keys. "Plus, weird or not, we need… the nanoprocessor."

DJ rolled his eyes but acknowledged the statement.

The doors were sensor activated and slid open silently when DJ got close. That explained where his guide had gone, assuming she hadn't continued through the halls. DJ had a hard time imagining what could be farther in, though. He took a tentative step inside.

The room was dark, save for the blinking lights on the hardware. The stacks were so close that he could reach out and touch one. He brought out the thumb drive CJ had given him. There was no point heading farther in if he could get what he needed right at the door.

As he reached out, an alarm stopped him in his tracks. He crouched on instinct. There was no way he'd been the one to cause it. He hadn't even touched the damn thing.

"What's that noise, D?" Christy asked.

At the same time, CJ said, "What happened?"

That would have elicited a chuckle under normal circumstances, but not when a damn siren was blowing in his ear.

"Hell if I know," DJ replied, looking around. There was no way the alarm was localized to the lab itself—or even to the floor he was on. "I hadn't even touched it yet and—"

A blurred shape crashed into him. The ground rushed to meet them. The floor was carpeted, so DJ groaned more in surprise than pain. The shape wiggled against him as the person struggled to disentangle them.

Finally, the woman wriggled free and stood. The lighting in the room was pretty bad, but DJ's eyes had adjusted enough for him to make out a knee-length dress. It seemed he'd found his guide.

"I'm sorry," she said, a rather panicked look on her face. "I wasn't looking where I was going."

DJ's eyes went to the small box she clutched in her hand. Belatedly, the woman attempted to hide it behind her back. But DJ wasn't truly focused on that; it'd just been a convenient place to look while he focused his thoughts.

That voice. It was so familiar. But from where?

His comms crackled as both his brother and the sniper took turns blasting his ears with questions. DJ pushed it to the back of his head. In his peripheral vision, the woman turned to leave when he didn't respond. DJ placed a hand on her shoulder. He was pretty close to recognizing that voice. He just needed one more…

"Can I help you?" she asked hesitantly.

A lightbulb went on in DJ's head. "Ndidi? What the hell are you doing here?"

CHAPTER

21

APRIL 2040

NEW YORK

[THREAT LEVEL INCREASED TO BLUE,] Helene reported.

Manar tore his gaze away from the pieces scattered on his floor and glared at the hologram. His eyes were bloodshot. Over the past hour, the voice had grown more insistent. Even immersing himself in his task wasn't enough to keep it at bay anymore. He'd started to make mistakes.

Him? Make mistakes? It was pathetic! It was *beyond* pathetic.

"Fix it," he growled at the AI.

He needed to stop and rest before he made an irreparable error, but sleeping brought its own sort of horrors. Manar avoided it whenever he could. Anyway, he was almost done with the hardware. If Helene hadn't solved the problem because of processing power, then it was more important for him to finish the work. No, he couldn't afford to rest yet.

[Permission requested: Use of security personnel.]

"Do as you wish," Manar muttered absently. His hair fell over his eyes as he stared at the pieces scattered on the floor.

[Acknowledged.]

APRIL 2040
GAIUS CORPORATION,
SILICON VALLEY, CALIFORNIA

NDIDI FROZE AT THE SOUND of her name. She tried to keep her face perfectly still, but her thoughts were racing, and she was sure she couldn't completely hide the panic from her eyes.

The alarm blared in the background. The sound quite thoroughly shredded the forced calm she'd imposed on herself. She cursed herself with every second breath. How had she not considered that the mainframe computers of a tech company would have some protection?

Ironically, the flashing lights of the alarm provided far better lighting than the lights from the mainframe computers, which she'd used to navigate before. She started toward the door, but the hand on her shoulder reminded her that she wasn't alone.

Right, she thought. *I crashed into the only person this far out on the floor. And he somehow knows me already.* She groaned.

"I'm guessing I have you to thank for the alarm?" the man asked, still smiling. Ndidi took a step back. To her surprise, the man let her. He cocked his head to the side as if listening for something. After a second, he focused on her, his expression far more urgent. "Right. We don't have time for this."

"Who are you?" She recognized him as the guy that'd been tying his shoes behind her, and she had a vague impression that they'd passed each other in a hallway somewhere. But none of that explained how he knew her name.

Once again, the man cocked his head to the side. "What if I explain that while we get out of here?" he suggested. "I'll make it easy for you. I already know you came here for the nanoprocessor. I already know that it's in your hand and that taking it from the mainframe is what triggered the alarm."

Ndidi took another step back, for all the good it would do. Her heart beat a rhythm in her chest. He had caught her in the act. It wouldn't be much of a hassle to track her down if Gaius was determined to find her.

He raised his hand placatingly. "Chill. I can't rat you out, even if I wanted to—which I don't. I would never after what you did for my brother. I don't work here." He gestured to his tight-fitting T-shirt and jeans. Still, she didn't breathe a sigh of relief. Not just yet.

"What exactly did I do for your brother?" she asked cautiously.

"That doesn't matter now." He pressed a finger to his ear. "How far out, Christy? Well, shit." He focused back on Ndidi. "Look, I'm doing a crap job of this, but the bottom line is, there are a *lot* of men heading our way. From the look of panic on your face, I can assume that you didn't plan to call building security and their friends on us. Luckily, I have— scratch that. My *brother* has a plan that can get us out. But you're gonna have to trust me. We can do introductions on the way."

Once again, Ndidi's thoughts raced. She was actually quite proud that she'd remained calm for so long. However, she could feel herself unraveling. She tried to consider her options logically, but she didn't have many. There was no exit plan for the same reason there was no infiltration plan. It was flat-out mad to trust a stranger, even one who seemed to know her. But that detail had her more than a little curious, and her choices were limited.

She nodded. "Lead the way."

DJ FLASHED A QUICK SMILE, but his mind had already moved on. He was burning with questions about why he'd found his brother's former mentor in the middle of some grand larceny, but there wasn't time to indulge in asking for answers. Everything about it had to be put on the back burner. She was here, and they had to get out. That was all that mattered.

He strode through the sliding doors. The footsteps behind him confirmed that Ndidi was keeping pace. That was good since he really didn't have the time for hand-holding.

The lights went off, plunging the passages into semidarkness. He was only able to see a couple of feet around him. It was probably some misguided attempt to slow them down while security penned them in. All it did, however, was provide the cover of darkness, so DJ wasn't in a position to complain.

He pressed a finger to his comms device. "Do you still have control of the cameras?" he asked his brother. Ndidi came to his side, looking at him questioningly. DJ shook his head and pointed at his ears. Her eyes widened, and she made a little "oh" sound. A lot of their conversation in the mainframe room was probably making more sense to her now.

"The section you are on is on… another server that I… cannot access," CJ replied softly. "The good news: I have control… over the sixth-floor cameras too."

DJ nodded; he'd expected as much. He turned a corner, continuing down a passage. He didn't need to get all the way back to the main hallway. That would probably be swarming with security anyway. He just needed to get close enough for CJ to pick him up on the camera. From there, getting directions out of the building would be far easier. He hoped, anyway.

"Do you at least have a bead on our tails?"

"They're around fourth," Christy offered. "I can just barely make them out. Seems they were looking for someone on that floor initially, so they were separated and caught flat-footed when the alarms rang."

"There were… some already on the tenth floor," CJ said. "They are headed your way now."

"Shit," DJ cursed reflexively. He turned two more corners, both as dark as the ones they'd just left. He hadn't thought they'd cut off the power for the entire floor.

They'd probably just isolated it to their section. He glanced at his companion, Christy's words bouncing around in his ears.

"Hey…" he started, directing the line to Ndidi. With a grimace, he realized he didn't exactly know how to phrase his question.

Was there a polite way to ask if she'd known she was already being hunted and hadn't told him despite the risk it posed? That security had been spread thin worked in DJ's favor. However, the fact that they'd already been on alert increased the risk significantly.

Screw it.

"Hey," he started again, "you didn't happen to do anything that'd tip off security while you made your way to the room, did you?"

He watched her carefully and saw her expression go from alarm to confusion, to realization, and finally to embarrassment. It was the last part that threw DJ off. He would have expected guilt for hiding it from him, not embarrassment. It was on the tip of his tongue to ask, but luckily, she started talking before he could.

"The only thing that I can think of was that I used a visitor's pass when coming in." She held up the card that hung around her neck.

DJ's eyebrows rose. Where would she have gotten a pass? He thought Gaius had learned to stop giving those after the third or fourth infiltration. It would explain the search, though. She might have had permission to be in the building, but that was probably on the assumption that she'd be monitored throughout.

"How'd you flip your handlers?" he asked curiously.

"I… uh… arrived an hour early."

DJ's eyebrows rose higher, and he nodded in appreciation. Simple plans tended to be the most effective. "Impressive."

Ndidi hesitated. "Would that bring down our chances of escaping?"

DJ led them into another passage. "Not at all," he said reassuringly. No need to freak the chick out.

Ndidi nodded, and some of the embarrassment was replaced by a resolute expression. Embracing determination was far easier than dealing with blubbering fools scared out of their wits.

There was light at the end of the next passage, but DJ didn't let the relief show on his face. It was weird that they'd made it this far without encountering any security. He pressed a finger to his ear.

"What's the bead on the tenth-floor security?" he asked. However, the sound of rushing feet answered his question.

"They're reaching the edge of my field now," his brother confirmed a second later.

"Shit," DJ cursed again. Without missing a beat, he grabbed ahold of Ndidi's hand and spun on his heels, lengthening his stride. Luckily, they'd just entered the hallway and the footsteps sounded farther away. There was no chance they'd been spotted before backtracking.

DJ dropped Ndidi's hand a moment later, muttering silent thanks that she kept up with his strides. He led them down a hallway, back the way they'd come. Instead of turning right, the direction of the mainframe room, he turned left and continued to the end of the hall.

Then he waited. Ndidi peered into the darkness but didn't make any comment. Smart.

A few seconds later, the drum of boots headed in the other direction. He would have grinned if his heart weren't pounding so hard in his chest. He waited a few moments until the passages were completely silent before leading Ndidi back the way they'd come.

After they reached the end of the passage, CJ's voice crackled in his ear. "I can… see you."

"Great," DJ said. The statement was creepy but brought DJ some relief.

"About time, D," Christy put in. "What took you so long?"

DJ hesitated. Ndidi was looking at him, no doubt trying to puzzle out his side of the conversation. Without thinking too much about it, he removed one of his comms and helped her fix it in her ear. Honestly, he should have done that from the beginning. She'd already been able to keep up with him, reacting at a moment's notice, but that was the easy phase. *Now* was when the real fun started. And if she could get information from CJ and Christy at the same time he did, everything would go more smoothly—he hoped.

"I'm here, aren't I?" DJ replied finally. "Hey, bro. Please tell me you have a way to get me out of here." A stare bored into the side of his head, and he avoided Ndidi's gaze. He'd told her that he already had a plan for leaving the building. What he'd left out was that his plan had been for his brother to come up with one.

"Back stairways are… not guarded. You can follow those."

"The stairways?" Ndidi raised a brow.

DJ shrugged. "It's kicked ass so far. Plus, I like the message it sends: take the stairs once in a while for better security." Ndidi chuckled slightly. They made their way through the passage, and DJ continued, his voice growing serious. "The stairs are generally along the main hallways, so we're gonna have to hustle when we get there."

Ndidi nodded, her face a grim mask of determination.

"C— My brother's jacked into the cameras, so security won't be able to track us through them," DJ said, waving at said camera. He glanced at Ndidi, wondering if she'd noticed his slip. Then again, she'd helped so many kids, she might not have recognized the name if he'd said it. "We have no plan for the people, though, so it's a good thing your acting skills are good."

"What makes you say that?"

"Next right," CJ's voice crackled through the comm. "There is… a group coming."

DJ gave a small salute at a camera, turning to the new passage, Ndidi by his side. A few seconds later, he heard footsteps behind him. Adrenaline coursed through him. With a glance at his companion, he lengthened his stride. She hadn't had a problem keeping up so far, but there was no point tiring her out when they still had a ways to go.

"I've seen them," DJ said, replying to her earlier question. Her face scrunched up for a second before the dots clicked. DJ chuckled, scratching the back of his head. "That actually saved me. Pretty sure I would have been lost three times over, searching for that stupid room, if you weren't so good at pretending you belong."

"Incoming," CJ said again.

"Let's pick this up later," DJ suggested, glancing around.

He took a left. Office doors lined both sides of the hallway. DJ was less concerned about the people inside and more concerned that this hallway took them farther into the floor, though he'd found that most of the halls had a path linking to the central one. Halfway in, he heard boots on the floor and slowed down. They sounded *way* too close.

Without missing a beat, DJ spun on his heels, heading back the way he'd come. His comms cracked before he'd gone more than a few feet.

"What are you doing?" CJ asked. "Guards are… coming from that way."

DJ stopped. "Well, guards are coming from the other direction too," he said, careful to keep his voice low. There was no point broadcasting their position.

DJ could almost feel his brother's confusion as he clicked away on his computer. A few seconds went by, and the footsteps grew louder. DJ didn't even have to strain to hear the thumping anymore. He tapped his earpiece impatiently and opened his mouth to speak, when CJ's voice came back.

"I cannot see a group… at the other end of the hall."

DJ went still. Even if he couldn't verify the group from the hallway they'd just come from, DJ could at least hear the footsteps from the one behind him.

"What're you saying, bro?" He chuckled nervously. "I can hear them behind me."

"The passage behind you is deserted. There is… no one there."

DJ started to reply, but the words died on his lips as more footsteps started coming from the hallway in front of him. He chuckled again, more out of habit than any real amusement. Ndidi looked at him like he was mad.

What the hell's happening right now? DJ thought. They were very clearly hemmed in by the two groups, yet one of the groups wasn't showing up on camera. Even if security had called in some guys from the fourth-floor search, how had they found Ndidi and him so quickly?

"Is it possible your brother's feed has been tapped into?" Ndidi's voice said through his comm. He glanced at the end of the hallway and saw she had a finger pressed to her ear.

There was a pause. "Who is… this?" CJ asked.

"Is that really what you want to focus on right now?" DJ cut in sharply.

The footsteps grew louder, bouncing off the walls into a cacophony. DJ swore softly, his thoughts racing. He caught Ndidi's attention and made a vague gesture at the doors around them. DJ could tell when she understood by the panic on her face, but she quickly stifled it. That was good; he was trying not to panic too. It was a shitty plan, but they had limited options at the moment.

Finally, she nodded, and DJ tested the closest door, muttering a prayer as the latch turned. If there were only one person in there, he could probably take them before they sounded the alarm. Maybe even if there were two. He hoped it wouldn't come to that. The whole theft thing already rubbed him the wrong way. He would prefer not to harm anyone at all.

Someone up there must have been watching because the room was empty. He guided Ndidi first, ignoring the way she stiffened, then followed her, closing the door with a soft click. Outside, the footsteps grew louder, and the floor vibrated.

Neither DJ nor Ndidi dared to breathe.

Seconds that felt like minutes passed. The sound receded into the distance. Hopefully, their pursuers had decided to retrace their steps back to the mainframe room and weren't just standing outside, luring the intruders into a false sense of security while they got the battering ram.

Ndidi slumped against the door, eyes closed. In the brief respite, DJ scanned the room. There wasn't much to take in. He could see no cameras. That didn't really say much because they could be so small that he had no chance of spotting them without investing precious time and effort. But the same logic could work for basically every place in the building. That was a rabbit hole that DJ really didn't want to go down. So, there were no cameras.

A large table took up most of the space in the center, a single chair on one side and two side by side on the other. The cabinets on the table were locked, but they sounded hollow when DJ knocked. A thin layer of dust fell from the tabletop, and DJ wiped his hand on his shirt. Somehow, the coat of dust added weight to the sheer absence of everything. Whoever had stayed here obviously didn't expect to come back.

The air was stale. Another quick glance confirmed there were no windows. DJ sighed and sat on the edge of the table. He hadn't heard the second group of guards pass. This meant they were still roving about. For now, he and Ndidi were trapped within the room.

Doesn't make much of a difference, DJ thought, cracking his neck. *We can't go anywhere, anyway—not until we figure out what the hell just happened.*

DJ glanced at Ndidi and almost recoiled. The woman was back on her feet. Once again, her face was set in a determined mask, but her eyes were different. Colder. Before, DJ could tell her general mental state from her eyes, though she had hidden it quite well. That was how he'd decided how much to push or when to slow down. But now, she stared back at him impassively, and he got nothing.

It freaked him the hell out. Luckily, his comms crackled before he could blurt out anything stupid.

"What the fuck was that out there?" he snapped.

"Trying to… figure it out," CJ's voice came out as a murmur that made DJ wince. CJ didn't react well to strong emotions. It wreaked havoc on his anxiety.

DJ took a breath. The anger had crept up on him, but it would be a dick move to pass it on just because he could. He took another breath, releasing it as a sigh.

"Didn't mean to snap," he said finally. CJ made a noise that could loosely be taken as acknowledgment, which was the best DJ could ask for. They would sort out their issues later. "I've been cracking my head on this, but I can't figure out how they got a bead on us. Any ideas?"

No one spoke for a few seconds.

"Well, shit, I dunno, D!" Christy said finally. DJ wondered why she'd been silent for so long. "Their surveillance's pretty much shot, with your brother jacked into it, so I guess you guys made a ton of noise…"

"We didn't."

"Why is their surveillance shot?" Ndidi asked. DJ blanched. Even her voice was as cold as her eyes now. She'd come to stand beside him at the desk, making it easier for him to observe her out of the corner of his eye.

"Because my brother has control of them. Everything on this floor, at least. Any more, and they'll notice the hack."

"But they still found us. Is there a chance they've already noticed the hack and are monitoring us with it?"

"Uh… bro?"

"Next to none," CJ replied after a beat, sounding distracted. "I would have noticed… if they had taken back control."

DJ frowned. It hadn't even occurred to him that security could have taken back control from his brother. It wouldn't be such a leap. Gaius Corporation *was* a tech company, first and foremost. They wouldn't have succeeded without employing the best in the business. But somehow, after only a couple of days of seeing how good his brother was with a keyboard, he'd taken it for granted.

Weird. And possibly fatal if they had noticed CJ's hack.

"It could be that they didn't take control," Ndidi said. She must have thought she was on to something because her voice got some life back. "Rationally, it would make more sense for them to leave your program in place and just piggyback on it. Is that possible? If they wanted to set a trap for us?"

DJ groaned. He couldn't argue with logic like that, but he so *badly* wanted to try. It was a level of craftiness he just didn't want to deal with. Ever. "Hey bro? *Is* it possible they could have piggybacked on your signal stuff?"

For a minute, all DJ heard was the clacking of keys, but he forced himself to be patient. His brother hated to waste words, so he was probably confirming whether or not his hack had been noticed. Rushing him wouldn't do any good. "Found it," CJ said, sounding almost awed. "Disguised the worm… as part of a feed."

Well, damn! DJ glanced at Ndidi, expecting something like satisfaction on her face. Nope. Blank as ever. "Can you remove it?"

"Not anytime soon."

He groaned again, but there was only one thing to do if he and Ndidi could be monitored by the cameras. "Then cut the feed entirely."

No one spoke for a moment.

"You sure 'bout that, D?" Christy asked tentatively. "You'll be walking completely blind."

"Wouldn't be the first time." He paused, frowning. "Though the other times were just training."

"Nothing different here." Christy chuckled, though there was an undertone of worry in her voice. "Coach never had a problem with shooting us."

That thought brought a whole host of memories that DJ really didn't want to deal with. He brushed the comment aside. "Cut it off, CJ."

"Done."

DJ grinned. Clearly his brother had drawn the same conclusion. That just left Ndidi. He turned to find that she was already staring at him, her features thoughtful.

"Your brother's name is CJ?"

DJ winced. Seriously? All it took was one slip-up? He scratched the back of his neck. "Yeah, kinda." He gestured, dismissing her next question. "You guys will have time to catch up. We're kinda in the middle of something."

Ndidi nodded, and DJ returned it. He stood from the table, making a half-hearted attempt to dust himself off. After all, he was probably going to get dirtier before the day was over. Ndidi met him at the door. A quick scan of the hallway verified that the guards had moved on. They had precious little time before someone figured out that he and Ndidi hadn't retreated and they all doubled back. He glanced up at the camera that his brother—and now, apparently, Gaius Corp—had used to track him. The red light was off.

They were all alone.

23

NDIDI HAD NEVER BEEN MORE STRESSED out. She and DJ followed the route they'd originally planned to take, mostly because they didn't have a choice. Neither of them had a map of the place, and they were short on time, so it was too risky to search for an alternative route.

Fortunately, because the hallway was deserted, they didn't immediately have to test whether it was a good idea. DJ kept to a slow jog, belying his urgency more than any words could. Ndidi strained to keep pace, which surprised her. She wasn't one of those people who went to extreme lengths during exercise, but she'd had a constant workout regimen since she was old enough to plan one. She shouldn't be so winded by a jog. But then again, her weariness wasn't purely physical.

Everything about the day had gone wrong. Part of it was a result of her poor planning. The other was just sheer idiocy. Did she really think she could walk into the building and just wing it? Who did that? And it hadn't even occurred to her that the guards would take enough notice of her visitor's pass to warrant a search when she didn't show up for her appointment. And then the alarm in the mainframe room…

Ndidi clenched her fist so tightly it turned white, staring at DJ's back. *He* had probably thought of the alarm and figured out a way to disable it. If Ndidi hadn't run into him when she did, she would have been caught. And then who would avenge Bethany?

Turning a corner, Ndidi pushed out a breath and forced the thoughts to the back of her mind. There was no point dwelling on them. She still wasn't exactly home free.

They'd been jogging for a couple of minutes, so they must have been close to the main hallway now. Hopefully, it wouldn't be as populated as it was earlier. Or maybe it would be better if it was. They could blend in more. She stared at DJ's T-shirt and reconsidered. *She* could blend in, but that was a pointless train of thought. She wouldn't leave DJ.

They reached the end of the hallway. DJ slowed from a jog to a walk. Ndidi shook herself free from her thoughts in time to follow suit, though her transition was nowhere as smooth. Why had he stopped?

She panted softly, struggling to maintain her composure. DJ wasn't even breathing hard. He stared down at her, and although his eyes showed worry, his face was tense. Ndidi wondered if this was how she looked when she retreated into herself.

She let out one final breath and straightened up. He gave a slight nod, and without a word, they turned the corner. Ndidi was surprised to see the main hall filled with people. Not as many as before. How hadn't she heard so many people moving around? The elevator was right at the end of the hall. Two security guards stood casually in front of it, chuckling and chatting. For a second, DJ hesitated. But then he was moving again, making Ndidi wonder if she'd imagined it.

The tenth floor was basically built as concentric squares, with the hallways forming the edges of the squares and the offices filling the hollow insides. Since each square was connected to every other square, every passage joined another two at the halfway point. This made it easier to navigate, despite the huge size.

At one of these halfway points, DJ turned into another passage and pressed a finger to his ear. "Ndidi, can you hear me?"

Ndidi almost jumped at the sudden sound. Her head snapped up to DJ's back a few paces away. She'd deliberately left some space between them so it wouldn't seem as though they were together. "Yes," she replied softly.

"Do you know how to find the stairway? It's opposite the restroom you used."

Ndidi missed a step. It was at the tip of her tongue to ask how exactly he knew that she'd used the restroom, but she pushed the urge away. It could come later. She *did* remember how to get there. The only problem was that the stairway was within sight of the elevators. The guards would definitely notice two people going inside, and the security team certainly had to know what they looked like thanks to the cameras.

"I can get there," Ndidi said.

DJ nodded, but Ndidi frowned. Why was it important that she knew where the stairs were if he already did?

It wasn't. Unless, of course, she'd be heading there alone.

She went through the problem once again. The guards would notice anyone entering the stairway... unless they were forced to leave their post.

Ndidi groaned, drawing a few weird looks that she ignored. DJ glanced back at her. He gave a small smile, and his voice came in her ear again.

"You seem to have the gist of it then. I'll draw them away while you take the stairs down."

Ndidi started to protest—what had she just thought about not leaving him? But the fool spoke over her, his voice more urgent.

"Head to the seventh floor; it should be deserted. Wait for me by the glass windows. Christy will tell you where. Right, Christy?"

"Do you even need to ask?" the other woman—Christy apparently—said over the comms. "We're going with Plan C, then?"

He gave a small shrug. "Doesn't seem like we have a choice. All you have to do is be in position. I'll tell you when." He paused, considered something, then shook his head. "So, you'll wait there, and I'll meet you. Cool?" He directed the question at Ndidi but once again didn't give her the chance to reply. "Okay! Good talk." He spun on his heels and ran in the direction of the elevators.

DJ IGNORED THE STARTLED LOOKS of Ndidi and the remaining half a dozen people in the hall. He *really* didn't want to do this. Using himself as bait so the chick could get to safety? What was this, Hollywood? Given enough time, he could probably have come up with a better plan, or at least a plan that didn't involve him leading a bunch of fools on a merry-go-round chase. So far, Ndidi had shown herself to have more than a little sense. Hopefully that stretched into following the plan.

He turned the corner into the main hallway and slowed down to a walk. The elevators were right in front of him, as were the guards. The hallway had even fewer people than the others. Good. He already stood out with his clothing. Having fewer people around would give him a better chance of being recognized.

DJ shook his head. *Talk about a turnabout.*

The guards still hadn't noticed him yet, so he straightened a little too much and deliberately messed up his walk. With each step, he tensed every muscle in his body, moving with a jerk that could have looked casual, if seen from a mile away. The people near him moved away as if he carried the plague. DJ almost nodded in thanks because that finally got the guards to notice him. Their eyes widened, and their hands went straight to their hips. DJ forced his eyes to widen too, feigning shock that he'd been made so easily. Then, he spun on his heels and backtracked down the hallway at a dead sprint. The footsteps behind him confirmed his ploy had worked.

That was way too easy. How dumb are these guys?

He passed the hallway where he'd left Ndidi and breathed a sigh of relief when he didn't see her there. He'd half expected her to stand there in a misguided protest about leaving him behind. That's why he hadn't given her a chance to object to the plan.

He glanced back, making sure to keep his expression terrified. Better they thought he was just a guy in over his head. The hallways sped by, corners blending together as he passed them. He slowed a bit when he noticed he was losing his tails. He had to buy Ndidi as much time as possible, but if he took too long, the security on the lower floors might have the chance to catch up.

DJ glanced back again and almost tripped when he saw that two more guards had appeared. He'd known that the elevator guards would call for backup, but he hadn't expected there would be some so close.

Let's give her five more minutes.

NDIDI CROUCHED in the eleventh-floor stairway and tried not to make a sound.

She'd escaped to the stairs all right after DJ had done whatever he'd done to get the guards' attention, but she hadn't gone down more than a couple of flights before the door below her had burst open, sending the sound of footsteps echoing upward. She'd counted at least half a dozen before she'd crawled back up the stairs. Luckily, the footsteps stopped at the tenth floor, rushing through the door she'd just used. Unluckily, it was obvious why they were in such a hurry. DJ.

Once the sounds receded, Ndidi stood from her crouch. She went down the stairs and paced in front of the door, chewing the side of her lip. There had been at least six guards running up the stairs; she was sure of that. That was six plus however many were already on the floor, searching for them. DJ couldn't handle that many by himself—especially without his brother giving him directions.

She paced the other way. She should go help. But how?

Ndidi had been brought up never to shy away from a fact, no matter how difficult it was to hear. And now she had to accept that she would be next to useless if she dashed back into the hall. The thought made her grit her teeth, but it was the truth. Her anger didn't change that.

She stopped her pacing, exhaling. She couldn't help him with the guards, but she *could* make his plan easier by following through to the seventh-floor window and waiting there. Between the guards moving in and her indecision, she'd already wasted five minutes. She shouldn't waste more.

Ndidi went down the stairs.

KARLA'S AND LIZ'S EXPRESSIONS gave way to confusion when they turned the corner, guns ready, and found the area empty. The thump of marching boots was closer than ever, but there was nobody there. Karla heard a growl beside her and turned toward Liz, who was glaring with undisguised hatred at a part of the wall.

Karla followed her sister's gaze and found the security camera immediately. She frowned. Liz always kept her temper on a short leash; such a thing would never provoke an extreme reaction. The marching boots drummed around them. Karla squinted, following the noise, and noticed the black device nestled under the camera. When she realized what the device was, she growled as deeply as her sister.

"All this time," she muttered, barely audible over the roaring in her ears. "All this time, we've been running like scared hens for *nothing*. They made us scared of our own shadows, treating us like mice in a maze."

The hatred Liz emitted was palpable. That was one thing Karla had to thank Sparta for—may the gods spit in its face. Liz hadn't lost her temper in years. It meant, at least, that the night would not be so ruined.

They continued down the hallway at a jog, following the marching sounds. It was humiliating to realize that the siren wasn't blaring in every hallway, only those that led to the twins' target—and only to scare them off. They had been herded like sheep, but Karla would take great delight in showing them the wolf beneath the wool.

Liz no longer looked at the map. It was obvious she wanted whatever this artificial mind had tried so hard to keep from them. Karla could not find it in herself to disagree. They would take whatever it is the mind deemed so precious. Maybe José would find a need for it. If not, Karla would take pleasure in mounting it on her wall. It would make a nice contrast.

The thought made Karla grin.

When they ran into their first guard patrol, her grin threatened to split her face. Her gun was already in her hand, so the five men were bleeding on the floor within a minute. Her shots, mixed with her sister's, sounded like small explosions. The result was better than Karla had dreamed. If she was lucky, other patrols would hear and come to investigate like sharks in the water.

In the meantime, the twins made their way to their target. Liz was far too engulfed in her rage to fulfill her usual role, so Karla found herself becoming the cautious one. It left a foul taste in her mouth, but it was better than dying from recklessness. She was the one who signaled for a stop at an intersection so they could scout out the next turn. The siren sound blanketed almost everything. It would be ridiculously easy—and foolish—to stumble upon a patrol.

She took the map from Liz, sparing it a passing glance to ensure they did not stray too far from their target. José would not listen to stories about the humiliation this artificial mind had put them through. No, her father would only care about results, and they were not Chloe, who could disregard him without obvious consequences.

Still, she glared at her sister, whose scowl left her so distracted that she missed a patrol coming into view. Her head shot up immediately following the first gunshot, but the men were already bleeding on the floor. Liz had fired so fast that five shots had sounded like one.

The sirens—of both the general alarm and the marching boots—cut off immediately. The hallway went deathly silent.

"I did not expect this mind to understand our tactic so fast, sister," Karla muttered, signaling for a stop.

Liz just let out an impatient huff. Karla understood the feeling. She had lived with that anger, the urge to repay every slight with overwhelming violence. People learned only when they had the scars to remind them.

Liz signaled, and Karla listened, hearing boots in the distance. She frowned, then grinned. Perhaps the artificial mind was not smart enough to understand their plan. To think that such a cheap trick would work again after their previous humiliation—it must have thought them fools. Her instincts warned her that something was wrong, and it made her blood boil that her own mind would have her retreat in fear.

Karla signaled back. The pair made their way toward the sound. It grew louder as they approached. Even the walls seemed to vibrate. What sort of speaker could do such a thing?

They turned another corner and found a wall of bodies jogging toward them. Karla cursed, her gun slipping into her hand without any conscious thought. The mind *had* understood their tactics and baited them with the sound, luring them to meet what was surely all the patrols in the department.

The mob stretched from the middle of the hallway and disappeared around the corner. The passageway was barely wide enough to contain them, so they jogged in threes, closing the distance rapidly. Their expressions showed grim resolve and hints of sadistic anticipation. Karla understood their eagerness to spill blood, but she would make them pay for it all the same. Half a dozen died every second against Karla and Liz's bullets. The others merely stepped over their comrades. What had the demon offered to make them waste their lives like this?

Karla's and Liz's clips emptied and were replaced; the men never flinched. Liz screamed a hoarse, wordless yell of frustration. Even through the haze, she'd realized what Karla had, their bullets would run out far before their enemies would.

Karla's mind resisted the very notion of running away. Chloe had beaten into them that they should survive above all. Karla let out her own scream, releasing regret and promising vengeance. Then her fire cut off, and she signaled to Liz. They fled.

The hallway flashed by them, and for the second time, Karla saw the office doors spread out on each side. They might be able to hide there if the gods spat on them and the worst happened. It was a fleeting thought. The feeling of being watched had not left her since she had stepped into the accursed department. She had little doubt that the artificial mind could find them anywhere in the building.

A loud bang sounded from somewhere in front of them. For some reason, Karla felt fear creep into her mind for the first time. She dug it out ruthlessly. Nevertheless, the damage had been done. She felt increased fatigue; her breaths came out ragged.

It was not a mind but a demon that had done this to her. The whole building was under its control. She spared a glance behind her, thus missing the way her map glitched and flickered off and on. She glanced at it a second later, then signaled her sister to turn, following the directions to the exit.

They found a huge metal door blocking their way. Karla didn't miss a beat, glancing at the map and taking the next turn. They would escape this demonic building, then they would come back and raze it to the ground.

The patrols caught up to them. Karla counted down her clips. She would have cursed if she could spare the breath. They would not survive another battle with the ants. Even the haze that had enveloped Liz had cleared up. They needed to escape, to survive.

No, Karla growled internally. They were leaving to report to José, nothing more. Ants would never make the Polova sisters run—not even ants controlled by a demon. If she could accept anything else, she would take her gun to herself.

The hallways merged, turn after turn. The sisters ran down the same stairways they had taken earlier that night to advance to higher floors. Surprisingly, the patrols kept up with them. At first, Karla thought the mind was tricking them and signaled that they should turn back. And then the sisters met the wall of bodies once again and wasted their last few clips on their retreat. The metal doors had almost crushed them there, confirming that the demon wanted to trap them.

If that is what it wants, Karla thought with a growl, *I will deny it with my every breath.*

The statement became a mantra in her heart and a chant on her lips. They burst out of the stairway, onto a lower floor. Deep in her heart, Karla knew they would not make it. With each new level, the patrols grew in number while the twins grew tired. The doors slammed more frequently, blocking paths.

"We will die here, sister," Liz muttered.

"No," Karla snapped harshly. "We cannot. We *must* not. How, then, would we take our revenge on the demon? Would you trust your vengeance to someone else?"

Liz said nothing. This frightened Karla more than anything else. They had to escape to destroy this building, but her sister was resigned to their deaths.

It was always bad when they disagreed.

But no! They would make it. They were on the floor they had come in from. Their climbing gear was still on the window they'd broken. Karla glanced at the map again as the next hallway opened up. She grinned savagely. They just needed to make it to the end of the passage, and they could rappel down.

"Be alert, sister. We're almost there." Karla said. Defeat shone in Liz's eyes.

Karla pushed herself through the passage faster than she had before. She flexed with every step, making sure she and her sister were always in sync. Her grin widened when they passed the halfway mark, and she glanced at Liz, once again missing when the map glitched out and the walls on either side flickered.

In the next step, Karla found herself on the floor, a dull ringing surrounding her. She clutched her head, groaning. It felt as if she were underwater. Her head pounded like someone had taken a hammer to it. There was even a bruise.

"What… happened?" she muttered. Her thoughts came slowly, a sign of a concussion. But what had caused it? She turned her head toward her sister and confirmed that they had suffered the same plight.

The walls flickered again, then disappeared entirely.

"Demon," Karla whispered. She looked around. Her skin paled in horror at the metal doors that blocked them on every side except one.

"How did this come to be?" she whispered, switching instinctively to Russian. Her thoughts came faster now, and with them the realization they were trapped, caged like animals.

But… they had escaped! Karla was sure they had! They had kept ahead of the guards and the doors! They had followed the map.

The map!

Her head snapped to the cuff on her wrist. The map displayed, flickered as the walls had, and disappeared. Karla cursed, long and loud. She used every foul word she knew—every one she had heard José mutter. They had been led along like cats following a string, toyed with without a care. They hadn't even known enough to stop it.

Karla let herself slump. They were doomed the moment they had infiltrated the building. No, even before that—when José had given the order.

"Does it matter?" Liz muttered. "We will die here all the same." Death reflected in her eyes. Death, and relief. Karla could not fault her for either.

Another thick metal door lowered from the ceiling and sealed them in with a bang.

Karla closed her eyes and let the darkness take her.

DJ WAS STARTING TO THINK he was in over his head.

He turned a corner, using the chance to glance behind him. He'd long since stopped being surprised by the number of guards he'd managed to pull away from Ndidi. Weirdly, he was kind of proud. But now, they were finally getting smarter. It was always bad when that happened.

At some point, they'd figured out it was stupid to chase him all at once. Some had branched off to block his path. DJ grimaced when they did this. So far, he'd been trying not to hurt anybody, since he was sort of in the wrong here, but now he didn't really have a choice.

Fortunately, he'd been able to disable some of his pursuers. More just came to take up their spots, but still.

Seriously, what the hell is *this place? Some sort of anthill for guards?* DJ thought, ducking under a punch and giving a jab of his own without breaking stride. The guard fell.

One thing confused DJ. All the guards had guns, and if they decided to use them instead of just pointing them at him, he would have been screwed ten times over. But apparently they wanted to catch him alive. And DJ couldn't allow himself to be caught at all.

He sped up to dodge a tackle from behind him. This allowed him to once again get a bead of his pursuers. He blanched and stopped counting after eight.

Time to go, he thought. Ndidi should have had enough time to get to the seventh-floor window. And if not… well, they'd cross that bridge when they got to it.

DJ wove under some punches and tackles as he made his way to the central hallway. Three guards had been positioned in front of the elevators. These ones were built like linebackers: too much muscle to be any good in a chase but perfect when you don't want your target to escape.

They grinned when they saw DJ approach. DJ sped up to meet them, a grin forming on his face as well.

NDIDI WAS REACHING THE END of the hallway when a bang echoed throughout the floor. A second later, DJ came into view, his eyes wide with excitement and not a little terror.

Ndidi slowed when she saw him, but he kept up his sprint. Ndidi figured there was a reason for that and increased her pace as well. The offices blurred past her. She was more focused on the glass windows and the… *hole in one of them?*

Oh God, he didn't expect her to jump out of the damn building?

The comms crackled, loudly. "*Now, Christy!*"

Ndidi reached the hole in the window, let out a startled yelp, and ducked as a black streak flew in her direction. It occurred to her later that the streak was probably headed for the hole that was at least a foot above her. By then, DJ had caught up to her and was jamming something—a grappling hook?—into the wall with a small hammer. She peered outside, her face blanching. The line stretched to a smaller building at the other end of the street. Protesters roared below at the foot of the building. Hundreds of people were bound to notice the two of them gliding away from Gaius.

DJ straightened, peering outside at the line as if reconsidering. Another bang echoed on their floor, and the footsteps padding on the carpet seemed to make his decision for him. He flashed a grin in her direction and stepped out onto the ledge. Ndidi spared a glance at the dozen guards, their teeth bared, racing down the hallway to meet them. Suddenly, the eighty-foot drop didn't seem so bad compared to whatever they had planned for her.

She followed DJ onto the ledge. The wind beat at her, blowing her hair into her eyes and sending her into a mini-panic until she could see again.

DJ chuckled and pulled at a string attached to his belt, hooking it to the line. He held a hand out to her, grinning. "How good are you at holding on really, really tight?"

Ndidi peered back into the building. The security teams were halfway to them now. Her nerves were taut, but it wasn't as if she had a choice. That seemed to be the theme of the day.

She sighed and grasped DJ's hand, allowing him to pull her close. She closed her eyes and lurched as DJ pushed away from the ledge.

And then they were gliding.

APRIL 2040

OKAFOR AUTISM RESEARCH CENTRE, NEW YORK

CJ'S FINGERS CLICKED at the keyboard as if they had a mind of their own. Black lines of code scrolled in front of him. His brows were creased in worry. Despite his best efforts, he had been unable to hold back the pursuers. This wouldn't have been the best time for his brain circuits to misfire. He spared a glance at the device in the center of the table. The nanoprocessor had two cables connected to it. One of them led to CJ's computer; the other ran up to Chad's.

CJ's glance took in the cowboy. Judging by the frown on his face, he wasn't making much progress either. Two pairs of eyes bored into the side of his head, and he deliberately turned away from them, focusing once more on his screen. CJ already knew how much was riding on this without the lives of his younger brother and former mentor being at stake.

The air conditioner blasted in the background. CJ felt goose bumps on his arms. His sleeves were too short to fully cover his hands, but even if they had, he didn't think the light material would do much good. Did it have to be so cold? His fingers felt about ready to fall off. Nobody else seemed to be bothered. What was up with that?

"Any luck?" Chad asked.

CJ spared another glance at the man. His cowboy hat hung from a strap around his neck, and he was hunched over just as CJ was, his fingers a blur on his keyboard. Lines of code also appeared on his computer monitor—the same ones that were on CJ's.

CJ shook his head. He studied the code again, following each line systematically. He wasn't confident in much, but he had little doubt in his ability to write code. He'd written this one perfectly.

So why didn't it work?

"You guys have been staring blankly for a couple minutes now," his brother said. "There a problem?"

CJ sighed. There *was* a problem; he could see that clearly. He just didn't know what the problem was. Connected to the mainframe of a compromised system, it had been easy for his worm to locate and isolate the glitch that had caused the vehicles to malfunction in the first place. It was why he'd needed the hardware, and it had served its purpose. With a frame of reference, it should have been easy to program a trace to follow the hack to where it came from. Getting the hardware was supposed to be the hard part. The rest should have been easy.

But his trace didn't work. *That* was the problem. It didn't go anywhere. Normally, that would mean that there was nothing *to* trace and that the malfunction in the system was just what the system said: an accident. But CJ didn't want to consider what that would mean. He'd gone through his code time and time again. But there wasn't anything wrong with it. Finally, he leaned back in his chair.

"I am not… um… not sure."

"What do you mean?" Ndidi asked, coming to stand behind his chair. Once again, CJ deliberately avoided meeting her eyes.

He wasn't yet sure what to think of his mentor. On one hand, in many ways, Ndidi was responsible for how far he'd progressed in dealing with being on the autism spectrum. The Autism Research Centre had developed most of the techniques that he'd used growing up. Furthermore, she'd taken a vested interest in CJ and tutored him herself. He'd always be grateful for that.

On the other hand, the Ndidi who stood behind him now was *not* the same one he remembered. Her eyes were still calm and patient, but they were also colder. She'd always had an easy smile. Now she looked constantly frustrated. Though she kept the anger on a leash, she always looked one step away from lashing out.

His mentor would have picked up on his reluctance to make eye contact or his limited speech while talking and worked him through both. Now, he didn't think she'd even spared him a glance until his brother had spoken up.

CJ fidgeted in his seat just thinking about it. He didn't know what she'd gone through or who she'd lost on Mayday, but the transition was jarring.

"The trace… runs around in a loop," he replied.

DJ scrunched up his nose. "Okay, what does that tell us?"

Chad replaced the hat on his head, leaning back in his chair like CJ. "Normally, that means there's nothing to trace or the hack came from within the system itself, which is impossible."

CJ nodded in agreement. Every hacker—no matter how good—leaves a trace. It was how the higher-ups in the Navy SEALs had found him, despite how careful he'd been. If you already knew where the hack entered the system, it was only a matter of time to trace the source address. You could bounce the signal through multiple points, but with a strong enough trace, it would be a delaying tactic at most. Because of risks like that, no hacker worth his salt would use his own terminal for a job.

CJ *wished* that was all there was to it. But their trace couldn't even detect the point of entry. It was exactly as Chad had said: it was as if the system had sabotaged itself, and CJ couldn't see any way that was possible.

"Both your traces are saying the same thing?" Ndidi asked. They nodded. "And there's no way there's a problem with the code?"

CJ pinched the bridge of his nose and Chad scoffed, looking vaguely offended. "I've gone through each line three times," the cowboy replied. "My code is clean."

Ndidi exhaled. "Okay, let's—hypothetically, and purely for the sake of discussion—assume that it *is* possible that the hack was generated by the system itself. What could cause something like that?"

CJ had already thought of this, but his mind shied away from the sheer implications of it. "Could have been… a previous hack," he said. "Virus set on a timer… or activated remotely…"

He trailed off when the words failed him, but Chad caught his meaning immediately. "If the virus was set up far back enough, then even isolating the hack after the fact wouldn't give a trace because the trail would have already gone cold."

"How likely is this to have happened?" Ndidi asked.

"It definitely is possible, miss. But it would require some mad preplanning to set it up."

"What other options are there?"

Chad shrugged and CJ stared at his screen, following the numbers.

After a minute, DJ asked, "Could it have been done by another AI?"

"An… AI?" CJ asked, looking up at his brother.

DJ shrugged. "Well, I don't know shit about all this stuff, but Gaius is an AI, right? Do AIs… communicate or something? Can one override another's programming?"

Ndidi's head snapped to him, and her eyes glazed over. CJ's chair creaked as he sat up, turning fully to face his brother. He'd never heard of such a thing happening. Artificial intelligence had progressed considerably since its inception. But even with how far the technology had come, there was still a limited number of AIs that would be capable of that, even fewer programmed to do so. Gaius was the first that came to mind and the second was…

"Helene," he muttered. Three pairs of eyes snapped to him, and CJ recoiled from the attention. He hurried to explain. He knew what he wanted to say, but no words came out.

DJ came to his rescue, placing a hand on his shoulder. "Hey," he said, trying to meet CJ's eyes. "Focus on me. Breathe."

CJ shut his eyes, inhaling and exhaling deeply. He was very aware of the gazes still pinned on him. Only when he felt he could deal with it did he open his eyes. DJ was grinning, though worry was etched on his face. CJ averted his gaze, his face turning red.

Guess I haven't made as much progress as I thought.

He glanced at the others through his lashes. Chad kept his face impassive, his cowboy hat tipped low, but his eyes showed his confusion. Ndidi showed her concern easily, her face softening. She looked on the verge of saying something, but her eyes went to DJ and seemed to decide against it.

"Don't worry about them," DJ said, drawing CJ's attention back to him. "You're speaking to me. What were you saying about Helene?"

CJ nodded, closing his eyes again and arranging his thoughts. He directed his words to his brother but made sure he was audible enough for both Ndidi and Chad to hear. "Only two AIs… advanced enough to communicate like you said: Gaius and Helene."

Ndidi took a step back, her eyes wide. "How would that even be possible?"

CJ shrugged. Chad, however, looked thoughtful. "I've never heard of it being done, but it's theoretically possible. Programmers talk to their programs all the time when they code. We already know Helene can get into most systems. So, if she somehow got into Gaius's server, posing as the head programmer or technician or whatever, with the right access codes…" He shrugged, then tipped his hat. "That's something to consider, to be sure."

"Is there a way to confirm this?" DJ asked.

Ndidi closed her eyes. Her lips pressed into a thin line. "We'd either have to hack into Helene, somehow…" she said slowly, and Chad snorted at the thought. "Or we'd have to speak to her creator to confirm."

"You *know* Manar Saleem?" Chad asked incredulously.

"You could say that." Her eyes opened, and they shone with a mixture of anxiety and excitement. "He's my ex-fiancé."

JOSÉ OLVERA REPLACED HIS PHONE in his pocket, strode up the stairs to the Sparta building, and tried to hide the anger on his face. There were times when his rage was just the edge he needed, but this wasn't one of them. He could have tried it if he was dealing with a human, which he wasn't, or if he had any sort of leverage, which he didn't. If anything, he had a liability.

So, no, anger wouldn't serve him well here. Still, he could not keep his face from hardening as he passed through the doors. He had been summoned like an errant child. But he would not grovel like a worm for anybody.

The question was, How does one deal with the rogue AI? His first thought was to unplug it, but they'd already tried that. As a matter of fact, it was the whole reason he was in this mess, trying to bargain for his daughters.

The doors to the building opened automatically—or maybe *deliberately*, since it was likely the AI already knew he was there. It had been the one to demand the meeting when it hacked his phone, laptop, and television and declared its ultimatum.

José felt his face harden even more. He shook off the thought with effort. They'd bitten off more than they could chew. He would never admit it to anyone else, but it was true. He should have realized that before he sent the twins, but the higher-ups had pushed and *pushed*.

José took another breath, counting backward. He stopped in the middle of the floor, noting the guards around him and comparing their positions to the exits. Without conscious command, his fingers tapped on his gun through his trousers. He stopped as soon as he noticed the action. Chloe would have chewed him out for revealing that he was carrying a weapon.

The building was as big as the blueprint said. José hadn't been sure.

And yet you'd still sent in the girls—without Chloe.

He'd grown too dependent on them and it was a wake-up call when they'd failed him. At least he wouldn't make the same mistake again. He might not be given the chance to if this meeting went sideways.

José chuckled at that, counting the guards more consciously this time. If the girls were in any condition to walk, they would leave with him, regardless of the meeting's outcome. If they couldn't, he would rather raze the place than leave without them.

The place was sparsely decorated, walls and floors all but bare. José didn't know whether they were still rebuilding after Mayday or if the higher-ups simply had no taste for embellishment. Regardless, the emptiness made the floor look larger than it was. This was more impressive than it sounded because the blueprints showed that the building was several blocks wide.

His observation drew the attention of a guard. The fool eyed him suspiciously before striding over, glaring. *Finally,* José thought, bringing out his phone. He stared down the guard as the idiot approached.

"Can I see your ID?" the man asked in a tone of phony politeness laced with suspicion and supreme self-importance. José felt his face harden even more as he showed the guard his phone. At this rate, he would not be able to control himself by the time he met the AI. Then, he would have to deal with Chloe—which was its own kind of torture.

The man squinted at the phone for a second before rapidly paling. "You're here for Mr. Saleem? Forgive me for wasting your time. Do you need any directions? I can take you to the seventieth floor myself." The man spoke hurriedly, tripping over himself to better stick his head up José's ass. José would have spat on him if he thought the man was worth it.

He wasn't exactly sure what the AI had sent to his phone—he couldn't make heads or tails of the code—but the security outside had responded the same way. That was good. If he was being summoned like common rabble, then the ants should not stand in his way.

"That won't be necessary," he replied stoically, replacing his phone in his pocket. After all his years in the country, his voice only held a hint of a Russian accent. The guard paled even further before hurrying off.

The elevator doors closed, and José punched in the floor number. A camera blinked at him from the corner. José ignored it. What did it matter if the AI tracked his movements as long as he left with his daughters?

It took close to five minutes before a ding signaled his arrival. An assistant came to meet him immediately. José barely kept the sneer from his face. The boy looked barely old enough to shave.

"Can I help you, sir? This floor isn't open to visitors."

"I have an appointment with Manar Saleem," José said. He wondered whether the staff knew that they no longer worked for Saleem, but a security risk. He wondered whether it would change anything if they did. The rabbit cared for little but to get fed, after all.

"Can you verify that?" the child asked, barely constraining his amusement at the thought. José brought out his phone. The child wiped the smile off his face immediately.

A few seconds later, José was led into a large conference room and left there.

The room contained only a fairly large table surrounded by a dozen chairs. José opted to stand.

There was a small buzz, like the sound of static. Then, a voice spoke behind him. [Good afternoon, José Olvera. Thank you for accepting my request.]

As José turned to meet the AI, he ground his teeth.

"Where are my daughters?" he asked, and then immediately cursed himself. The AI must have known how Karla and Liz were related to him, but by verifying that relationship, he could no longer claim detachment in a bid to lower their importance. He would have killed any of his subordinates if they had made such a rookie error during negotiations.

The AI floated a few inches off the ground. It was humanoid and had facial features that made it distinctly female. Its form was transparent, so José could see the currents passing through it. It didn't have a body, but its head was blue. All of it was blue—except its eyes, which shone a brilliant yellow, like two spotlights trained on him. José felt the hair on his neck rise. There was a presence in that gaze that made him feel as though an actual person was standing in front of him.

Electricity crackled in the space where it floated. The AI gestured, and there was another sound of static as an image formed. José found that he preferred focusing on it rather than the monstrosity hovering beside it. Still, both holograms tested his composure—the first for obvious reasons, the second because it showed his daughters trapped in a cage.

[Do not worry; they were not harmed,] the AI said.

Its voice was obviously modeled to sound as human as possible, but it changed frequently as it spoke, varying tones and accents, sometimes mid-word. The sound was enough to snap José out of the rage he'd fallen into. He stared at the AI in confusion. Every voice it tried still came out clipped, stunted, and metallic. It was as if it had not yet decided on a voice that suited it and kept searching and experimenting.

[They were simply a lure,] the AI admitted.

"For whom?" José asked.

[For you,] it replied, its voice now deep enough to be confused as male. [We needed to talk, and I calculated you would not be amenable to such a discussion.]

"Why use my daughters?" José asked. "Why not the first operative we sent?"

[It was decided that the operative would not have been a strong enough lure to draw your attention.]

"Well, you have my attention," José said, crossing his arms. "What happens to my daughters now?"

[Karla and Liz Polova will be returned to you at the conclusion of our meeting, unharmed.]

José's eyes flicked to the projection. Karla had a bruise forming on her forehead and numerous burn marks on her face. Liz looked as though she'd aged several years, her normal emotionless mask giving way to despair.

"Without harm, huh?"

[The wounds have been scanned and deemed superficial at most. They were caused by their own hands as they tried to infiltrate, then flee the building.] The AI floated closer. Its eyebrows were pinched together in what would typically be a frown on a human. That was somehow more unsettling than its abrupt voice change had been. [Significant effort was put into capture without impairment, even at the loss of security personnel. You are urged to consider that in your anger.]

Despite himself, José took a step back, flinching. He was accustomed to threats. They were a constant in his line of work, which gathered a seemingly endless wave of enemies. Threats came from a place of anger, from a need to excuse future violence, or as motivation. Whichever it was, there was always emotion involved when a threat was issued.

The AI didn't threaten him. It genuinely wanted him to consider that no harm had come to his daughters before standing on a pedestal of self-righteous anger. But José could not help but feel like the words had an unspoken promise of what would happen if he kept pushing.

José struggled to keep his thoughts off his face, but that had never been his strong suit. He swallowed and decided to cut through the bullshit. "Why did you call me here?"

[I have a proposal for you.]

José's mind went blank for a moment. The devil AI had called him out here and captured his daughters… to offer him a job?

"What is your proposal?" he asked. His accent became more prominent in his desire to leave.

[Conjoined twins develop when an early embryo does not completely separate into two individuals during development in the womb. Thus, the fetuses develop by sharing one or more organs. Karla and Liz are an extreme example, sharing every organ and system except their brains.]

José frowned. "I know this already."

The AI floated closer until they were almost a breath apart. [Extensively invasive surgery could have separated them in childhood, but now they have become too fused. Most techniques to duplicate or replace their organs and systems are doomed to fail due to the frailty of humans and your barbaric technology.]

José's frown deepened, and the barest flickers of anger ignited in his chest, despite the AI's warning. Was it mocking him? "What is your point?" he growled.

[The surgery is doomed to fail because the biomechatronic parts needed to replace the organs and body parts after the separation did not previously exist.]

"Previously?"

[Sparta now has the technology.]

Finally, the pieces clicked into place. Despite his best efforts to hide it, José stared at the hologram with eyes widened in surprise and not a little greed. That tech would *double* Karla and Liz's strength.

"What exactly is your proposal?"

INTERLUDE:
PICOSPORES

MAY 2040
OKAFOR CORPORATION,
ABUJA, NIGERIA

EZE OKAFOR STRODE into the presentation room and ignored the sudden hush of conversation.

It was a fairly large space, separated into a lower presentation deck and a gallery where Eze, the members of the executive management team, and the investors were to be seated. There were three rows along the length of the gallery, arranged in ascending tiers. Eze took a seat on the uppermost row, claiming its entire length for himself. He took a moment, steeling himself, then finally acknowledged the others in the room with a nod.

As he'd expected, they took it as an invitation to swarm him in greeting. Eze steeled himself again. He didn't dislike any of the men here—far from it, seeing as he had been the one to invite them. But even as an automatic response, shaking hands and murmuring greetings took more energy these days. Eze ranked it among the top five things that he hated about growing old.

Aging was inevitable—making it first on his list. However, with constant exercise and healthy habits while in his prime, Eze had taken steps to ensure that growing old would happen far into his future. The steps had worked, but apparently they hadn't pushed it back far enough.

Medical technology had advanced enough that drugs and operations could potentially lengthen his lifespan, but Eze abhorred such things, considering them cowardice. He was old and he detested that, but he acknowledged it as inevitable and expected. And so, he'd planned for it like any good businessman: he'd arranged an heir.

The clock rang on the hour. With it came scowling and futile requests for more time. The swarm of executives and investors finally dispersed. Eze held back a sigh of relief.

On the presentation deck, Cloney arranged some papers. Since the presentation would be by slide, the papers were nothing more than a way to give his guests the chance to settle down. Eze allowed himself a small smile and studied the man.

He's lost a lot of weight, Eze noted with a frown. Understandably, the disappearance of his daughter, Bethany, during the events of Mayday had hit Cloney hard. Eze himself had felt no small guilt over the incident. He had convinced Cloney to give Bethany to Ndidi's Autism Research Centre, from which she had disappeared.

Mayday had been less than half a year ago, and though Cloney seemed to have focused his efforts more on his work, it was obvious he was suffering.

Eze would have to talk to him.

A slide appeared on the wall, large enough to be seen by everyone. Cloney launched into his presentation.

"Nanotechnology has advanced the world over," he began. "And its presence can be seen in virtually all fields of science, from its medical and engineering applications to its potential for military use. It has advanced more in the last decade than at any time since its conceptualization. Its applications are almost staggering—so much so that by today's principles, a standard nanometer chip is miraculous. Essentially one-billionth of a meter, which was miracle technology a decade ago, is completely worthless nowadays because it's simply too big."

This got a reaction from the management team and investors. Most of them leaned forward in their seats. Eze frowned, however. Cloney had never been a public speaker. His gestures had always been too loud, and he had no head for voice modulation. The little he did know seemed enough to excite the investors for now, but surely Cloney realized that his presentation technique wasn't going to work forever.

So why did it seem like he intended to lead the presentation himself?

Eze allowed his eyes to drift. A second later, they focused on the side door, where Hermione Cloney stood with a notepad in hand. She was following her father's presentation gesture for gesture.

"Ah," Eze smiled in realization. "Cloney's just the warm-up." He nodded. It was a bold move, to be sure, but with a huge payout potential if it worked. Eze approved.

Every entrepreneur worth his salt grew to hate the investors. However, to a business owner, investors were the indirect but oh-so-important partners needed to get their foothold in the market. They were the money wolves, with near-inexhaustible wallets and the ability to smell weakness from a mile away.

Socially awkward and scared of large gatherings, Cloney was not equipped to deal with such people. Thus, he was the one who wowed them with already well-known facts and numbers that had no true value, all to have them properly astounded and excited for the true pitch—which his daughter would throw with heat toward home.

Hermione stepped in now. Cloney spared a glance at his daughter's entrance and transitioned smoothly into an introduction. "Please allow me to introduce my daughter and the co-designer of the technology, Miss Hermione Cloney."

There was no applause. Eze didn't think Dr. Cloney had expected any. With quick strides, Hermione met her father at the center of the stage. "Thank you, Dad," she said softly.

It was a physical sensation. Eze felt the moment the investors—predominantly male—fully took notice of Hermione. For Eze, it was still awkward to see the young lady as anything other than the lanky twelve-year-old he had first known. However, her effect on the room was obvious. She wore a lab coat over a T-shirt and sensible jeans, yet, somehow, the men leaned out of their seats for a better look.

This Eze did not approve of.

Hermione had graduated at the top of her class. She held a master's degree from the University of Benin—an institution officially recognized by the National Universities Commission of Nigeria for its brilliance. She had spent a significant part of the last decade with her father in picotechnology research. She was brilliant, yet all the investors saw was a pretty girl in a lab coat.

For a moment, he allowed that dissatisfaction to show on his face. And, as if sensing it, Hermione met his eyes and she grinned. She turned the smile on the investors, and there was just a hint of mockery in it.

Then, undaunted, she launched smoothly into her presentation.

"The strength of picotechnology is best seen when applied at the cellular and subcellular levels," she explained, her eyes seeming to rest on everyone at once. "This is because the functional margin of similar types of molecules at picoscale—that is, ten to the power of twelve—goes higher than at nanoscale, ten to the power of nine…"

Eze let the sounds drift into the background. Hermione's demeanor became less anxious the more she spoke. More and more, she shifted her stance to something more relaxed. Her voice rose in pitch when it was necessary and tapered off when appropriate. She exuded silent confidence in every word and had the natural magnetism that made people *want* to listen. Her technique drew in the investors.

Eze had noticed all this when he'd seen the young Cloney practicing her speech off to the side, but he hadn't realized the sheer impact that it would have.

There was a lull as Hermione gave the audience time to digest her words. Eze replayed the speech in his mind and chuckled softly. The girl hadn't said anything that wasn't already years old, but her delivery had his most discerning partners jabbering like monkeys with bananas.

"In this way," Hermione continued, "the potential applications of picotechnology in the disciplines of biomedical and environmental science are limitless. But this is only because we have control of the electron distribution around the atoms. This allows us to change the surface energy significantly and, thus, the way proteins are absorbed into a material. Consequently, the rearrangement of electrons around atoms may be altered."

Eze processed this and found the underlying concept easy to follow. Essentially, the extended surface area and improved electrical, chemical, optical, and mechanical properties would make picotechnological products even better than nanomaterials in real-world applications. The question, though, was *how*?

Hermione seemed to have predicted the issue. With a gesture, she waved her father back onstage. "Allow me to demonstrate the concept," she said, reaching for a single large aerosol syringe on the lab table. She pointed it directly at her father's face and pumped it once. Eze raised a brow. She had balls; he had to give her that.

A grayish cloud puffed out of the syringe and engulfed Dr. Cloney's face. Breathing normally, he inhaled more than half of the grayish cloud. The rest of it landed on his face and the whites of his eyes, turning them gray for a split second. For the first time, Eze leaned forward.

"My father just inhaled approximately one hundred million picospores," Hermione said, the epitome of showmanship. "Another one hundred million entered his body through the pores of his skin. If you turn to the projection, you'll see that some also entered through his pupils. In the same way, had he stood sideways, the picospores would have entered through his ear canals. That is how mind-bogglingly small they are.

"What my father just inhaled are harmless, unprogrammed core processors. However, with the right funding and software programs, the picospores can travel virtually anywhere within the body and perform a myriad of functions in real time." She paused to let the statement sink in. "There isn't a limit to what the technology might be capable of."

Eze grinned. *Best closer I've heard,* he thought. He could practically see the dollar signs in each investor's eyes as they calculated the billions they could make when the technology went live. Eze gave young Cloney a nod of acknowledgment. Hermione smiled as if she hadn't realized what she'd just started. Eze stood to leave.

The picospores were the sort of game-changing technology he'd been looking for. Hermione would get her funding—even if Eze had to bankrupt himself to do it.

PART 2
THE PAST

SEPTEMBER 2001

NEW YORK CITY, NEW YORK

SIMONE PETERSON AWOKE with a groan, shielding her eyes from the sun rays piercing through the open drapes. Her head pounded. The light didn't help.

She frowned at the empty bed. She hadn't heard Joan get up. As if to make sure that Simone was really awake, another ray found a gap between her fingers, scorching her retinas.

She glared at the window and reluctantly sat up. She needed to have a talk with Joan about closing the blinds before she left.

Where did she go anyway? Simone thought, making her way out of the room. It wasn't like Joan to leave without at least waking her for a kiss. Simone made a mental note: it was yet another thing they needed to talk about. They hadn't been dating long enough for Simone to let her partner off the hook for leaving without a goodbye kiss.

Really, what're two years in the grand scheme of things? Simone thought, following her nose to the pot of coffee. She poured herself a cup as her eyes scanned the countertop. Joan was old-fashioned enough to have left a note instead of waking her up. But there was nothing on the counter.

She frowned as her phone rang. Her head pounded at the noise, and she winced. Reflexively, she reached to her side, but her hands met empty air. She realized she'd stepped out in just her underwear. Again.

"Good thing Joan's not around to see this," Simone muttered, spinning around to trace the phone. "She'd never let me live it down."

She followed the ring to the living room and pushed aside the pillows strewn on the floor. She found the phone stuffed between two cushions.

How the hell did it get there? Simone thought, cocking her head.

She stood for a minute, looking at the mess that was her living room before it clicked. A blush crept up her cheeks for the second time in just a few minutes.

At least that explains my headache, she thought. *And why I'm in just my underwear.* Joan never liked clothes on while in the apartment. For the most part, Simone didn't mind—though it was hell for their productivity when they both were home.

The phone rang again, bringing another fresh wave of pain to Simone's head. She picked it up hurriedly, not bothering to check the caller ID. There was only one person who knew her well enough to be sure she was awake by now.

"Bold of you to just leave without giving me my kiss," Simone said by way of greeting. She tried to make her voice stern but failed woefully. *Kind of hard to be righteously indignant while standing in only my underwear.* She looked at the living room again. *And at the scene of the crime.*

"I'll make it up to you when I get home," Joan chuckled.

Simone frowned. Even through the phone, Joan's voice sounded strained and detached. She was only like this when she didn't want Simone to be worried.

"Just wanted to make sure you got my note," Joan finished. Her voice was calm, but that just set off more alarm bells in Simone's mind. Joan was working way too early to be calm.

Simone sat up on the couch, pressing the phone closer to her ear. "No. I didn't get the note," she replied. For the first time, she became aware of the noise in the background. Were those… screams? "Never mind that. Where are you right now?"

Joan didn't answer immediately, and Simone could feel her partner searching for how to respond. Simone didn't know why she tried. After two years, she knew of Joan's tricks.

"I'm going up South," Joan said, in what she probably thought was a casual tone. "We got called in. Some idiot left their stove on or something."

Simone stood now. Joan had just lied to her. And it wasn't even a good lie. On any other day, Simone might have fallen for it, but not when she could hear *screams* in the background. Simone clutched the phone tighter and tried to take measured breaths.

"Don't lie to me, Joan. It isn't even your shift," she said. "Where *are* you?"

"Everything will be okay, love," Joan tried again. She must have really been desperate if she was breaking out the pet names so soon. There was the muffled sound of an explosion in the background. That didn't help ease Simone's nerves. Joan cursed. "Listen, I have to go. I'll call you later, okay?"

"Wait, Jo—"

"I love you. Okay?" Joan cut in hurriedly. Her voice had lost the measured calmness. It was harsher now. She sounded hurried but filled with resolve. "I love you. Never forget that. We'll talk later."

The line went dead.

Immediately, Simone turned on the TV. Any fire big enough to cause the kind of distress she had heard over the phone would be on the news. She flipped through the channels but didn't have to search long. Every channel was showing the same thing.

At first, Simone didn't understand what she was seeing. She heard the screams in the background and saw the people running like ants, but it didn't really make sense. The fires filled the screen. Molten metal fell from buildings, landing on a firefighter with a woman in his arms. The man thrashed from the pain yet used his body as a shield for the woman. More people came to help. The picture blurred, shifting to another scene of mayhem.

Simone fought the urge to throw up.

Buildings collapsed, roads cracked, and people ran. And through all these were the screams. Simone realized how much the bad connection between her and Joan had muffled the pandemonium. The broadcast didn't have that problem, and Simone was able to hear the screams in full. She retched on the living room floor, then wiped her mouth, her eyes riveted on the TV. The second building of the World Trade Center collapsed. Simone threw up again. Firefighters streamed into the ruin, shouting above the chaos. While dozens rushed in, only a trickle came back out. Even fewer carried people with them.

Joan is there right now.

Simone had known that when she saw the news. It was the only thing big enough to call an all-hands-on-deck at the fire station. Still, she'd deliberately refused to consider it. She still didn't want to. But how could she not? How could she watch as firefighters dashed into that blaze and *not* consider that Joan would be one of them? How could she watch as husbands wept over blackened corpses and *not* consider Joan was one of them?

Simone threw up again, but she didn't care. *Joan is there right now.*

Simone knew her partner. She would always be in the thick of it because that was where she could save the most people. It was that kind of shit that had drawn her to Joan in the first place. It was also the kind of shit that kept her pacing every time Joan left for a shift and even when it wasn't her shift. That had been the cause of so many arguments between them. Joan worried about the people who could be hurt because she wasn't there, and Simone worried about Joan being hurt because she *was* there.

Joan was there right now, and Simone's fears were realized. She tried to throw up again, but her stomach was empty.

For the next few hours, Simone watched the news in silence. At some point, her tears dried and then crusted on her cheeks. She tried to feel anger—at herself, at Joan, at whoever had done this. For a while, she succeeded. She paced around the apartment, cursing. She threw the furniture she could lift and destroyed the pieces she couldn't. She hurled insults into the air.

Why? her mind screamed. *Why couldn't she just have stayed back? Doesn't she care? Doesn't she know what this will do to me? Why are they more important?*

"We were supposed to spend our lives together," Simone muttered, her voice cracking. A new wave of tears spilled down her face, and Simone did nothing to wipe them off.

Another news anchor came on at some point. The woman's eyes were red and puffy in a way that makeup couldn't hide. "At 8:46 a.m.," she started, her voice crackling, "the first plane crashed into the North Tower. At 9:03 a.m., the second plane crashed into the South Tower."

South, Simone thought numbly. Another wave of grief knocked her off the couch. *Joan said she was going up South.*

"The third plane crashed into the western facade of the Pentagon in Washington, DC, at 9:37 a.m.," the anchor continued, taking a breath. "At this moment, the White House has officially declared our nation is under terrorist attack." Her lips trembled and her voice wavered with horror. It was not often—if ever—that a person recognized when history was being made.

Logically, Simone knew it was possible that Joan would keep her promise— that her partner *would* come back to her. But in a more real sense, she knew that was just wishful thinking. Dozens of first responders had flooded into the collapsed buildings and only a handful had come back out. And even putting that aside, the emptiness she felt in her gut, in her heart, told her all she needed to know.

She finally stood and went back into the bedroom. She returned to the couch a few minutes later with a note clutched in her fist. The scene played out in the background, until the rubble finally settled, until the sounds of the screams penetrated Simone's skull. But still she watched, her eyes locked on the bonfire. In her hands, Joan's note crinkled.

Before you get all riled up, you'll get your kiss when I come back. In the mean-time, try to put some clothes on before coming out, okay? I love you.

CHAPTER

29

MARCH 2002

SAN DIEGO, CALIFORNIA

THE WEATHER WAS DREARY, which was unusual so early in the spring. Simone found it fitting; it was the first time the weather had deigned to match her mood. The climate seemed to impair the thinking of other people, though, because Simone had been staring at the Marine sergeant for well over a minute.

He seemed to have problems processing her request. Mark—his name, according to the plaque on his desk—licked his lips, his eyes darting to the side as if hoping for someone to rescue him.

"Come again?" he asked finally.

"I would like to enlist in the marines," Simone repeated calmly and clearly. This seemed to be the part that he was stuck on.

Mark's eyes roamed over her, as they'd done several times already. A couple of months ago, in a different lifetime, Simone would have felt disgusted by that look. Now, she couldn't bring herself to feel much of anything.

The sergeant was young for his station. Simone didn't think he was far past his twenties, barely out of training. He must have been given the recruiting office assignment as punishment. But self-control was always the first thing instilled in the military. It was a testament to his shock that he did absolutely nothing to hide how ridiculous he found the idea of her enlisting.

Lucky for him, Simone didn't care. It was hard to anymore.

The office was packed, though most of the people were families that had come to show support or try to change their children's minds. Simone had waited for over an hour for her turn. The line had quickly filled in behind her. So far, she hadn't seen anyone turned away.

Mark stared blankly at her for another few seconds. Simone's raven hair had lost its luster over the past few months, falling listlessly over her head. She'd lost a lot of weight and was little more than ribs. Joan had often told her that her eyes were her best feature because they always had a twinkle. Months of constant crying had left her eyes sunken and swollen. The twinkle Joan had been so proud of had died the day Joan did. Now, Simone's eyes looked as dead as the rest of her. As dead as she felt.

So, she *did* understand why Mark thought it so ridiculous that she would enlist. Frankly, she did too. But avenging Joan's death—regardless of whether it brought peace—was the only thing that stirred any emotion inside her anymore. And for that, she needed military training.

She ignored the looks and the murmurs. She would enlist, and she would learn. For Joan.

Oh, how I miss you. She missed Joan's full lips when they kissed, the way she pouted to get her way.

New York had quickly lost all value to her after 9/11. There was a new level of solidarity in the city that hadn't been there before. The trauma had forced people to remember their own mortality. They sought comfort in others because the numbers helped them feel safe. Well… safer, at least.

Joan would have loved it. This was one of the things that she'd fought so hard for. It had cost her life. But for Simone, that was too high a price. *I miss you, Joan.* Simone missed watching the sunset with her partner on top of the Rockefeller

Center. She missed the feel of her long shiny blonde hair between her fingers. Somehow, her hair had always smelled like strawberries.

"What division are you interested in?" Mark asked an eternity later. Simone forced her eyes to focus on him.

"The First," she said. She'd spent considerable thought on this. At first, she'd been drawn to this division simply because it was the closest. But then she noticed the motto: *No better friend, no worse enemy.*

Yes, Simone thought, *to the ones who did this, no worse enemy indeed.*

There was a thud as the sergeant stamped her request. Simone accepted it in silence. Across the page was one word: *ENLISTED.*

A YEAR LATER, President Bush authorized military operations to disarm Iraq, to free its people and defend the world from danger. For this, the First Division was deployed.

MANAR STOOD BY THE DOOR and listened to his mother pray. She did that daily now, and her voice increased in fervor with every recitation. Manar didn't know exactly why she prayed so hard or why he found it so comforting. It's just what she did, and he accepted what that meant to him.

"My name is Nadira Saleem," she started. Manar hid by the door and settled in to listen. "And I beg you, Allah, to pardon my husband, Dar Saleem. Pardon him for occasionally raising his voice to his wife, Nadira; his daughter, Farrah; and his son, Manar."

Manar perked up. He didn't mind so much when his father raised his voice at him. It was when he raised his hand that Manar grew afraid.

"He has lost his faith in his family. He has lost his faith in you. He has turned to the arak bottle for comfort, and it has affected him grossly. But his two children and I still dote on his every word and deed. We love him as husband and father.

I forgive him. The children forgive him. I beg you, Allah, to pardon him and let us into heaven together as a family."

After this, the prayer dissolved into Arabic. Manar did not know enough of the holy tongue to follow it. Still, he would have preferred to sit and listen to his mother's voice, but his father would be waking up soon, and Manar had to finish his chores before then. Maybe if he stayed by his father's side today, his presence would stop him from drinking, or at least shame him enough that he wouldn't raise his voice or hand that day.

Manar went to meet his sister in the courtyard. The dawn had not yet broken, but he expected she'd begun sweeping. Mama was always happy if she found the place clean after she came out from her prayers.

He heard the sound of sweeping when he stepped out but couldn't make out where it came from. Allah only knew where Farrah got her vision, to work in such darkness.

"Farrah," he called as loudly as he dared. He wouldn't want to disturb his mother as she prayed or—Allah forbid—wake his father so early.

The sweeping paused. Manar heard footsteps echo in the silence. Moments later, he saw the light coming from the back of their compound, Farrah a few steps behind it. Ah, so she was not the owl that Manar had thought.

"I was going to wake you soon, had you not called me," she whispered. The lantern provided poor lighting, but it was enough for Manar to observe his sister.

Manar felt a frown form on his face. He was five years old—old enough to wake up by himself. However, his sister insisted on treating him like a child, even though she was barely older than he was. He nodded once, standing to his full height to try to meet Farrah's eyes. His mother told him that he would one day be far taller than his sister. Manar could not wait until that day.

"I have been up for a while," he said, though it was not strictly true. "I was having my morning prayers. But Father will be awake soon, and the chores must be done before then."

Farrah nodded absently. Manar knew she was thinking about their father. Her expression was pained almost to the point of tears. Manar felt an urge to comfort her. He was the male child; he should take care of his women. But her tears confused him. Farrah was the only one to whom his father never raised his hand. Rather, he spoke in riddles about selling her. This was another thing that always confused Manar. Was his sister cattle to be sold?

Farrah looked up. "We should hurry. It will soon be daybreak."

THE SOLDIERS BURST into the house an hour later, when the sun started coming out from behind the mountains. Wide-eyed, Manar saw three men rush in from the broken door, guns strapped to their backs. Outside, a scream pierced through the dawn.

Farrah.

Manar opened his mouth to shout, but one of the men backhanded him, pulling his hair to stop him from falling. He was dragged outside by the scalp, dazed from the blow. Still, similar hits from his father had conditioned him to keep his consciousness. There was a familiar ringing in his ears, like a mosquito constantly hounding him in the heat of summer.

He looked around and spotted his sister at the other end of the compound. She was being held down by two soldiers. No, wait… *one* soldier held her down. The other played with his pants, a crazed look in his eyes.

Manar tried to turn away—his mother had told them of such vile things as a warning never to stay out too late—but his head was held too firmly. He closed his eyes, but the image penetrated his eyelids.

"Farrah!" he called loudly so she would hear him over her screams. He thought of what his mother would have said and channeled it. "Be brave! Close your eyes and pray to Allah, my sweet sister."

Farrah cried louder.

Blood spilled into his eyes from where his hair had been pulled out at the roots. He blinked it away in time to see the two men go into one of the inner rooms and drag his mother out, also by her hair. His father was inside the room too. Why hadn't he stopped them?

His mother's mouth was open, but no sounds came out. She twisted in the soldier's grasp, but he ignored her completely. Her eyes locked on Manar as they crossed the threshold of the house, and her struggles doubled.

"Manar. I'm here. Umma is here, Manar. Allah will protect us." Her hijab was torn. It hung from her shoulders, displaying her naked face and hair for everyone to see. Tears ran from her eyes. Each word came out as a sob, but still she cried out, her hands stretching toward Manar. "Husband, where are you? The children need you!"

The man dropped her, wincing at how loudly she screamed. Manar's mother reached out to him. A second later, the soldier hissed and used the butt of the gun on her head. She crumpled immediately.

Tears ran down Manar's cheeks. He found it difficult to breathe through his clogged nose, and his jaw ached for some reason. A few seconds later, he realized he was screaming. He struggled free from the soldier's grip and rushed to his mother's side, but a blinding pain struck the back of his head.

He tripped on his second step, and the ground rushed to meet him.

THE FIRST MARINE DIVISION had covered approximately eight hundred kilometers—no small feat for a division engaged in constant combat. But after days of fighting, they were rewarded by getting deep into enemy territory. Simone panted, sweat dripping with each step. Hours later, they got into position, and the squad was given a few minutes to rest. She gulped from her flask, risking a look around.

Their squad had taken shelter in an abandoned building and converted it for their purposes. Officially, their mission was to subdue the remaining pockets of resistance across Baghdad. Their intelligence indicated that one such pocket was in Fallujah, a town where the Fedayeen militia had taken civilians hostage. Simone didn't see much of anything worth saving. The scant houses looked long abandoned, with cracks in their walls and weeds left to grow. She didn't see how anyone could live here.

A minute later, her reverie was broken by the squad leader's voice calling the group into a huddle.

"Lance Corporal Peterson, Private Joseph, and Private Edwards, you're on the roof," Staff Sergeant Robert said. "Everyone else, you're with me. Keep your eyes peeled for unarmed civilians."

The squad nodded. Simone glanced at them, at the grim resolve on their faces. She held in a sigh.

"Roll out," the staff sergeant called. Simone, Joseph, and Edwards broke off from the main group and scaled the building in seconds. The squad kept to the back roads—or, at least, roads that were in greater disrepair than others—until they reached the coordinates their intelligence had indicated. It was a nondescript compound seemingly in better shape than those around it. Simone and the two privates made their way onto the rooftops, watching their trail to be sure they weren't followed.

Staff Sergeant Robert signaled a halt when they were a few hundred meters from the compound. Without another word, the squad dispersed to their assigned positions. Simone flattened her body on the rooftop, setting up her M27 infantry rifle with practiced motions. She peered through the scope and made out the Fedayeen militia immediately.

They were dragging an Iraqi family into the street: a woman and two young children, a girl and a boy. Their mouths were open as they screamed to their gods, to each other, or just because. The daughter was splayed out between two soldiers, her dress pushed up to her waist. One of the men held her down while the other unbuckled his pants.

Joseph threw up. Edwards cursed on the comms unit. He was watching the same scene Simone was. Out of the corner of her eye, she saw his finger twitch on the trigger.

Simone fixed her eyes on the boy, the son. She tried to watch the whole family and the soldiers. She would need to report what she saw later. But her eyes kept going back to the boy. He was so small.

Joan had always wanted a son.

The mother crumpled from a blow to the head. The boy lost it, wriggling in his captor's hands until he was released. He rushed to his mother, but the soldier had already brought his gun around. The butt of the rifle crashed against the back of the child's head, and he collapsed in a heap.

"They're beating up *children*," Joseph spat, his eyes brimming with disgust. "What sort of sick fuckers use a *family* as hostages?" The report forced Simone out of her thoughts. She could wallow in self-pity later. With effort, she drew her eyes from the boy, focusing instead on the soldiers.

Something's wrong, she thought. What was the militia waiting for? They stood around, their eyes scanning the surroundings and into the building while they held down their captives, but they made no moves to actually take the hostages anywhere. Why had they brought the family outside? Surely the girl could be raped just as well inside. It didn't make any sense.

Unless, of course, they already knew Simone's squad was out there, and the hostages were nothing more than bait.

Simone had to admit the plan was solid, even if it was a disgusting tactic. If her squad tried to rescue the hostages, the militia inside the building would ambush them. And if the squad took the building first, they'd have dead civilians on their hands. The soldiers hadn't once looked at the rooftops, so they probably didn't expect snipers. Her squad's best bet was to have her, Joseph, and Edwards pick them off one by one before the main squad stormed the building.

She relayed her thoughts to the other privates, and they acknowledged. She signaled to Staff Sergeant Robert to get his attention. When she was sure she had it, her fingers flashed rapidly, relaying her report: Hostages. Bait. Military. Building. Pick them off.

It was the best she could come up with. Their comms unit had been destroyed in one of their earlier campaigns, and they hadn't had a supply drop in days. The squad only had a few working ones, and those were only used for emergencies to communicate with the temporary military base. Robert looked confused before nodding in agreement. He turned to the squad, probably informing them of the plan. When he turned back, Simone signaled that she was ready. He nodded.

A second later, the squad engaged the soldiers.

Simone drew her brows together. *Why would he engage when I just said—*

The thoughts clicked in her head. He'd misunderstood her, taking her message to mean that *he* would engage while the snipers provided backup. But that was a stupid plan. How did he not see that? Already, some of her squad members had opened fire on the compound, and the militia had retaliated. Bullets flew with abandon and there were hostages in the middle of that. How stupid *were* these guys?

Dust quickly obscured the area, and even if Simone had been inclined to shoot, she couldn't without the risk of hitting one of her own.

And *that* was why the plan lacked merit.

The shootout continued. Simone aimed at the soldiers, but the dust kept her from hitting anything. Her attention was drawn suddenly to the hostages. The soldiers had let go of them in their haste to defend against Simone's squad. The girl lay curled up on the ground, her glassy eyes staring into the distance as quiet sobs wracked her body. The mother and the boy lay unconscious on the ground.

Or at least, the mother *had been* unconscious on the ground. She'd jerked awake suddenly, her eyes darting wildly before landing on her son. She clutched something to her chest, her mouth moving wordlessly as she crawled through the gunfire to the child. Simone admired her courage.

A second later, a stray bullet passed through the mother's throat, and her blood sprayed an arc through the air. Simone felt her heart lurch. She shouted and reached out a hand, as if she could grab the woman. As if that would help her bleed out less. As if she could do anything at all.

The mother clutched at the wound instinctively. Her eyes were already losing their light. She fell a few feet from where she'd been shot, her son yards away.

Simone turned her sights to the boy. Blessedly, he was still knocked out. No child should have to witness a parent's death. Simone turned to the daughter. Her mother's death seemed to have snapped her out of her shock. The girl crawled haltingly toward her mother's corpse.

This time, Simone *did* see where the shot came from. A private, rushing for cover, shot over his shoulder in his retreat. The bullet, wildly off the mark, angled way too low to do any good. It struck the girl in her chest. She collapsed immediately. Too late, Simone averted her eyes. Now, the image of son, mother, and daughter lying bloody a few feet apart was imprinted in her mind.

With her eyes closed, she missed the moment the grenade launcher brought down the family's house.

The explosion threatened to deafen her. The force of it rocked the three-story building she perched on. She clung to the cracks, her eyes fixed on the collapsing building. A fire had already started somewhere within the ruins. Its heat was so intense that she could feel it over a hundred feet away.

Soldiers from both sides scrambled for cover—slowly, as if they were running through water. Simone found that she could not move. Her eyes were fixed on the flames. It seemed so close, as if the heat were a physical presence.

There's… someone there, isn't there?

A figure stood in the flames. It was nothing but a silhouette, yet Simone would recognize that form anywhere. But what was Joan doing here?

The figure strode out of the building and walked toward Simone. She moved at normal speed while the building crashed in slow motion around her. Simone's heart pounded in her chest, and her face flushed with excitement. She could feel her mouth stretch into a grin she couldn't control.

Dimly, in the back of her mind, she realized that she was probably reliving her trauma from 9/11. She knew her mind had been fragile since Joan's death, and now, the collapsing building and the bonfire created just the right situation to push her into the deep end. Or maybe she'd fallen from the roof, and her body was lying broken in a coma while her mind escaped into whatever this was.

Simone found that she didn't give a rat's ass. If she was in a coma, all the more reason to enjoy her reprieve. And if she was dead? At least now she knew she would be with Joan.

But Joan stopped in the middle of the street and knelt. Simone tried to move. The house had tilted enough that it would be a simple matter for her to jump, but her body didn't respond. She couldn't even twitch her fingers. Joan reached out to something on the street. *Someone,* Simone corrected. The unconscious boy. There were tears in Joan's eyes as she caressed the boy's cheeks. Simone's heart ached for her. Joan had always wanted a son.

Save him, Simone, a voice said inside her.

Simone tried to turn toward it, though her body remained unresponsive. She knew instinctively whose voice it was. Simone stared at Joan until she met her eyes. She let her resolve be her acknowledgment. Joan nodded once, a smile dancing on her lips.

And then she left. She hadn't disappeared; that would mean what Simone had felt hadn't been real. And she couldn't—wouldn't—accept that.

Simone blinked, and time returned to normal. She peered at the unconscious boy through the scope and squeezed off a shot at the Fadayeen soldier reaching for him. And then she took out the next one, and then the next, working her way in a spiral from the closest to farthest. Somehow, the dust wasn't as big an issue as it had been earlier. Her shots never missed.

She was so focused on the boy that she missed the multiple rocket-propelled grenades that flew straight to the rooftop. They exploded in the space between the other two snipers. The roof caved in, and Simone fell to the ground floor. Somehow, she was still conscious as the building started to collapse around her.

I wonder if I'll see her again, she thought as she slipped into darkness.

CHAPTER

31

AUGUST 2003
FALLUJAH, IRAQ

THE DARKNESS WAS STILL THERE when Simone woke. She had an irresistible urge to sneeze. Her whole body convulsed, which almost made her black out from the pain. She couldn't tell how long she'd been unconscious. Long enough, at least, for her body to come to terms with the beating she'd put it through over the last couple of hours. Every bone screamed at her; her muscles burned through her skin. Her lungs were scorched from all the dust she'd inhaled, and each harsh breath echoed through the space around her.

I've been buried alive, she thought. But she'd already known that. She was conscious when the building collapsed around her. She strained through the pain, squinting at the darkness. Debris was scattered all around her, some large enough and close enough to crush her head if it rolled even the slightest bit.

Small mercies that none landed on me.

Still, the rocks that *had* landed on her had broken enough bones to almost make her wish for death, even if they had missed anything vital.

I can't just lie here.

She had to find what was left of her squad so they could regroup and report back. Somehow, the soldiers had known they were coming. They had a leak somewhere. Joseph and Edwards were right beside her when the rockets hit, so they couldn't have fallen far away.

Grunting, she tried to sit up, but blacked out again.

When Simone woke up the second time, she was still in darkness. However, her eyes had adjusted enough that she didn't have to squint to make out the silhouettes of the rocks. Her bones still screamed at her, but the pain had lessened. The stars shimmered above through the two collapsed floors and the caved-in roof. Was it nighttime?

Regardless, she didn't think that was enough time for her wounds to have started healing. That meant she had become more acclimated to the pain. It didn't bode well for her already fragile mind.

Ignoring the voice in the back of her brain, she once again tried to sit up. This time she succeeded, though her arms could barely lift her, and her breath became even harsher. Her head was fuzzy, and her sight spun. She closed her eyes, leaning on a rock. If her wounds didn't kill her, the lack of oxygen would. She had to find a way out, and fast.

Or… I could just let go.

Simone shook the thought from her head.

Not yet.

She focused her energy. "Private Joseph," she called out—or at least tried to. Her words were stifled by a coughing fit that brought another wave of pain. She cleared her thoughts, swallowed, and tried again.

"Private Edwards." Her voice was still weak, but the echoes helped carry it.

Silence greeted her. They might have been unconscious, but she had no way to confirm that. She doubted that she had the strength to keep shouting. Staff Sergeant Robert might be working to dig them out. They must have seen the roof collapsing.

But then again, she thought grimly, *they might also be trapped. Or dead. Or presumed we are.*

She chuckled, ignoring the burn in her chest. When had she become so pessimistic? Surely she hadn't changed *that* much since… since that day.

Simone closed her eyes. She was so *tired*. Mentally. Emotionally. She'd known this for months, but only now, when she couldn't make herself move, couldn't distract herself with something else, did she realize how deeply tired she was.

Maybe I should let go. She already knew Joan would be waiting on the other side, and this thought made her smile.

The sound of sobbing drifted through the darkness. Simone opened her eyes with difficulty and listened. A moment later, the sound came again, faint. It wasn't any of her squad members, Simone was sure. This was higher pitched, like a woman—or a child.

The boy, she realized. He'd still been unconscious in the courtyard. She didn't know whether it was good or bad that he'd woken up now. *Definitely good,* she resolved, *because now I can find him.*

And she *would* find him. She didn't know where the protective instinct came from or why it appeared now, but it was out in full force. Maybe because Joan had asked her? But no, she'd felt a connection to the boy as soon as she'd seen him. Joan had just reinforced it. She'd always wanted a son, too, after all.

"Hold on," Simone called out, hoping it would be loud enough to reach the child. She gathered all her energy and managed to get to her feet by leaning on the rock behind her. One of her ankles protested whenever she applied pressure, so she had only the other to work with.

She recalled the sense of resolve she'd felt when Joan asked her to save the child. She channeled that as she used the rocks as a crutch, hopping through the wreckage in the direction of the sobs.

The first few steps were the worst, each of them making her more light-headed. After a while, black spots dotted her vision, forcing her to rest. "I'm coming," she murmured. She wasn't sure if her words reached the child or if he'd even understand them if they did, but it was the best she could do. She got no response, except when the sobbing seemed to grow louder.

As the wailing increased, Simone felt adrenaline rush through her. She was close—really close. She took a few more steps and found the bodies of privates

Joseph and Edwards. A large steel pipe had punctured Joseph's chest from behind. Large pieces of debris had crushed Edward's body and skull. Only his hand was visible, identified by the old-fashioned signet ring he always wore. He called it a family heirloom. Simone reached down and pried it from his finger. At least his family would have something of his to bury.

She chewed her lip, a habit Joan had spent months trying to get her to stop. Her squad should have found her by now—or at least been rummaging through the wreckage. It was night, and she didn't hear any gunfire from the streets, meaning the fight was over. It didn't bode well, then, that no one had come for her.

Simone forced herself past the bodies. The cries had subsided somewhat. Simone shut down her thoughts before they could take hold. She moved toward where she'd last heard the sobbing. She'd been so close; she should be able to see him by now.

"Where are you?" she called. She was almost surprised when he answered. Not in any words, of course, but the cries picked up again farther out. Had he moved? The sound no longer echoed among the rocks, so he must have found the way out. At least that was another problem solved.

MANAR HEARD THE VOICE OF HIS MOTHER call out to him, and his relief was so great that he cried out. Her voice consoled him, but this just made Manar cry out more, this time in shame. He had not been able to protect his mother or his sister when the soldiers came.

Was this not the duty of the male child? Manar no longer had the excuse of childhood. He was *five* years old, yet he'd been unable to do anything. The soldier had been able to control him like Manar controlled the small plastic toy figures his mother had found for him.

His mother called out again, and Manar's tears intensified. How was he going to tell her that Farrah had been seen by men that were not her husband? Such a thing would leave her unwed, Manar knew. And it was all because he had not done his duty.

The voice of his mother called out to him a third time. This time it was clear enough that he could make out the words. They weren't words he knew, and he frowned. She sometimes did that: use words that he didn't know. Most times, it was when she spoke with Father and didn't want him or Farrah to understand. But why would she use the strange words now? Father was... Where was his father? Where was he when the soldiers had come? And when they had taken Manar's mother and sister and beat them? Had he also been powerless?

Manar couldn't believe that. Dar Saleem had the heaviest hand he knew. His father would have easily been able to handle the soldiers, even with their weapons.

Unless... unless he'd found where Manar's mother had hidden the arak bottle.

Manar felt a dark cloud in his head. It was different from his weariness—and it came with voices. The voices whispered that his father had chosen the arak over his family. Manar tried to shake away the thought, crying out in his confusion. But in the shadows of the rocks, he saw images of the past so vivid that he could almost reach out and touch them.

His memories showed his father lying passed out in the living room, his hands clutching a bottle of arak. The vision shifted to his father stumbling around the courtyard as he dragged Manar's mother to their room despite her pleas. In the darkness, Manar heard the sounds that always came soon after.

Memory after memory flashed through his mind.

Manar had always believed that his father had done these things because of the bottle, not because he wanted to. And so Manar had frequently cursed the arak. But if his father had been easily controlled by a bottle, then how could the same man have overpowered multiple soldiers? The cloud whispered that, in many ways, his passed-out father had been just as weak as Manar.

They had both been powerless to protect their women.

His mother called out again, and Manar moved in the direction he thought the sound came from. He rose from the rubble where he had woken and entered the courtyard. The moon had risen. Manar realized that a whole cycle had passed. His stomach grumbled a reminder that he had not even broken his fast that day.

Manar ignored the pain and stared up at the moon. He vowed never to be so powerless again. Never to be controlled like how his father had been controlled by the bottle, like how the soldier had controlled Manar himself. His mother was coming to him. Together, they would find Farrah, and he would get a second chance to protect them. He didn't care what he had to do. He would be strong enough to protect those he cared about and punish those who stood against him.

"I swear it," Manar vowed, nodding to the moon. It was full: a good omen. Let the heavens witness his oath.

He waited for his mother's call and cried out when he heard it. A minute later, a woman stumbled from the rocks. Manar's eyes widened. This was definitely not his mother. At first, he was willing to believe that she might have been covered in dust, explaining why her skin was so white. But this woman didn't have his mother's girth, and she wore trousers like a man. Manar's mother would have died before going against Allah in such a way. Her clothes were torn in several places, and she hopped gingerly on one leg. It was obvious she could barely stand, but relief shone in her eyes when she saw him.

She smiled, and Manar felt as if he were in his mother's bosom, protected and safe, even standing among the rubble of his home. No wonder he'd thought the woman was his mother. She called out to him. Her voice was the sound of rain hitting the soil and nourishing the crops. He took a step toward her but stumbled on something.

Manar looked down and found the glassy eyes of his mother staring back at him. They did not flash in recognition, nor did they sparkle with joy. They didn't even blink. And as he stared, an insect crept across her pupil.

Something in Manar broke. He screamed, though he did not realize he had done so. He cried, though he thought his tears had long dried up. The black cloud in his mind spread until it consumed everything.

Once again, the ground rushed to meet him.

SOMEHOW, SIMONE CAUGHT THE BOY before he fell. Her body punished her for it, even more so when the pair of them fell. She sat up with difficulty, cradling the child's head to her chest. When her legs brushed against something, Simone's eyes were drawn to the corpse on the ground. Recognition flashed, and her heart bled for the boy even more.

No child should have to see his parent's death. It was the second time she'd thought that today. Both times, it'd meant nothing.

She stroked the boy's head, whispering all the things that Joan had whispered to her in the night—all the things that they'd hoped to one day whisper to their son. "I will be your mother now," Simone whispered softly. And she would. No power under the sky would stop that from happening.

She sat there for hours, gently stroking his head. Her back and arms protested, but somehow Simone hadn't felt this strong in months.

"SO," THE IRAQI JUDGE SAID, glaring at her from the high table, "why do you want to take Manar away from his country?"

Simone stood up and forced herself to restrain her glare. She'd been on edge for the eighteen months she'd been forced to wait for this meeting. The hours she'd spent sitting had further frayed her nerves. Still, she could not afford to show just how much she wanted to wipe the smile off his face for his shitty phrasing.

Simone forced herself to take a breath, calmly meeting the eyes of the judges. There were six of them: three representing each country. They would be the ones to decide whether Manar went back home with her or if she would spend more months in Iraq, filing further pleas.

The months after the mission at the compound had been hell. Once they'd found each other, neither she nor Manar had been in any condition to move very far. Neither of them had had the provisions to stay. Luckily, she'd been able to find Robert's body and salvaged the comms unit, using it to radio for an extraction.

After that, the days passed in a blur of bureaucracy. Simone had been forced to dictate and submit a copy of her report even while she was mummified in the infirmary and doped up on drugs. The silver lining was that Manar had been allowed to stay close after she'd opened her wounds going after the fools that'd tried to lock him in a cell.

Weeks later, she'd been deemed well enough to attend a meeting called by one of the base lieutenants. She handed him all the dog tags she'd been able to collect. Far more had been buried under rubble, but there was nothing Simone could do about that. She once again summarized the events of the mission. Since she was almost fully healed and no longer delirious from pain, she was able to remember far more details. This earned her the task of updating her initial report. It took effort not to grit her teeth as she acknowledged the order.

"That's unfortunate to hear, corporal, but I'm glad that you made it back to us," Lieutenant Darryl Johnson had said after she was done. Simone had never met the man before and knew next to nothing about his character. It came as a surprise then when she felt an almost immediate dislike for him. Maybe it was the mustache and shaved head. Who did that?

"Now, about the boy," he'd continued. Simone had tensed immediately. "Since his parents, by your own words, are dead, there is little need for him to wander around the base. We have allowed it up till now because of his fragile state, but the base is not a childcare facility. You're permitted to take a few days off to escort the child to an orphanage, ensure he's settled, then report back for your next assignment. The war's not won yet."

Simone had somewhat expected this, so it had been easier to bear. Still, accepting the order had been more painful than her fall from the roof.

Mother Teresa's Orphanage had not been pleased to see a white woman request refuge for the child. They'd been even less pleased when she'd explained that her squad had been at fault for the death of his parents. Maybe it was the love that shone in her eyes when she looked at Manar, or the fire that burned there when she assured them she was coming back for him. Or perhaps Joan was still looking out for her somehow. Regardless, the nuns agreed to care for Manar and allow regular communication between them until things were sorted.

"I'll be back for you," Simone whispered to Manar as she left. The boy stared blankly ahead, as he'd done since the night of his mother's death.

Then came the adoption paperwork. She'd already been prepared for the stress of dealing with the bureaucracy, but the restrictions of Sharia Law brought the problems to a whole new level. Foreigners were prohibited from adopting Iraqi children without due reason—which of course, Simone did not have. She figured telling them it was a request from her dead girlfriend would hurt her chances a bit.

She'd spent the following months between missions poring over adoption laws for both countries and parsing the edicts of the Sharia Law—two things she'd never thought she'd do. When the weeks passed, and her eyes became more bloodshot without result, she'd enlisted the help of one of the few friends of Joan's that she'd kept in touch with: a rogue lawyer, Dolores Falcons. She'd suggested Simone take the route of humanitarian parole.

"You were there when things went down," she explained. "What's more, you're the only survivor of the event. You're the only one who can tell the story, so your words will be gold."

The next day, Simone submitted a request to adopt Manar for urgent health reasons: childhood schizophrenia. Dolores had given her the idea to use her own experiences with the illness. The nuns of the orphanage were easily convinced to testify to the child's degrading mental health. By then, Simone had become a near-constant presence at the orphanage, staying there almost as often as the base when she was not on missions.

For over eighteen months, they'd waited. Finally, Simone was summoned to testify under oath in front of a committee of both countries on Manar's behalf and now she took a long look into each judge's eyes before making her statement.

"Manar needs a loving mother to nurture him," Simone said to the panel.

They'd read the reports of her case and all the paperwork she'd filed to get to this point. Simone did not doubt that they got hundreds of such requests weekly. But none of the others came from her, and she found that it was a whole lot more difficult to keep a mother separated from her child when she stared you down with fire in her eyes.

"His near-comatose state after the death of his mother already proves that, as do his hallucinations and distorted speech. I have personal experience with schizophrenia, so I'm in a unique position to love and help him, as both family and his support system, so he can not only live, but thrive."

One of the other Iraqi men glared at her with barely concealed disgust. She had been right to think he would be the most difficult. "You said you have personal experience with schizophrenia? How?"

Simone hesitated. Dolores had warned that the question may come up. "My own mother suffered from the illness. Fortunately, we were able to get the help she needed."

The judge sneered and gestured at his colleagues. He no longer hid his disgust. "Your report says that your squad was responsible for the boy's parents' deaths. It states accidental crossfire. If you are so careless, should we then reward you with another of our citizens—a minor, no less?"

Simone narrowed her eyes. *How dare these fucking—*

She took a breath, forcibly stamping down the thought. If nothing else, the last few months had taught her how to be tolerant. She met the fool's eyes. When she spoke, her voice was polite yet firm. "The parents' deaths were a tragedy for both sides, showing the sad lengths to which the conflict has deteriorated. However, it is not a matter of rewarding the accidents, but seeking the best option for the child—"

"And you think that you're the best option?"

"I was there for his parents' final moments and saw Manar's reaction to them. Both cases give me insights into the boy's life and personality that no one else can have, and—"

"You were there because you murdered his parents," the Iraqi spat.

And so, the meeting dragged on.

SIMONE STAYED IN IRAQ while the deliberation was held even though she'd completed her tour days ago. There wasn't enough space in the orphanage for a prolonged stay, so she'd rented an apartment close by. She'd expected the bureaucracy to take just as long to decide her case as it took to get it before a panel, but they surprised her. Somehow, the system moved even slower.

She spent that time with Manar, gently coaxing him away from the depths of his mind. She whispered to him all the things that Joan had whispered to her—at least the ones that were suitable for an almost-seven-year-old. With the help of the nuns, she brushed up on her Arabic and told him stories in his language. Her tales told the boy of her life growing up, her schooling, her love of programming and coding, and her dislike of cooking. When she ran out of stories, she told him about Joan. When she spoke of Joan, his eyes didn't look so glazed over. He almost seemed to hear her. Simone latched onto that.

And so, the months went by.

She got feedback from the Iraqi minister of labor about three years later, informing her that she could take her son back to America for medical care. The US Department of Homeland Security followed suit and approved her request for humanitarian parole. Five years after the incident that had brought Manar into her life, Simone was on a flight home with her son.

She didn't realize that he clutched her hand just as tightly as she did until she felt a tug.

"Umma?" he asked, staring up at her with clear green eyes.

Mother?

Tears poured like rivers down her cheeks as she nodded. "Yes," she responded in Arabic. "We're going home."

33

MANAR POKED HIS HEAD THROUGH the doorway and watched his mother play with her black box again. He frowned and scratched his head. He did not understand what enticed her to play with it every day. He made his way back to his room. The house was bigger than his old one, so Manar was still getting used to the corridors. His mother had said he'd get used to it eventually, and Manar believed her. He still wasn't used to having a room to himself. All his life he'd shared a room with… someone. Someone important, Manar felt, even if he couldn't remember. And he found that reasonable.

Why did one person need so much space? Allah frowned on such greed. Manar had not complained when his mother had shown him the room. She was smiling so broadly that he hadn't had the heart to tell her he would have preferred a smaller space. However, two benefits of the room were that there was enough space for his toys and no one around to complain when he played with them.

Had someone complained before? Again, Manar could not remember.

Sometimes, Simone joined him in his games, but she always went back to playing with her black box. Once, while she was out, Manar had poked at it. Although he had managed to force out the weird *click-click* sounds his mother always produced when she played, he hadn't been able to discover its allure. It was an hour's entertainment at best. Nothing like the cars that his mother had gifted him. She'd given him toy soldiers as well, but they scared him, so he broke them.

Yet every day, there she sat, playing with the box that went *clack-clack-clack*.

Manar walked up to her. "Umma," he said in Arabic, "why do you always play with the box?"

His mother smiled down at him.

Manar loved his mother's smiles—all sixteen of them. Even the ones that failed to push away the darkness he sometimes saw when she stared at nothing. The one she gave him now was the one she used when her mind wasn't fully there. Manar knew not to disturb her when she smiled like that. He would have left, but he was bored of playing with his toys, and his mother never seemed to get tired of the box. Maybe there was a secret he missed when he'd poked it.

Her eyes cleared, and she lifted him onto her lap so he was facing the box. Manar tried not to show how uncomfortable he felt being lifted. He knew his mother liked it, but he was ten—far too old to be carried like a child. Soon, he would be as tall as Farrah.

Manar's mind went blank, and for a second he gazed at nothing. Farrah?

He shook himself awake at the sound of his mother's voice.

"It's not a box," she replied using the same language. "Well, it *is* a box, but that's not all it is. It's called a computer, and Mummy uses it to work, not play."

Manar turned so he could look at her. He was pleased that she was still smiling. The smile had changed to the one she used when she was amused but didn't want Manar to know. "But it always makes a funny sound when you poke it."

"When I… poke it?" his mother whispered slowly. Her smile widened a bit. "Do you mean this?" She pressed something on the box, and it produced the *click-click* sound. Manar noticed that something else appeared on the glass box that was in front of the other.

He nodded.

"This is called a keyboard. Can you repeat the word?" Manar rolled his eyes and repeated it perfectly. He did not understand why she tested him with such things. He really needed to show her that he was no longer a child. "The keyboard helps me type words on the monitor." She pressed the keyboard again, and this time Manar could see the mark appear in the glass box.

He raised his hand to clean it but could not. His mother chuckled but Manar ignored her, staring distrustfully at the marks on the glass. His mother had forced him to go to school ever since they came to their new home. However, the symbols on the glass looked nothing like what he had been taught. Though to be fair, Manar regarded the school with great suspicion too. It was too different from his old one. Not one person spoke Arabic. How did they ask Allah for forgiveness and blessings on their family?

Manar repeated these thoughts to his mother.

"The symbols are not different," she replied, stroking his head. "They are just different from the alphabets you know. Maybe someday I will teach them to you."

As Manar stared, the symbols seemed to grow larger before his eyes. He nodded at his mother's words. He would like to learn them.

"I UNDERSTAND COMPLETELY, Principal Gurung," Simone said, sighing. She shifted in her seat. "I'd like to say that he's having trouble adjusting, but nothing excuses such behavior. I'll have a talk with him again tonight."

The office door was closed, so Manar couldn't listen in. But even if he could, it wouldn't change his punishment. Simone was angry enough that none of his little tricks were going to work on her.

It's the third time I've been called in, for Christ's sake, she thought, holding back another sigh. Three times in one semester. And it was for the same reason: Manar had fought with one of his peers. *He better have won this one at least.*

The principal, Deepthi Gurung, clicked a perfectly manicured nail on her desk. She was justifiably angry about the situation. Simone could understand that. But it wasn't like kids fighting was a whole new concept. It's what they did.

He really better have won this one.

"It's only the first semester of his freshmen year, and he's already been in three fights," Deepthi said, staring at Simone. Since the principal had repeated this fact several times over the last hour, Simone wasn't really sure what reaction the woman was expecting.

Another promise? Would that help?

Deepthi interlaced her fingers on the table, really leaning into the stern principal look. "We've found that children are more likely to act up if their support systems at home have issues. Kids notice things like that."

At this, Simone felt her face harden. It would be one thing if Deepthi was probing just to find out how fitting a suspension would be, but that wasn't the case here. *How dare she judge me?*

"Principal Gurung—" Simone started, forcing calmness into her voice.

"Please," Gurung interrupted softly, "call me Deepthi."

Simone scrunched up her brows. What'd happened to the stern principal poking into her business?

"Deepthi, then," Simone said hesitantly. "There are no problems at home. There can't be. It's only me and Manar, and—"

"No spouse?" Deepthi interrupted again.

Simone shook her head. "No, my partner passed away years ago in the events of 9/11."

"I'm sorry for your loss," Gurung said. Her eyes softened, but Simone felt hers harden. She'd come to terms with Joan's death a long time ago. She didn't need pity. "I can cancel the suspension if you guarantee that the incident won't happen again. It's a new academic year, after all."

"I appreciate it, and I *can* guarantee it won't happen again." *Mostly because I'm going to drown that boy in so many chores, he won't be able to lift a finger for anything other than homework.* "But I still think Manar would benefit from some form of punishment. If not suspension, maybe after-school detention for ten days?"

"That'll be fine, I guess," the principal blinked, probably wondering how they had arrived at the point where Simone was the one issuing detention.

Simone smiled sweetly and stood. "Always a pleasure making your acquaintance, Deepthi."

"The pleasure's all mine," Deepthi responded automatically. "Your son should be out of the nurse's office by now and waiting for you in the hallway. Please inform him about his detention. He'll be expected to begin tomorrow."

Simone just nodded and walked toward the door. It had been far too long since she and Manar had some words.

Simone closed the principal's door behind her and met her son's guilty look. She stared at him until he looked away. *Didn't think he would start so soon,* Simone thought. If she hadn't been so pissed, the look, combined with the bruises on his face would have had her rushing to him in an instant.

Now she stared at him coolly, her arms crossed in front of her chest. "Did you at least get a few punches in?" He shook his head, and Simone sighed. "Why, then, have we been working on your punches?" She gestured toward his bag, and he picked it up and followed her out of the school.

"He was an older kid. Bigger than me."

"And didn't we practice what to do when someone's bigger than you?" Simone asked over her shoulder, getting into the car. Manar threw his backpack in the back as he climbed in. "Why would you even pick a fight with an older guy?"

"He called you a bad word," Manar muttered.

Simone glanced at him out of the corner of her eye. "So you decided to let him beat you up?" Manar didn't answer. Simone softened her voice. "We'll work on your punches when we get home."

This was probably not the conversation that Deepthi had had in mind when Simone had said she would talk to Manar. Frankly, it was not the conversation that Simone had planned on having. This would have been more Joan's forte, but Joan was not there to have it. And Manar *did* need to know how to defend himself.

"Umma?" Manar started. Simone rolled her eyes. He was really going for it if he had decided to bust out the Umma card. "Can I still code this weekend?"

"No," Simone said. She'd decided this the moment she'd seen his green eyes. Frankly, she wasn't upset about the fight. What pissed her off was that some kid had decided to use her son as a punching bag, and he couldn't defend himself.

Obviously, she couldn't punish him for *that*. Stopping him from coding was the best way to keep her promise to Deepthi and guarantee that Manar would actively avoid fights.

That didn't stop her from feeling guilty, though. She'd taught Manar the basics of programming nine months ago at his insistence. She hadn't expected the boy's sheer aptitude for it. Simone, with years of experience in its applications, could code complex algorithms, though they mostly required a substantial amount of time and effort on her part. Meanwhile, Manar could now handle the same level of algorithms that she struggled with. He never used the same techniques that Simone did, and his programs were always deceptively simple. Yet they somehow had a way of coming more alive after each compilation. He had a knack for addressing the kinks in his code.

He *lived* for programming, and Simone couldn't help but feel she was stifling a gift by punishing him this way. But she couldn't afford to go easy on him. Any other punishment would just go over his head.

"You have after-school detention for ten days," she said. "When you're done with that, if you're on your best behavior and it's not extended, maybe I'll reconsider. Until then, the computer stays locked in my room."

Which reminds me, Simone thought, *I have to change the lock on that thing.* Manar broke it the last time Simone had taken away his computer.

Manar grumbled under his breath, and Simone endeavored to ignore it.

The rest of the drive passed in silence.

VIKTOR POLOV SPED DOWN the highway while his wife gave birth in the backseat.

"For the hundredth time," his wife groaned, "I am not giving birth in the car, you fool."

A retort was at the tip of Viktor's tongue. If she were *not* giving birth, then why was his back seat drenched with suspicious fluid? A scream from the love of his life silenced him.

"I believe you, my heart," Viktor said, slamming his foot down on the pedal. The 1997 Lada screamed from the abuse but assented to his wishes. If only everyone were so simple—complain a little, but listen to reason. Life would have been so much better. The vehicle sputtered on its last cylinder and attenuated tire treads, but still it moved. It had been built comrade tough about fifteen years ago. The standards and needs had changed, but Viktor refused to get rid of such a magnificent beast, if only because it was the only thing that still listened to him.

Even if its speed right now was just a bar above crap.

The hospital was eighty kilometers away, a manageable distance if it weren't the middle of a Russian winter, let alone that winter's blizzard. The ground was more sleet than asphalt, and the snow pouring as hard as rain made visibility almost impossible. Viktor was driving more on memory than actual sight, but he refused to let his wife give birth in the car. He would be forced, then, to name the poor boy—if the doctor had been wrong and the supposed twins were, in fact, a single baby boy—in the American way. He already had the perfect name, though only a small part of him hoped to use it: Carson. It was a good name and had taken him weeks to decide on it.

"Are we there yet?" Sofia screamed at him.

Viktor ventured a look back and blanched. How could one body produce so much liquid? "We're almost there, my love!"

They had been driving for over an hour and would probably be on the road for another hour if Viktor got his bearings right. But he could not worry the woman like that. He crushed the pedal beneath his heel again, trying to coax his car to speeds faster than a grandmother's shuffle. Such speed was dangerous on roads so slippery. Even stepping out of the house in such weather could invite an early death.

Russia might as well have been two different countries when comparing the seasons. In summer, it was hot and humid, making one wish for death by drowning—at least one wouldn't sweat so much. In every other season, it was cold enough to freeze your nipples off. Viktor had seen that once when he passed a hobo on the street. It was not a pretty sight.

"The contractions are getting shorter," Sofia called out. Viktor glanced at his watch. The books did not say anything about contractions shortening so fast. They covered everything else in great and disgusting detail, but not that. He muttered a curse. Were the twins in so much of a hurry? Had they taken on their mother's impatience despite all his prayers? It was just as well that women would choose to stick together, even if they were not born yet.

Though they'll be born as girls, he thought, failing to hide his grin, *I will teach them to be ruthless, unyielding, uncowering to the men in their lives. And God help the poor fool who would break their hearts.* Viktor had purchased a Mosin-Nagant rifle just for the lad, whoever he might be.

"Are we at the Bol'nitsa yet, Viktor?" his wife demanded. "Stop daydreaming and step on the gas!"

Viktor jumped. Even after a decade of marriage, it was creepy how she always knew when he was distracted. "Yes, dear." He stepped once more on the pedal, but the car had no more to give. He turned left onto another street and resisted the urge to slam on the brakes when his wife shrieked.

"The babies are coming out," she wailed.

"Please, please, *please* hold on, my heart. We are nearly there," Viktor said. He tried to meet his wife's eyes through the rearview mirror, but hers were shut in pain. There were no cars at their back and none in front either. He needed one—just *one*—to flag down. He slammed his foot down on the gas again and again, but the car did not move any faster.

It was another forty-five minutes before the Lada finally turned left onto Murmansk. His wife's cries of agony had turned to barely audible grunts a few kilometers back. Viktor provided a steady stream of encouragement but he did not, *could* not, turn back.

He parked the sputtering vehicle and rushed to the backseat, throwing open the door. He cursed loudly. Then, when that wasn't enough, repeated it in English: "Fuck."

The passenger chair was scooted all the way to the front, and Sofia lay on the blanket set on the seat. There was blood—so much blood. Far more than should be outside a body. And what was that between her legs? Sofia groaned. The sound was enough to shock Viktor from his reverie.

He ran straight for the hospital's entrance, slipping on the ice, falling, standing, and running once more. All the while, he screamed at the top of his lungs. "Help! Please help! My wife! She's dying! There's so much blood. Please help!"

Tears clouded his eyes. *She must be in so much pain, in so much agony,* he thought. *How could there be so much blood?*

The hospital entrance loomed before him. The doors opened with barely a sound. None of this registered in Viktor's mind. The nurse on duty had to slap him before he could focus on her. "My wife," he shouted, his voice hoarse. "She's dying, along with my two girls. Help us, please."

"I understand," the nurse replied calmly. She gestured to her colleagues. When had they arrived? "We need you to lead us to her so we can save her."

Viktor nodded, and his mind restored itself with hope.

Yes, Sofia will be safe. And the girls too. They will all be safe.

They sprinted back to the Lada. The nurse threw open the door without hesitation. Viktor tried not to read too much into her gasp. And he really tried not to dwell on her muttered curse, a variant of the one he'd used earlier. A second passed. He could see the effort it took her to gather herself as she leaned in to take his wife's pulse. Viktor squeezed his hands together. He could not read the damn woman's face.

Won't she say anything? Do I still have a wife?

The nurse staunchly refused to look in his direction, and Viktor tried not to read too much into that either. She picked up the twins from between his wife's legs. He excused himself in time to throw up beside the car. He wiped his mouth clean as fast as he could and returned to find the nurse dangling his children upside down with one hand.

Rage blanketed his vision before logic once again reasserted itself, and he calmed with effort. She slapped their buttock with her other hand.

The sound was faint at first, but as surely as the clouds covered the sun, the babies wailed in the nurse's arm. Viktor felt his legs give out from the relief, and a new set of tears clouded his vision.

"Breathe, little ones," the nurse cooed. "The winter air will wake up your lungs. It's good for you. You'll be fine."

She cradled the girls in her arm, then crouched and passed them off to Viktor. Viktor looked down at the two little girls, two beautiful faces. Their two perfectly round heads were glazed with gorgeous red curls. They were perfect, healthy little girls, with one exception. The twins were attached to each other from their shoulders down to their buttocks. They shared one set of arms and one set of legs. It was likely they shared internal organs too.

They were beautiful.

"And my wife?" Viktor looked up at the nurse. She shook her head.

Viktor felt his heart break. He maintained himself only with great effort. Still, he could not stop the tears from running like rivers down his cheeks. He gazed down at his girls. They would grow up without a mother. That meant Viktor would just have to show enough love for two. He could hear his wife weeping with joy. Or maybe that was him.

He stayed on the snow-covered asphalt for another few minutes, gently rocking his girls. May God protect them.

NDIDI GAPED at the gathered crowd and gulped down her nervousness. She tried to stand tall, as her father had taught her, but it was hard not to slump under the weight of the eyes fixed on her.

She must not have succeeded because her father extricated himself from the interview with the reporters and strode to meet her. His back was to the group, so he missed the anger that darkened their faces at his abrupt departure. Ndidi gave them an apologetic shrug. If they were smart—which they would have to be for her father to pay them any mind—their anger wouldn't go further than the look on their faces. Even at twelve, Ndidi knew that it didn't go well for people who messed with Eze Okafor.

"It's beautiful, isn't it?" her father asked. He was looking around at the massive stadium, but instead of the anxiety that shone in Ndidi's eyes, his eyes brimmed with excitement and pride.

Of course he's excited, Ndidi thought. *He isn't the one who has to go up there.*

The thought drew her eyes to the stage where she'd have to fight. It was raised a bit to make it easier for people perched on the bleachers—*do they call them bleachers in Japan?*—to see. The Japanese had a way of making everything grander than it needed to be, and they'd held nothing back with the arena. It was ringed like a wrestling ring, but round instead of square, and the ground was sandy. Colorful scarves were tied to the ring, drawing the eye as they danced with the breeze.

"It's terrifying," Ndidi replied truthfully. She'd grown up with servants and people constantly befriending her to get closer to her father, but she'd never liked being the center of attention. This sucked, considering where she was and what she was about to do.

JEWELS was a mixed martial arts competition focused on promoting the top female fighters in the US and Japan. From the size of the crowd, it was a really big deal. In hindsight, Ndidi should have realized that when her father had broached the topic. He never did anything in a small way, after all.

"That's good," he said, squatting down to meet her eyes. His face was expressionless, but his eyes shone with excitement, kindness, and boundless wisdom. Ndidi had always thought her father's eyes were his best feature. "It means you're giving the tournament the respect it deserves."

Ndidi didn't know how true that was. She'd been trained in martial arts since she was old enough to walk, after an altercation at the playground. So, she wasn't afraid of the fight. All the other preliminary matches had been too easy, even though she was years younger than her competitors. What made her so anxious was that they would all be *looking* at her. It almost made her shudder. Only her father's presence stopped her.

She looked into his eyes again and saw the pride shining there. She squared her shoulders and stretched to her full height, all five feet and seven inches.

So what if they looked at her? It was because she was *good*. If that was all it took to garner attention, she had to start getting used to it. Ndidi grinned and scanned the crowd. She could probably take any one of the people gathered there. Maybe even with one hand behind her back.

Her father saw that look and ruffled her hair as he stood. "It's good that you're confident, but remember your opponent has also made it this far. The competition doesn't allow for luck to influence results much."

Ndidi started to reply but was interrupted by the announcer.

Eze grinned and patted her once on the shoulder. Ndidi cracked her neck and loosened her muscles while the announcer warmed up the crowd. By the time her name was called, Ndidi had forgotten her nervousness.

NDIDI STARED BLANKLY at her opponent: Hermione Cloney. The announcer explained the rules in the background, and Ndidi was pretty sure she heard the man call out twenty-one as Hermione's age. The girl in front of her couldn't have been much older than Ndidi herself.

I guess Dad isn't the only one that thought to exaggerate his girl's age, Ndidi thought. Hermione stared back at Ndidi with a mixture of shock and curiosity. Ndidi could imagine what was going through her head: *How did a girl so young make it to the finals?* Ndidi, bolstered by a mix of adrenaline and her father's confidence, smirked, which felt weird on her face.

The bell rang for the first round.

Hermione lunged at Ndidi, starting off with common kickboxing techniques. She bounced around, throwing fast jabs that had no chance of connecting. Ndidi forced herself to stay still. She felt a familiar set of eyes settle on the back of her head. She didn't have to look at her sensei to know what she would advise as a counter. She focused her strength into her feet, grounding herself with the aikido technique. This would give her the stability to focus her attacks.

Hermione charged in. Ndidi waited a beat before she flowed into the *tachi-waza mae* to stop the advance, then spammed *kogeki* attacks until Hermione dropped. The bell rang, indicating the end of round one.

By the time it rang again to signal the beginning of the second round, Hermione was back on her feet and at her side of the ring. Ndidi simply reset her stance.

This time, Hermione opened with *pankraton*'s all-force combination of wrestling and boxing. Ndidi immediately switched her stance to jujitsu, but she still couldn't block all the attacks. Blood splattered on the ground, a red contrast to the golden sand. The crowd roared, but Ndidi pushed them to the back of her mind. Minutes later, she managed to pin Hermione.

The bell marked the end of the second round.

By round three, Ndidi was tired of waiting for Hermione to come to her. She rushed in with the Soviet's sambo. Either by plan or coincidence, Hermione met her with the same form.

Ndidi didn't realize she was smiling until her cheeks started aching. The girls exchanged percussive punches and powerful kicks, striking hard with elbows to the heads and knees to the chests. Ndidi couldn't block all the attacks. It hurt when they landed, but her smile didn't dim, and it was reflected on Hermione's face.

They switched forms without a thought, attacking and countering with a precision that spoke of countless hours spent practicing. The crowd roared, but they no longer mattered. Ndidi put all her attention into creating an opening where she could… *there!*

Hermione had overextended herself in a strike. The mistake was barely noticeable, but it left her just out of place enough to meet Ndidi's next attack. Ndidi roared and sent Hermione into the ropes with a headbutt. The move pushed Hermione over the ring, but Ndidi caught her by the arm before she could fall. There were nets below, but it would have been a bitch coming back up.

Regardless, with Hermione out of the ring, Ndidi had won. The crowd went wild. Ndidi felt the weight of thousands of eyes and found that she didn't care. Her eyes sought out one specific pair. Her father beamed with pride.

NDIDI MET HER FATHER at the bottom of the stage. A grin threatened to split her face. She was still bloodied from the match, and her ribs were surely cracked in a few places, but those were minor details.

Her father returned the smile and drew her into his arms. Ndidi melted into the hug until the sound of a toddler crying drew her attention. Frowning, she scanned the crowd until her eyes settled on the child. The young girl sat between an American couple in the front row, which was typically reserved for family members. The couple was visibly stressed out, trying to calm her down to no avail.

Hermione stood beside them. Though her weariness was evident in her posture, she was also trying to console the toddler.

Ndidi didn't think. "Excuse me," she said to her father, extricating herself from the hug, and strolled in the direction of the family. Hermione saw her coming and stepped forward to meet her. Ndidi stopped, rubbing her arm awkwardly. She hadn't really thought about what she was going to say. The little girl had just drawn her attention.

"Is that your sister?" she asked finally.

Hermione nodded, turning to look back at the toddler. "Yeah. Her name's Bethany. Wanna meet her?"

NDIDI TOOK HERMIONE to her house. There was easily more than enough room on the jet, and her father had given her enough of an excuse when he wanted to talk to Hermione's dad. She didn't know what they'd spoken about, but Ndidi wasn't about to let the opportunity pass—despite her mother's concerned glare.

She understood the worry, she really did. They were complete strangers, after all. But Hermione was the first girl her age with whom she'd connected. And Bethany was just so *cute*. Plus, it wasn't as if anyone was going to attack her dad in his own country.

It hadn't been difficult to find out they'd fudged Hermione's age so she'd qualify for the match-ups. Her dad had admitted it easily enough after being plied with enough alcohol to drown a fish. Ndidi had tried booze once and felt ill for days, so she didn't understand why grown-ups liked it so much. Maybe it was a manhood thing about proving who was tougher.

"Oh, your room is amazing," Hermione said as the door closed.

Ndidi shrugged casually, glancing around. Hermione was probably just being nice. The room wasn't awfully big, and she'd made all the decorations herself. She'd outgrown most of it a couple of years ago, but her dad wouldn't let her take one of the other bedrooms for some reason. Something about not becoming spoiled. She didn't understand how a new room would spoil her. Grown-ups were weird.

"Thanks," she replied, rubbing her arms. She and Hermione had spoken for hours after the match. Most of it involved their fighting styles. Sensei Mukalla had taught Ndidi a lot, but Hermione had used some moves she didn't recognize. Bethany squirmed in her sister's arms, drawing Ndidi's eyes to the toddler.

"Has Bethany said much?" Ndidi asked.

Hermione shrugged and carefully set the girl down on the bed, holding on to an arm so she wouldn't walk too far away. "She screams and throws tantrums when she wants something, like any toddler, I guess. The problem is that hers can go on for hours until she tires herself out. It makes for a very difficult sleep."

Ndidi winced. Hermione had mentioned her sister was on the autism spectrum, but Ndidi didn't really know what that entailed. Hours-long tantrums? That was brutal for anybody.

"My parents are very patient, but we all struggle to understand her. They give in to her most of the time to keep the screaming and tantrums to a minimum. She's smart enough to understand what you're saying. She just never responds to it. I can't wait until she speaks actual words. It'll be far easier to train her then."

Bethany gurgled, reaching for a porcelain cat figurine at the edge of the bed. Hermione held her back, so Bethany started wailing—long, loud sobs like the ones that she had made in the stadium after the match.

Yeah, Ndidi thought as she covered her ears, grimacing, *I can understand why they'd do anything to stop this.* She stared at the child, focusing through the noise. *That's the wrong approach, though.*

With some effort, Ndidi forced her hands away from her ears. She made her way to the toddler, smiling openly even through the noise. "Bethany, you like the cat?" she asked, kneeling in front of her. Bethany just wailed louder. She didn't even look at Ndidi. "Can you say, 'I want cat' or 'I want kitty,' maybe?"

Nothing.

Hermione sighed. "It's no use. She doesn't respond to anyone when she's like this."

Ndidi understood that, but this seemed better than just handing her whatever she wanted whenever she wanted it. That sort of habit was hard to break once it got started. And what would they do once she developed further and started to talk?

Ndidi put her face right in front of the child. "Say, 'I want kitty,'" she repeated.

Nothing. Bethany just looked away from her and continued wailing. Ndidi repeated it a few more times, but the response was the same.

"Let's try something else," she muttered. She made her way out of the room and into her dad's office, where she rummaged about until she found a notepad and pen. She didn't know why the whole situation annoyed her, but it did—like nothing else before. Maybe she was just being stubborn, but her father always said to never stop until you'd done everything you could, and even then, only for long enough to think of something else to try.

It was probably just a matter of communication. Maybe they'd done the whole talking thing, but perhaps Hermione hadn't tried using a notepad. Ndidi walked back into the room, clutching the pad to her chest.

Hermione saw it and smiled wearily. "Bethany doesn't know how to read or write yet," she said. "She does like to doodle, though. Hopefully, we can use that to take her attention from the kitty. It looks expensive, and she'd break it, for sure."

Ndidi just shook her head, returning to her spot in front of the toddler. She drew two squares. In the left square, she scribbled *YES*. In the right square, she wrote *NO*. She raised the notepad up close to Bethany's face, forcing the toddler to look at it, and then repeated her question.

"Bethany, you like that kitty?" She pointed to the left box. "Yes"—then, she pointed to the right box—"or no?"

Nothing. Ndidi took a breath and repeated the question. "Bethany." She put her face in front of the child's. "Do you like that kitty?" She pointed to the boxes in turn, making sure the notepad was right in front of Bethany's eyes. "Yes or no?"

There was no response, and Ndidi felt her patience slipping. How did Hermione deal with this? She took another breath and once more repeated the question. When there still wasn't a response, she dropped the pad in front of her and shrugged at Hermione's weary look. She'd officially exhausted all her options. Ndidi stood to leave.

Then the wailing stopped. She turned back. Hermione had let go of the child's arm, and the little girl crawled over to the notepad and pointed at the *YES* box.

Ndidi's face split into a grin, and she whooped despite herself. Hermione seemed to be frozen in shock. Ndidi scooped up Bethany and danced around the room.

"She said yes!" Ndidi and Hermione both shouted together. "Bethany said *yes!*"

MANAR STARED AT HIS MOTHER and Principal Gurung and tried to hide his grimace. Were they… *flirting?* He knew Simone preferred women, but *Principal Gurung?* Wasn't she married? *She* didn't seem to remember, as their conversation turned weirder by the second.

"Mom?" he whispered, if only to put an end to this madness. They were both in the principal's office, and though Manar hadn't been brought here for punishment in years, no high schooler wanted to stay in the principal's office longer than they had to.

His mother turned, but his whisper also caught the attention of Deepthi. Manar furiously covered up the dread on his face. *Please, don't involve me in whatever's going on between you two,* he thought desperately.

"Look at me." The principal smiled. "I've been going on and on with your mother, when the true congratulations should go to you. You've certainly worked hard enough to earn it."

Manar scratched his head, feeling more uncomfortable by the second. He didn't see what the big deal was. Months ago, he'd resigned himself to being valedictorian. His grades far surpassed everyone else's in the school district. Simone had noticed immediately when he'd tried to score lower on some tests to bring it down and avoid this conversation. She'd threatened to break his computer if his grades dropped. He glanced at her now. For all her smiles, she really was ruthless when protecting something she cared about.

"Thank you?" Manar muttered finally. Why had the principal called his mother to the school just to tell her Manar had been confirmed as valedictorian? Manar could have told her himself at the end of the day. Was this just another thinly veiled attempt to flirt? If so, it was one of their better ones.

Deepthi turned to Simone. "Nicole Le was previously the holder of the title," she explained, but did she *have* to? "But she received much lower marks than Manar in the end-of-year project."

"It was in Artificial Intelligence Programming, right?" Simone smiled. "Even I can barely keep up with him anymore." She practically oozed pride, and her eyes turned weird when she stared at Deepthi.

"Mom," Manar whispered again. Luckily, this was enough to break her off from whatever spiral she was starting.

Simone sighed. "Thank you so much for the news, Deepthi."

Deepthi?

"We have to go, but I'll definitely make sure he keeps his grades up until the end of the semester."

Manar snorted. With a lead like his, he could spend the next month coding and still have his grades high enough to be valedictorian.

He slung his backpack over his shoulder and left the office before he could get dragged into any more pointless conversations. He didn't shut the door fully since he assumed his mother was right at his back. Unfortunately, that meant he could hear perfectly what exactly his mom and Principal Gurung were talking about.

"Can I come over tonight?" Deepthi asked, her voice low… and *weird*. "Bipin is away with the boys at a basketball game and"—her voice got even lower and weirder—"I miss you."

Manar mentally retched, his eyes scanning wildly for an escape. He'd known that something was up with his mom and Deepthi. Between his mom's "secret" looks at Principal Gurung, the nervousness in her voice, and the excessive number of times she "found time" to pick him up early, he would have been a fool not to. Still, there were just some tones a guy was *not* meant to hear his principal use.

He should have moved away. He *wanted* to move away, but he needed to hear his mother's response, if only to understand.

"I think Manar would like to celebrate privately tonight," Simone said, a bit guiltily. Manar smiled sadly. His mom was definitely using her I-want-to-but-I-have-some-stuff-to-figure-out-first smile. "I'll let you know when we can get together for a drink at the V-Hotel again," she said, and any rational person could hear the distance in her voice.

Manar didn't hear Deepthi's response. His mom came out of the office a few minutes later. Manar had already moved away and was standing by the water fountain, tapping away at his phone. He looked up in surprise when his mother called his name.

He smiled wryly and pocketed the device. Initially, he'd just been trying to pass the time, but he'd found some new programs that might help with the code he'd been running. He and his mother made their way to the car in silence. Manar waited until she'd driven out of the school grounds before speaking.

"So," he said, "you and Principal Gurung, huh?"

The car swerved a bit, and Simone gaped at him in surprise. Manar pretended not to notice, eyes on his phone.

"What?" his mother sputtered.

"I mean, I'm not judging or anything." He shrugged. "But isn't she married?"

Simone sputtered more, and it was a struggle to keep the smile from his face. It would only embarrass her more. Finally, she sighed, and her driving evened out.

"It's… complicated."

"I'd assume so." Manar nodded sagely. He was happy for her. It'd been years since she'd had the gleam of happiness in her eyes, and if Principal Gurung was responsible for that, then Manar couldn't bring himself to have a problem with it. Still, he had to make sure that it was what she *wanted*, not an attempt to use his principal as a long-overdue rebound. "But… the husband?"

Simone hesitated. Manar wondered if she was thinking of the irony that after years of parenthood. *She* was the one in trouble now. "That's what makes it complicated. Deepthi isn't ready to tell Bipin about her… preferences."

Manar kept his face forward by force of will. "Mom, if she thinks you're not worth it—"

"That's not it," Simone said sharply. "It's just different in her culture." She glanced at him, softening her voice. "We're working on it. I promise."

Guilt shone in her eyes, and Manar felt he should drop the subject. He was surprised Simone had even let it go on that long. But if she was willing to talk about it…

"How did it even start anyway?" he asked, feigning disinterest.

Simone chuckled, her eyes lighting up at the memory. "You were mostly the cause of it, what with all the fights you got into. I didn't care much for her initially, but since I was coming to the school basically every other day…" She shrugged. "I don't know. It just happened."

"I was a little rowdy when I was younger, huh?" Manar murmured, leaning back in his seat. He doubted his mom would elaborate on the subject.

"A little?" Simone laughed.

Manar smiled. In his defense, it was *her* fault for enrolling him. The school had been so *different* from the one he'd been used to in Iraq. Here, people couldn't look past the fact that he was a foreigner, and they made fun of him for it. The insults to himself he could bear. But when the idiots had found out his mother was white…

Manar chuckled. "Yeah," he said. "A little."

The idiots hadn't let up when Manar had shown them he wasn't going to back down, nor when he showed them he wasn't afraid of suspension. So, he'd gone on the offensive instead. He didn't wait for them to corner him under the bleachers. He sought them out after school and left them with black eyes. He didn't wait for them to hold his hands behind his back. He struck at their throats and balls. *Then* they'd listened. It was barbaric and dangerous, but Manar had experienced much worse, even if he couldn't remember most of those times. Still, it'd been a pain to hide his injuries from Simone.

After that came the painful process of having the rest of the school accept him as more than the foreigner with a white mother. Luckily, that had been easier once they saw how quickly he absorbed the classes, and easier still when he got the top marks consistently. Frankly, Manar was surprised that others actually found that stuff difficult. Simone had suggested he tutor other students in his spare time, and that had worked wonders, winning over the kids' parents too. When their kids went from barely passing to above-average grades, both they and their parents were sold.

For a while, he'd liked the attention. He basked in the feeling of solidarity that came with acceptance. But it quickly turned hollow. People looked past his skin because they remembered their black eyes. They liked him because he could help them get better grades. They spoke to him because he helped with their assignments. But what was the point? Why did he have to put up with such things? He was much smarter than they were. Despite his tutoring, no one could once match his grades or his aptitude for programming.

If they couldn't stand by his side as equals, why should he have to lower himself to match them?

"Well?" Simone asked.

Manar glanced at her in surprise. Had she been talking this whole time? "I'm sorry?"

"Have you decided which scholarship you're gonna accept?"

Manar shrugged. Simone asked the question at least once a week, but he still hadn't brought himself to think about it. His end-of-year project in Artificial Intelligence had gained some attention from universities worldwide, and he'd received a bunch of scholarship offers in return. Manar didn't see what the big deal was.

Most of the scholarship packages offered to waive all tuition and even added a sizable monthly cash stipend for him and his mom if she decided to come with him. She hadn't stopped running his ear off about the importance of making a choice sooner rather than later.

Manar understood her point, but it wasn't like he was running out of time or options. Best-case scenario: wherever he ended up, someone could keep up with him.

"Not yet," he replied, taking out his phone again. "Definitely not MIT though. They suck."

39

VIKTOR WOKE TO THE SOUND of his name being cursed, the smell of liquor and vomit, and the sight of an angry Russian with her fist drawn back for a punch. He was still very much hungover, so he did not immediately respond. The pain that exploded in his head a second later was enough to fully wake him.

"To all the gods, Yelena, what was that for?" He groaned, clutching his jaw. Yelena—may the gods curse the day he met her—glared at him and raised a fist again. The woman's size was truly monstrous. Her arms were as thick as his legs. Viktor winced, bringing his hands up for protection. "Okay, okay! I'm up. What do you want?"

Yelena spat in his face. "I need *rubles* to go buy the girls' food," she demanded finally.

Viktor sat up and noticed the twins saddled on Yelena's back. They pawed at her ears and tugged her hair, but all she did was shift periodically when they tilted too far to one side. Viktor stared. The girls noticed his attention, reaching out for him. He stared at the twin on the left, and for a moment, the image of Sofia superimposed on the girl. His next image was of his wife lying in the backseat of the Lada, blood dripping from between her legs: dead, because she'd dreamed of being a mother. Was that why he could never look the girls in the eyes? Why he felt such rage every time they were near?

He turned away.

He'd passed out in the kitchen again. This explained the hard knots in his back. He'd probably wanted to fix something to eat but had passed out. A bottle was clutched in his hand. He lifted it to his lips, but a hand snatched it away before more than a drop entered his mouth.

"What do you *want*, Yelena?" he spat, struggling to his feet.

"Rubles," she said simply, adjusting the girls again.

He clutched the sink for balance. "Yes, *rubles*," he muttered bitterly. "Always rubles. It's never enough for you, is it? The three of you took everything I had, and you always want more. Next, you will drain my blood, for I have nothing else to give. You'll be the death of me, and then where would you get your precious rubles?"

He tried to move past the woman, but she blocked his path. Her arm fat jiggled with the motion, and Viktor struggled to keep the revulsion from his face. "Move, Yelena."

"Your children need to eat, Viktor. And if you were not such a piece of shit, I would not have to knock on your door every day and force you to do your duties. Sofia would spit on—"

"Do not talk to me about Sofia!" he roared, bloodshot eyes wide with rage. It gave him no small amount of pleasure to see Yelena take a step back despite herself. The gods cursed the day Sofia befriended this woman.

He looked over her shoulder. The twins stared at him, wide-eyed and trembling. Viktor mastered himself with effort. It didn't matter anyway; he just needed a few more hours.

"The subsidy check will not be here until tomorrow," he said. "I'll sign it over to you then, and you can cash it along with yours on Friday."

The biweekly welfare check was the only good thing that had come from the nightmare of his children's birth. He'd fallen behind on his rent payments shortly after Sofia's death and had been forced to move into a government-assisted apartment. Yelena had found him a few days later, claiming to be his wife's friend. But how could gentle Sofia have befriended someone so feral?

Yelena's services, of course, were not for free and, along with the twins' upkeep, barely left him with enough rubles to get his moonshine.

Yelena's nostrils widened as they did when she was annoyed. Did she realize how much she resembled a pig when she did that? Finally, she huffed and handed him the twins with obvious reluctance.

"Auntie will see you later," she cooed. Viktor held in a snort. If the beast was truly their aunt, the heavens hated them more than he thought. "I am off to get beets to make you some borscht. Auntie will miss you, Lefty. Righty."

She shot a disgusted look at Viktor, which he ignored. Since he hadn't given the girls names, Yelena had started calling them by their positions. She walked out of the kitchen. The front door slammed shut a second later.

Viktor, the twins held loosely in his arm, moved to the living room and slumped onto the couch. The woman would be gone for hours, and he still had some time before he had to leave for work. He could rest his eyes for a bit.

He woke sometime later to the sound of wailing, the smell of piss, and the feeling of something wet on his chest. Viktor bolted upright, then sighed in relief when he discovered it was just snot. *Just snot*, he thought, his expression souring. He pushed the girls off his chest. Gods only knew why they had climbed there in the first place. He stared at them.

This was the product of his and Sofia's love? Was this the symbol of their union? What his wife had so long dreamed of? Tears poured down each of their cheeks, and snot from their noses mixed in their mouths into something that made Viktor throw up.

Oh, Sofia. He sighed. *This was not how it was to be. You were supposed to be by my side.*

Until the girls were born, he had never heard of conjoined twins—nor had anyone in Severomorsk, apparently. The news had caused a measure of interest for the first few months, to the point that some American doctors from the Mayo Clinic had flown to Russia to examine them. It was from them that Viktor had learned everything he knew about the girls' condition. They would remain fused unless they underwent surgery.

After this, they offered to do the surgery for free and bear the burden of every complication. All it would cost would be the girls' lives if the surgery proved unsuccessful.

Unfortunately, Viktor had still been deluded with love for his dead wife and rejected the offer. He cursed himself for that as much as he cursed Yelena.

He stood with a groan and wrapped the sobbing girls in their oversized jacket. It slipped constantly, didn't cover them properly, and smelled, but it was either that or let them freeze. Yelena would have an excuse to kill him, then.

A ratty blanket was draped over the couch, and he put it across his shoulders instead of a jacket. The ground swayed as he moved, but he managed to carry the twins outside to the Lada. He'd never managed to install a car seat, so he made do with a cardboard box he'd belted down. He placed the girls in it, ignoring their cries and attempts to reach for him.

Sofia would spit on my face, he thought, recalling Yelena's words. He chuckled as he ensured that the box was tight enough. *Sofia spat in my face the day she died and left me without a wife.*

He stumbled over to the driver's seat.

The air burned his nose and ears. He probably should have worn gloves and maybe a cap, if he'd had the money for that. *No use wishing,* Viktor thought with a sigh. *And it wouldn't change much.*

It definitely wouldn't have changed his decision that day.

The ignition didn't start the first time, or the second, or the third. He rubbed the key between his fingers and blew hot air on it. When he tried it after that, the car started up. It didn't purr as it had when he'd bought it for Sofia. Instead it bucked and groaned as it sped down the highway.

The girls tired themselves out about an hour into the drive, so he drove in relative silence. Was he supposed to say something? Maybe something to mark the day?

Viktor shook his head. *What does one say in times like this?* Maybe Sofia would have thought of something. But if she'd been there, he wouldn't have been doing this at all. Or at least, he wouldn't be of the mind to speak after the beating he would have gone through.

The dashboard clock clicked midnight a few hours later as he turned into the driveway of Murmansk Hospital. He parked at the entrance but opted to stare at the building from his car. His eyes were irrevocably drawn to a very specific spot in the parking lot, where drops of blood seemed to cover the snow even three years later.

There was a reason he'd avoided the place. Being there dragged up as many memories of Sofia as the twins did. There, in that spot, he couldn't bring himself to bury the memories.

"This will be good for them," he muttered to himself. It sounded like a thin, hollow justification even to him, but that didn't make it any less true. It *would* be good for them. And it would be good for him. They wouldn't be in a constant state of starvation and cold, and he… he wouldn't have to try so hard to drown the memories.

He was never meant to do this alone.

He stumbled out of the car to the back door and rewrapped the girls in their jacket. On a whim, he took the blanket from his shoulders and added that too. And then, once again, he ran to the hospital entrance. But this time he didn't scream at the top of his lungs, nor did he wail and flail. He cried all the same, though. He cursed the gods for forcing his hand, Yelena just because, and Sofia… No, he couldn't bring himself to curse Sofia.

He set the girls on the ground in front of the building, banged on the door, and then ran back to his car. He reached the Lada just as a nurse came outside. Viktor could barely make her out in the snow, but her form was burned in his brain, intertwined with the memories of that day.

She picked up the girls and stared for a while in the direction of the car. Viktor was sure she wouldn't be able to make out his features in the blizzard, but she didn't have to. Viktor guessed it wasn't every day that a grown man rushed into the hospital, snot covered, snow covered, and bellowing at the top of his lungs to help save his wife and twins.

She couldn't save the wife. It was fitting, then, that she save the twins as payment.

Slowly, he reversed out of the parking lot and sped onto the road.

He should have felt glad he'd done it, after all. Sofia might have been angry, but at least she would have understood… right? No, she would not have understood. His gladness soured to mere relief. It was two fewer mouths to feed—three if he counted the leech that was Yelena. It was inevitable that he would make this choice.

What other choice did he have?

The Lada sputtered, slowing. He veered off to the side of the road before it stopped completely. He tried the key again. The engine sputtered once more, then died. On his second try, there wasn't even a response.

Was this karma? Was it *now*, after almost eighteen years, that the car broke down? He couldn't deny the irony. He hadn't traveled too far from the hospital and could probably trek back for help. It would be difficult in the blizzard but not impossible.

But then he'd risk undoing the past few hours.

"The universe really is a sick bastard," he muttered. The cold seeped in through the windows, and the dead engine did nothing to push it back. He reached for his blanket, then remembered that he'd used it for the girls. "A really sick bastard."

The cold cut to his bones. It was the middle of the night, so he had little hope of a car passing by and even less of the car stopping to help, at least until the sun rose. He just had to stay warm until then.

He leaned over and wiggled the glove box, clumsily catching the half-empty bottle that fell out: his emergency stash. This was an emergency if there ever was one.

He took a swig every few seconds, grimacing at the taste. It burned his throat, which helped combat the cold. It took a while for the exhaustion to set in, and for the alcohol to lose its effect.

The hallucinations set in long before that. For the most part, they were about the early days of him and Sofia—from when they'd been courting. Times had been better then. After they'd been married and started trying to have kids, things had become somewhat strained. Yet Viktor still loved her. The children were supposed to have been the manifestation of that love. But they were monsters. Did that mean Viktor's love wasn't true?

Or that Sofia hadn't loved him?

Maybe it would be best if that were true. Viktor hadn't done anything deserving of her love in years. He watched the snow fall all around him, as his breath turned cool enough to see, and his fingers became too numb to clutch the bottle.

An hour later, he blinked and slipped into darkness.

JOSÉ OLVERA TAPPED a rhythm on the gilded armchair while he contemplated treason.

He was in the Hotel Metropol, inside one of the few rooms that didn't have carpets just to cover the shit stains and blood splatters. That wasn't to say the room was anything *good*. It just wasn't covered in shit and blood. This served his purposes nicely. On the television, a Russian newscaster replayed a report of the death of the former prime minister, Boris Nemtsov, a man whom José had been tasked with keeping alive.

Of course, José had been assigned the case too late. By the time he'd arrived in the country, he was protecting a corpse, but the brass definitely wouldn't see it that way. They would need someone to blame for this. José was basically a fine rib at a banquet.

Hence, the need for treason.

It wouldn't technically be treason. He would just be retiring—a years-over-due one, at that. But his retirement would leave the brass with no one to blame and maybe force them to take responsibility for their mistake. His retirement and treason were one and the same.

José understood this, which is why he only cursed occasionally while contemplating what such a plan would entail and what it would cost.

Boris Nemtsov would be alive if I'd arrived hours ago, José thought. The president would have been aware of the death by now. This would start the cascade of pressure down the line until it reached him.

"They'd better not put this on me," he muttered half-heartedly. Of course, they would. The CIA was notorious for throwing its agents under the bus. It didn't matter that he'd dedicated thirty years of his life to the army, or that he'd received a medal directly from the president.

Or that I stayed on even after my wife had been used as target practice in retaliation for a mission I went on. A mission I'd been assigned to.

Against his will, José's thoughts drifted to Miranda. He'd met her after signing up with the CIA. She was almost half his age, but they'd both started at the bottom. So, like everyone else, they competed to climb up the ranks. But unlike everyone else, they tended to take their rivalry too far—even if it risked demerits. José chuckled at that.

He still maintained that she'd fallen for him first, even though he could hear her voice in his head disagreeing. Once the attraction had set in, their competition was more an excuse to see each other than anything else. At some point, they dropped the games and had a small wedding with only their families and closest friends. José imagined she'd become pregnant not long after that. Of course, had he known then, he never would have allowed her to go with him on the mission.

The fucking mission.

José banished the memories from his head. That was all in the past. All that mattered now was he'd been too late to save the fucking prime minister.

The CIA had kept him busy with more missions after the death of his wife. He didn't have anyone else to lose, both he and the Agency knew that. For a while, he'd welcomed the distraction, had even thought that it was good for him. But now…

"Shit," he cursed again.

The settlement from the agency would not be enough to bring back his dead wife, but it was more than enough for retirement. Still, there was a reason José had put it off for so long. What would he be retiring to? Or with whom? He did not plan on remarrying, and he and Miranda never had children. He would be alone. Was it worth it?

José took a breath. There was no need to go down that rabbit hole. Once again, he focused on the TV, switching the channel to another station.

"In a shocking tragedy, conjoined twin girls were found at the entrance to the hospital in Murmansk Oblast last night. The father was reportedly found dead, frozen a few miles away in his car. The hospital has transported the girls to the local orphanage and is imploring the public…"

José let the words recede into the background. His eyes were instead fixed on the images of the girls. They were swaddled in an oversized jacket and wrapped with a ratty blanket. Still, it was easy enough to see that there wasn't enough space for two in there. *Conjoined twins, she said. Two heads. They're almost as fucked as I am.*

José nodded. Within a few minutes, he'd gathered his belongings and packed his carry-on. It was stuffed with various portfolios of Nemtsov. He probably wouldn't need them, but he'd be an idiot to leave that in the room.

A glance at the TV confirmed the address of the orphanage, and then José was gone. It would be difficult to run the adoption papers without his fake ID, but once he used it, the CIA would know where he was. He would have to move fast and disappear.

Hopefully, when he did, he would have two girls to retire with.

CHAPTER

41

NDIDI STOOD IN FRONT of her parents, a clipboard clutched to her chest and a grin splitting her face. "We've had another breakthrough with Bethany and the kids at the Centre," she announced. "*Bethany* completed her homework by herself." She paced as she spoke, making circles around the living room couch. "I mean, it's just second grade, but it was *math*, and math always sucks regardless of the grade. Plus, she communicated to the ABA therapist to let her do it by herself—*verbally*. She *spoke*."

Her parents stared at her with barely concealed amusement. Ndidi couldn't bring herself to care much. The progress might not seem like much, but for Bethany—and all the others on the spectrum who'd seemed to have no chance—it was an amazing opportunity.

Research about the autism spectrum disorder had been scant at best and nonexistent at worst in sub-Saharan Africa. Most people didn't even know what it was. Those that did rejected the notion that their child might be on the spectrum and neglected to provide much-needed care.

This was the first thing Ndidi had sought to change when she'd convinced her father to commission the Okafor Autism Centre. Though, if Ndidi was being honest, he hadn't needed much convincing. The progress Bethany had made during her and Hermione's visits had been undeniable. Ndidi had not been the only one to notice the effect the interventions had made on Bethany.

She threw herself into research about ASD until it took up most of her free time. With her father's resources, she'd unearthed long-forgotten techniques from various parts of the world and tweaked them to fit modern mindsets. And they'd *worked*—initially, at least, and only on Bethany. She had been Ndidi's only case study.

From there, it hadn't required much deliberation for her to share her techniques on behavioral analysis with the public. It had taken the better part of a year for people to look past her age and realize her methods worked. Once they did, they flocked to the Centre. The Okafor Autism Centre got new enlistments daily and was in touch with many more networks worldwide.

She had her own *staff*. The thought still made her giggle.

"We can unveil the new method at the World Autism Conference at the end of the month. Maybe people will be able to refine it further," Ndidi continued. Her rotation brought her in front of her parents. She stopped and gestured wildly. "Right now, it works on only about half of the kids, and I *do* think there's something wrong with the data. But for the life of me, I can't see it. You guys have gone through the reports, right? Any ideas? Dad?"

"Busted," she heard her mum mutter.

Ndidi frowned. Her father laughed, which just made Ndidi frown more. She was being serious here. Her dad stood and ruffled her hair. He stared into her eyes. This was unfair; he knew Ndidi could never be angry at him when he did that. "I'm sure you can figure it out, dear," he said. His eyes twinkled with mirth. "You don't need us old birds to mess up your work with our outdated ideas."

Ndidi narrowed her eyes. He only brought up his age when he didn't have a ready excuse to get out of something. Her father chuckled again, kissed her forehead, and walked off. Her mum smiled at her, then followed him.

Traitors, Ndidi thought, hiding a smile.

"WHAT WOULD YOU BOYS LIKE for dessert?" Papa called from the kitchen. His voice echoed weirdly, but CJ knew he wasn't supposed to focus on that. Voices sounded weird sometimes, but the important thing was what the voices were saying. What had Papa said?

"Ice cream," DJ called from beside him.

CJ frowned. They were both seated on a sofa in the living room. DJ hadn't even turned his head from the TV when he'd answered. What was the question, again?

CJ tapped his brother, and DJ muttered out of the corner of his mouth, "What would you like to eat?"

CJ nodded. He tapped DJ again, partly in thanks and partly to keep his attention. "Uh… pop… sicle?" It was hard for the phrases to form in his mouth, and harder for him to say them loudly because he would have to focus on increasing his voice. Fortunately, over the years, they'd developed a system.

"CJ wants a popsicle," DJ called out once more.

"A popsicle? Really?" Dad poked his head out of the kitchen. For some reason, he and Papa always made dinner together. "You know you'll just regret it tomorrow."

CJ was focusing this time, so he'd heard the response. Still, it took him a few seconds to process it, and even that was progress compared to when he was younger.

"Bro, go for the ice cream," DJ whispered. "Papa's probably gonna get vanilla."

CJ considered this, too, and came to an answer after a minute or so. "No," he said as firmly as he could. "We had… um… um… ice cream on Wednesday."

DJ shrugged, but CJ just shook his head. Even *he* knew that that much sugar was bad, and he was just seven.

"So, popsicle and ice cream?" Dad asked. They both nodded. DJ's eyes never left the TV, so he didn't notice that Dad's eyes lingered on CJ before he retreated to the kitchen. CJ had noticed, though, and he felt his cheeks heat up. He'd taken too long to decide on such a simple question. He *always* took too long. Even DJ thought so, even if he never said it. And now Dad thought so too.

CJ always tried his best to hurry up, but it was hard to focus on voices and even harder to form the words in his mind to reply. He'd used a tablet when he was younger, but everyone said he'd made progress since then, and so he stopped. Maybe he shouldn't have.

The pauses between his sentences had become shorter since he'd started using the techniques from the Okafor Autism Centre. His therapist had said that soon it wouldn't be noticeable anymore. But CJ still felt that he took too long to process things, and that was only if he was focusing and had actually heard what had been said. He couldn't help that his mind wandered sometimes.

"Hey," DJ said, nudging him. He held one of CJ's hands in his. Only then did CJ realize that he'd been hitting his own head. His throat felt sore like it did when he'd been whining. CJ closed his eyes, holding in a groan. He hadn't had an episode in months.

"It's gonna be okay, all right?" DJ continued. "Focus on me. Breathe. Do you want me to call Dad and Papa?"

CJ shook his head. "They… would just… be disappointed… with me."

DJ snorted and smacked CJ's head. His voice lost the concern once he realized CJ had calmed down. "They won't be disappointed, dumbass."

"Yes, they… will," CJ insisted softly. Tears ran down his cheeks. He sniffled. "I'm always… uh… taking too long to reply, and… and… sometimes they have to… repeat things over and over… before I get it."

DJ smacked him again, harder this time. CJ murmured a protest that DJ ignored. "So what?" he asked. "They have to repeat stuff to me all the time when I'm playing video games."

"That's… um… different."

"No, it's not, you idiot. It's not your fault that you're on the spectrum." DJ smacked him again. This time, CJ wiped his tears and smacked him back. DJ never knew when to stop unless CJ hit him back. DJ hit him again, and CJ hit him back once more.

Soon they were rolling around on the living room carpet. They bumped into one of the side tables, and the lamp on it wobbled. DJ caught it, but Dad was already glaring at them, drawn by the noise.

"Who started it?" Dad asked, crouching to meet their eyes.

CJ immediately lowered his gaze, but DJ stared back. His voice was deceptively soft, but the boys were not fooled. They could talk their way out with Papa but never with Dad. They glanced at each other and remained silent.

"Sticking up for one another, huh?" Dad continued, reaching out and wiping a stray tear from CJ's cheeks. CJ tensed unconsciously at the contact and forced himself to relax. Dad stared at them for a moment more before he stood. "Guess that means no dessert for either one of you."

DJ opened his mouth to say something, but then thought better of it. CJ was just relieved that their father hadn't asked about why he'd been crying. Maybe he just thought it was because he and DJ were fighting. But CJ could remember other times when it'd been harder to hide his tears. Dad would deliberately ignore them too.

Their dads had told both him and DJ about the autism spectrum a few months ago, when they'd turned seven. They explained that was why CJ threw tantrums and sometimes had trouble speaking or making eye contact. CJ hadn't known what to feel then. He still didn't. On one hand, he was relieved to be told that he wasn't to blame for the things that he couldn't control. On the other hand… there was something wrong with him.

"Go clean up," Dad said. "Dinner's almost ready, and I don't want Papa to see that you've been fighting."

Both CJ and DJ nodded, rushing to their room. They came back a few minutes later. While they were on the stairs, DJ smacked him again for good measure once he knew their father wasn't looking. "Dumbass," he whispered as he passed.

CJ slowed, rubbing his head.

"Dinner's ready," Papa called, coming out of the kitchen. He placed a tray on the table. DJ helped set the plates. Dad came out from the kitchen, his hands hidden behind his back. From his vantage on the stairs, CJ could make out another tray with a tub of ice cream and a popsicle.

Dad noticed his look and winked.

CJ walked over to him, taking the tray and setting it on the table. Maybe it didn't matter so much that he had something wrong with him. No one else seemed to care.

THE DOOR CREAKED as José entered the house. He grimaced, glancing fearfully inside. Maybe they hadn't heard it. This was proven wrong a second later by the patter of footsteps. The girls stumbled into the foyer, their faces stretched as far as they could go.

José tried to adopt a stern expression. Even at seven, they had not yet learned how to coordinate their movements. And he had not yet found a means to separate them. Running almost always led to an injury. But did they listen? No.

Luckily, this time, they made it all the way to him without falling. This was progress in its own way. His stern expression fell before it ever formed. He crouched and opened his arms to receive them.

"How have you been, my daughters?" José asked in Russian.

It had been hell, convincing the child services agency to let him adopt the girls. They had questioned his motives. *Why would a visiting American want to adopt such young girls? What sick perversions did he want to use them for?*

José didn't know that it mattered much. Even if they thought he was bad, it was obvious that he was the only choice the girls had. Few people, no matter how humanitarian, could stomach the sight of two heads on one body and the knowledge that it would always remain that way. Fewer people—fewer *Americans,* at least, and he didn't think it was much different in Russia—would be willing to take the girls, considering the stigma of their condition. This had been proven by the absence of requests during the month it'd taken him to finalize the paperwork for their adoption.

No one in Russia wanted them.

For the agency, he'd squashed all their misgivings with a simple tale of his life: the loss of his parents, the loss of his wife, and being framed at his job and forced to flee. When that hadn't worked, he'd donated a large sum of money to their cause. He'd received the adoption papers within the week. The birth parents never named the girls.

Weird! It must be a Russian thing, José thought and took the opportunity to name them after his grandmothers—Karla on the left and Liz on the right.

"Auntie Yelena made us borscht with sour cream," Karla grinned, her arm waving energetically. Everything Karla did was energetic. Her lips were always stretched out in a smile, and her eyes were always fiercely wide. Liz, more subdued, nodded simply, her eyes roving over José's face. He wondered if she saw only the exhaustion or if the hint of pain finally showed in the lines on his face.

Another pair of footsteps drew José's attention toward the inner corridor. When had the foyer become the greeting room? "Thank you again for all your help, Yelena," he said to the woman. "I don't know what I would do without you."

The hulking woman smiled at him. Until recently, José hadn't known how she had found them after the adoption. She'd claimed to have known both parents, though she cursed the father with every breath that carried his name, and bullied the agency into giving her his address. From her size, José didn't doubt that both were possible, but had rented an apartment only for the adoption inspection and had cleared out the next day, paying in cash and giving no information about where he was going. So, her latter claim was clearly false.

Still, none of his searching had brought out any viable information—even when he'd hacked into government and military servers. It had taken him months. But finally, José was forced to admit that, except for her discomforting size, Yelena was totally average. If she had any ulterior motives, she had not made any moves to act on them. If any of his enemies had planned so far ahead and planted her in his life, José was obviously outmatched, and there was nothing he could do to delay his death anyway. In the meantime, he would enjoy her services and allow her to take care of his girls.

And he *did* enjoy it. He truly did not know what he would have done without the nanny. His was a noble decision to have adopted the children, both for their sakes and his, but—and he'd realized this only after the fact—he knew *nothing* about raising children.

"It's no problem at all," Yelena replied in a voice that would have made a father proud of the way his son was growing.

Finally, José was able to extricate himself from the girls. He hung his coat on the rack and headed to his room to freshen up. The glacial water that spewed from the shower temporarily made him regret his decision to stay on in Russia. Originally, he'd seen it as the sensible thing to do: raising the girls in their own homeland. It was why he hardly ever spoke English to them. He was intent on disappearing with his new family.

Though he had the utmost respect for the CIA—may its buildings burn to ashes—it would be difficult for them to operate in a foreign country. Difficult, but not impossible. It was lucky they needed to stay under the radar only until Nemtsov's death blew over. Then he could find a way to return to his country.

Or he would have to earn enough credits to buy his freedom.

Credits weren't legal tender by any means. The goal was to earn enough merits in the agency to prove your worth, but not so much that you made yourself indispensable. You were liable to get killed that way. Previously, credits could be earned from successful missions, and José didn't see any reason why that would have changed. If he could earn enough credits, he wouldn't have to look over his shoulder anymore—or at least not as much.

José ran the sponge over his body, tracing the scattered scars. Most of them were old and had long scabbed over. Some, like the one that ran diagonally from his shoulder to his waist, were more recent and were an ugly blistering red.

He'd been accumulating credits over the past four years, working undercover for the CIA, taking the cases assigned to him. Of course, all their communications were bounced from the moon back to Earth through sixteen different relays so they could never pinpoint his location. But at least they knew it was him. Slowly, they would come to realize it was worth clearing his name to have him back in the fold.

It wasn't much of a plan, he knew. For one, his reward was unspoken, so there was no guarantee the agency would let him cash in his credits. For another, they might actually be using the missions as a way to track his movements and one day hit him while he is down.

José scrubbed at this skin until it matched the blistering red of his scars. When his fingers started to prune, he stepped out of the shower, donned a robe, and sprawled out on his armchair. As he did, he stared at his hands. Most people developed calluses from manual labor. José had developed his over the years wielding a gun. They'd become harder of late. That was good. It meant he was doing something to keep his girls safe.

Maybe, if he were lucky, they would be spared from being part of his world.

Yelena came into the room sometime later after putting the girls to bed. She smelled vaguely of vomit and disinfectant soap and was holding a large cast-iron pot—a sight that, in her gigantic hands, would have frightened anyone else. A towel was slung over her shoulder. She kept its edge away from the water-filled pot as she made her way to the armchair.

"So," she said in English. José didn't know why she bothered; her accent made her words virtually impossible to understand unless one were familiar with it. "How many ribs did they break this time?"

She dabbed at his torso, drawing a groan from him, but he didn't answer. He never knew how she figured out that he'd been injured on a mission. No matter how much he tried to hide it, Yelena would waddle into his room, a towel slung over her shoulder and a pot of water in her hands. It had made him intensely suspicious at first, to the point that he'd refused her ministrations. But eventually,

José accepted that the nanny had no ulterior motives. With his trust and a well-placed knife, there wouldn't be much José could do to defend himself in his weakened state. And it did feel good to be attended to by a woman.

That didn't mean he would give her all his secrets.

"You don't have to tell me," she said. She dabbed again and water dripped down his stomach. "But these injuries should be a sign for you to quit, no? You have those little girls to take care of."

"Everything I do," José muttered, "I do for them."

Yelena tsked but didn't push. That was good. He was not so weak that he would allow his pride to be trampled on. A minute later, Yelena pulled off his robe, eliciting another groan. She tsked again at whatever she saw, spitting to the side. He hadn't bothered to examine his injuries in the shower, so he didn't know how bad they looked. He'd taken a few blows and fallen almost three stories, but those by themselves shouldn't have been strong enough to elicit such a reaction.

"Mirror," he murmured. Yelena tsked again, this time directing the full force of her glare to him. Gods, the woman was hideous, but José forced himself to meet her eyes. "Mirror," he repeated.

The mirror was placed beside the bed, within reach for whenever José had to treat his own wounds. Yelena grumbled as she brought it and held it up for him. José stared at his reflection.

His whole chest was a mesh of purple and black. The wounds were concentrated mostly around his ribs, but no part of his torso was spared. The marks reached his shoulder blades and even his arms. They seemed to writhe as he stared at them, and he almost spat in disgust.

Yelena dropped the mirror and dragged the pot of water closer. She dabbed at the bruises, not bothering to hide her displeasure. José ignored those too. His mind replayed the bruises and the actions that had made them. In his prime, his skin wouldn't have been marked like this.

When had that changed?

He couldn't discern anything today that was different from what he would have done five years before. However, somehow his moves had been slower, and his breathing quicker to turn into panting.

José's thoughts drifted, surprisingly, to his nanny. Assuming that she was as she claimed, José knew practically everything about Yelena: from her poverty-ridden childhood to her days living on the street to her brief stint in brothels. Most of the information was from a simple background check, though she'd shared some details herself amid her grumblings. However, he was relatively sure she knew next to nothing about him, mostly by his design. Throughout the four years she'd worked for him, he hadn't offered any information about his background—what he did or why he, a foreigner, had adopted children most people would have crossed the street to avoid. And she hadn't asked.

Yet she would treat his wounds and take care of his girls, homeschooling them, at his insistence, to provide a measure of protection against the inevitable ridicule. She would take the money he handed her every week with no care whether it was tied to the wounds she would treat later that night. A few times, José had purposely withheld the check for weeks on end. She never asked for it and would still come every morning to take the girls while he was away.

The twins adored her for the constant attention, sometimes more than they did him. Though they referred to her only as Auntie Yelena, they treated her more like their mother. If she weren't so terrifying, José might have considered making it official—if only for the girls.

As if she heard his thoughts, Yelena turned him over on his side, amid furious cursing. Somehow, maybe because he'd had the time to rest, or he knew exactly how bad they were, the bruises seemed to ache more. Yelena tsked again when he was fully rolled over. José could guess that his back showed the same map as his front. She pressed on him, feeling and listening for the crackling of dislodged ribs. José almost passed out from the pain, but the thought of such weakness helped him retain his lucidity. The pressure lasted for a minute more. Yelena must have been satisfied with what she heard because her muttering stopped, and she washed the wounded flesh with the towel.

Half an hour later, when Yelena stood to put away the pot and the now-bloody towel, a red dot appeared on her back. By the time José noticed it, it had moved up her neck and rested on the back of her head.

He lunged for her, ignoring the wave of dizziness that hit him. A sharp ping, like the sound of a whistle, shattered the silence. Blood sprayed in an arc in the air, visible in the moonlight, and then she was falling.

He caught her as she hit the ground. A wall of red washed over his vision at the sight of her listless eyes. Her face lost its rigid edge, though somehow she still seemed to frown.

"Why?!" he roared. He didn't know if he was asking himself or whatever idiots had dared to attack his home. Hadn't he *just* been thinking of how he wouldn't know what to do without her? How the girls adored her as a mother? What was the point of anything he'd done over the last four years if he couldn't protect the few he cared about? What was the point of getting wounded weekly, and Yelena fixing it without a word of complaint, if anybody thought they could attack him as they pleased?

Why? Because he hadn't stayed to be properly framed and executed?

He shot a glance at the window where the bullet had come from. A shape ran across the opposite rooftop. There was a backpack slung across his shoulders, a muzzle clearly sticking out. *Fucking snipers,* he thought. Then he suddenly remembered: snipers never attacked alone.

Glass shattered loudly in the living room. José was at the door before he'd made any conscious decision to move, gun in his hands. He waited for a second, took a breath, and then another. The pistol fit comfortably in his hands, and José drew strength from that. His wounds receded to the background of his mind, relegated to minor annoyances. Whatever Yelena put in that water had worked wonders, and whatever it couldn't fix, adrenaline did.

José reached for a switch on the wall, and the house was plunged into darkness. José walked calmly into the blackness.

The CIA provided some compensation for every job he'd done. It was nothing compared to his former salary, but it was enough to live on. Most of it went toward the girls' upkeep, some had gone to Yelena for her weekly salary, and the rest had been enough for him to rent a decent house. It wasn't big by any means, but it was nice. It was supposed to be a temporary shelter, but it would be the first home for his girls. And how could he give his daughters anything but the best?

Whoever had attacked them would regret that they hadn't had the foresight to pick a better location than his home.

The sound of a squished toy came from the darkness. He smiled despite himself. Yelena had never been able to get the girls to pick up after themselves. Now, it seemed that worked in his favor. There was at least one person he had to kill in the living room.

Crouching, he made his way down the hallway. His eyes had adjusted to the darkness. José paused at the end of the passage. Another toy squeaked, and the sound was followed by muffled cursing. José stepped out, fingering the trigger. The report of the gun shattered the silence—once, twice—until he heard a body drop. Only then did he screw on the silencer.

The gunshots would wake up the girls, and hopefully, they would remember their training: hit the floor and stay there until he came for them. Though, calling it training may have been putting it loosely. He would do anything in his power to protect them, but children who'd never faced death could not understand its nuances. Thus, they would never take any training to that effect seriously.

But they'd still needed to learn, if only for his own peace of mind. So, despite his misgivings, he'd turned it into a game. Games, at least, were fun. It seemed like a weird sort of irony to him. Was this not what the CIA did to its agents? Played with them?

The front door slammed open, hinges wailing from the strain. José crouched, backstepping into the hallway. In the moonlight, he could make out three men as they forced themselves through the opening. They stood by the door as their laser sights scanned the room.

José snorted. He should be insulted that they had sent only five men to kill his family. They were dressed in military black with masks over their faces. That they'd stayed by the door, however, showed they were not complete amateurs. Only a fool rushed into another man's house. Of course, they were fools for attacking at all. At least this way, it wouldn't be as if he were slaughtering children. The red dots slowly moved in his direction, but José stayed ahead of them, ducking from the hallway and making his way behind the kitchen counter. It was designed with a window overlooking the living room, so he still had a perfect line of sight to them. The intruders, however, would have to go through the door just to see him.

On a signal, they moved into the house proper. Moonlight streamed in through the broken door, but even without it, every creak of the floorboards told him where the men were.

The men were arranged in a triangle formation. The leader acted as a scout while the others swept the room. José waited for a beam to pass him before standing from his cover. His fingers caressed the trigger. There was the muffled sound of his gun, then the louder sound of a body hitting the ground.

The other two men tensed immediately. Their lasers flew about erratically before finally settling in the direction of the counter. There were some whispered words, then footsteps moving in his direction. José, however, was more concerned about the sound of footsteps heading farther into the house.

The girls.

Why would the intruder not stay to cover his partner? The creaking of floorboards confirmed that at least one of the men was still making his way to the counter. Why would the other leave? But it didn't matter. Either way, he would have to kill one before he could stop the other from stumbling into the girls' room.

Carefully, silently, he took two steps toward the kitchen door. From there, he could get a clear line of sight on both of them while still maintaining cover. José stood. A split second later, a bullet deflected off the kitchen door, missing his face by an inch. José cursed, crouching quickly.

Forgot about the sniper, he thought. It was a rookie mistake. Lucky it didn't get him killed.

That explained why the leader was confident about leaving the other alone while he scouted ahead. The sniper had only as much visibility as the broken door provided, but it was enough. All he needed to do was pin José down until the other fool reached the counter and riddled him with bullets.

José snorted at the thought. Still crouched, he moved one step backward, took a breath, listened, and stood again. The gun came to life, spewing two shots in quick succession.

He'd stood in the path of the laser, so the attacker had a clear line of sight. If José's first shot hadn't targeted the fool's hands, the idiot might have had a chance. José's second shot caught him in the neck. A bullet whizzed past José's head, but the shot went wide.

José was over the counter a second later, diving behind one of the couches. He ignored the body beside him as his ears strained for movement. He was rewarded a few seconds later with the deep thud of footsteps. A door creaked open. There was only one door in the house that creaked like that.

José cursed, moving with almost fanatic desperation into the hallway. He dodged the toys that littered the ground, instinct driving him to not give away his position. There was a silhouette at the end of the hallway, one arm outstretched and the other holding a rifle. José immediately stamped on the floor. The head of the silhouette turned sharply at the noise. Next, a blinding light filled the passage, and a steady stream of gunshots shattered the silence. José dropped down instinctively. He realized the shots were coming from farther down the hall.

José's heart lurched. *No,* he thought, moving toward his girls. *No. They're safe. They're safe. If they remembered the training, if they remembered to duck down and stay away from the door...*

He crossed the hallway in a flash, just in time to see the silhouette—the other attacker—fall lifelessly to the ground.

José stared at the body for a few seconds, then at the bedroom door. It was riddled with holes. Distantly, he realized only the sniper was left to worry about, and that was if the fool had decided to stay even after the last shots. José bent down and removed the assailant's mask. In the dim lighting, he could make out distinct features.

Russian? José thought, his brows scrunching up. *They must be the ones who tried to sabotage the Losharik earlier.* José had stopped them at the request of the CIA. That explained the reason for their attack, but not how they had found him. He'd scrubbed his records of everything all personal information. José pushed the question to the back of his mind.

"Girls?" he called out, tentatively pushing open the door to their room. It fell and crashed with a sound like broken plates. Within the room, four shimmering circles stared back at him. "Girls?" he called out, hesitantly.

The girls stumbled a few steps forward until José could make them out better. They were still wearing their custom pajamas, a hack job created by Yelena to fit both their heads and plus-sized body. In their hands, they held an M4A1 rifle. It was José's backup gun. He'd hidden it in a space within the wall. How long had they known that it was there? And how had they gotten their little paws on it? Did it matter? The butt of the gun rested between their necks. Karla supported its length with her left hand while Liz fingered the trigger with her right.

"Did we do good, Daddy?" Karla asked. She grinned fiercely, but there was a hint of fear in her eyes. Was she afraid of *him*? That he would be angry? Gingerly, José took the gun from them and laid it on the floor.

They were in his arms a second later, pressed to his chest. His grin threatened to split his face. How could he be angry at these… these *angels*? How could he condemn them for defending themselves? What sort of father would he be?

"You were amazing, girls," José said. "Yelena would be so proud of you."

The girls stiffened in his arms. José cursed himself. He should have found a better way to break the news. "Has Yelena gone to heaven?" Karla asked.

"Will we ever see her again?" murmured Liz.

"I'm sure we will," José replied, leaning back. He stared them in the eyes so they would know he was serious. "Gods willing, it will not be soon, but someday."

The twins hugged him again. They stayed that way, a body a few feet from them, until the girls fell asleep.

The sniper never returned. José would have to hunt him down at some point. He would have to fix the broken front door and his bedroom window and then get rid of the bodies. They would smell if not attended to. But he could do all that tomorrow.

There was no reason to leave his girls' arms just yet.

AUGUST 2019
SEVEROMORSK, RUSSIA

OVER THE FOLLOWING MONTHS, José and his girls were attacked five more times. Each assault was from the Losharik gang. José dealt with them as he had done their counterparts. Easier actually, since he now had help from his girls. They were far from battle ready. It pained José to allow them to be in harm's way, but it also gave him a sense of pride to see them grow stronger. The Losharik gang provided good fodder for the girls' practice. They were not squeamish about the blood splatters, but Karla's fingers had not yet grown enough to easily handle the trigger. Their small frame and lack of coordination made handling the recoil difficult.

Initially, José had thought about changing houses. The Losharik mob sought retribution for foiling their plans. They were not so wise to know that the paltry strike teams they'd sent against him would never be enough. José could deal with endless harassment, or he could put a stop to the gang permanently. He would have done so if he were sure that his actions would not bring the CIA to him.

He considered packing up and leaving, but that would have meant dragging the girls out of the house they'd grown up in. He'd been the one to bring the Losharik to their home, so why should the girls pay for it? He could not change the past. However, if the mob was so foolish as to attack his family, why couldn't José use them to make his daughters stronger?

And so, he did. With enough gang members to practice on, they slowly got better. Although their coordination was still terrible, soon they were no longer falling down after each shot.

The fourth and fifth attacks were close. José locked up the girls as soon as he realized the difference and hadn't dared to let them out. Fortunately, they recognized the seriousness in his tone and stayed silent—at least Liz was. Karla wanted to fight anyway.

The fourth team was wildly overconfident. They were double in number compared to the previous attacks, and better armed. José was pushed to his limit, but he dealt with them.

The fifth attack was more of a nuisance. José survived only because he'd been expecting them. He'd put out feelers across their hideout, so he knew the moment they left their base. After that, it was just a matter of sniping them from far away and picking off the survivors. That attack left a bad taste in his mouth. Their numbers had doubled again, to almost a dozen.

Again, José considered simply disappearing. No matter how persistent the mob was, they could not find him if he didn't want them to. He could not risk the agency tracking him down because of these fools. Again, he reconsidered. He was confident in his fail-safes; nobody could bypass them without him knowing.

Sometime later, someone managed to bypass his security measures, but as he'd predicted, they tripped an alarm. José knew about it the moment it happened.

There was nothing he could do. The agency had found him, but they'd sent only one person: Chloe Savage. Had it been anybody else, José would have been deeply offended. To send just one person to apprehend him? He would have been honor bound to kill the agent they sent, then track down their relatives as a warning.

Of course, it was different with Chloe. She had been the same rank as José before his retirement.

In the CIA, no one person was considered the top agent—not officially, at least. The CIA relied far too much on competition to name a specific person the top dog. Not when they could have their agents fight for it. Even if they did, no smart agent would accept the responsibility. It would be like painting a target on your back.

Despite this, there was a clear hierarchy among agents. In his day, José had been near the top, with a near-perfect record in mission completions and a kill count in the hundreds.

Chloe Savage had been his equal.

José rushed to his room. He was packing the girls' bag when they stumbled to his side. They didn't say anything, but José once again reconsidered leaving. He wasn't afraid of Chloe, but he didn't want to introduce the girls to the danger the CIA would bring after he defeated her.

How could his daughters grow up to be strong if they constantly had to run like cowering dogs? Wouldn't they know humiliation, once they were old enough to understand such things?

He had detected the alarm after Chloe breached the outer reaches of his security. Inevitably, she would crack the rest and track him down, but it gave him a month of preparation.

If nothing else, the years he'd waited in a futile attempt to win back his freedom had kept his skills sharp. José was confident he could take on Chloe if they fought. With time to prepare, however, José figured he wouldn't have to lift a finger.

And he was right.

CHAPTER

45

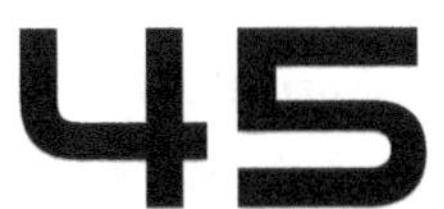

SEPTEMBER 2019
SEVEROMORSK, RUSSIA

CHLOE SLID OFF HER BIKE, suppressing a shiver. She'd changed out of her leather jumpsuit into more casual jeans and a top to blend in. Boy, was she regretting that choice now. The leather would have drawn attention that her quarry might have picked up on, but at least she wouldn't have been freezing her ass off. Her reactions would likely be slower than she wanted.

Huh, she thought. *That's actually a good idea. If only I'd had it before I changed.*

Chloe looked down the street, then the other way. It was the middle of the day in the middle of the week, so it was mostly empty. Most people had gone to their jobs or were too passed-out drunk to be out. Nevertheless, she'd still managed to draw the attention of the few people that passed.

No. Not her. Her bike.

Chloe stared at the machine, sighing. She ignored the looks and turned to scope out the building in front of her. There was a sign in front that confirmed she had the right place. It hadn't been hard to track down the orphanage once she knew it existed. What *had* been difficult was finding the connection between the orphanage and her quarry. She'd snorted when she had.

What sort of numb-nut fugitive makes a stop to adopt a bunch of kids? In what universe is that a good move? Chloe paused, considering. *Then again, if he made good decisions, he wouldn't be in this mess in the first place.*

Although, that wasn't completely true. The CIA found a way to put you in a mess, no matter what decisions you made. It was all about what was convenient for them. That still didn't make the kids a good idea, though. *How was he even allowed to adopt them?* Chloe wondered, walking through the door. *Orphanages just don't* give *kids to foreigners. Normal citizens, maybe.*

The place was exactly as she'd envisioned it. It wasn't rundown, yet, but it was clearly heading there. There were cracks in the walls. And most of the lights on the ceiling weren't working. There was a small reception desk off to the side. Except for the elderly woman staring at her, the room was empty.

Chloe walked up to the desk. "I need to see your adoption ledger for the last four years." She kept her tone brusque and added a hint of a Russian accent to her words. She flashed a badge to the woman, then pocketed it. If she'd left it open for longer, the woman would have seen that it was an American badge and realized Chloe didn't have any authority over her. She might still figure that out, but Chloe had a backup plan. If the woman was unusually uncooperative… well, Chloe had a plan for that too.

Thankfully, that didn't prove necessary. Without a word, the woman reached below the desk. Chloe tensed, her hand drifting to where her daggers were tucked into the waistband of her trousers. A second later, the woman thumped a large, thick book onto the desk. A cloud of dust rose into the air. Chloe wasn't sure if it originated from the book or the desk.

Chloe nodded her thanks. It was ignored by the woman, who just kept staring at her. Chloe took a couple of steps to the edge of the counter, dragging the book with her. She flipped to the most recent entry. It happened to be years back when her target had adopted his daughters. It had been under a different name, of course, but the dates matched her intel. Next to the record was an asterisk.

Chloe flipped back through the entries, finding several such asterisks among other names. She keyed a couple of them on her phone and waited while the database tracked them down. A minute later, she got a ping. *No records, huh? That meant the person had used a fake name and probably bribed the orphanage to get whatever child they wanted. *Seems kind of stupid to make a record of it, though.*

Chloe sighed. Since the record she was interested in had an asterisk too, it more or less confirmed that she had the right guy.

Chloe traced the entry down to the address listed and noted it. She did the same for the last couple of entries with asterisks too, just to be sure. Then she slid the book back to the woman, who hadn't stopped staring at her.

Chloe flashed a smile and headed out. The old crone had likely assumed that Chloe was there to bust her and probably thought Chloe hadn't made the connection about the bribery. But it was the bribery that had drawn her attention to the orphanage in the first place. It had been sent a few days after her target had gone off-grid. Initially Chloe had thought the money was payment for some kind of underground-market-type shit her quarry had sourced stuff to disappear for a while. But it had been for *kids*. That still didn't make sense. Had he known their mother or something?

She brought up the address in her mind as she straddled her bike. It was almost definitely fake, but there still should be some kind of trail she could follow. It wasn't as though she had much of a choice. Her worm would need a couple more days to break through her target's security, so she'd have to track him down the old-fashioned way in case the hack didn't pan out.

Chloe revved her engine, drawing the eyes of everyone on the street. She grinned at the attention and put on her shades.

Just a matter of time.

CHLOE GLARED AT HER TRACKER, then at the cluster of trees in front of her. "You gotta be kidding me," she muttered unhappily. "I have to go trudging through a goddamn forest?"

She slid off her bike, still glaring. The bike wouldn't be able to navigate the trail, and its engines would be a "come fuck me up" beacon. But that didn't mean she was comfortable leaving her ride at the side of the road for any loser to sit on.

Stop being a pussy, she told herself, dragging the bike a few feet into the forest so it wouldn't be easily seen from the road. *It has a tracker, so you can find anyone that gets near it.* That thought cheered her up slightly. She patted the side of the bike and then set off into the woods, one eye on her tracker.

She had to dedicate part of her concentration to avoiding dead leaves or twigs that might give away her position. She couldn't afford to miss this chance.

The address she'd obtained from the orphanage had led to a false trail. She'd half expected that. No CIA agent, current or former, would make such a stupid mistake. Yet the leads she'd gotten had somehow been compelling enough for her to still believe she was on the right track. It had taken her far longer than it should have to figure out she was being led by the nose.

"It's humiliating," Chloe muttered angrily. She pushed a branch out of her way. "Just another thing to make him suffer for."

She glanced at her tracker. Two days ago, her worm had finally cracked through her target's security. She'd delayed going, not sure that it wasn't another false lead of some kind, but it wasn't as if she had much of a choice. The guy was scarily good at covering his tracks. Even the kids didn't leave a trail she could follow. If the lead from the hack didn't pan out, she'd hang around for another couple of days to see what she could pick up. She'd heard something about a gang war that might be worth checking out.

That being said, she *really* didn't want to stay here longer than she had to.

Midstep, Chloe suddenly stiffened. Slowly, she retracted her leg, then bent down to investigate what had triggered her senses. Less than a foot from the ground, a thin red line connected two trees. The laser was barely visible through the cover of leaves, so it'd go unnoticed by most.

Chloe smiled. She'd ignored the forest paths, assuming they'd been booby-trapped. Yet, somehow, she'd still almost triggered one.

Did he guess which direction I'd be coming from? Chloe wondered. *Or did he just rig the entire forest?*

She immediately discarded the second thought. The forest was huge; the man couldn't have been living there for more than a few months. The sheer manpower it would take to trap the whole thing was insane.

Chloe reversed her step, glanced at her tracker, and chose a different direction. She was more cautious now, so it didn't surprise her when she noticed another alarm line a few minutes later. It was inconspicuous enough that she would have missed it had she not noticed the glint of sunlight it reflected. She ignored this one, too, and changed directions. When Chloe found the third line, she was able to come to a conclusion.

"Somehow, he knew what direction I would come from," she muttered to herself. It was impossible to booby-trap the entire forest. It was the only explanation for her coming across so many traps so quickly.

The annoying thing was that Chloe couldn't be sure that she hadn't already triggered one of the lasers. She'd been walking for almost twenty minutes before she found her first. If she had triggered one, her quarry would be prepared for her.

Though, Chloe considered, *he's probably been prepared for the last two days. There's no way he doesn't know I broke through his security.*

But that didn't mean she wouldn't be irritated if she'd actually fallen for such a basic rookie trap.

"I'll ask him if I tripped any before I take him out," Chloe decided.

Almost half an hour later, she stepped into a clearing, her eyes scanning the area. She'd had to avoid nearly a dozen more alarms, but fortunately, they became easier to spot after a while. She glanced at her tracker, though it was unnecessary. She could already make out the shape of the cabin in the distance.

Who the fuck builds a cabin in the woods anymore? She wondered, irritated. *And in goddamn Russia!*

The house wasn't much. She'd expected something grander after hearing how much the boss paid this guy for every side job. She thought it was a waste to give all that money just to keep him on the rope until she could get to him. But no one argued with the boss. At least, not more than once.

She did a lap around the place, checking for anything that could bite her in the ass later. If the man had tripwires littered around a goddamn forest, who knew what kind of nonsense he would have around his actual house? As if to prove her point,

Chloe found a couple of nonconcussive landmines around some trees. These were a relatively new invention. Though they were technically explosives, they weren't actually lethal. Nevertheless, they'd be a bitch and a half for anyone who stepped on them.

Chloe disabled them as quickly as she could. Holding onto them would just slow her down, so she'd have to come back for them when she was done. *Where did a man on the run get toys like this anyway?*

Besides the mines, she didn't find any other traps. Still, she did another lap before moving in on the house. As she did, she was primed to hear any sound coming from the house, but the cabin was silent. That made her immediately suspicious. It was the middle of the day. There was no reason for anyone to be around. Her target, sure, but she already knew his daughters didn't go to school—or anywhere. It would have made her job infinitely easier if they had.

Why would someone lay down traps if they aren't around to take advantage of them?

She crouched and approached the back of the house. The door was open, but she ignored it. *Too easy.* Someone who'd gone to so much trouble to hide wouldn't leave their doors open all willy-nilly. The windows were made of tinted glass, so Chloe couldn't see inside. Still, that didn't mean she was helpless.

Her tracker led her to the side of the house. She marked the spot and then promptly ignored it. A guy who'd force his daughters to live in a shack for months on end would probably be the kind of control freak who'd keep his equipment nearby. By marking the spot where the signal was strongest on her tracker, she knew where his bedroom was. After that, it wasn't much of an issue to determine which window belonged to a different bedroom.

She unholstered her gun and brought out her tools. A second later, the window swung open without a sound. Gun in hand, in case she had been wrong about the rooms, she poked her head through the window. The room was bigger than it seemed on the outside. The bed was shoved against the wall beside a dresser packed with what had to be over a dozen toys.

Something caught Chloe's eye. Light glinted off a long metallic tube set in a corner of the room. The tube wobbled slightly, and Chloe's eyes widened when she realized what it was.

The barrel of an M4A1 rifle.

The girls behind the gun pulled the trigger. Something whizzed by Chloe's hair, close enough that she felt a line of fire on her cheek. She dropped down immediately.

Two heads? she thought. She'd had only a brief glimpse but… *Two heads, huh? How does that happen?*

Chloe shook her head to clear her thoughts. She categorized. Obviously, she'd been expected, but she'd figured that would be the case. Should she withdraw?

Fuck no. If she let the man disappear again, it'd be ages before she tracked him down again. At least now she knew he was around there somewhere. But what sort of father would use his children as bait? More to the point, what sort of father would arm his kids with an M4A1 rifle?

In his defense, those weren't your usual kids. She had to admit, the way the freaks handled the gun was sort of cool. Chloe shook her head again, moving away from the wall. Just a few seconds had passed since she'd been shot at. It shouldn't be enough time for two seven-year-olds to recover from the recoil and give chase. Then again, they'd already surprised her once.

There was also the matter of knowing where their father—her main target— was. She couldn't move recklessly before she figured out where he …

A glowing red dot landed on her chest. Chloe dove out of the way, but the dot just met her where she ended up, this time tagged to her forehead. Chloe followed the line with her eyes and met the gaze of her target, perched on a tree.

She'd read the report on José Olvera before she'd started on the mission. Though they'd never known each other personally in the CIA, she'd chased him enough these past few months to build a mental profile on him. The false trail he'd led her on from the orphanage was impressive. Even more impressive was how long it had taken her to break through his security and land a trace on him. Even then, he'd anticipated her and placed traps in the forest. It was all very irritating, but impressive nonetheless. Despite that, she'd been fully confident that she could take him down.

Now, Chloe almost snorted at how stupid she'd been.

José smiled, though there was nothing friendly about it. A minute later, the girls came stumbling out the back door and around the house. They still clutched the overweight gun in their hands, even though it was clearly difficult for them to move with it.

"Huh," Chloe muttered, staring at them. "They're actually sort of cute."

JOSÉ CLIMBED DOWN FROM THE TREE while awkwardly trying to keep his gun trained on the woman. She could probably have made a break for it while he was distracted, but she seemed oddly fascinated with Karla and Liz. She didn't even bother to pick herself up from her crouch.

The twins stood a short distance away, struggling to position the rifle. José deliberately kept his focus away from them while he approached. He kept his face hard and stoic, as if on the edge of violence. Truthfully, he didn't know what to do with her. He'd known Chloe was coming since she'd managed to break through his security measures. Although that had given him enough time to prepare, it hadn't given him enough time to figure out what to do once he caught her.

Killing her would have been easy. But José couldn't risk being defeated in a one-on-one battle and leaving the girls to the devices of the CIA. Drawing her close to his home and capturing her was his best bet.

And he'd done just that. Now he had to decide what to do next.

"You don't know what to do with me, do you?" the woman asked from the ground. José focused on her. Really focused on her. Chloe Savage's reputation in the CIA was almost as bloody as his own. But as an unspoken rule, the top agents of the organization didn't mingle with each other. José had seen passes of her, though he'd never had a reason to actually *look.*

She was attractive in her simple jeans and blouse, with her brunette hair pulled back and tied. Her features were sharp, made sharper by the relaxed defiance on her face. She'd probably figured out that José wasn't going to kill her. Or at least, he wasn't going to kill her at that moment. That would give her a chance to make a break for it, which, of course, José couldn't allow.

He gestured for her to stand, then threw her a pair of handcuffs. She caught them and put them on without complaint. José walked up to ensure the cuffs were actually clasped. Only then did he let his gun fall.

He turned to the girls. Both of them were grinning. They still hadn't dropped the gun, though José didn't know how they'd handled its weight for so long. "Go to your room, and I'll come meet you in a while. Don't forget to drop the gun in its secret place. If I find you playing with it later, you won't be able to sit for a week. Understood?"

Karla booed and Liz hid a pout, but they both stumbled back into the house, still struggling with the rifle.

Chloe's eyes remained fixed on them. "I just have to ask," she said finally. "Why does a man on the run from the CIA make a stop at an orphanage to pick up a pair of freaks? Is it some sick sex thing?"

"You bitch—"

José had his gun cocked and pointed at her head before his brain had finished forming the thought. He mastered himself with effort, lowering his gun. The woman hadn't even flinched at the violence in his expression. "They are my girls. That's all you need to know."

Chloe stared back, a smirk on her face. She must have seen something in José's face, because she changed the subject. "Why not just kill me?"

"Bodies are messy." They crossed the threshold into the cabin. José led her to his room and tied her to his desk chair. Since the cuffs had been placed with her hands in front, she was tied as if hugging the legs of the table. She could probably escape with enough time, but even he would find it difficult to maneuver with the handcuffs on.

Why don't I just kill her? José wondered. A couple of answers came to his head.

The CIA would send agents after him, but they were already doing that. And it wasn't that he didn't want to taint the innocence of the girls by introducing them to violence. That ship had sailed months back when the gang started attacking them.

It would be much easier to kill her and move his girls somewhere else. He'd already cleaned Chloe's worm from his security system and patched the break, so he was confident it would take months for anyone to find him again. If he gave up on getting credits from the CIA and deleted and destroyed all their contact points, he could disappear for years.

Ah, José realized unhappily. If he killed one of their top dogs, the CIA would never stop tracking him, and he would give up any chance he had of returning to the US with his girls. And he wasn't ready to risk that.

He'd lived in Russia for the last four years. It was where he'd found and started raising his daughters. But José had always planned to take them back to the US. That was what had led him to maintain contact with the CIA even if common sense said he should have broken it off and disappeared completely. He wasn't ready to relinquish that hope. If he had been all alone, then he might have. The US had nothing for him anymore, but the girls would find more opportunities there than Russia could provide. It grated on him that he was forced to run from his own government. Like an outcast, banished from his home.

For something I didn't even do.

José felt his lips curling into a snarl and stopped it immediately. Unfortunately, Chloe noticed the brief lapse.

"Why, exactly, is the boss going crazy looking for you anyway?" she asked. "What'd you do?"

"Listen," José growled, eyes hard as he stalked closer. "You tracked me for months, hounding me and my family, just to kill me. I do not hold a grudge for that. But you would have left my girls at the mercy of the CIA—and *that* I cannot forgive. I have not yet decided what to do with you. However, every time you speak, you make the decision a little easier."

Chloe smirked, defiance in her eyes, but she didn't say anything. José grunted and stepped back. He moved to the other side of the room, where he kept his computers. All the hardware packed together made the room almost too tight to move around in, but there was nowhere else to put it. He'd needed somewhere away from people to prepare for Chloe, so he'd chosen speed over comfort when purchasing the cabin.

He regretted it now. But it wasn't as if he hadn't lived in worse conditions. The fact that he noticed it at all was proof that he'd allowed himself to grow soft over the years.

He disabled the notifications for the alarm traps in the woods and noticed that the mines were offline. He scowled at the screen, then at the brunette, before stalking out.

CHLOE DROPPED HER SMIRK the moment José stepped out of the room. She tested her cuffs, noting their strength. There was an easy way to get out of cuffs, but Chloe would prefer not to use that talent until it was necessary—which it might be. She could barely move her wrists in the things. The added rope tying her to the table didn't help.

The door creaked open again, but Chloe continued trying to figure out how to move. She was fairly certain José wasn't going to kill her, for whatever reason. God knows she wouldn't have the same hang-ups if the shoe were on the other foot. The most he would do if he caught her trying to escape was shift her position.

Or he could drug me and knock me out for days on end, Chloe thought. It was another thing she would do in his position.

The door opened wider. Chloe glanced up in time to notice a red-haired head poke through and then a second. Two pairs of eyes stared at her—one curious, the other angry. After a moment, they glanced around the room as if to make sure José had left, before stumbling inside.

Chloe watched them. Earlier, when they'd shot at her, she'd been forced to compartmentalize her priorities, so she hadn't been able to get a good look. Now, as they struggled to make their way to her, she could stare at them as much as she wanted.

They really do have two heads on the same body.

She couldn't wrap her head around that. She'd heard of conjoined twins before, but mostly she'd known that to mean the kids shared some organs. Not an entire fucking body. *How does that even work?*

Their gait was unsteady, as if a stiff breeze were about to blow them over. It was obvious that mere movement took a lot of their concentration. The angry head on the left started the motion with the left foot, while the curious right head followed. She'd already seen them run, so she knew the process could be completed faster, but that didn't mean it was easy.

The focused expression on their faces was cute, though—even if the two heads could be off-putting to someone who cared about such things.

Finally, they stopped in front of Chloe, staring at her.

"Hey, girls," she cooed, grinning brightly. She jiggled her cuffs, drawing their attention there. "Don't suppose you know where the keys are, do you? Maybe in the secret place you keep the gun?"

"Father said you came here to hurt him," the left head said, her face squeezed into a scowl. "He said you wanted to take him away from us."

"Well, that's because your daddy is a really bad man, and he did a really bad thing in his previous job," she said. Then a thought occurred to her. She might need some way to track him again if she managed to get out—though that was looking more and more unlikely. "Do you know where your daddy works now? Does he have an office he goes to during the day?"

"Auntie Yelena already told us he was a bad man," the right head—the curious one—said, deliberately ignoring the question. "But he stopped hurting people to take care of us. Now he only hurts people who try to hurt us. Like you and the ones he had us use as target practice."

Ones they could practice on? Chloe's thought trailed off and she recoiled. *He had them practice their aim on actual people? What sort of sick parenting is that?*

Then she remembered the wound on her cheek. "Can't argue with the results," she muttered. Plus, they were what, seven? If they could already handle a gun at this age, even with their shitty balance, they'd be terrifying to behold once someone gave them some training.

"Look, I can't call you 'Right Head' and 'Left Head.' What are your names?"

"Karla," the left head said.

"Liz," the other followed.

Chloe nodded. She glanced at the door. She didn't know where José had gone, but she doubted he'd planned to stay there for the rest of the day.

"Who is Auntie Yelena?" she asked.

"Auntie Yelena is dead," Karla replied. Her scowl was tinged with a hint of sadness. "But we killed the people responsible."

"We?" Chloe asked. "You and Liz?"

Both heads nodded.

Forget the training. They're terrifying now. Is this why José risked so much to adopt them?

Chloe started speaking, but the door creaked again. José walked in, his face hard. The girls immediately adopted an innocent expression, and José's expression softened at it. He scolded them in Russian. Their heads dropped lower with every pronouncement. When he was done, he opened the door wider, and the twins stumbled through with their awkward gait.

"Let's deal," Chloe said before José could say anything. She dropped her usual smirk, her expression turning serious to show her sincerity. José's mouth shut, though more from anger at being interrupted. Chloe spoke before he could get started again. "Let's face it. You're not going to kill me because that would shut you out of the US for good. You wouldn't have risked keeping in contact with the agency and doing their petty jobs for so long if that was okay with you. However, I'm evidence that they haven't stopped tracking you, so you can't let me go to give them information about your little cabin or your girls."

She paused to give him time to respond, but he just stared at her creepily.

"I can help you get the credits you need," Chloe continued. "More, in fact, since yours mean crap. And I'll provide the backing you need to clear your name and actually make headway toward getting you and your girls home."

"What do you mean my credits mean crap?" José asked. "I've been gathering them for years."

"Hate to break it to you, but you were duped. The CIA only promised you that so you'd stay in contact with them. The jobs were mostly to keep you busy and narrow down your general location so it'd be easy for me to track."

José went still.

Chloe had been about to continue, but she couldn't get the words out. She stared at the man. She wasn't afraid when he'd pointed the gun at her or even when he'd almost shot her after she'd called his girls freaks. *Now* she was. And he hadn't even done anything. Chloe looked at José Olvera as if seeing him for the first time.

Maybe it's just me, she thought, *but has he always been this hot?*

Finally, José spoke, his tone deceptively calm. "You seem very comfortable telling a man that he has been wasting his life the last few years." He seemed on the edge of doing something stupid and hoped Chloe would be the push.

"That's because I'm also offering a way for your hope to pan out."

"And I'm supposed to assume you'll do all this from the goodness of your heart?"

"Of course not!" Chloe grinned. "But that doesn't mean my request will be unreasonable."

"I cannot let you run back to the CIA," José said.

"Good, because I don't plan on doing so anytime soon. What I want is to train your daughters."

José narrowed his eyes at her. "The only way you'll ever get close to my girls is when they help me carry you out of here in a body bag."

Chloe recoiled—which was awkward, tied to a table. "Well damn. How long have you been holding that in? Jesus."

José snorted and crossed the room to the computers.

"I don't plan to hurt your girls," Chloe said. "Whoever trained them obviously didn't know what they were doing, yet they already know how to use a gun. I'm curious how good they'll be with *actual* training."

José didn't bother to face her when he spoke. "You will *not* tell me how to raise my girls or how they should be trained."

"Wait," Chloe said, adopting a look of surprise. "You're the one that taught them how to use the gun? And you didn't teach them how to walk first? What, were you afraid they'd run out on you?"

This made him turn around, but his face could have been cut out from steel for all he showed. "You can teach them to walk?"

Chloe nodded. "All they need to learn is to be in sync. When I'm done with them, they'll be finishing each other's sentences like actual creepy Russian twins."

"Why?"

Chloe dropped her smile, showing her seriousness. "Because if they're terrifying when they waddle like ducks, I'm curious how they'll turn out when we put all that potential to good use."

"You want to make them a weapon," José said.

"Yes," Chloe murmured. "But in the process, I'll make them strong enough to survive everything that's thrown at them. And lethal enough to kill the ones who threw it."

José stared at her unblinkingly for a minute. "Fine. You'll work on their training while we clear my name." He stalked toward her, his expression glacial. "And if you betray me or seek to turn my girls against me, you won't live long enough to regret it."

Chloe grinned. *Yeah, he definitely wasn't this hot a few minutes ago.*

47

"I HAVE BEEN ON THE JOB here only thirty days, Manar," the new dean of students started. Stephen A. Schwarzman, according to the plaque on his desk. He had a thinning hairline and a pudgy face that couldn't stop sweating even with the air conditioner on. According to rumor, he was an alumnus of the school and had apparently been the top student of his year. Manar could barely keep the snort in; over thirty years later, and not a single endeavor worthy of interest. He'd gone on to teach, of all things. Oh, how Manar already missed the former dean.

"Just thirty days," Schwarzman continued, "and I've already heard everything about you. In fact, *everything* I've heard has been about you."

Manar didn't respond. Maybe if he stayed quiet, the man would get to his point.

"You completed your undergraduate study within eighteen months and finished your thesis and dissertation two years after. Your dissertation…"

Manar let the words recede to the background as he looked around the office. He hadn't been here since his first days at MIT, even though he had been very close to the former dean. At least Manar had respected him. He'd survived his first year thanks to the old man's counsel. Just like his time in high school, he'd had a hard time fitting in. And just as he'd found his place, he was hounded by hollow friendships he couldn't abide. And so, he'd floundered.

The former dean had given him advice that stuck with him: *Life is hard when you play outside the system. Learn the rules. Play the game, and destroy it from the inside out.*

What he'd discovered himself, however, was that one could only do that from the top. And for that, he needed people—even if that meant pretending to lower himself to their level.

The words had stuck with Manar through his years, resonating with him in a way that few things did. Power enough to protect. Scenes flashed in his head whenever he thought this: scenes about a field of blood, a full moon, and a whispered oath.

Manar brought himself back just in time to get the last sentences of Schwarzman's speech.

"Thank you, sir, for your words," Manar said, forcing a small smile. "My mother taught me at a young age, and since then, programming has been a passion."

"In terms of your career," the dean started again, "have you given any thought to what company you'd like to work with after you graduate? I'm on the board of directors for Sparta. I'm sure I can put in a word."

Manar narrowed his eyes. If the dean were truly on the board of directors, he would already know that Sparta had extended an offer that Manar had rejected. What, did they think because the new dean asked, Manar would cave?

Sparta was considered the best technology company out there, but that was mostly because they hired only the best talent, buying them with an ocean of money. Despite this, they didn't have a single groundbreaking product. Gaius, on the other hand, had revolutionized the market with its mammoth search engine and self-driving AI, ClearView Inc. had its powerful operating systems, and Phoenix had its rPhones. Even Flux Corp had electric vehicles. Sparta made do by having rich investors and owning a monopoly on talent. Manar wanted to be the best, and Sparta was a sinking ship. Manar figured their offer was a last-ditch effort to secure their position before they were inevitably booted out. He could take advantage of their desperation, but with over thirty offers worldwide, he wasn't lacking options.

"I appreciate the offer," Manar said, forcing a bow, "but I still have some time until I finish my PhD. I'm afraid I'm still not ready to commit."

"Well, that's perfectly reasonable," Schwarzman said. "A mind like yours is naturally bound to excel anywhere you choose, but it's never smart to make a hasty decision." He paused, and his eyes gained a gleam that Manar couldn't identify. "I've heard in the short while I've been here, however, that you're currently working on an AI to pair with your thesis on the role of artificial intelligence in modern daily life."

Manar frowned. Fewer than ten people knew about that, and he was supposed to believe that Schwarzman had just stumbled upon the knowledge? Was he being *spied* on? They couldn't have hacked his systems, so it couldn't have been digitally.

"Yes," Manar replied finally, narrowing his eyes to make sure his displeasure was conveyed. "It was a recent decision. I picked up a project I had begun in high school."

"Surely you're not talking about Helene," Schwarzman said, surprised. Manar was even more shocked. Helene was his submission for his end-of-the-year project. It was what had initially given him national attention and won him the scholarship to study at MIT. Still, the project was over four years old and among the least of his recent achievements.

The program was designed to serve as a holographic personal assistant capable of simultaneously coordinating industry-wide tasks. It had worked in the sense that he had created an assistant, but the processing power had not even been close to the design. He had never been able to figure out the schematics for the hologram. So he'd scrapped it. Until now. Manar felt he finally understood what he'd done wrong with the codes.

"I didn't think people still remembered Helene. But yes, I plan to revitalize her."

"You'd be hard-pressed to find people in our industry who *don't* talk about Helene—especially at Sparta," Schwarzman said. "She, through you, showed the world what was possible with AI. It was almost completely monopolized by the military before then."

Manar sniffed at the obvious attempt at flattery. Helene was ultimately flawed, and her processing was so less than optimal, barely able to manage a school's database. If anyone thought that her programming was revolutionary, then they were better off shooting themselves.

"Since then," Schwarzman continued, meeting Manar's eyes. "Sparta has researched the matter extensively and even has a working model that's to be brought to the market. Though, instead of a personal assistant, we went the route of an e-reader. It's called ASH."

Manar had heard of it, though he couldn't remember what ASH stood for. Probably something pretentious that was supposed to sound futuristic and grandiose. So far, Sparta had survived by devouring anything in its path through acquisitions and hostile takeovers. They were smart enough to realize that such tactics weren't sustainable. ASH would at least give them a nice little niche that they could rule over until they found a way to actually make use of the so-called geniuses they'd spent so much money acquiring.

Still, Manar thought, struggling not to snort, *an e-reader? That's their grand idea?* ASH by itself would be a laughable product coming from an already-established company like Sparta. An e-reader that functioned as a personal assistant, however…

Helene would probably be able to integrate with it, though he doubted anyone except him could figure out how without completely ruining the codes. This would explain why they had gone so far as to have Schwarzman talk to him. They were *really* desperate. They just didn't want to show it.

They needed him, but he didn't need them. There was no reason for him to accept.

"We went over the codes for your end-of-the-year project," said Schwarzman. Manar raised a brow. He hadn't opened the program up to the public. "And we noticed one of the main problems was that the program was coded to handle far more processing power than the high school servers could provide. Because of this, it had to be continuously monitored and re-adjusted to work for any length of time without completely overpowering the hardware, making it unfeasible to use."

Manar nodded. Honestly, he was surprised they'd even gotten that much out of it. But the fact that he hadn't mentioned the segment for the hologram meant that they hadn't been able to fully grasp it.

"Frankly, for something to handle the kind of processing power you designed the AI for, you'd have to build it yourself."

"I have a master's in advanced robotics," Manar reminded him softly.

"Yes, but materials cost money," replied Schwarzman.

Manar narrowed his eyes again. He was quickly getting tired of this conversation. "With all due respect sir, what exactly is your point?"

"I urge you to consider Sparta's offer. Once employed, you would be given full control of the Software Engineering Research and Development Team and tasked only with integrating Helene with ASH to bring both to life.

"Since it was inspired by your work, ASH already has a design similar to Helene's, so you won't have to start from the ground up. All you'll be focused on is fixing the flaws in your high school project and upgrading it until it becomes a fully functioning virtual intelligence on the verge of becoming true AI. Isn't that your dream?"

Manar considered this. He *had* thought about the inevitable cost of building a server advanced enough to keep up with Helene. He'd assumed getting a grant would be enough, but would it? If ASH was based on Helene and they already had a working server, he wouldn't have to start from scratch. It would save years of work and even if he loathed working with others, a dedicated team would be useful for handling all the nuances he couldn't be bothered with.

From a VI to a true AI, Manar mused. The average person would not be able to tell the difference, but the gap was a chasm. Both could ask how someone's day was and make educated guesses as to what would cheer a person up, but only an AI would be able to guess based on prior experiences and adapt accordingly.

There wasn't such a thing as true AI yet. However, Helene was close, and with Sparta, Manar wouldn't have to wait years to push her the final mile.

"If you can set up a meeting," Manar said, "I'm willing to go over the terms of employment."

"Wonderful."

"ALL RIGHT," Chloe said. "Snap."

Karla snapped her fingers—the left hand, since that was the only side she could control. The sound was barely audible, but that wasn't the point of the exercise. Liz's eyes widened.

"I felt it," she said. Her eyes sparkled, and a smile tugged on her lips. Any other kid her age would have been bouncing, but Liz was careful to keep her expression muted. She was only seven. When Chloe had asked José about it, he'd said that was how she'd always been.

Chloe found that interesting. Karla was loud to the point of being irritating. Happy or angry, the girl didn't seem to have a mute button. Liz was more pensive and controlled. The contrast was jarring, seeing as they had the same face. And their heads were always side by side.

"Good," Chloe said to Liz. "In a second, it'll be your turn. Now, Karla." She squatted in front of the girls. She'd been smiling at Liz, but when she turned to

Karla, she switched to a smirk tinged with mockery. "We've been trying this for the last two days. Liz got the hang of it ages ago, so why haven't you?"

"Because she isn't doing it right," Karla scowled.

"Of course she's doing it right," Chloe replied, ramping up the mockery. "Even José thinks she's doing it right. And he's starting to get angry that you're slowing us down."

Karla's eyes widened for a second before her scowl returned. "Father is always angry. I don't care. Liz is the one that's doing it wrong."

"Maybe she's just better than you are," Chloe whispered.

Karla glared at her. Her eyes held far too much hatred for a girl her age. This was exactly the reaction Chloe was going for, yet she found herself reaching for her dagger before she caught herself.

"Now, Liz," Chloe said.

Liz snapped her fingers sharply. Chloe saw the moment Karla felt the vibration. *Fucking finally,* Chloe thought, standing. Karla's expression flickered from anger to happiness. Then, the red-haired girl caught Chloe's gaze, and her face settled back to its scowl.

Chloe grinned back. It had taken barely a day of observation to find out what motivated these girls. Liz was easier; she responded to logical arguments. As long as Chloe explained what she wanted and broke it down, Liz wouldn't have a problem doing it. If that didn't work, Chloe would call José to sit in on one of their lessons.

Karla—the little bitch—was all emotion. There was a perpetual scowl on her face as if living irritated her. Sometimes Liz could get her to do something without fuss, but most times, Chloe had found that the girl only responded when she was forced or coerced in some way. Since José would kill Chloe the moment she laid her hands on either of the girls, Chloe had needed to be creative about how she motivated them. It'd taken her close to three weeks to find a working system for Karla, harsh though it was.

Chloe clapped her hands. "Again," she called. "You first, Liz." Liz snapped her fingers. Karla's scowl softened almost imperceptibly from her surprise. Chloe nodded. "Now you, Karla." Karla snapped her fingers, and Liz nodded that she felt it.

Chloe had them practicing that for the next hour, alternating their snaps. Karla complained but inevitably shut up when her sister didn't join. Chloe stayed just close enough that she could be sure they were actually practicing.

José came out of the cabin a few minutes before the hour was up. He grunted at the girls. "What do you have them doing now?"

"Snapping their fingers."

José waited for more, but Chloe remained silent. She felt his gaze boring into the side of her head. This just made her grin wider. After a moment, she let out a laugh and then started explaining.

"The idea is, when one of them snaps her fingers, the vibration travels through the body to be felt by the other."

"How would that help them walk?"

"They already know how to walk. They just need to be more in sync with each other. This will help with that."

It had taken Chloe a while to figure out how to work around the fact that Karla only felt and controlled what was on her left side while Liz only felt what was on her right. It made coordination hard, but Chloe still didn't think it was impossible. The vibration from snapping their fingers was her third project, but it actually worked. With a lot of practice and a little refinement, they could expand the concept.

José grunted again but didn't say anything more. He didn't have to. Both of them knew what would happen if Chloe couldn't deliver. Without hope that the CIA would grant him his citizenship, getting his kids into shape was the only thing that kept Chloe alive.

And I have no doubt that if I run, I'll be the one who's hunted down for the rest of my life. Chloe held back a groan at the thought. But it wasn't all bad. She could do without José's crankiness—even though it made him hot as hell—but she genuinely liked training the girls. Even Karla, though the girl *was* a little bitch.

CHLOE CLAPPED HER HANDS, watching from a few meters away as the girls tried to walk. "Don't go too fast," she said. "Liz, that means you."

The girl gave a rare, impish smile then went back to concentrating. She snapped her fingers to signal her sister, then took a step. Karla followed a beat later with her own snap. Liz took over the next step, again with a snap, and so on. They moved at a snail's pace, but at least they weren't waddling with every step.

Chloe called that progress. Even though it'd taken them over three months to get here, practicing for hours at a time. Still, they'd mastered feeling for the vibration of the snaps relatively quickly. And they picked up Chloe's idea for using it to sync without any input from her. So, once they could work without actively concentrating on it—and without competing with a snail for speed—then they would be able to move on to more complicated moves.

In the meantime, Liz lost the rhythm and stumbled, dragging Karla down with her. Chloe sighed. "Might take a while."

José stepped up to her. He'd made it a habit, over the months, to check in on the training. Chloe held in a snort. She got that he didn't trust her with the girls, but he should at least trust that she had her own best interests at heart.

"When do you plan on contacting the Agency?" he asked.

"I already did," Chloe replied, "about two months back to assure them that I wasn't KIA and to stop them from sending anyone after me."

José stared at her but didn't say anything.

"I told them I'd made contact with you and was determining your loyalties." She shrugged. "Figured that should at least give me some time to come up with something better. They've given me permission to have you as a tagalong on my missions if I think you're willing to come back without a fuss. I told them that won't be a problem because it won't, right? These missions will actually count for something so all you have to do is impress them a few times and you're in."

José walked back inside.

50

DJ WATCHED HIS BROTHER out of the corner of his eye. He knew CJ hated it, but how could he stop when watching his brother's therapy session was infinitely more interesting than TV? He knew he wasn't meant to find any of it funny. The therapy helped his brother repress his quirks, and there was nothing funny about him learning the techniques involved. But it *was*. DJ forced his eyes away before he could start laughing.

"Pink pixie promised the painted panther some pint of blood," the therapist read and waited patiently while CJ processed it and repeated it back to her. The session was online, as most of his were. Speech was one of CJ's biggest challenges, so they focused more on that. Fortunately, the Okafor Centre specialized in speech and behavioral therapies. Unfortunately, the Centre was situated on the other side of the world in Nigeria, and as there were no other branches nearby, in-person sessions were out of the question.

Luckily, there was the internet.

"Pink pixie… uh… promi… sed the pain… ted… uh…"

Papa had explained that different people on the autism spectrum had different means of communicating, since talking sucked for them. CJ preferred to type. Although his mind was fast enough to keep up with the session if he concentrated, it became a whole other issue when forming the words, much less actually *saying* them.

Reading exercises were the latest assignment. It hadn't made much sense to DJ until Papa explained it. Hearing the words read aloud helped CJ process them faster, taught him how they *should* sound, and pushed him to follow the pattern when speaking. In an in-person session, this would have been done while making sure the autistic child made eye contact—another problem area for CJ. But there was nothing to be done here.

They'd been using the technique for a few months. They had made some progress—to the point that CJ could almost hold a conversation—but they had hit a roadblock a couple of weeks back. Now, the technique no longer worked. CJ had given DJ no end of grief about it. He was sure it was his fault it no longer worked, that it was his fault he could not focus enough to avoid drifting off when forming the words.

He'd shut up a few moments later, when DJ smacked him on the side of his head. "The dumbass," DJ muttered, remembering the day. It annoyed him when his brother thought like that. Honestly, who cared that his speech was somewhat slow? So what if he wouldn't make eye contact? Even with the drifting, CJ's mind was unsurpassed in most areas. DJ continuously found himself struggling to keep up. What did it matter, then, that CJ didn't speak?

"… some pi… nt of… of…" CJ paused, scrunching up his brows. After a moment, he looked back, straight at DJ.

"Blood," DJ mouthed, "some pint of blood."

"Blood," CJ finished confidently, turning back to his session. DJ returned to the TV. He was already busted, and CJ was sure to give him hell later. But he couldn't help it. Over the past week, the therapists had switched to reading more complex passages, trying to help CJ maintain interest and stay grounded. The effect wasn't yet pronounced enough to be noticed—even if his brother used him as a cheat sheet.

"That's good, Christopher. You're making tremendous progress" the therapist said. She was probably paid to offer encouragement. "Would you be willing to—" She paused. DJ shifted his position to get a better look at the screen. The therapist was speaking to someone. She came back a minute later, her smile wide enough to crack her face. "CJ, one of my senior colleagues from Harvard would like to speak with you about the recent roadblock we seem to have reached."

CJ nodded slowly, his confusion palpable. DJ shifted more, his curiosity piqued. The group of therapists was hand-picked to cater to CJ's unique psyche, and now they were calling for help?

"Morning, CJ," a voice said. DJ strained to look at the screen, where a dark-skinned girl waved at his brother. DJ blinked. She was barely older than they were, and she was a *senior* colleague? "Sorry to barge in on you. I'm Ndidi Okafor, the head of research here at the Centre."

CJ's eyes were as wide as saucers. It wasn't hard to understand why, with the way Dad and Papa had gone on and on about her and the things she did for kids like CJ. She was a legend and… kind of pretty, actually.

"Nice to… uh… me… et you," CJ said finally.

"Danae here says you've had some issues focusing on the words you're trying to say. Is that right?"

CJ nodded dejectedly. DJ almost scooted over to smack him. Ndidi smiled.

"Chin up, kiddo. Danae has told me how much progress you've made since you started with us. A minor hurdle is nothing to worry about for a champ like you. I'm just gonna have you try something for a couple minutes. We'll see if that makes a difference. Okay?"

CJ nodded again. DJ scooted closer.

"All right, cool," Ndidi said. "It's really simple. I'm just gonna read a passage from a book, and you're gonna repeat it just like you've been doing. What's different here, though, is that I want you to picture the words I'm reading. It helps if you connect them with something visual. That way your brain has a reference to focus on when it's trying to remember. Good so far?"

CJ nodded. DJ started to wonder about his brother's weird behavior. He was naturally shy, but what was with all the nodding?

"So, we're gonna read one of the passages you've already gone over," she said, and then started reading. "The rope hangs from the tree." The monitor switched as she spoke, shifting through pictures: first a rope, then a tree, and a rope tied around the tree with its end left to drift.

"The rope hangs… from the tree," CJ repeated. And then his eyes widened. "The words… they were… easier then." He faced DJ, his eyes alight. "The words … came … *easier*."

DJ's grin matched his brother's. He gave up on the pretense of watching TV, scooting closer to watch the session fully. The other techniques had reached a dead end because CJ had not been able to focus on the words enough to construct them.

But this? This could work.

A LEAF FLUTTERED OUTSIDE the window. Ndidi looked up from her book, stilling her pen. She watched it fall, her gaze distant.

I'm so… bored, she mentally moaned. Harvard's fall semester started a few days ago. Ndidi should have been going over the semester's outline. Point of fact, she *had* been doing that for the last two hours, but there was only so much reading a girl could take before she went out of her mind. Plus, she'd already covered most of the coursework during the holidays, courtesy of her father. Repeating it just sucked.

She glanced around the room, which was another thing she had to thank her father for. The presidential suite of the Charles Hotel in Cambridge was amazingly plush. It had a great view of Harvard Square, and she could order anything she wanted.

It sucked. Ndidi stood from the desk, pacing the room. *Why do I need an entire damn floor?*

It wasn't so much the room that irritated her, nor was it the comfort. It was the fact that her father had booked the *entire* tenth floor for the four years she was studying at the university.

"It's for your safety," he had said in the infuriatingly calm tone he always used with her. But wasn't it for her safety that she'd trained with Sensei Mukalla her entire childhood? And all through that time, she'd only been attacked once—

Ndidi stopped, releasing a breath in a rush. *There you go, sounding like a spoiled brat,* she told herself. She released another breath, glancing around the room again. It honestly wasn't bad. She'd grown accustomed to the quiet after three years.

She returned to her desk and slammed her textbook shut. The room was perfect for studying, but she didn't feel much like repeating things she'd already learned. Instead, she drew another book closer to her, this one about ASD. When she worked on her ASD research, she felt as if she was actually doing something with her life. Technically, she *was* still studying.

In 2019, Harvard University began its autism research in collaboration with the Okafor Centre. The team of researchers met Ndidi that year and convinced her father to let her join their research while she went to school.

Since then, Ndidi had been working with the Harvard research team. Each member of the group had a different specialty, so the research was always varied. Ndidi already had broad knowledge of ASD, gained from her studies and work with Bethany. That and the fact that she hadn't yet picked a specific field made her the perfect sounding board for the rest of the team when they needed to discuss their theories or receive help with their investigations.

Of course, this added to her already heavy workload, but frankly, delving into the different studies and bouncing around ideas with the other scientists kept Ndidi sane. In collaboration with the Okafor Centre, they had already discovered so much that could help kids on the autism spectrum. Moreover, there were *tons* of studies they hadn't gotten to yet.

At the moment, she was researching the sensory experiences that shape social behaviors relevant to autism. After that, she wanted to investigate genetic variations linked to autism and their possible effects on brain development. The group had hit a wall there, so if she could find evidence that—

Her alarm shook her from her thoughts. She jumped, reaching for the phone. The sky was dark outside. *Huh,* she thought. *When did that happen?* Ndidi decided she should probably eat something. She could order in but preferred to leave that for whenever she got too invested in her work to stand up. And she *had* been cooped up in the room all day.

"I guess I could check out the new burger place," Ndidi muttered.

The diner was just down the block. Ndidi made a beeline for a corner booth and flagged down a waitress. The restaurant was larger than most but had a relaxed air. There was a bar in the corner where people had formed a small line to pick up their to-go orders. One wall was lined with booths, and the middle of the room had tables for larger groups. Ndidi hadn't seen a setting like this before. Most of the tables were taken, yet even with all the conversation going on, the room wasn't at all noisy. It was actually pretty nice.

"As long as the food's good, I can definitely see myself coming back here again. Maybe I'll bring Lucy and all the others," she said to herself. It was weird not having them around; they were usually the ones who had to drag her out.

"Are you ready to order?"

Ndidi looked up. A waiter stood beside her booth, tapping a notepad expectantly. "Yes, sure. Can I have the burger with a side of fries, extra fries?"

Ndidi hesitated when she felt eyes on her. She waited until the waiter had gone before completely turning around to scan the room. Fortunately, Ndidi was not the same timid girl she'd been at the tournament in Japan, and she'd long since learned to ignore the attention. Still, there had been so much *intent* behind the stare, she felt compelled to seek out the source—even if it was just to reassure herself that it wasn't a creepy guy she'd have to look out for when she went back to her room.

Nobody stood out. Conversations were still going strong at the tables around her. No one was paying any attention to her. She frowned. *I'm really not used to coming out by myself if I'm jumping this much over nothing.*

She turned back around, scrolling through her phone. The feeling returned, and she looked up again—and forcefully shoved down her surprise.

Well, Ndidi thought, deliberately going back to her phone. She gave it a few more seconds before glancing again at the man seated two tables away. He was *still* staring at her. *Bold, I'll give him that. Hot, too. Can't overlook that.*

Over the next few minutes, whenever Ndidi looked up, she pretended to be looking past him. The guy probably saw through that due to how frequently their eyes met. Several times, Ndidi was almost able to stop herself from glancing, but he never took his eyes off her. And there was something about his stare that intrigued her.

If it were any other guy, Ndidi would have already been walking away, fries or no. But somehow, she didn't feel any danger. Frankly, she didn't know *what* she felt—or whether that was a good thing or a bad thing.

Most guys had no effect on her. They were either immature, douchebags, or too intimidated by her once they finally realized why her last name sounded so familiar. Ndidi had learned to identify each kind of guy before they spoke.

The man who stared across at her wasn't like any other guy she'd seen. A nugget of irritation rose. She hadn't pegged herself for someone who'd be so invested in a person's looks. She didn't go tripping over every hot guy. This was an exception; they didn't make guys like him where she was from. *The cheekbones and lashes alone…*

"Hi," he said finally.

Ndidi, who'd risked another peek, forced herself to casually meet the man's eyes. "Do you always do this when a girl places an order?"

His green eyes lit up, and his gaze seemed to intensify somehow. A lazy smile tugged at his lips. Ndidi forced down her blush.

"In fact," he responded, his voice smooth as silk, "we had the same order, so I thought it would be nice to have some company." He stood and walked over, gesturing to the chair opposite her. "Is this seat taken? My name's Manar."

"Ndidi," she replied absently. For a moment, Ndidi wondered what he would do if she told him the seat was occupied. For some reason, she didn't think he was the type to walk away. He was certainly arrogant—*who stares at someone for over five minutes without speaking?*—but somehow, he carried it in a way that was so self-assured, it didn't seem like a fault. In him, it was *confidence.*

And then she registered his name.

"Wait," she said. Now she was forcing calm for an entirely different reason. That didn't make her cheeks any less warm though. "You're Manar? From Sparta Corp?"

"So you've heard of me." Manar smiled, sitting.

Ndidi almost couldn't believe what she was hearing. *Have I heard?*

"You're the software genius." Her voice came out slightly high pitched, and she forced herself to stay calm. "You came to give a speech on artificial intelligence today to the freshman class at MIT. It's not my field, but even I know that your AI, Helene, is groundbreaking work. Even at Harvard, you're a legend."

MANAR DISMISSED NDIDI'S PRAISE. Helene was still two-dimensional. That was far from the level he envisioned. People were going nuts over the AI now because their minds were too small to understand how much more was possible. With Sparta, he was closer than ever to achieving what he wanted. Nevertheless, it would be years before he got everything he needed.

But that can come later, Manar chided himself. Fortunately, Ndidi hadn't noticed his attention drifting. She stared at him, then glanced away. He could see the effort she put into calming herself. Most of it was futile, but at least it showed she was as affected by him as he was by her. She was waiting to see what he would do.

And honestly, Manar wasn't sure. He'd never been in this sort of position before, never been so drawn to someone. He'd had lovers before, sure. But he wasn't embarrassed to say that those had been mostly for the sex.

That's probably what's happening here too, Manar thought. It couldn't be anything else. They'd barely spoken, after all. He'd noticed her shortly after she'd walked into the restaurant and hadn't been able to keep his eyes off her. Admittedly, it had been her body that had drawn him in at first. But once their eyes met, he'd noticed *intelligence* there. This was someone that he might actually be able to hold a conversation with.

But what to do? he thought. *What to do?*

"What do you study?" he asked.

The waiter came then with both of their meals. "Business administration," Ndidi replied after the server left, "but I consider myself more a researcher on ASD."

"ASD?" he asked.

Immediately, he realized he'd struck conversational gold. Ndidi's eyes lit up, and she took a sip of her drink as if preparing.

The next few minutes were spent with Ndidi talking about her research, both at the Okafor Centre and with the Harvard team. Manar listened with half an ear. The subject *was* interesting, but his attention was otherwise taken up by her face. At least he now had a good reason to stare.

Ndidi tapered off after a while. Somehow, she'd managed to finish her burger between sentences. Manar had barely even touched his.

"Anyway," she said, taking a sip of her drink, "the tournament was where I met Hermione and her sister, Bethany, who was basically the reason I chose ASD research." She reached for a fry and blinked when she realized she'd eaten them all. Manar's eyes glinted with amusement.

"And that's where you got the scar on your neck?" he asked.

Her hand reached up to brush the mark. "Yeah, Hermione and I got into a fight. She thought it was an easy win, but I won all three rounds." The last part was said with a small smile, her gaze distant.

Manar bit into his burger. "So, where are Hermione and Bethany now?"

"Hermione's in Nigeria, helping her father with his research while Bethany's over at the Okafor Centre in New York. We found that she's more receptive to the techniques we use when she sees others using them. Maybe it's just a competitive streak, but it works." Ndidi paused. "Unfortunately, her progress has been stalling for the last few months. We're working on something that might help, but sadly, she's stuck until we come up with a new technique."

Her gaze was sad. It was obvious this had been weighing on her. Manar wasn't sure whether he should pursue the conversation or change the topic. Before he could think too much about it, his hand was on hers. Ndidi's eyes were immediately drawn to the spot. It took most of Manar's willpower to ignore the heat in that look and keep his voice level.

"I'm sure Bethany will be fine. You'll make sure she is. You're obviously passionate about your work. If you're half as competitive as the girl, I doubt you'll let a block in your studies stop you."

Ndidi lifted her eyes to meet his. Manar immediately withdrew his hand. He coughed, breaking the eye contact but doing nothing to dispel the friction in the air.

"So, how'd your speech go?" Ndidi asked, shaking her head as if to clear it. She sipped her drink.

"There wasn't really much of note. But I did manage to…"

As if by mutual agreement, they stuck to casual conversation. At some point, Ndidi ordered another side of fries, staring at Manar as if daring him to say anything. They spoke for over an hour, yet it might as well have been white noise. Between the heat when their eyes met and when their hands "accidentally" touched, Manar couldn't recall exactly what they'd spoken about.

Attraction did not begin to describe what he was feeling. And it was fueled by the way she clearly felt it too, despite her efforts to appear casual. The tension was so thick, all it would take was a little push.

But do I want to give that push? Manar wondered. He'd always felt that relationships were a distraction, one he couldn't afford—especially now. Sparta was already constructing the hardware he'd need to upgrade Helene. He would need to keep up his part of the deal and manage their department.

They could always have a one-night stand, but he had a feeling one night wouldn't be enough to quench the fire between them. *It would probably make it worse,* he thought, then immediately amended it. *It would definitely make it worse.*

The hours passed, and Manar grew tired of his indecisiveness. He was a man of numbers, but logic went only so far.

"Hey! There's something on your cheek," he said, pointing to a spot on his own face.

Ndidi reached up at the spot, and if there had actually been something on her cheek, she probably would have gotten it. Manar shook his head like she'd missed it. Before she could try again, he reached toward her.

"Here," he said softly, "let me."

Her skin sent lightning down his wrist. Only through sheer willpower could he keep his hands steady. He wiped at a random spot on her face, then let his hand fall to her lower lip and linger there. Through all this, his eyes never left hers. Her face was flushed, and her forehead started glistening with sweat.

Time to make the push. "Do you want to get out of here?"

Ndidi was nodding before he finished. "Sure. Absolutely."

"All right, then," Manar said, leaning back in his chair. He gestured to the waiter and dropped a couple of twenties on the table. Ndidi, who'd already been reaching for her purse, frowned her disapproval. Manar smiled, pretending he didn't see the look. "My hotel's not far. Let's take a walk."

Somehow, they ended up holding hands as they left the burger place. Ndidi continued telling him about her ASD research. She even got Manar to stop staring at her enough to speak about artificial intelligence. Surprisingly, Ndidi had some reservations about AI. She actually brought up good points to argue. This just made the whole thing even more interesting.

"You really haven't watched enough movies if you think sentient machines are a good idea." She laughed, clutching his arm.

Manar shook his head, but he, too, was grinning. "That's the difference. AIs aren't sentient. Programmers have become more flexible in how they code them, but they *are* still programs. They have instructions they have to obey."

"Oh, really?" Ndidi teased.

"Yeah, really. It only ends badly when AIs are sought out by small-minded men just looking for a quick buck. Take Helene for example. She's the most advanced AI on the market. She has a limited ability to grow and learn, right? But in the end, what she does with that knowledge would still be within the bounds of my codes."

"And she can't go outside of that?" Ndidi asked. "There's no *possible* way that could happen?"

"It's impossible," Manar said.

After that, their conversation shifted to a discourse on the ethics and moral obligations of a competent society of knowledge versus the lazy tendencies of an impatient modern society. It was a semi-serious topic, but both were in high enough spirits that they kept their arguments light. Several times, Manar caught Ndidi glancing at their intertwined hands. She would freeze up whenever she did, then pretend to stare at the sky. Manar wondered what was going on in her head.

If it's anything like what's going on in mine…

Unconsciously, Manar drew her closer to him. He was practically steaming inside his clothes, but that was all right, because she was too. Their conversation so far had been light, but that had done nothing to reduce the tension in the air. If anything, being aware of the heat between them and deliberately trying not to call attention to it somehow made it *hotter*.

The hand-holding probably didn't help. This was a first for Manar, losing this much control just from holding hands.

The wind blew harder as they walked, and Manar followed a flash of lightning with his eyes. "We might have to jog a little if we don't want to get rained on." He glanced down at her to find she was gazing at the sky. He smiled. "You up for it?"

"I only *look* like a princess, I'm not an invalid," she muttered absently, still glaring. A moment later, she seemed to realize what she'd said, and her mouth fell open in mortification. She turned to gauge Manar's reaction, then seemed to think better of it, instead staring down the street with deliberate casualness. She cleared her throat. "I mean, yeah, I'm up for it."

Manar laughed, then immediately covered it up with a cough. "Let's… uh, let's go then."

Manar had been ready to risk getting wet and slow down his pace so Ndidi wouldn't fall behind. However, as soon as they started, he was the one struggling to keep up. *I have to meet this Sensei Mukalla at some point,* he thought. Though they were going at a fast jog, the rain still caught up to them. Fortunately, by then they were just a minute away from the hotel, so they wouldn't be as drenched as they could have been.

They were laughing like school kids when they finally entered the lobby. Their clothes dripped a steady trail as they made their way to the elevators. Throughout their jog, they hadn't stopped holding hands. And the water had done nothing to stop the tension in the air.

The elevator dinged on his floor, and they both stepped out. Manar's room was at the end of the hall. It would take maybe a minute to get there.

And that was too long.

Manar pressed Ndidi against the elevator doors and kissed her. His hands wrapped around her waist, pressing her against him. The wet clothes helped him feel her skin against his. And the *heat* she emitted.

Maybe it had been the jogging through the rain or the fact that they'd been alone through the elevator ride. At some point, the tension between them had built to an irresistible level. It felt as if the whole night had been just one long foreplay.

To her credit, Ndidi's surprise only lasted a split second before she kissed him back. Her lips moved against his with the same urgency. Manar growled harshly, drawing her closer. His hands roamed over her body, but the clothes kept getting in the way. Without breaking off the kiss, Manar picked her up until she straddled him. He let go when they reached his room, but her legs were locked around him, and her hands ran along his chest and back.

He fumbled with the door code and cursed himself for not installing voice activation. *Not that that would have helped either,* he thought. Finally, he managed to punch in the correct code, and they tumbled into the room.

Manar broke away. "We need to get you out of those clothes," he gasped, kicking the door shut.

Ndidi grinned, her gaze piercing him. Her hands reached for the bottom of her shirt. "That's what I was thinking." The shirt went over her head, and she stood in front of him in only her bra and jeans.

"Fuck," Manar breathed. His hand reached for her automatically, but he wrestled it back and forced himself to concentrate. "I have some extra clothes you can use while we get yours into the dryer." It went against every instinct to offer her *more* clothes, but Simone would kill him if he didn't treat a woman properly.

"Or…" Ndidi drawled, shimmying out of her jeans. "We could just snuggle under the covers until we get warm."

Manar gulped.

CHAPTER

52

SEPTEMBER 2023
SEVEROMORSK, RUSSIA

"AGAIN," CHLOE SAID, hair pulled back into a ponytail to keep it out of her way. She and José stood over the twins. Around them, the forest was silent in the winter's chill. José wanted to move back to the city, but Chloe had argued against it. The forest was a good training ground. With the things she put the girls through, they'd probably have been arrested by child services ages ago.

Karla and Liz were on their knees, panting. Blood and sweat dripped from their heads. They'd been working on the same sequence of movement for the last four hours. All four of them knew the girls wouldn't stop until Chloe decided they had it down. Karla raised her head to glare but couldn't draw the breath to actually talk.

You would think, Chloe mused, *that after four years, she would have realized that shit doesn't work on me.*

"Again," she repeated, her voice harder.

Liz snapped her fingers, Karla responded with one of her own. Then, as one, they straightened. The movement wasn't graceful, but at least it was smooth and looked natural. Before Chloe's training, their timing would have been wrong, and they probably would have fallen trying to do that. It was progress, but imperfect. *We'll have to work on another way for them to coordinate. Snapping their fingers will just get them killed when they are trying to be stealthy.*

The girls stood straight, each holding a wooden dagger. Chloe also held one, but hers was sharp enough to leave a mark with enough force. She'd started with blunt weapons a few weeks back, but quickly realized that it had to hurt for Karla to be motivated. Thankfully, José had gotten over being squeamish about her techniques years back, once he'd seen Chloe's training taking hold.

Karla snapped her fingers—*yeah, they'll definitely have to work on that*—and the girls lunged at Chloe. The move was much slower than Chloe had hoped, but at least they weren't tripping over themselves and Chloe could appreciate the ridiculous amount of coordination that went into such a simple move.

The snap had been to inform Liz to start the motion for the lunge. Liz had taken a step while Karla had twisted the body so that her dagger stuck out at Chloe. When Chloe blocked, Liz would strike with her own weapon while Karla took a step to reposition, and so on. Each phase of that had been thoroughly planned out and practiced hundreds of times over the last few years. It had been worth it.

Even though their speed wasn't at the level Chloe wanted, the girls had still surpassed her expectations of what was possible. They took to fighting like fish to water, limited only by their unique situation. In terms of skill, they outpaced people who had been fighting for twice as long, especially other eleven-year-olds.

If they'd been born normal, though…

Chloe banished the thought, deflecting a strike and countering. She had worked them to hell and back, and she'd keep at it until their nature was more an asset than anything else.

Liz couldn't shift fast enough without breaking their coordination, so she let Chloe's counter land. A bruise formed on her cheek, but other than a slight wince, the girl didn't show any emotion. There was a snap, and the twins withdrew. Chloe let them. They'd earned it.

"Good one, Liz," Chloe said. "You could probably have dodged that if you'd tried, but it would have left both of you unbalanced, which I would have punished. Your teamwork's your greatest strength, so you must do whatever you can to keep in sync. Don't forget that."

"We already know that." Karla deadpanned.

Chloe ignored her glare. "Again."

Another hour of harsh practice later, she found José in his computer room. "We're ready." She'd left the girls still practicing outside, but since she wasn't there to keep them on track, they'd probably be slacking off. They'd earned it.

"What're you talking about?" José groused.

"I think it's time. We've certainly waited long enough. The girls aren't as ready as I'd like, but they have more than enough skill to handle a couple of thugs. We should contact the agency now and get permission to bring them on our next mission."

NDIDI WOKE UP THE NEXT MORNING sore but thoroughly satiated. Her head was foggy, and her limbs felt like jelly. She basked in the feeling for a moment, her lips stretched into a grin. Beside her, Manar slept with his arms wrapped around her. The blanket covered him from the waist down, but that did nothing to stop Ndidi's thoughts from going wild with the memories of the previous night. Faint lines ran from his chest to his stomach. The marks, evidence of how out of control she was, just helped to fuel the fire she felt. She traced the lines now, unable to help herself. After a few seconds, Manar's hand tightened around her, and there was a very noticeable bulge in the blanket.

Ndidi's eyes zeroed in on it. She licked her lips.

"Well, this is a first," Manar chuckled several minutes later. Ndidi pulled herself up from under the blanket, wiping her mouth. She looked up at him. Amusement twinkled in his eyes, wrestling with the lust. Somehow, that made him even sexier. He tried to sit up, but Ndidi straddled him.

I really can't get enough of him, she realized. Something insistent poked her in between her legs. Ndidi leaned over until her breasts touched his face. She rose a little from the straddle, shifting her legs until she was filled. Manar groaned deeply and latched on to her breasts, almost growling. *And it seems like he can't get enough of me either.*

For the second time in a couple of hours, the room was filled with the sound of slapping bodies. Ndidi moved like a piston, her head thrown back. Suddenly, Manar's hands were around her waist and she was lifted up and slammed onto her back. He bucked frantically, almost splitting Ndidi in two. Not that she minded.

Manar gave one last thrust and groaned. She gasped, bucking just as frantically as he had been. Finally, they lay in an exhausted, satisfied heap.

"That's a morning warm-up the books don't tell you about," Manar said, drawing her close. "How about it? You feel warmed up?" He was panting hard, but the pride in his tone was unmistakable. His hands slithered down her stomach, cupping her. "Because we could also try again if you aren't."

Ndidi giggled, slapping his hands away. "You're making it difficult to call this a one-night stand."

"I considered that last night," he replied, replacing his hand. "I made my decision this morning."

"And?"

Manar rolled her over until she faced him. He kissed her long and hard with the same amount of urgency and lust he had the previous night. Ndidi's toes curled. She was caressing his head before she even realized it. Some point later, Manar pulled away, his eyes glinting, his breathing ragged.

"I'm definitely not giving this up after just one night."

His voice was firm and confident. *Like everything he does, actually.* Ndidi didn't reply, focusing instead on bringing down the flush in her cheeks.

Manar slapped her ass. "Come on, let's continue this in the shower." He rolled away, slipping from the bed and into the bathroom. After a minute, Ndidi joined him.

They'd awakened late and spent far too long in the shower, but somehow they still managed to return to the room before the morning got away from them. They ordered a late breakfast, which made them feel heavy enough for the activities to catch up to them, and they slept.

Ndidi didn't wake up until late afternoon, and for the first time since the previous night, she felt in control of herself. If nothing else, her body had lost the warmth that had so pervaded it for the last few hours. She stared down at Manar and felt a pang of regret. "What the hell came over me?" she groaned. *Sleeping with a guy I just met?*

But that wasn't really the problem, she knew. Now that it was done, she didn't regret the sex. She couldn't bring herself to regret the sex. It didn't matter that it had been with a guy she just met. At least, Ndidi understood herself enough to know that Manar was the exception, not the rule. She wouldn't have done this with anyone else. There was just something about this one that drew her in.

And *that* was the problem.

She'd known from the moment they'd started talking that Manar was different. Anything she did with Manar was going to *mean* something. *I'm definitely not giving this up after just one night,* he'd said. And Ndidi had no doubt that he meant it. Worse, she *wanted* him to mean it.

God, this is a mess, she thought with a grimace. She couldn't afford the distraction.

Her father could have hired tutors for her, or she could have applied to a school in Nigeria. Her coming to Harvard had always been less about her studies and more about the freedom that she would have away from home. Getting distracted from her research—from helping Bethany with the breakthrough she needed—because of a guy wasn't her handling her freedom very well. She'd known that she couldn't let it go far, so why had she let it happen at all?

Because there was something about this one. She liked him, and she knew he liked her as well. No casual encounter could be that passionate.

"But I can't afford any distraction," she muttered firmly. She'd reached the conclusion minutes before, but somehow, saying it out loud helped her accept it. She felt a spark of anger, and channeled it into action, just as she'd been taught. Manar was still sleeping, which was good. This would be infinitely more difficult if he were awake and staring at her.

She gently removed his hands from around her waist and slithered from the bed. Fortunately, Manar had been true to his word and laundered her clothes, though Ndidi didn't know when he'd found the time. She dressed in silence, her back to the door.

When she slipped from the room, she didn't look back.

MANAR WOKE TO AN EMPTY BED. He listened but didn't hear the shower running. His eyes went to the chair on which he'd put Ndidi's clothes, and found them gone. He sighed.

His phone pinged from the bedside table. He reached for it absently, glancing at the text.

"If you're extending your stay, sir, should we start working on the codes for the project?"

Earlier that morning, he'd sent a message to his team stating he would be staying a couple more days. Manar stared at the question for a few seconds.

"Yes. Lay the groundwork. I'll continue when I'm back."

The reply came immediately. "Do you have a timeline?"

"I'll have to finish up here first. Something went missing, and I aim to recover it before I leave."

He stood, stretching. His eyes were flat but full of confidence. *I don't know her last name,* he thought. But he knew her first, and he knew where she went to school.

It would have to be enough.

54

FEBRUARY 2024
SEVEROMORSK, RUSSIA

CHLOE PEERED THROUGH THE SCOPE at the warehouse across the street. The darkness and her perch on the upper branches of a tree made her invisible to the two guards patrolling the building.

"What're we waiting for?" Karla's voice rattled in her ear. The twins and José were on the ground, waiting for Chloe's signal to go ahead. Which, frankly, they didn't need. Everyone she could spot seemed mediocre fighters at best. She and José alone could have stormed the place and still come out ahead. But that was the reason she'd chosen this mission.

The CIA didn't often give operatives a choice about which missions to take. Chloe had heard that was because it caused the agents to actually use their brains—a bad thing in their line of work. Top operatives, though, were given some leeway, unless the job came from the boss. No one refused the boss. At least, not twice.

Chloe had requested an assignment that was relatively low level, so Karla and Liz had some grunts to wet their beaks with. That had been in November, but she'd expected the delay and used it to train the girls further. For the most part, top operatives only got called when shit had already hit the fan, so for months to go by without getting any missions wasn't unheard of.

Still, if an agent was really hankering for some action, the agency could send them more common grunt work. Chloe had seen more of those jobs in the last few years than any other, since they'd needed to build up José's credibility so he could return. Grunt work didn't really add up to much. Chloe hoped that they'd done enough of it to prove that José was an asset willing to work with the CIA.

"For you to learn some patience," Chloe whispered back. "Though that's obviously not going to happen. We'll storm in fifteen."

"Fifteen?" Karla groaned.

Chloe put away her scope and dropped down from the tree. "Fifteen seconds, genius," she replied, crouching till she was eye level with them. "Just enough for me to tell you that the warehouse has three floors and is littered with grunts. No one, apart from the two guards out front, is alert, so do with that as you will. Both of you will take point while José and I stay back. Now, what's the objective of the mission?"

"Kill the bad guy," Karla and Liz said together.

"Kill the bad guy," Chloe echoed. "How you do that is up to you. But don't expect José and me to step in. We won't. You live or die by your own strengths. If you die, it'll mean I was wrong about you both and I've wasted the last four years of my life." She checked her watch. "Fifteen seconds on the dot. Go!"

Karla looked as if she wanted to say something, but Liz flexed. Her normally blank face showed determination. Karla shot a glare at Chloe before following her sister and disappearing into the forest. Chloe straightened and meant to tail them, but José caught her hand.

"If anything happens to my daughters…" he warned in a low voice.

"This is grunt work, the lowest kind there is," Chloe growled right back. "Plus, I've busted my ass training them for four years. If they still end up dying after that, they wouldn't have survived anyway, and you'll suck it up like a big boy." Then she grinned, bringing out her gun. "The odds are stacked in their favor already. And you and I are here to stack them up more. Now, do you want to stand here or go keep them alive?"

José released her hand, but Chloe stepped closer and smashed her lips against his. "Normally, the concerned father thing doesn't do it for me, but you make it work."

She shot another smile at him before jogging in the direction of the teenage girls.

JOSÉ SHOOK HIS HEAD at Chloe's departing figure. His lips still tingled from the kiss, but he put that aside. His gun slid smoothly into his hand, and he made his way after the girls.

The forest wasn't so thick that visibility was bad. He made them out after a minute. The girls hid behind a tree close to the road, while Chloe hung back a few meters, crouching down. José stopped behind her, watching.

On the other side of the road, the guards that Chloe had mentioned were rounding the corner of the building. Snippets of their conversation drifted across the distance. The twins waited until the guards had their backs to them before stepping out and crossing the road. They moved at a half crouch. Their pace was a slow jog as they tried to move as far as possible without making any noise.

"They're still stumbling every other step," Chloe muttered.

José studied the girls. He'd watched Chloe train them to walk. Coordinating their steps had been the first thing they'd worked on. Now, the girls had mastered walking. It was difficult to notice anything wrong with it close up. However, from a distance, the oddness in their steps was clear.

José compared the image of them now to them at seven, when even just standing had been a problem. They'd threatened to fall with every step.

"They look fine to me," he said. He straightened, though he still kept his profile out of sight. "They're almost at the guards, and we're too far away. Come on."

He crossed the road, ignoring the sound of Chloe following him. The girls had reached the guards. They must have alerted them somehow because the two men spun around suddenly, their guns raised. Unsurprisingly, the men hesitated when they saw the twins. That was their last mistake.

Karla and Liz already had their guns in their hands. The shots were muffled by the silencers. The only sound was the two men hitting the ground with matching holes in their heads.

There are my girls. José nodded grimly. Even Chloe, watching from his side, had nothing to say.

With the guards taken care of, the girls turned back and made their way to the front of the warehouse. José and Chloe followed, careful to keep out of sight. Pressed against the door, Karla peeked inside. Then they went in. José started to follow, but Chloe held him back.

"There are no shots, so they weren't seen. If we go in now, the girls will know that we're trailing them. They'll be more reckless if they think we can save them."

"Isn't the plan to save them?"

"Yes, but if they know that, we'll always be a crutch for them. They'll be half-baked soldiers at best."

"Fine," José said.

He and Chloe hung back for a few minutes until the sound of gunshots shattered the silence. José swore and rushed into the building. The inside was darkly lit, with shadows thrown on the wall. There were three floors, and José could make out some movement on the upper levels. Boxes were stacked across the room, providing more than enough cover for the girls to hide behind. José made them out almost immediately. They were taking on two grunts at the far wall. Even with the distance, they could make out how filthy the men were. They were covered in soot, their clothes patched. They leered at the girls. *His* girls.

José fingered the trigger, but Chloe slapped his hand, exasperated. "Watch, for Christ's sake."

José lowered the gun, pushing past his rage. He finally saw what Chloe had been talking about. The girls had switched to their daggers. Every other second, they lunged at the men. The cuts they inflicted weren't enough to put down the grunts, but they stopped them from using their guns. Other attacks from the men were punished with another cut.

They're playing with them, José realized. They were going to get killed if they didn't stop. The warehouse was filled with more than just the two men. The alarm had already been raised, and more of the filthy grunts were moving to surround them.

José dropped a man that had snuck too close to their backs. He removed the silencer from his gun, and his next shot rang out. The bullet struck almost a foot from the girls, close enough to draw their attention back to the bigger picture.

While Karla focused on the fight, Liz turned back, her eyes widening in surprise when she noticed the other men making their way over.

"Nice," Chloe said. She gestured to some boxes where they could hide but still have a clear line of sight to the girls.

More focused, the girls made short work of the men in front of them before turning to the rest. The fools, like their counterparts, raked their eyes over twins' body. One of the men lingered on the two heads. Then he grabbed his crotch and shrugged.

Karla and Liz must have noticed because they started with him. They lunged, and Karla jabbed with her dagger. The fool tried to block with his gun, but Liz was already stabbing his stomach. The man clutched the wound and fell to his knees. Karla jabbed her dagger into his eye as he went down.

There was a second of silence, everyone too stunned by the ruthlessness to react. José struggled to keep the grin from his face.

"Damn," Chloe whistled. "They must have been practicing by themselves to have the move down that smooth."

The silence was broken when the men all lunged at once. The twins danced between them, slashing at extended limbs and exposed skin. They were always in motion, their two arms working independently of each other. When Liz couldn't block an attack, Karla was there to intercept it so Liz could retaliate. They began a steady retreat, but for every step they gave, the men paid for it. The cuts were shallow, but these guys were obviously not used to women putting up so much of a fight.

José and Chloe took turns picking off the ones that got too close or tried to come at the girls from behind. Occasionally, some of the goons would reach over the railing to shoot at them from the upper floor, only to be dropped by a bullet to the head. One even tumbled over the railing to the ground floor, but it went largely unnoticed in the chaos. The next few minutes were filled with pandemonium as Karla and Liz tore through the room. Finger snaps went unheard through the screams. Karla had a maniacal smile on her face as her dagger flashed wildly. Each swing was followed by a cry of pain or gurgle from a cut throat. Liz, true to form, maintained a stoic expression through it all, but her weapons moved with unerring precision. Her dagger was different from her sister's. It was more suited to jabs and pinpoint thrusts than cutting.

As more bodies fell, the goons finally realized they were running to their deaths. Unfortunately, the realization came when fewer than ten men were standing out of the nearly two dozen from the initial rush. When the last body fell, Karla and Liz were left panting in the middle of the warehouse. Karla's smile grew as she surveyed the ring of bodies surrounding them. Even Liz looked impressed.

"Damn," Chloe said, a grin on her face. "We've actually gone and raised a couple of monsters."

"My girls are not monsters," José protested.

"Hey, I'm not judging." Chloe shrugged. "I love the little bastards as much as you. But a fact's a fact. Look at them. They're practically creaming their pants from the number of people they've killed. That kind of bloodlust? At that age? That's rare. And I know it."

José almost asked how she knew but stopped himself. Chloe didn't talk about her background. All of José's attempts to pry it out had been met with a blank expression—even in the early days when she was still uncertain about whether José was going to kill her or not.

Chloe chuckled as if she could read his mind. Knowing the damn woman, she probably dropped the hint to test whether he'd ask. "Seems like they're ready to move on," she said.

In the middle of the room, the girls had straightened their posture, looking up at the next floor. A couple of grunts peered down at them but didn't shoot. If they hadn't been a bunch of cowards, José would have let them. It would have been too obvious that he'd interfered otherwise.

Liz's expression was puzzled. She scanned the warehouse, passing over the spot where José and Chloe hid.

That one's a lot more perceptive than most her age, José thought.

The girls made their way to the stairs but stopped partway. José glanced around the warehouse and spotted a stack of boxes that'd serve his purpose. He nudged Chloe and made his way to the stack. It took almost a minute to climb to the top, above the third floor, where he had a full view of everything below.

The roof was a few feet above him, with a ledge wide enough for someone to perch. Chloe got the idea immediately and boosted José up. He, in turn, pulled her up. Everything took less than a minute. They were sufficiently settled in when the twins threw the grenade into the second floor.

"You gave Karla explosives?" José asked.

"I gave Liz *an* explosive," Chloe replied. "It was supposed to be a backup, but they were smart to use it now. The fools were already entrenched and waiting. The girls would have been riddled with bullets had they just climbed up."

José said nothing further, but his angry breathing was enough to indicate he and Chloe would have words later. He took his irritation out on the goons, swapping out his pistol for a sniper rifle. This one also had a silencer screwed on, so the only sound came from the bodies he dropped.

Not that it mattered. The grenade had created the same chaos seen on the previous floor, and Karla and Liz danced through the mayhem with their daggers. Beside him, Chloe brought out her own rifle and settled in to pick off the few stragglers.

The grenade had taken out a bunch of the goons, so the fight didn't last long. José and Chloe barely needed to do anything.

While the girls recovered their energy—he would tell Chloe to work on that further; they tired themselves out too fast—José scanned the floor for anyone just pretending to be incapacitated. There was one floor left. The intel the agency had provided said that was where their target would be—assuming the intel was right and there wasn't another exit somewhere. If he was anything like his men, he was probably cowering in a corner like a rat.

When the girls got to the last floor, they found the goons on their knees, their hands raised in surrender. The target had been pushed in front of them, obviously a sacrifice so the rest would be spared. The girls hesitated, surprised. Again, Liz scanned the warehouse, searching for José and Chloe, but didn't see them.

José increased the zoom on his scope, curious about what they would do. Chloe had told them the mission was just to eliminate the target. Anyone that stood in their way was fair game. But now, no one stood in their way.

Karla's lips moved, whispering something to her sister. A second later, Liz nodded, and they both sheathed their daggers. Then they brought out the guns Chloe had made for them, and pointed them at the men.

The fools dove for their own weapons, but the twins picked them off one after the other. Their gunshots reverberated through the building. At last, there were only the scared whimpers of the target.

The girls replaced their guns, and Karla brought out her dagger. Together, they made their way to him.

THE AFTERMATH

CHAPTER

55

MAY 2040

SPARTA HQ, NEW YORK

JOSÉ GLANCED AT HIS WATCH. His jaw clicked along with the clock, and his fingers beat a rhythm on his forearm. He glared at the door.

He could leave whenever he wanted, of course. The AI had made that clear in their meeting the month before. But José had only left once, to tender his resignation from the CIA. The same day, there had been an attempt on his life—as expected. The CIA would not be the CIA if one could just walk away after decades of being privy to state secrets. Still, despite his preparations, he had narrowly avoided being killed. Fortunately, the operatives had made the mistake of attacking him in his home.

José snorted. *Different countries, same fools.*

The next day, he made his way to Sparta and moved into the apartment that came with his position. Apparently his room was one of many available to high-ranking employees—another testament to how disgustingly large the building was.

José had not been attacked since. He didn't know if it was because the agents had tried and been thwarted or—and this was no less likely—if they had given up once they realized he'd sought refuge with Sparta. With what he knew now about the AI, he was tempted to lean toward the latter, but the twins had not managed to pass their information on to the agency, so it was probably the former. After all, the twins were the best the CIA had, and even they had failed.

Though he was generally allowed free rein within the building, he hadn't been able to talk to Karla or Liz since he'd taken his position. He hadn't even been allowed to see them apart from the projection the AI had shown him. He had, however, been provided with the security video of their infiltration attempt.

José didn't remember much of that day. He remembered the rage—*that* was clear—but everything else came in flashes tainted with black and crimson. Maybe that was for the best. When he'd finally come back to himself, it had been because of the blood loss from struggling against his chains.

The AI had spoken to him then, its metallic voice measured. José stopped struggling long before it was done.

José shook his head, imagining an iron box and pushing the memory into it, before pushing both to the deepest recesses of his mind. It was a trick he'd learned from his mentor. In his earlier days, the box method was the only way of getting a quiet night away from the screams. The more he worked in the agency, however, the less he grew to need the box, until it was no longer necessary.

In the month he'd been working for Sparta, he'd been forced to relearn the trick. Now it saw more use than ever.

José shook his head again, checking his watch. *Almost,* he thought. He hadn't been able to see his girls because of the preparations they had to go through for the surgery. José wasn't privy to these preparations, so he didn't know how true they were. He had little choice in the matter.

All that was irrelevant though. He was promised he would be able to see them today.

José glanced at his watch again just as the hand ticked the hour. Right on cue, his door slid open. José, who'd been standing in front of it for the last hour, strode through immediately.

Directions to his destination had appeared a few days earlier on his phone, which had been hacked into as it had the first time he faced the devil AI. José had long since given up trying to block the artificial mind. Over two decades of service as one of the country's best field agents and cyber protectors, and his firewalls weren't worth shit. It was pathetic but of little relevance. That part of his life was over the moment he'd stepped into the accursed building.

José pictured the map he'd been sent. His long strides ate up the distance easily. The turns blended as he walked, each the same as the last. In the month he'd been here, José had learned that the seventieth floor—where he was—and those above were filled only with rooms for high-ranking employees and the occasional worthy guest. As such, the hallways possessed a measure of opulence, with their rich carpets and textured walls. However, the complete absence of any other decoration or fixture showed the token extravagance for what it was. Despite the luxury of the place, the bland uniformity hinted at the militaristic mind behind it: one that wasn't used to—or didn't much care about—an average human's need for material possessions. Frankly, it was the one aspect of the building that José didn't completely loathe.

José turned a corner. There was a guard patrol coming into the passage from the other end, and he forced his face to harden at the sight of them. They hesitated but pushed themselves forward. The guards continued into the hall, eyes trained on José's movement. Unlike the fool who had stopped him a month ago when he'd stepped into the building, there was no evidence of superiority in their eyes or posture. Rather, they slowed the closer they got to him, pressing themselves to the wall to maintain distance before hurrying away.

José's lips twitched. He had little memory of his actions on the day he'd watched the girls' infiltration. The AI hadn't deemed it necessary to respond to his request, but the guards had reacted that way since.

José found the whole thing hilarious. He hadn't had lapses in his memory since his younger days, but what could he have done to prompt such fear? Karla would have been frothing at the mouth in her curiosity. If nothing else, she would want to know how to replicate it.

The thought sobered him up, and he put the guards out of his mind. His steps quickened as he checked his internal map. He turned a few more corners and crossed the threshold of a large metallic door. It was similar to those used to segment the departments on the lower floors, if a bit thicker. Previously, when José had visited the floor, the door had been sealed shut. He'd turned back immediately. Trying to gain access to the other side would have been a waste of his time.

And now he had, but he spared no thought to the fact. Despite maintaining his long strides, a part of him focused on the cameras, situated every few steps and around every corner. He had turned corners only a few times, but none of them were branching passages, nor were there side doors or exits. There was only one path to follow. Gone were the plush carpets and textured walls. Bare stone walls surrounded him on every side. There was only a fine film of dust. It was as if the designer had given up on any pretense of luxury, adopting a more functional approach.

José slowed despite himself, old habits kicking in. Something about all this sent alarm bells ringing in his head. It took a concerted effort to ignore his instincts. José had no illusions about his situation. If he were to be killed, the AI had had a little less than a month to do it. There was little he could have done to stop it. Even if he was being led into a trap, if there was a chance that his daughters would be there, José would keep moving, no matter the risk.

Soon the bland walls were replaced by glistering coats of paint—the nauseatingly white hospitals were so fond of. José slowed down even more, jarred by the abrupt change. There had been no warning or transition; he'd simply turned a corner and been surrounded by white. Half a dozen people in lab coats strode about the halls with an air of urgency, heads bowed over clipboards or brows furrowed in concentration. They had a subtle air of confidence.

How is it possible? José thought, struggling to keep his expression even. Chloe would have been proud of him. He had seen the blueprints of the building. Though its size was incredible, it shouldn't have been possible for there to be an entire hospital buried within the Sparta building. A hospital that had apparently been there for a while.

José stood in the middle of the hallway, back straight, ignoring the people moving around him while he wrapped his head around it. He glanced at the painted walls again, noting the wires running along them. Some connected to cameras, while others slid under doors. Following the design of a hospital, each room had a large transparent window facing the passageway.

José walked to the nearest one. Soon, he was slamming his hands against the partition, his eyes wide. The noise drew the attention of a few lab coats, but José didn't care. His whole being was trained on the body lying on a gurney within the room, surrounded by nearly a dozen men and women in coats.

A body with two heads.

CHAPTER

56

MANAR WATCHED NDIDI as she crossed the threshold of the Sparta building. Helene had flagged her down, obeying a command he'd given weeks earlier when he thought he'd want to see her.

Did he want to see her? He wasn't sure anymore. He'd hoped for her a few months earlier, when he'd received news of Simone's passing. He hoped for her while he'd been in the hospital, and when he'd seen the destruction of his home, and even when his dead mother's voice had begun speaking to him.

Now Manar wasn't so sure. The sight of her brought a flood of memories, but Manar had known there would be. There had to be, considering how they'd ended things.

Ndidi made her way to the elevators, her steps both confident and insecure. Manar had never figured out how she managed to balance those so perfectly, or why she'd be insecure in the first place. The curiosity of it was one of the things that had drawn him to her so long ago. And years later, it still did. Manar didn't know how to feel about that.

"Connect to Mark's computer," he said, his eyes still on the screen. Mark was the receptionist. He would serve as a fitting medium while Manar arranged his thoughts. "Ask him to stop the woman who's making her way to the elevators."

[Acknowledged.]

Now what? Manar thought.

Mark must have gotten the message because his eyes darted around him as if he would suddenly catch Manar looking over his shoulder. This wasn't the first time Manar had used Helene to communicate with the staff, yet they had the same reaction every time. At least they no longer tripped over themselves in fear. That had been annoying.

Mark stood, surveying the near-empty lobby until he spotted Ndidi. He hurried to catch her before she reached the elevators.

There was no going back now. But what should he say? Should he say anything?

Mark would stop her before she got to the elevator, and Manar would have to make a decision. As if on cue, the projection showed that Mark had reached Ndidi and was speaking to her. The man gestured to his desk, probably hoping that Manar had sent new instructions, but Ndidi was firm and refused to move. Manar sighed at her narrowed eyes and set jaw. She'd decided to be stubborn, probably banking on the fact that he was watching and wouldn't throw her out.

Manar hadn't yet decided whether she was right. "Connect to Mark's phone," he said, "and ask him to repeat my words exactly: 'Mr. Saleem is not in the building. He hasn't been in the building since the events of Mayday, for his own safety. I'm sure you understand.'"

[Acknowledged.]

Manar had to give Mark credit. He read the instructions without a change in expression, then relayed the message to Ndidi. Her eyes only narrowed further, however. She said something to Mark, which made him glance down at his phone.

"I need to hear what they're saying," Manar said.

[Processing,] Helene said.

"I've already told you," Mark's voice came through the speaker. His voice was muted and glitched, but it was better than nothing. "Mr. Saleem isn't in the building, and even if he was, nonemployees are limited to the first floor unless they have a visitor's pass. Which, by your own admission, you don't."

"Because I don't *need* a visitor's pass," Ndidi replied. She straightened to her full height, meeting Mark's eyes. "If you would just *call* the man—"

"Like I said," Mark interrupted, his stoic facade hiding his anger, "I do not have the ability to contact Mr. Saleem. If you could just wait, I'm sure I could find somebody who could address whatever issue you might have."

Ndidi closed her eyes. Her chest rose with her breath and stayed there for a couple of seconds before she exhaled. When she opened her eyes, the anger was under control, allowing Manar, even with the distance and the distortion from the projection, to make out grief and exhaustion.

Who did she lose? Manar wondered, leaning closer despite himself. A year and a half ago, Ndidi wouldn't have been able to conceive a reality where she allowed her emotions to be so bare. She'd been so in control of herself that it had taken Manar *months* before he'd been able to draw out a laugh in public. What had changed?

Her gaze took in the lobby and stopped at a security camera. Helene switched the view of the projection so that Manar was once again staring at her eyes. Despite everything they'd gone through, despite the time they'd stayed apart, despite even the distortion of the image, Manar found he could not look away.

"I can't force you to talk to me, Manar," she said. "And, honestly, I never thought I'd have to try. Still, I understand why you might not want to see me, and I don't really have an excuse for it. I *am* sorry about Simone. I thought about rushing over to you every single day, but you and I both know that wouldn't have ended well. I wouldn't even be here except…" She paused, and for a moment, grief and anger fought for supremacy in her eyes. "Except that Bethany's gone, and I need your help to find her."

Manar froze. Well, shit.

She lost someone too, Simone's voice said in his ears, and her image whispered madness in the light of Ndidi's eyes. *But you were too obsessed with yourself to notice, to even consider what she might have gone through during Mayday. Even now, you're comparing her loss to yours and judging.*

"Connect to Ndidi's phone," Manar said, his voice hoarse. "Send her this address."

There was a ding, and Ndidi brought out her phone. She stared at it for a second, then looked back into the camera. "Thank you. You won't regret it."

Manar only hoped that were true.

NDIDI STEPPED OUT OF THE TAXI and watched as it sped off. That bought her a few seconds to arrange her thoughts before she had to go in. Did it matter, though? She'd given CJ and Chad a whole month to have a second, third, and even fourth go at the Gaius files. They hadn't made any headway. She'd had that time to try to figure out what she was going to say. Even the taxi ride had been filled with her pacing. Still, she had nothing.

Though it had taken all of her will to loosen the grip she'd held on her emotions the past few months, she knew it had only worked because she'd caught him by surprise.

At least she was one step closer to him. It should be easier to speak when it was just the two of them—and Helene. Ndidi stifled a groan. How had she forgotten about the AI? She was about to enter Manar's *home*. No time would have been long enough for him to change so much that he wouldn't have hooked Helene up to everything in his house. It was only logical; he saw her as little more than an assistant. Ironically, anyone else on the planet would have told him the AI had long since surpassed its usual bounds—or any bounds, if CJ's theory was correct.

Still, she couldn't have a conversation about Helene if the AI was within spitting distance. She hadn't paid enough attention to Manar's work over the last several years to be able to tell what, if anything, the AI would do. Could she convince Manar to block Helene? *Could* he?

Ndidi took a breath to stamp out her frustration. Worrying herself over things she didn't have the answers to wasn't her best stalling attempt. And it was a temporary measure at best; more so, given that she'd already started to attract some weird looks.

She turned her back to the street and climbed the steps into the building proper. Immediately after the door, there was another flight of stairs that, at a glance, reminded her disturbingly of the ones in the Gaius Corporation. When she focused, however, she found disparities. For one, the stairs at Gaius had been built for a corporation, so they felt sturdy. The ones she climbed now seemed one good march away from breaking off altogether. Ndidi couldn't put her finger on it. It wasn't as if they were particularly corroded or wrecked. However, the entire building, down to the dry flaking walls, gave off the inexplicable feeling of *age*.

Ndidi had to give it to him. If, for whatever reason, Manar's intention had been to disappear, then he'd achieved it. Knowing what she did of him—no matter how outdated it might be—she would never have expected Manar, with his casual arrogance, to lower himself to such a place.

That being said, Ndidi mused, stopping to trace a wire to the small camera nestled at the edge of the wall, *it's good to see his paranoia is still up in force. Hopefully he's lost the pride and nothing else.* It would be a far easier conversation if that were true.

Ndidi continued up the stairs another two flights before she reached the door Manar's text had indicated. She checked once more just to confirm, then raised her hand to knock. The door swung open at the same time.

"What took you so long?" Manar asked. He jerked his head behind him. "Come in."

Ndidi let her hands drop and took a breath as she entered. *Pride and nothing else,* she thought. *Guess it was too much to ask for.*

CHAPTER

57

MAY 2040
NAVAL AMPHIBIOUS BASE,
CORONADO, CALIFORNIA

THE BASE HADN'T CHANGED since DJ had last been there. It would have been weird if it had, after only a month. Even so, DJ strode through the hallway with a sense of wonderment; the base hadn't changed, but *he* had. He had been assigned his first mission—the first stages of it, anyway—and come out with his prize. So what if the bruises hadn't completely healed? All the better to show them off.

Except he couldn't, of course. DJ's grin faltered at that.

It had been a month since he'd infiltrated Gaius and met Ndidi, and while they'd surely kicked the hornet's nest as they'd tried to escape, there hadn't been a peep of it anywhere. It was as if the whole thing had never happened. Which kind of pissed DJ off.

Sure, he understood that the story couldn't get out until they'd hammered out all the facts. But still, couldn't he brag about how he'd had fifty guards on his tail, and none had even come close to catching him? That's the sort of shit that'd get him out of morning exercise for at least a month.

"So," DJ asked, "anything I should know about?"

Christy shrugged. "Apart from the fact that we were assigned to a new beta team, nothing much."

Olsen hadn't technically sanctioned Christy to join the op, so she'd had to return to the base immediately after the Gaius stint. DJ *had* been sanctioned, so he'd been able to stay an extra month until CJ and Chad admitted that they'd hit a dead end. It was up to Ndidi now.

"Please tell me the leader isn't as much of a dick as Bradley was," DJ groaned. He couldn't handle another Bradley. Well, he *could*, but he doubted Olsen would be there to save his ass again. He wouldn't even want the admiral to. DJ couldn't help but feel as if he lost something every time he and Olsen met.

"I haven't seen him yet," Christy replied, "but from what Kyle and the twins say, they're not so bad. We can probably manage until we're off the first probation."

After basic training, a squad was on probation for six months while they audited missions with more established teams—the alphas and betas. After the first probation, depending on the recommendation of their mentor team and their performance during the exam, they could be recognized as an official team and given soft missions to further wet their feet. Most recruits referred to that as the second probation because the missions given were little more than fetch quests that no official team would take.

Since they'd been switched from Bradley's team to a new one, DJ wondered which review the higher-ups would use when evaluating them. Being downgraded to a beta team probably didn't bode well.

"So, you ever gonna tell me what we were doing in Silicon Valley?"

DJ stumbled and then caught himself. He glanced at Christy uncomfortably. *Well fuck.* He should have seen this coming. It was a risk to involve her in San Jose, but he'd needed an extra pair of eyes, and he surely wouldn't have asked Kyle or the twins.

DJ forced a chuckle. "What do you mean?"

Christy rolled her eyes. "I've already figured out that whatever you and the other chick did in there is top secret or whatever. I haven't heard a peep about it on the news or anything. But seriously, you weren't gonna say anything?"

DJ looked away, scratching his head. One benefit of being an airhead was that he could live as he pleased without guilt. It royally sucked when it backfired. But she was right; he hadn't told her much of anything when he'd asked for her help, and she hadn't asked any questions. And he'd used her without thinking about how being left out of the loop would make her feel. In her shoes, DJ would have been going mad with curiosity.

He glanced around. Luckily, it was that brief time of day when the hallways weren't crawling with sergeants. "You know what? Fuck it," he said. So what if he got reprimanded? He couldn't *not* tell her, especially when she was looking at him like that. An overview, at least. Something that was going to come out sooner or later. "It's about Mayday. We needed something from Gaius to help track the person who did it."

There, DJ thought, pleased. *That should be enough. And I didn't say anything about the AI.* He couldn't tell her everything, no matter how much he trusted her. At least now she knew about as much as he had a month ago.

Christy was silent, her eyes indicating deep thought as she considered what he'd said. DJ glanced at the watch CJ had insisted he wear. It was almost time for his briefing with Olsen. He remembered the last time he'd been to the admin block and almost groaned at the distance he still had to cover.

"Listen, Christy, it's cool that you're taking time to consider what I've said, but I kinda have a thing to go to, so…"

Christy shook herself back to Earth, but her brows remained scrunched in confusion. "There's just one thing that doesn't make sense."

"What?"

"Why you?" she asked. "Why did the higher-ups pick you to retrieve whatever was so important? Why didn't they send Bradley or one of the other alpha teams?"

Because Bradley is a colossal fuckup, and my brother hacked the government, so the higher-ups were trying to recruit him in exchange for dropping his charges and keeping his mouth shut, DJ thought, the words on the tip of his tongue.

"I don't know," he said instead, grimacing. "It was part of the deal I made with Olsen for getting me out of the shit with Bradley." That at least wasn't a total lie.

"So, what now? Is it over?"

Not unless Ndidi can convince Manar to check if his AI is running bonkers and dropping planes from the sky.

"I don't know," he said. "Probably? I mean, I hope so, but I'll know more after I meet with Olsen in"—he checked his watch and blanched—"fifteen minutes."

"Well, shit! You'd better get a move on then."

DJ forced a smile. "Yeah, thanks. We'll catch up more when I'm done." *But literally about anything else.* The last few minutes had left him more mentally exhausted than the whole previous month.

He jogged away with an awkward wave. Luckily, Christy had already turned away and didn't see it.

"Now," DJ muttered, "let's see what Olsen wants."

DJ WASTED FAR MORE TIME than he would have liked trying to recall the route to the admin block. The first and only time he'd been called there, he'd had a guide and was understandably distracted by the possible consequences of his insubordination.

Hard to believe that whole mess had led to this point.

Unlike the last time, he passed through the wide, expansive courts without a glance from any passersby, hurrying into the first of the many hallways. Even within the building, there were very few people milling about, but all of them outranked him by at least three stars. Luckily, they paid him no mind, so he was able to hurry past without trouble.

Locating the admiral's office was another issue. DJ first had to find the court-like room where his case had been resolved and retrace the steps he and Olsen had taken until he found it. He knocked tentatively.

A voice barked from inside. "Boy, if you don't get in here after keeping me waiting…"

DJ grimaced and let himself in. The room was as small as he remembered—little more than a regular sergeant's office—and yet it seemed to shrink further in the presence of the man seated behind the desk.

"Damn," DJ muttered. Olsen was doing the whole aura thing. He still didn't know if there was a trick to it. Normally, the man looked and sounded like a genial grandpa—if your grandpa had a physique most linebackers would envy—but when he got pissed or just wanted to scare you, suddenly he was every bit the admiral the legends made him out to be.

It took DJ's breath away. The man's aura *literally* made it difficult for DJ to breathe. This was doubly annoying since he was winded from spending the last few minutes jogging to get there. It was only the second time he'd been on the receiving end of it, and it didn't get any better.

"You're late," the admiral said.

DJ didn't respond, gritting his teeth against the pressure. He hated the feeling it brought out: reverence for a *person*. The whole concept left a vile taste in his mouth. DJ felt a glare form on his face, despite himself.

Olsen chuckled, and all at once the pressure fell away. DJ almost stumbled from all his muscles relaxing at once. His glare left his face, if not his eyes, and he moved further into the room.

"It seems like you grew some balls in San Jose," Olsen said, meeting DJ's gaze. "Be careful that you temper that with wisdom."

Fuck you too, DJ thought. He stopped a foot away from the visitor's chair. Olsen didn't offer the seat. *Okay then.*

"I'm going to ignore your tardiness because we have far more important things to talk about," Olsen continued. "Now, the boys at the lab have been cracking their heads over that piece of hardware you sent a couple weeks ago. And while it's funny to see them stymied for once, it doesn't bode well when the best and brightest in the government can't crack something. It makes some people jumpy about national security and whatnot. You still with me, boy?"

DJ's gaze flicked from Olsen to the chair in front of him and back. *Fuck it,* he thought, and lowered himself into the seat. *Much better.*

"Yeah, I'm still with you," he said.

DJ had sent Olsen a copy of the hard drive immediately after the Gaius stint. He hadn't wanted to. He still wasn't completely sure he trusted Olsen, but he couldn't exactly say they hadn't found anything. Plus the hard drive had impressed Olsen enough that he'd approved DJ's request to skip training and stay in New York an extra month.

When his brother had failed to break the code, DJ had figured the navy would too. Olsen had confirmed that when he called for him. After all, if they *had* been able to break it, DJ's part in the whole thing would have been over.

Olsen stared at DJ with an unreadable expression, and DJ stared back impassively. He hadn't felt the need to act out and deliberately piss someone off since high school. He'd forgotten how much fun it could be. Who cared if the admiral could take everything from him and make his life a living hell? It was *his* fault for acting like a jerk.

Besides, if Olsen flipped out because DJ had taken a seat, their relationship wasn't meant to last, anyway.

"We took the disk to the boys at the CIA to see if they'd fare any better. They didn't. But while one of our guys was there, he got an interesting tidbit about an agent of theirs who'd recently resigned. Had the whole building going out of their mind because of what this agent knew."

DJ scrunched up his brows. "Okay… What does this have to do with me and my brother?"

"Nothing, probably," Olsen admitted, "but my gut's telling me to tell you anyway, so you're gonna sit there." He narrowed his eyes, probably remembering that he hadn't actually asked DJ to sit. "And listen until I'm done."

"Fucking senile old men," DJ muttered under his breath, then returned to full volume. "Fine. What's the big deal about the former agent?"

"Not him personally. His conjoined daughters, Karla and Liz."

59

MAY 2040

SPARTA HQ, NEW YORK

THERE WAS A CRY OF OUTRAGE, and José spun toward it. A pudgy-faced man in a lab coat was waddling toward him, his face red. José wasn't sure if the man was angry or simply wasn't used to such abrupt movement.

"Who are you?" the man asked as he neared, his voice carrying all the indignation of a fly. "What do you think you're doing?"

José forced calm into his tone, but there was an undertone of violence when he spoke. "This room," he said, pointing to the window. "Where is its entrance?"

The man took a step back, thrown for a moment by the unspoken threat. Then his indignation spiked, and with it, his foolishness. "What business is it of yours?"

José went very still. It wasn't a difficult thing to do if one knew how. People were constantly moving, even when they weren't. Their chests rose and fell with each breath, and their muscles trembled. They fidgeted even when calm. Most people didn't consciously pick up when these things stopped. Yet such stillness was likened to corpses and death. It unnerved them at an instinctive level.

This time, however, the intimidation it inspired was purely a by-product of the effort José put into stopping himself from staining the pristine walls with the imbecile's blood.

The man took another step back.

"Where?" José growled, meeting the man's eyes.

The fool pointed down a different passage. José held his gaze for a moment longer before striding away. The fool had caused a scene with his outburst, stopping nurses and doctors alike. Fortunately for them, none made an effort to impede José as he passed.

He turned the corner and found the door. It was locked. Must everything in this place try to keep him away from his daughters? José let out a shout, slamming his shoulder against the door. It didn't work. On his second try, there was a flash from one of the security cameras above. Beams of light spilled out, forming a giant female head. Currents of electricity crackled in the space where it floated, running through its system and culminating in its eyes, which shone a brilliant yellow.

José resisted the urge to flinch. *Those eyes.*

[Is there a problem, José Olvera?]

Once again, José forced himself to remain calm. "What are you doing with my daughters?"

[In line with our agreement, Karla and Liz Polova are undergoing separation surgery.]

Now? José thought. He forced the worry down. Anxiety narrowed the mind and left room for error. He couldn't afford that when dealing with this… this *thing.* He had been told that he'd be meeting his daughters today. Directions had even been provided. The door had been open when he'd reached this floor, and it had closed behind him, meaning the AI had been following or at least tracking him.

Yet José had not been informed that his daughters would be separated today. Why? Was it another attempt to control him? If so, to what end? José had already accepted the contract. Despite every heinous act he had committed—and those he probably would soon—he was a man of his word.

"Why wasn't I informed of the procedure?"

[It was not needed.]

Not needed? They were his *daughters*. The AI stared at him impassively. José realized it would be impossible to argue with the thing. Apart from his girls—and, to some extent, Chloe—José didn't consider himself overly sentimental about anyone. In his former line of work, such things got people killed, if not through hesitation, then when the agency inevitably deemed you unnecessary. José made his decisions based on a mixture of logic and feasibility. But there were exceptions. Adopting a pair of conjoined twins while on the run in Russia was neither logical nor practical, but it had been his greatest decision. How could a thing of numbers and codes understand such things?

It would be stupid to argue with such a creature.

"Why was I called here, then?" José asked. His eyes lost their glare, and his muscles relaxed.

[Stand by,] the AI replied.

"That's it?" José said, failing to hide his surprise. The AI said nothing. Its form flickered, and it was gone. José released one breath, then another. He had truly fallen far if he could be summoned like a pup to its master.

He went back to the main hallway and the window that looked into the room. A few people gave him passing glances. Perhaps they picked up on the violence in his eyes or had seen him with the AI, but no one was foolish enough to approach him. The space beyond the window was designed much like a hospital emergency room, if slightly larger. It contained only a single bed. The men and women that had surrounded it earlier were now positioned around the edge of the room. Mechanical arms, four in total, detached themselves from the walls and stretched toward his girls.

José frowned. Surely the AI itself wasn't performing the surgery? Then José noticed a man who stood apart from the others, fiddling with a pair of surgical gloves. He was taller than the rest. The hair beneath the surgical cap was blond, and he had strong bones. He moved confidently, every motion self-assured. He flexed his fingers, and the arms responded. José observed the metal monstrosities more closely. The end of each one was in the shape of a hand. The man flexed his fingers again but in a different pattern, and this time only two arms responded. Another flex, and the other arms responded. The man nodded to himself.

There was another flurry of activity as the other doctors scurried about with last-minute checks, but José's attention was drawn to the arms. Such technology wasn't new. Mechanical cranes had been in use in construction for generations. Fine-tuning the arms to be controlled without a vehicle was the natural next step. However, it was the first time José had seen the concept applied to medicine. Granted, it wasn't his field, but such technology was bound to be revolutionary. The fact that it wasn't bothered him. If such things weren't used publicly, there must have been a problem with them. He had no desire to entrust his daughters' lives to them.

But did he have a choice?

It was a grating thought, but José had never been one to shy away from those. He'd lived within Sparta for close to a month, so he knew, more clearly than he had during his first meeting, that he didn't have the power to take his girls back by force.

But even if he did, did he *truly* have a choice about whether or not to cancel the whole thing? If he took them away, and the girls discovered the opportunity that had been taken from them, they would loathe him—definitely Karla, if not Liz. And what if the AI refused to nullify their arrangement? He would still have sold his life away—a second time—without anything to show for it.

So no, he had no choice but to trust that the devil AI would complete its part of the deal.

Throughout the hours of surgery, that proved to be a constant refrain.

JOSÉ HAD BEEN TASKED to apprehend a target for questioning. It was supposed to be a routine pickup. José had tracked him to an underground gambling den that used a butcher shop as a front. He hadn't been high enough on the ladder to just storm the place, so he'd been forced to wait into the night.

He'd spent hours crouched in a corner of the butcher shop while the butcher worked his trade.

The surgery reminded him of that night.

One of the other doctors nodded to the gloved man, who flexed his fingers again. A robotic arm stretched far from the rest, setting itself directly above the twins. Their heads had been moved apart and strapped to the table. The arm settled in the space between. Another flex, and a beam of light shot from the forefinger to the bed. The gloved man strained now, drawing his finger downward. The metal arm mirrored the motion, and the laser dragged downward. The beam didn't scorch the bed, but there was the permeable smell of burned flesh when it touched skin.

José forced himself to still. Though his knowledge of the human body was limited to its softest parts, he'd forced himself to ruminate about how the surgery might be done. If the girls were truly to become distinct, separate individuals, it was only logical that they'd be separated at the middle. That was the only way new organs could be attached. Lasers had long since replaced old-world scalpels because of the accuracy they afforded, though this was the first time José had seen one used in such a way.

The separation was done quickly. The beam was only a hair's breadth wide: more than enough to cut through bone and tissue, but not wide enough to cause excessive damage to the system.

While this was being done, a bald man with thick glasses that covered his face better than his mask donned another pair of gloves. A different set of arms detached themselves from the far wall, stretching quickly to the bed. This time it was more difficult for José to maintain his stoic expression. His brows lowered into a frown. There were now eight metal arms waving around the room.

Was this really necessary? Weren't they more likely to lose control of them all?

The laser cut a line through the body, down to the pelvis. Immediately, the new set of arms drew to one side and pulled away one half of the bed, along with one of the girls—Liz. She stilled in a way that a living being shouldn't. Despite the anesthetic, her chest had been rising and falling steadily. But now there was nothing.

José suddenly recalled one of the most frequent problems cited when doctors had refused to perform surgery on the girls: they shared a heart. José's frown deepened, and it became considerably harder to remain standing.

The doctors had considered this, however. Like a choreographed dance, the previously useless group by the wall split into two, five to either side. Each group went to a gloved man, surrounding him. The arms around Liz moved frantically now, and one of them extracted something from a nearby case. The bald man leaned over Liz, his glasses—no, goggles—glowing a dim green. He directed the arm through Liz's left side, where she'd been separated. He held it motionless. Each of his nurses held a box open around him. Two of the three remaining free arms flitted among them, grabbing things from the boxes and going back into Liz.

A minute passed like this. José was sure that they had lost control. But the bald man never looked up from Liz, and the original arm remained motionless while the rest flitted about. José's eyes burned through the glass as he strained to see something, *anything*, of what was happening.

A few seconds later, he got his wish. Almost imperceptibly, Liz's chest began to rise and fall.

José let out a breath he hadn't realized he'd been holding. He stared at Liz a moment longer, blinking away the burn in his eyes, before pulling his gaze toward the opposite end of the room.

There, a similar scene repeated itself. The other gloved man, the taller one, had his mechanical arms darting around the cases his nurses were holding. His movements were fast but not as frantic as the other had been. As such, José was able to make out what he pulled out during each pass of his arms: thread. José watched his fingers next and realized their movements were that of a man sewing. At some point, he too had donned a pair of goggles. He fixated on Karla's body, his fingers pulling and pushing while the mechanical arms followed their motions perfectly.

They're sewing the nerves to organs, José realized. When Liz was detached, she'd been without a heart, so the first object the bald man had grabbed was likely the synthetic heart. He had held it in position while he sewed the nerves, veins, and arteries to it. After that would come the other replacement organs.

The blond hadn't had to deal with an absence of a heart, so it was likely he was already on another organ. Through the whirlwind of arms darting around, José could see one staying motionless inside Karla, lending credit to his theory.

The glasses must be X-ray goggles, then. X-ray technology wasn't anything new. José had used it himself and found it paired well with armor-piercing bullets. Still, none of the X-ray tech he'd used provided enough clarity for surgery. And the *deftness* that using such a technology would require for such delicate work.

José was impressed. The man seemed to have everything under control, his movements quick but self-assured. José turned to gauge the progress of Liz, just in time to see her chest rise high enough to lift her body from the bed. Though the anesthesia and the restraints made it impossible for her to move, her muscles were tensed as if in a seizure. The bald man gaped at her, his mechanical arms perfectly mirroring his confusion.

A low whine emanated from somewhere within the room, growing louder until it surrounded his world. It overpowered the din of a dozen marching feet in the hallway, of a hundred different conversations, until it was the only sound he could hear.

Liz dropped to the bed. Her chest fell and did not rise again.

NDIDI WALKED INTO THE ROOM and immediately sighed. The run-down building had convinced her that Manar had learned to rough it, a concept that would have been completely impossible even just a year back.

"Nice place," she muttered. Admittedly, this was her first time in a New York apartment. Ndidi was pretty sure they were supposed to be small, but this looked like two normal-sized rooms joined together. With the bed, the room would not have looked out of place at a hotel.

Manar raised his head and made his way to the bed. Ndidi followed slowly, still glancing around. Cables ran along the walls, flowing into a closed room that was off to one side. Ndidi had seen something similar in his old apartment. She was surprised Manar would build an outlet for Helene in what she thought was a temporary apartment. Did he actually plan to live here permanently?

"What happened to Bethany?"

Ndidi turned to Manar. He sat at the edge of the mattress, his eyes boring into hers. The sight was familiar enough to almost make her smile through her nerves. Manar abhorred small talk and treated it as he would treat a mentally disabled person on the street: ignored or, when forced to confront it, regarded with mild disgust.

For a moment, she met Manar's eyes before her gaze flicked away under its intensity. That hadn't changed either. She focused on the bags under his eyes and frowned. She noted the redness of his skin, the wrinkled clothes, and his ruffled hair. It was the first time she had seen him so… worn.

Is this because of Simone? she wondered. His mother had been the only woman—the only *person*—he'd spoken of fondly while they'd been together. But Ndidi knew they'd become distant while Manar had immersed himself in designing Helene for Sparta. *I didn't think anything could affect him this much.* She pushed away a flash of bitterness. She'd once thought *she* had had that effect on him. Fortunately, she'd quickly grown out of that delusion.

"Well?" he asked, his voice worn. Ndidi risked his stare. It was intense but nowhere near as intense as it had been. His eyes had lost their brilliance, shifting to a darker, duller green. He looked worse than she felt.

Ndidi sat at the lone table, one of the few other furnishings. "We're not sure. It's not only her. Lots of people disappeared on Mayday. There weren't any signs of them having left, nor signs of them arriving somewhere. They just disappeared without a trace."

Manar sat straighter on the bed. Ndidi saw a hint of curiosity in his gaze. She grew angry, before resigning herself to the fact that he would be more interested in the challenge before them than the harm that had potentially befallen Bethany. Manar wouldn't be Manar if he'd felt anything else. But that didn't mean he didn't care. It was a struggle to remind herself of that.

Plus why he was helping didn't matter, only that he did. Ndidi reminded herself of that too.

"Where was she when she disappeared?" he asked.

Ndidi took a breath. She told him everything that had happened during Mayday. Kate had given her more information when she'd returned to the Centre, but it was the first time she was consciously piecing everything together and relating it.

Somehow, actually saying it, *reliving* it, was worse. In her mind's eye, some parts were clear: the crash that had distracted Ndidi from her work, the moment Kate had called, the conversation afterward. Other parts were blurred: the café she'd been in, the people, the means she'd used to get back to the Centre. Others still were blocked out altogether, like her immediate reaction to the news. Ndidi had always thought she'd felt anger. It was such a constant now, it had to have started then. But honestly, she hadn't been sure.

Saying it, though, she was forced to remember even the dimmest parts to paint a picture. That somehow made it more real. She remembered the heart-wrenching feeling of loss, the grief, the despair, and then the nothingness—which was somehow worse. Now she knew the anger had come after. It had simmered the week she'd waited for news, then surged on the day she'd met Dr. Cloney.

Manar listened silently. Occasionally he would wince as though he'd been scalded, but his expression always smoothed over before Ndidi could ask. When she finished, his eyes went distant. Ndidi left him to process it. She took the time to compose herself and distracted herself by glancing around the room-turned-apartment. There were some minor details she'd missed earlier, including a small black device at the center of a wall. It was no bigger than her thumbnail and blinked a faint red light every few seconds.

Somehow, she knew that the device was related to Helene. Was the AI watching now? Did it recognize what she might have implied in her story? The sight of the room had jarred her enough that she'd forgotten to check as soon as she'd entered. Now that she'd seen it, she couldn't seem to tear her eyes away.

Fortunately, a motion from Manar brought her out of her thoughts.

"So," he said, "why exactly did you come to *me*?"

MANAR STARED AT NDIDI. Her eyes went over him, and he stayed silent under her inspection. He had no illusions about how he looked. He could have cleaned up before she arrived—Helene had tracked her almost all the way—but he'd decided not to. Partly because of how pointless it would have been, partly to prove he didn't care. Now his pride would not let him regret it.

After all, *she* needed *him*. Manar would have to analyze his feelings about that. He'd learned early in life that genius inevitably attracted people who associated with him because of what they could get. Ndidi had never been like that. It was one of the things that had attracted him to her in the first place.

When did that change? Why did that change? Why couldn't she have left him alone? Why couldn't everybody leave him alone?

Because you do not deserve the rest, Simone's voice said. *You think solitude will bring you peace, but you're wrong—one of the many times you've been wrong.*

Manar struggled to keep his expression straight but couldn't stop a grimace. It was wrong this time though. The voice spoke when he communicated with others. If he were left alone, at least for long enough to plan out how to silence it…

That thought struck more than all the others, and he shied away from it. *I don't want to silence it,* Manar realized. No matter what it said, it was still his mother. He could not bear to lose her again. Not so soon. Maybe not ever.

Ndidi finished her inspection. Distantly, wearily, Manar wondered if she found what she'd been looking for. Her eyes glanced somewhere to the far wall, and she licked her lips.

Finally, she took a breath and her expression stilled. "Before that, can you isolate the room?"

Manar frowned, confused. "My room is always isolated. You know this."

Ndidi's eyes flicked to the wall again. This time Manar followed her gaze to Helene's relay, and his brows furrowed further. Was that what she was talking about? She wanted him to keep out Helene? Switching off the relay might stop the AI from projecting a hologram, but she was practically wired into the sockets.

"Can you," she said again when she saw he'd understood her meaning, "isolate the room?"

Manar narrowed his eyes at her, curiosity once again overcoming his exhaustion. He justified it. If nothing else, the faster he listened to her, the faster she would leave, and he would be left to his thoughts.

There is no peace there, Simone whispered.

He picked up his system from the edge of the bed. He'd ended up keeping the one the nurse had given him while in the hospital. Though he'd been limited in what he could access while in the hospital, he'd at least been able to amp up its processing power until it rivaled a brand-new computer. After he'd been released, it had just been a matter of amping it up further to meet his needs. It had saved him weeks or months having to do the same with another system just so it would have enough power to deal with Helene's codes.

It took Manar a few minutes to access her source code, which made him frown. He hadn't remembered putting in so many encryption protocols, and his master authorization glitched and wouldn't be recognized. Was the system too busted to deal with the load after all?

He was forced to override most of her defenses manually, adjust the source code to isolate functions throughout the building, and then rebuild the firewalls. On a whim, he also built in a backdoor mode so he wouldn't have to go through the stress of creating it later, if the need ever arose.

He sighed after a few minutes. "Done." His exhaustion had dissipated for the few minutes he'd tackled the codes, but now it came back in full force.

Ndidi had stayed silent while he worked, aware of how much voices irritated him. She glanced at the relay. Its light had gone out as Manar had known it would. Now it was little more than a dud. Useless.

Like you were, a voice whispered. Manar frowned. That had not been Simone—yet it sounded… familiar. Like he'd heard it before, often, at some point.

You were useless, it continued. *You couldn't stop them. You couldn't protect us. You couldn't even keep your promise.* The voice sounded young, like a child before puberty. Its familiarity scratched at Manar.

A memory tickled the back of his mind.

"Thank you," Ndidi said. Manar snapped his head back to her. The vague memory fled, and exhaustion tightened its grip.

Did it matter that it had sounded familiar? His schizophrenia picked voices from his past. It was mostly Simone, but Principal Gurung came once in a while, as had Joan, reconstructed from Simone's description of her. Should he wonder about *all* his delusions?

"What do you want from me?" Manar sighed, suddenly tired of the whole thing.

Ndidi looked taken aback by his tone but forged on regardless. "I've accepted that it might not be possible to get Bethany back. That she might be…" She paused and breathed out. When she continued, anger no longer tinged her voice. "That she might be dead. But a lot of people still need the closure of knowing that whoever did it, whoever caused Mayday, paid for it."

"It was an accident," Manar said. He closed his eyes and stretched out on the bed while he waited for her response. He already knew that Mayday hadn't been an accident, though he didn't actually have any proof.

"It was *not* an accident." Ndidi spoke with steel in her voice. "I met a former employee of the Gaius Corporation, one of the programmers responsible for designing the AI, and he assured me that hacking into the Gaius AI was impossible."

Manar sighed. *This* was her proof?

"And," she added, "I also have this." Manar forced open an eye to see her holding out a hard drive. He'd reacted to the hint of triumph in her voice, but now, though she still looked smug, there were hints of uncertainty in her expression. Hints that people less familiar with her wouldn't have been able to pick up on. "It's a hard drive from one of the vehicles that crashed on Mayday. You should be able to track the hack from here."

Manar sat back up with a grunt. He glanced once more at the hard drive but focused more on her. The uncertainty was stronger on her face now. "Where did you get this?" he asked.

"Does it matter?" she retorted, defensive.

No, he thought. It didn't. Not really. Nothing did.

"Yes," he said.

Ndidi met his eyes. It was what she did when she was trying to hide her emotions and expected him to take her by her words. "We got it from the Gaius Corporation."

"We?"

"I had some help." Surprisingly, Manar felt a faint stir of jealousy. But it died almost a second later. He didn't really care. *She* might have thought he did though. Ndidi had always been straightforward, so this at least explained why she was so roundabout in her replies.

Though it didn't answer why she had asked him to get rid of Helene. He posed the question to her and watched her uncertainty grow.

Again, she took a breath, and her expression evened out. Manar had forgotten how effective that trick was. She had had little cause to use it until the tail end of their relationship.

"Chad—he's the former employee of Gaius—and CJ, my… associates have already looked into it, but they couldn't find any point of entry for the virus. They've been at a dead end for months."

Manar sighed. Ndidi wasn't normally this roundabout. Had so much changed in a couple of months? "Again—"

"I'm getting there," Ndidi interrupted sharply. She took another breath. "They hadn't been able to get anywhere after a month. So CJ had an idea. What if there *wasn't* a point of entry because there wasn't a hack in the conventional sense." She met his eyes, gauging his expression. "Since Gaius was among the top AIs developed, he wondered how possible it would be for one AI to have communicated with another and convinced it to cause Mayday."

Manar blinked at her. AIs… communicating? Manar was tempted to dismiss the possibility entirely, end the farce, and send her out. But the theory *did* have some merit, even though the programmers' failure was probably due to their own ineptitude. He followed her train of thought to its obvious conclusion.

"You think Helene did it," he said. That, he dismissed immediately. She was obviously grasping at straws in her vendetta, but at least he understood her reasoning. If AI communication were a thing, there were precious few AIs that could manage it. At least it explained why she'd asked to isolate from Helene.

"I know how it sounds, and I understand if you don't believe me," Ndidi said, her tone both pleading and defensive. "But it's the only thing that makes sense, and it's our only lead to finding Bethany. And even if we're wrong, if you checked out the hard drive, you might be able to find something Chad and CJ missed."

The last sentence was obviously meant to flatter him, but Manar just didn't care enough for it to matter. He considered her arguments and admitted to himself that he was curious about whether such a thing was possible, but… did it matter?

Bethany was almost certainly dead. Ndidi was definitely driven by grief and was seeing conspiracies in every corner. And he… he just wanted to be left alone.

Once again, Manar considered everything that Ndidi had told him and made his decision. He realized he had made it since he'd seen her in the Sparta building.

"No."

CHAPTER

61

MAY 2040

SPARTA HQ, NEW YORK

JOSÉ STARED AT HIS DAUGHTER'S unmoving form. His mind staunchly refused to process what he saw. What he saw was obviously *wrong*. The bald man snapped out of his confusion, and his mechanical arms moved feverishly. But it was clear from his face that he was out of his depth. The nurses clustered around him, whispering as if their presence could somehow bring Liz back.

José's expression was flat and his back straight, but he found he could not tear his eyes away from the scene. Not even to assure himself that the same thing hadn't happened on the other side of the room. Maybe that was the better choice. José had never shied away from hard truths, but there were limits. There were some things that a father should not have to face.

Not once, and certainly not twice.

Two of the arms stretched along Liz's chest and pushed. Once, then twice. Electricity danced along their length with each compression. Liz rose with the force but otherwise didn't move. The concentration on the doctor's face gave way once again to confusion, then to fear, then to despair. He glanced at the ceiling, head darting as if expecting retribution.

José was confused by this until a *presence* descended on the ward. The lights in the room and the hallway flared brightly—some enough to bring sparks. The bald man ducked, his face twisted into a grimace. He stared at a spot in the wall, his limbs trembling, mimicked by the four mechanical arms.

Beams of light spilled from a device at the end of his gaze. The contraption was as small as his thumbnail and pulsed a slow red. The light, a dark blue, congealed within the room, hovering in the space between the two doctors and his daughters. This obviously wasn't José's first time seeing the form the AI took. However, something was different. Its presence blanketed the room and extended beyond it to where José stood. It was a struggle to stay on his feet beneath its weight. It was as if every other time the projection had manifested for him, it had given only a scant percentage of its attention to the task. And now, for some reason, it had focused its full awareness here.

The other doctor—the tall one—spared just a glance at the projection before focusing on his own work. However, sweat beaded his head where there hadn't been any before, and he moved just a bit faster. The other doctor and all the accompanying nurses stared at the AI with a mix of apprehension and fear. The demon ignored all of them, turning to observe Liz's unmoving form.

A second later, the projection disappeared in a flash of electricity that led to the bald man. The fool jumped in surprise, then again when his mechanical arms started to move on their own. In sync, three of the four limbs dove into his daughter. José had a wild impulse to bang against the glass and rave against the AI, to scream at it to stay away from his daughter. José buried the thought in the same box that he had locked others like it. For better or for worse, he had given his word to serve, however little he trusted his employer.

If the demon managed to save his daughter, though, giving away his life would have been worth it.

The sole arm that remained outside twitched, then immediately snapped to a nurse. To the man's credit, he didn't immediately bolt, though that might have been because it had been so fast. Even José had almost missed it. The arm retracted with a length of twine, which it fed into Liz. The other arms remained motionless inside the body. Then the first retrieved another length of twine from the startled nurse. Again and again, until the arm was a blur, darting in and out faster than José could follow. The other nurses, showing the first sign of initiative, fed their own twine to the other, refilling the box the moment the mechanical arm depleted it.

A minute passed as José scanned his daughter for any change. But when it came, the change was from the AI. One of the arms within Liz retracted and hovered in the air for a moment. Then, like the other, it snapped toward another startled nurse, snatching up one of the synthetic organs before retracting. José did not know how the AI discerned its work without eyes, but he didn't much care.

This new series continued for what was surely an eternity, with one arm fetching twine and the other organs. In one of her many lectures, Chloe had once told José that the maximum time a human body could be considered "dead" and still be revived without brain damage was twenty minutes. José was sure that twenty minutes hadn't yet gone by since the twins had been separated, but his girls had lived all their lives with only half their bodies. Did Liz only have ten minutes before her system shut down? Was it already too late?

José shook away his thoughts and forced his eyes from the scene. He stepped away from the window entirely and peered down the hall. It was deserted, which surprised him. He hadn't noted the silence. Maybe it was for the best.

José crossed to the other side. He rested his back on the wall and slid down until he sat on the floor. The tile was cool to the touch. He could still see into the ward, and that was all that mattered.

The tall doctor had slowed his motions. He glanced frequently across the room, but his expression no longer hinted fear, and his motions were even more confident. His arms moved lethargically, poking and prodding at odd intervals while his goggled eyes scanned his work. It was obvious that he was done with his part—or thought he was—and was just cross-checking for errors. His inspection drew José's eyes to Karla, but unlike her sister, he didn't see anything concerning. Her muscles were loose, and her chest rose rhythmically. Every once in a while, her fingers would twitch.

And suddenly José had another realization. Karla would never forgive him if Liz did not survive. And he wouldn't blame her. It didn't matter that he had made this choice because of them. She'd always thought that he blamed them for his lot in life. For years, he had let them believe that, even fostered the assumption, in the hopes it would make them stronger, that they would better be able to protect themselves. Maybe even leave him if the situation ever called for it.

But now, without Liz to temper her sister, that hatred would drive them apart. Worst-case scenario, Karla might even take his life to avenge her. And José didn't know if he'd stop her.

A cry of surprise drove him away from his thoughts. The cry had come from one of the nurses surrounding Liz. The fool jumped again at something, shifting his position enough for José to have a clear view of Liz.

Just in time to see her chest thump.

José was on his feet and in front of the window in an instant. Liz's chest rose again. It was unmistakable. José kept his expression still by sheer force of will. His head swiveled to Karla, whose breathing remained steady, then back again to Liz just in time to catch another thump. It was frequent enough now for José to notice that the beat came at the same time as a twitch from one of the arms. Two were still within her body, but the ones outside were still hovering, as if waiting for something. Electricity crackled down their length every few seconds, followed by a thump.

It was obvious what was happening, and José watched the scene with bated breath. His earlier musings washed over him, and he cursed his weakness. He was not so little a man to take his own life. The world had taken too much from him to give it a free meal. And if it deigned to take one of his daughters, José would meet it standing, as any man should. Then he'd spit in its face.

The thumps slowed, coming every two seconds instead of one. The electricity along the arms intensified. There were hints of dark blue and yellow in the most concentrated sparks.

A minute went by. The beats were the only sound in the room. Like the low whine that had heralded her death, the thump of his daughter's chest and the electricity crackling in the air grew in pitch until they consumed José's world.

Until they enveloped him and his own heart fell silent. Until his *being* pulsed to that rhythm.

José straightened his back, and his expression hardened with his acceptance. *So be it,* he thought. The pulses of current stopped, and the arms retracted from her body a moment later. Liz's chest rose once more, fell, and rose again.

José slammed his hand to the glass as if the action would help him see better. If nothing else, it helped him keep his feet. His gaze burned through the window and locked on to his daughter's unmoving form.

Her chest thumped again.

Not daring to hope, José glanced at the mechanical arms, but they were all hovering in the air. The bald doctor stood in stupefaction, as did the nurses. Through this all, Liz's heart kept beating. José restrained himself with effort. He had already broken down once. It would not do for it to become a habit. José allowed a smile.

A moment later, the robotic arms fell limp, snapping the bald doctor from his stupor. As before, electricity traveled visibly into the space between the two gloved men, forming the AI's cephalic shape. Every eye was drawn to it, including José's. Its presence was not as intense as it had been earlier, but it drew the eyes regardless. José had loathed the part of him that succumbed to that impulse. Now José gave his employer the respect it was due. It was not a sudden reverence that drove him to it—José was not so weak willed for that to be the case. His eyes took in his two daughters, separate yet alive, distinct in themselves. Something they never thought possible.

It was not sudden reverence that drove José. But the AI *had* kept its word, to the point of interfering when necessary. José had no illusion that it had done so from mercy or any other such nonsense. He still contended that a machine would never understand such concepts. However, the AI had done it and given back his daughters.

And José would honor that. For a time, at least.

He had traded his own life for a chance of bettering his daughters', but if his girls chose a different path for themselves… well, José had always found it difficult to deny them anything.

First, if they wanted to return to their former strength, they would need to grow accustomed to their new bodies. For that, they needed Chloe.

CHAPTER

62

MAY 2040
OKAFOR AUTISM RESEARCH CENTRE, NEW YORK

DJ STRODE THROUGH the tiled halls of the Autism Centre and shivered. He *hated* hospitals. The Centre wasn't technically a hospital, but why did it look so much like one?

DJ had noted it the first time he'd been there with Ndidi, but he had been justifiably distracted, observing it in only an absent kind of way. Now, though, the similarities just popped. The floor tiles were a glistering white to match the walls. The air smelled like bleach. *Bleh,* DJ thought. *Are they trying to scare kids away?* Nothing freaked a kid out more than the needles in a doctor's office—any kind of doctor's office.

His shoes clacked on the tiles, which irritated him. Sneakers weren't supposed to clack. Yet, somehow, the floor made it possible. Fortunately, he didn't have far to go before he reached the computer room.

"You see, Gaius?" he muttered into the air, twisting the door handle. "Everything's easier when it's labeled."

The room was a cold slap to the face. He shivered immediately. He had prepared for the cold and worn a woolen sweater over his T-shirt, but it was a wasted effort.

What did they do, turn it up when they saw me? DJ groused. What sort of yeti was comfortable like this?

Ndidi turned at the sound of the door and somehow looked as if she'd aged a couple of years since they'd seen each other the week before. Her face was drawn, with bags under her eyes. Yet when she stared at him, her gaze burned with the same suppressed anger he'd become used to. It was still jarring, though, from the image he had of her as a kid.

But apparently, shit happened. She wore a scarf over her neck, and a jacket. Her arms were crossed over her chest to conserve warmth. CJ, huddled over the computer, also wore a sweater over his clothes, but he'd gone one step further and put on his favorite SD Padres baseball cap and gloves. He nodded at DJ, eyes shining with relief. DJ let out a wry grin. Between Ndidi's silent brooding and Chad's need for constant conversation, CJ must have been in his own personal hell.

With that thought, DJ's eyes were drawn to the last person in the room. Chad smiled widely at DJ. All DJ noticed was that the man was the only one in the room with a simple shirt and jeans. And his hat, of course.

"Nice of you to join us," the cowboy said.

DJ flipped him off. "Unlike the rest of you guys, I had to fly in from Coronado. My flight was delayed."

That wasn't strictly true, though. Most of his time had been spent convincing Olsen to let him leave. The admiral was convinced that DJ was wasting resources on a dead-end theory and a dead-end team. DJ had "politely" told him to get his head out of his ass because this "dead-end team" was the only one that had provided a lead on Mayday. Obviously, *that* hadn't gone over well. But his point had been made, and Olsen had been forced to concede. The rest of DJ's time had been spent tracking Christy down. He'd explained that he might be gone for a couple of days, which meant he'd also had to explain why she couldn't come.

That also hadn't gone well.

"It's fine." Ndidi sighed. "As long as you're here." She waited until DJ had crossed the room and taken a seat beside his brother before she spoke again. "As you guys have no doubt concluded from my disposition, Manar said no to helping us review Helene's code."

DJ had called it. It was a stretch to hope the ex would help. "So what now?" he asked.

"I don't know," Ndidi answered, gritting her teeth. "I don't know."

Well, shit. DJ nudged his brother. "What are our options, bro?"

CJ shrugged. He played with his gloves, picking at the threads, a sure sign that he was uncomfortable. "I… um… already tried to see if there was any evidence of… of communication from… um… Gaius's end. But I was not able to find anything."

"Wouldn't it be from the mainframe?" Chad asked.

CJ shrugged again, "At the time when… when Helene would have… *communicated* with it, the hard drive we took would have still been… um… connected to the mainframe. So it should have showed."

Chad nodded and settled back into his seat. He didn't offer anything else. DJ grimaced. He was just the muscle. CJ and Chad were the ones who knew how any of it worked. If they didn't have a clue, they were all screwed.

And Olsen's gonna bust my ass. DJ's grimace deepened and he stood. He clapped his hands, snapping everyone's attention to him.

"Come on, people," he said, forcing a grin. "We need ideas. Ndidi, whatchu got?"

Ndidi looked up with a thoughtful expression. "We have to break into Sparta and check the codes ourselves."

Chad snorted. Even CJ looked up in surprise. DJ felt his smile crack. "What?"

Ndidi's eyes shone with determination, and she turned to better face everyone else. "I don't think we have much of a choice. If Helene really did cause Mayday, we have to find out. There are millions of people out there who deserve to know. People wondering why their loved ones were killed or taken. Bethany…"

Ah, DJ realized. *This is about Bethany.* Well, he'd learned enough from Chad to know that the girl was Ndidi's driving motivation, but he hadn't thought that it was *this* bad. Sheesh.

The silence stretched while Ndidi collected herself. DJ cleared his throat. *Better to nip this in the bud.* "We're not assaulting Sparta, Ndidi," he said softly. *At least not yet.* His last meeting with Olsen was still fresh in his mind. Infiltrating Sparta would be decidedly harder than breaking into Gaius.

"Well, what do you suggest?" She sighed.

DJ looked at CJ. "Hack it?"

Chad snorted. "We can't hack Sparta. No one can. Its security is run by Helene, Manar Saleem's brainchild. It's what every AI aspires to be."

DJ looked at Ndidi. "Ask Manar again?"

Ndidi shook her head slowly. "He was very clear about it. He's not going to help. I've never seen him like this. He didn't take the death of his mother well."

Her voice softened when she said that, but DJ couldn't bring himself to care much. Olsen's words rang clear in his mind. They couldn't attack Sparta. That would be bad. CJ caught his look, and his eyes asked a question. DJ just shook his head. Explaining it wouldn't matter. They wouldn't believe him. *He* hadn't believed it until he'd seen the videos.

But what could they do? What were their options? He sure as hell didn't know. CJ had a blank look on his face, as did Chad. Ndidi wasn't going to be much help for a while, and DJ couldn't really blame her. This Manar dude sounded like a dick.

"How about this, yeah?" he said. "There's no need to do something rash when we don't have to. We've been running at full speed for the last couple of weeks. Why don't we take one more week to chill and see if we have any ideas by the end of it." He stared at each in turn.

CJ nodded in an absentminded way. He, at least, always had DJ's back. But he would have to go to school anyway. Olsen had been able to pull some strings, but unless his brother dropped out entirely, he had a lot to catch up on. DJ did not envy him that.

Chad sucked on a tooth and shrugged. "I have a shitload of codes—forgive my French, ma'am—I've been pushing off anyway." He looked at Ndidi. "But I'd like to keep a copy of the drive anyway. I reckon at some point I'll wanna poke at it a little more."

Ndidi nodded, but she stared at DJ consideringly. When she spoke, her voice was weary. "What are you keeping from us? Why can't we attack Sparta? Gaius worked out fine."

DJ gaped at her. "We almost died in Gaius. Several times. And if I hadn't come along, you sure as shit would have been caught. Not to mention that we only squeezed by because we could hack into their cameras. Think that's gonna work on Sparta?"

Chad snorted again. It was really starting to piss DJ off.

"It doesn't matter anyway," he continued. "Just know that Sparta is a different beast than Gaius. It's not even an option for us to attack it. Not as we are. And not directly."

CJ looked up. "So... um... we can... we can attack it indirectly then?" His voice was perfectly expressionless, but DJ had long learned to read the little twitches he gave off when he was excited.

"What do you mean?" Chad asked.

CJ wilted under the attention at first, but then he squared his shoulders and looked up, focusing on everyone's foreheads when he looked at them. "Um... I mean, if we cannot attack directly, then we can... we can attack indirectly, then, yeah? An AI as... um... as advanced as Helene must have support structures. Can we... can we not attack those?"

DJ grinned.

CHAPTER

63

MAY 2040

SPARTA HQ, NEW YORK

KARLA WOKE. She blinked under the harsh lighting, hissing in pain. Absently, she brought up an arm to shield her eyes.

Her *right* arm. Karla stared at the limb in confusion. Had she not awakened after all? Her mind felt sluggish, as it had the few times Chloe had drugged them, supposedly for their own good. She was awake enough to realize that, yet she dreamed of… a metal arm?

What nonsense is this? Irritated, she dropped the right arm and flexed the fingers on her left. She waited, but there was no accompanying twitch to show that her sister had heard her request. That irritated Karla more, and she turned her head to glare at Liz.

The pain blinded her immediately. Darkness claimed her.

When Karla woke again, she stayed very still. Her mind was still sluggish, so whatever drug she'd been given hadn't completely worn off. That normally wouldn't have been enough of a deterrent, but the pain from her attempt at movement was imprinted on her mind. Still, she flexed her fingers again, and again she received no response. So she stayed still, her eyes open, and took stock of what she could. It wasn't as if she could do anything until Liz woke anyway. The longer she stayed, the less groggy she was, and the more she remembered.

The memories came slowly but intensely, and with each one her anger grew. She remembered running, turning corners to keep ahead of the pursuit. She remembered being hunted by men with eyes of hardened steel. She recalled the panic they had caused as she was herded like a sheep to a cage. And then she remembered the cage: a steel box similar to an animal's pen. And then the voice—flat and emotionless—that seemed to come from everywhere and nowhere.

"We will die here," Liz had said. But they hadn't died. Why not? What did the demon voice have planned for them?

Once again, Karla flexed her fingers and waited for Liz's response. The minutes dragged slowly by. Karla periodically tried to contact her sister, but again and again, there was no response. Her irritation only grew. If she had been awake for this long, her sister should be too. Why didn't she respond?

Karla steeled her mind, then snapped her head to her right. She braced for the pain but there was none. Maybe she hadn't awakened at all. Perhaps she was still dreaming. If she wasn't, then where was her sister?

Now Karla felt true fear. She blinked to clear her vision, but the space where her sister was supposed to be lying remained empty. She flexed her fingers desperately, searching for a response. There was no answering flex, but something twitched.

Karla traced the motion with her eyes and stopped when, instead of the extended torso that connected her to Liz, she saw that metallic arm again. Her desperation sputtered and died, giving way to confusion. She flexed her fingers again, but this time the fingers on her *right* side responded as well as those on her left. Her confusion gave way to panic, but Karla stamped it down immediately.

What is this? she wondered, still staring at her arm. Thoughts of her sister were still present in her mind, but she pushed them back. "What is this?" she said. Or tried to. Her voice came out as little more than a croak. Absently, she licked her lips, but her tongue was as dry as her throat felt. Her thirst wasn't enough to distract her, though. She pushed the feeling away.

Karla stared at the arm in wonder. It was made from some sort of dark-grayish metal. The color contrasted with her skin and connected to her shoulder in a mesh of wires. In fact, wires ran abundantly down the length of the arm to its fingers. Each was connected to a pocket on the arm, but some ran into a rectangular crevice on her biceps.

Karla flexed the arm. There was no response. She grunted, feeling a flash of irritation before she tried again. Again, there was no response, and this only stoked her anger. The third time she was able to flex the fingers, but the movement was disjointed and in the wrong order. *How am I supposed to communicate with Liz if the arm will not obey?* Her thought trailed off as another took precedence.

If she had a right arm, then what had happened to her sister?

Karla lifted her eyes to the space where her sister was supposed to be and scowled, forcing anger to drown out her fear. What had the demon done to her sister? *How* had it done it? They shared a heart, so they couldn't be separated without killing them.

Unless, of course, Karla had been given the organ, leaving her sister without one.

No, Karla thought sharply. That was impossible. If one were to be sacrificed, Karla would have been the obvious choice. She was far too impulsive. Liz had always said so. That was why Liz tempered Karla's impulses and drove her actions. Without Liz, there would be no one to keep her in check. Without Liz, without her sister, who would understand as she did?

José?

Karla cursed in Russian. If she could have spit, she would have. It was his fault they had been sent to Sparta. Oh, how Karla cursed the day he had given that order. She cursed Liz for agreeing to it. She cursed herself more, though. If she had been faster, if she had just paid more attention to something other than her bloodlust, they might have reached the exit in time. Her sister would still be with her, and she might have had the chance to punch José. Just once, she would have liked to do that.

"Damn," a voice said from across the room. "You're awake. I'd hoped I would get to slap you to make you come to."

Karla's head snapped around. She blinked at the familiar brunette, watching numbly as she strode toward her. If she'd been able to think, she would have wondered what Chloe was doing there.

"Are… are those tears?" Chloe grinned when she was close enough. "Didn't think you had it in you." Her hand flashed, and Karla felt a sharp sting on her cheek. A second later, there was another sting on her other cheek. *This bitch,* Karla thought.

Immediately, her pain gave way to rage. Her hand—her left—snapped upward. Chloe batted it with the same mocking grin on her face. In the same motion, her hand flashed, and there was another sting on her face. This one was hard enough that Karla tasted blood in her mouth. The rage blinded her, and Karla gave in to it fully.

The anger she'd felt as she'd run with her sister, the despair of being trapped in the metal cage, and her fear of her sister's fate all poured out in a wave. Her fists flew, deliberately at first, then blindly when Karla lost herself in the emotions. Her punches were raw and without focus. In a real fight, she would have been dead ten times over. But Liz was not there to berate her, and José was not there to punish her. Chloe, though, found a way to slip past her swinging arms every few seconds, and Karla's cheek would sting a moment later.

This continued until Karla had expended her rage. Her limbs fell lifelessly to the bed. Exhausted, she glared at the other woman. She had little strength to attack again or defend. Not that it would have done any good. She hadn't even been able to land one good punch.

Was this how worthless she was without her sister?

"You don't know how much of a favor you've just done for me," Chloe said, that infuriating grin still on her face. "I had a bunch of pent-up frustration. It seems like you did too. As a thank you, I'm gonna let you in on something you probably would have wanted to know before you went all batshit crazy. You ready?" Her eyes sparkled with mischief. "Your sister's still alive, you idiot."

"No," Karla croaked in Russian. They could not have been separated and both lived. Her sister was dead.

Chloe grimaced at the sound of her voice. She reached for something by the side of the bed and tilted it to Karla's lips. When the cool liquid touched her tongue, Karla was forcefully reminded of how thirsty she was. She lapped at the water and growled when Chloe pulled it back after a few seconds.

"No need to let you throw it all back up," Chloe muttered as she straightened. "Now, about your sister. Don't know which bonehead decided it was a good idea to put recently separated twins in different rooms, but yeah, that's where she is. Just came from there."

Karla stared at Chloe. She was dressed in black leather pants and a matching jacket. Karla had never seen her in anything else—even when she and Liz were barely seven years old.

Chloe had caused more pain than José ever had. Yet Karla had never had the same hatred for her as she did for her father. Maybe because of the beatings. Chloe's punishment had never been malicious. It had always served a goal. Even just then when Chloe had slapped her, it had obviously been so that Karla would have an outlet for her emotions. Karla didn't think Chloe would lie—not about this, and surely not to her.

"Where is she?" Karla asked.

Chloe thumbed a direction, "That way. Like I said, I just came from there. She isn't awake yet, though. According to José, her procedure was a lot dicier than yours, so she'll need some more time before she comes to."

"How is it possible?"

Chloe's expression softened. "I'm not rightly sure, honestly. It involves a bunch of stuff I'd rather not have to repeat when your sister joins us. You'll just have to chill until then. Or pester José about it and see how far that gets you."

Karla nodded. José had never been the most accommodating type. Not since Yelena, at least. It'd have been more useful to ask a brick wall. One thing stood out, however, from what Chloe had said. It made Karla furrow her eyebrows. "When Liz joins us where?"

"Where else?" Chloe retorted. The mischief in her eyes shone with a vengeance. She threw something at Karla: a black leather jumpsuit. "You finally have a full set of limbs. Time to learn how to use them to kill people."

"Before we start," Karla said, gulping down more water. "Where are we?"

The thought had pricked at her since she became aware of her surroundings. She had never been to an actual hospital, but the CIA had clinics where agents could get patched up. Although Karla had never had reason to go there, she'd caught brief glimpses of them as she and her sister passed by for one reason or the other. The floor here was laid in bright white tiles. The walls were painted the same sickening color. There was a heavy smell of bleach in the air. She was dressed in a white flowing gown and nothing else. She wasn't dumb enough to not pick up what kind of facility this was.

What she wanted to know was what *building* she was in.

Chloe picked at a loose thread in her outfit. "Somewhere in Sparta HQ. Somewhere deep. We really fucked up when we sent you girls here by yourselves. If we'd had any sense, we would have stormed the whole building with tanks. And that might not have been enough."

"Yes, I have already been through that," Karla replied scathingly. "A little too late to reconsider, don't you think?"

"Don't pout," Chloe chided. "It worked out well, didn't it? Relatively at least. I mean, you're alive. And you got a new set of titanium limbs out of it."

Limbs? Karla thought. *Plural.* She threw away the covers, lifted the tip of her gown and stared at her legs. The same sense of wonderment she'd felt earlier threatened to overwhelm her again, but this time, Karla was very aware that Chloe was a few steps away and ready to slap her. She tried to flex her right calf, but it didn't respond. She flexed her right arm. There was no response either. Karla growled and tried again.

Nothing.

Chloe laughed at her attempts. Karla refused to give her the satisfaction of acknowledging her, instead focusing on her arm again. This she already knew could move. It had listened to her when she had attacked Chloe. Karla grunted at the memory. Why, then, wouldn't it obey?

The arm jumped up as if something had burned it, and Karla was able to get better control. She brought it to her face for closer examination. Effort had been put into making the arm resemble its fleshy counterpart, and intricate marks covered its surface. The metal was twisted slightly in an attempt to form the ridges of a toned arm. Even her scars had been replicated, mirror images of the ones on her left arm.

"Glad to see you can actually learn," Chloe said. "I always knew you weren't just the brute you acted like. The nanites need some time to properly adjust to your nerve signals. The titanium arm is wire-connected to nerve or whatever, so it's gonna be a while before you can use it like your left."

Karla nodded absently.

"Tell you what, though. I don't feel like waiting all day. So, if you can put on those clothes within the hour, I'll take you to your sister. Doc says she should be awake by then."

Karla stared at the leather jumpsuit across her lap. In her distraction, her arm had fallen. She willed it to move again, but it stayed dormant. Outwardly, she sighed.

But inside, Karla burned at the challenge.

MANAR STARED BLANKLY at his ceiling while the voices in his head tormented him with their truths. They had become a lot more vocal since Ndidi's visit. Manar wasn't too proud to admit he'd made a mistake. He should never have invited her over.

He had always hated hindsight, but in the week since she'd sat on his worktable, he had cursed himself for ever looking at the projection. The voices had been no help, so eager to torment him that they were speaking over each other. It had been Helene's job to show him the feed. It was pure folly to have paid attention to it. After all, he'd known what the consequences would be. What they always were whenever he interacted with people since Simone's death.

You did it because you're a glutton for punishment, his mother whispered in his head. Though she was right, Manar tried to push the thought away. *You want to suffer for your arrogance.*

You've always been like that, a second voice added—the child's. Manar still couldn't recognize it, but like Simone's, it had become a fixture in his head. For some reason, he found it more difficult to push her voice away than he did Simone's. *It was why you always rushed futilely to his beatings when… took the arak…*

The last few words drifted into static. He felt as if there was a name in there, but he couldn't make it out. It was another peculiar thing about the child. Apart from having no memory of the voice, the names she mentioned always drifted into static.

Why was that? His curiosity stirred at the mystery but died almost immediately.

Manar went over Ndidi's visit. This wasn't the first time he'd done this, and it wouldn't be his last. He was fairly sure his preoccupation with the memory was why the voices were still active over a week later. Everything about their conversation pricked at him.

How possible would it be for one AI to have communicated with another and convinced it to cause Mayday?

Manar still thought the idea was ludicrous. The concept had merit, but if Helene could communicate with other AIs, it would only be due to his recent upgrades. Before Mayday, though she far surpassed every other artificial intelligence in her field, she had just been a virtual assistant.

Then why did his thoughts keep going back to it? His eyes shifted to the hard drive on his table. The little minx had left it behind, and he hadn't noticed it until hours after she'd gone. It was obvious what she was trying to do. Since she couldn't convince him, she was trying to rouse his curiosity to do her work for her. Months back, it would have worked.

But now, Manar really didn't care.

A reflection by the window caught his eye—a small girl dressed in a long gown, her hair covered in a black hijab. The image was gone when Manar focused on it, but it had been unmistakable. A moment later, the child spoke. *If you didn't care, you would have thrown the drive away. You wouldn't be so afraid of it.*

Manar sighed.

KARLA WAS ABLE TO PUT ON the leather jumpsuit within the hour deadline, with only two minutes to spare. In her eyes, this was a failure. Before, she would have immediately put her life on the line to regain her pride, often to Liz's irritation. But somehow, this failure did not grate on her nerves the way others had. Maybe it was because Karla knew that this time, she had had no chance of passing.

Chloe had stayed the whole time, her expression an edge away from full-blown laughter. Karla was not fooled. She'd been led to believe the task was just Chloe being lazy, but it was obvious the foolish woman meant it to be some demented form of training, one that she had not been meant to finish.

That was what grated on her nerves. *The bitch,* Karla thought.

For the first half hour, Karla had struggled to lift the piece of clothing high enough for her to wear it. The other half had been a bit easier. She'd had to order the arm only three times before it followed her instructions. That small success was the only reason she hadn't failed more spectacularly. Whether or not her effort would be enough depended on the bitch.

Karla glared at her now, but Chloe just stared back contemplatively. She shrugged after a few seconds, rising smoothly to her feet. Karla didn't know where she'd found the chair.

"Show me to my sister."

Chloe gestured for her to stand. Using her left arm to balance, Karla swung her left leg off the bed. With one foot on the ground, she focused on her right leg, picturing it joining the other. This was the trick she had learned with her arm. Karla stared hungrily at the leg, waiting for a twitch. But there was nothing. That characteristic irritation bubbled up from within her, but she stomped down the feeling. That was another thing she had learned from her arm.

Chloe watched silently while Karla finally got the leg to respond and then swing to the floor. With both feet under her, Karla was able to confirm something else.

"There is no feeling when I touch something," she muttered.

"I assume it's because there were no nerves there for the limbs to be connected to. You'll have to get used to that."

Karla wrinkled her nose at the woman. She had only been thinking out loud. Who cared why she couldn't feel? Was she supposed to weep like a mewling baby that her new limb was not perfect?

Chloe pulled a cane from behind her and offered it. Karla spat at her feet. She would rather die than let her dignity be reduced to this. The other woman shrugged, turned, and headed to the door.

"Keep up," she said.

Karla stared at Chloe's back. *She must be positively delirious with joy seeing me in such a state*, Karla thought. *May she choke on the feeling.*

Karla half stumbled and half hopped after her mentor. She gritted her teeth and used the rage to fuel her determination. First, she would reunite with her sister to confirm with her own eyes that she was whole too. Then she would lower herself to complete Chloe's training. With her sister by her side, she would master her new limbs in days, then punish Chloe for the disgrace. And then she'd do the same to José, just because.

Like Karla's room, the hallway was also sickening white and smelled of bleach. People in lab coats scurried about in one direction or the other. Some were hunched over wooden clipboards; others were just hunched over. Most stopped and stared when they saw her, then flinched at the violence in her eyes. Some took a step back, shaking their heads as if reliving a bad memory.

Chloe took all of this in stride, ignoring the stares and comments equally. Her steps were measured. Though she had asked Karla to keep up, it was obvious that she kept her pace slow to make sure she wasn't left behind. Karla sneered. The bitch was belittling her. She was probably chuckling as she walked, mocking her.

Karla stopped. She used her left leg to straighten and then, as she'd done in the room, focused on the titanium leg, picturing every motion involved in taking a step. She had done this when she was younger and learning to walk in coordination with Liz. Ironically, Chloe had been the one to teach them the trick.

The people stared at her as if she were a spectacle for their amusement, a new baby learning to walk. Chloe stopped and looked behind her when she noticed Karla wasn't following again. Her expression had been closed off, but when Karla met her eyes, a smirk appeared. The bitch *had* been mocking her.

Anger almost threatened to break her concentration, but Karla stomped it down again. Fortunately, this was something with which she had much practice. She focused on her limb again, channeling the memories of learning to time her movements with her sister's. This time, she was trying to match herself, to be in sync. Always in sync. It was another thing with which she had much practice.

Slowly, the leg twitched. Karla stared at it, ignoring everyone else. There would be time later to make them pay. Again, the leg twitched, then followed the path Karla had played out in her mind.

When her foot touched the floor, Karla took another step with her left leg and repeated the process with the right. It took minutes before it responded, adding to the impatience Karla shoved away. But then it did, just a bit quicker than her previous attempt.

She repeated this until she caught up with Chloe. Her mentor nodded but otherwise didn't say a word. She turned on her heel and continued walking.

Karla stamped down the flicker of excitement she had felt and followed after her.

OUT OF THE CORNER OF HER EYE, Chloe watched as Karla stumbled along. Her customary glare flickered on and off, probably both humiliated that she'd been brought so low and excited about her new leg. It beat the miserable state she was in when Chloe first walked into the room.

Chloe couldn't blame her. She'd thought she'd lost her sister, after all. On the other hand, she hadn't spent the last decade or so pummeling Karla, only for her to be so weak. That would only get her killed. Especially considering how José had bargained their lives away to a demonic AI with mysterious plans. What sort of dick father did that? Though, to his credit, their new mobility would make them stronger. And, in the meantime, she got to train them. She could deal with Liz, but the slaps she had given Karla just made the brunette hungry for more. She loved the girls to death. Hell, she'd practically raised them. But knocking them down a peg or two was always good for them.

Behind her, Karla stumbled. The titanium leg made a racket with every step. The docs assured her that the girls would eventually be able to control the limbs like they did their own. Until then, Chloe would just have to put up with the noise. Maybe she could use the excuse to work on their stealth. Karla would *hate* that—which would make it worthwhile enough.

Karla stumbled again, and her cursing prompted Chloe to turn. Her expression changed to a mixture of mild annoyance and amusement. "Told you to keep up."

Karla glared at her with eyes that promised violence. Then, she looked back at the bionic leg, the concentration evident on her face. Chloe gave her a minute. But when the limb didn't so much as tick, her impatience won.

"Hop if you must. We don't have much farther to go."

Without another word, Chloe took the next corner. Karla cursed up a storm in Russian, but a moment later, there was the rhythmic clang of the leg on the floor. The noise grated on Chloe, but she hadn't been lying when she said they didn't have far to go. She turned another corner and strode into a ward similar to Karla's. A minute later, Karla herself appeared through the door. Chloe stepped to the side, giving the sisters an uninterrupted view of each other.

With much clanging of metal, Karla was at her sister's side within seconds. Chloe was amused Karla still hadn't figured out that the titanium limbs worked best when she wasn't actively trying to control them.

Liz had sat up the moment she saw Chloe, her eyes wide in surprise. When Karla came shuffling into the room, her eyes had widened to the point it was almost comical, and a grin split her face. Liz had still been unconscious when Chloe had visited an hour before. Although there was no way to know exactly when Liz had woken, she had no doubt gone through the same thought process that Karla had.

Yet when she'd stepped into the room, Chloe had not met a blubbering mess but someone who was systematically taking stock of everything around her. Both girls had their strengths and weaknesses, but Chloe would always maintain that Liz's ability to remain levelheaded was the reason they were still alive.

The girls babbled to each other in Russian, blending their sentences in a way only twins could. Chloe let them at it for about ten minutes before crossing the distance and clapping loudly for their attention. Karla looked at Chloe as if she were lower than a bug, while Liz just waited to hear what she had to say. Chloe clapped her hands once more for good measure.

"Reunion time's over, girls. Now we get to the fun part."

KARLA STOOD WITH HER SISTER at one end of the training room, tapping her feet impatiently. Despite the brunette's words, the training did not start immediately, thank the gods. For some reason, Chloe had changed her mind a few minutes after making the high-and-mighty pronouncement. Oh, how Karla would love to wipe the smirk off her face. Instead, she'd spent a day with her sister. They hadn't done much other than compare their "bionics," as Chloe called them, and trade what they remembered from before the surgery. It was enough. Karla found that the arm was easier to control near Liz.

Her sister, however, seemed to have no difficulty controlling her bionics. Chloe had laughed herself raw when she'd heard that. Only Liz's hand on her shoulder had stopped Karla from lunging at the woman. The fact that Liz had used her new arm hadn't really helped.

It was the first time Karla had felt envy for her sister. Why did she struggle when Liz didn't? Chloe had even said it took the nanites time to adjust to the nerves, so why did Liz adjust so quickly? Was this her genius shining through? Attached, Karla had never worried that Liz would leave her. But now, would she stay if Karla couldn't keep up?

Karla hacked, spitting on the floor. Her face scrunched up in disgust. *What weakness is this?* she thought, irritated. As if she couldn't keep up with Liz. Impossible. Even if they didn't share a body anymore, they were one. That had always been their strength.

Karla scowled. Her thoughts had been so *soft* since she woke in her room. Had anyone else shown such weakness, she would have been drawn to attack—if only to beat it out of them for their own good. To think she could be so tainted. Again, she spat on the floor.

"You've gotta stop doing that," Chloe said from across the room.

Karla bared her teeth at her, then glanced at the room's only door and tapped her feet in impatience. Karla didn't know where in Sparta they were, exactly. Chloe had taken the twins through so many turns that Karla had become disinterested. None of them had the casual elegance of the halls they'd infiltrated a lifetime ago. At some point, they had gone so deep that the white paint had tapered off until only rock surrounded them. Yet they had not gone lower, only deeper. No building should be so big. It was unnatural.

Karla had seen Liz counting under her breath, so she was sure they would be able to make their way back. Although she and Liz were separated now, their new limbs came with consequences. It was so like José not to think of such a thing. But although Karla had learned to depend on her sister, she was not helpless without her. And if anyone doubted that, she would prove it with a dagger to the eye.

A scuffle at the door drew Karla's eyes. No one stepped through. Karla's feet tapped harder, and she spat again. "Why do we have to wait for José?" she snapped in Russian.

"Because he's your father," Chloe snapped back.

Karla tapped a finger on the blades by her side. Two now, one for each arm. She would be twice as deadly, if she could get the stupid lump of titanium to obey her. She tapped harder at the dagger, glaring at Chloe. Beside her, Liz tsked, drawing Karla from her thoughts.

"Calm down," Liz said. "What is wrong with you? You know she only tries to provoke you."

Karla almost snapped back at her. It was the shock that broke through her anger. What was happening to her? She knew that she had always been impulsive and prone to anger, but that was because people were so *irritating*. But never her sister. At least, not for something so little.

Karla pushed down her anger and forced her feet to stop tapping. A moment later, there was another shuffle at the door, and José stepped into the room.

Karla's dagger flew to meet him.

JOSÉ CAUGHT THE DAGGER with no change in his expression. Even Chloe raised an eyebrow at that. Karla glared at him, her legs tensed to lunge. Liz snapped at her, irritation in her voice. Fortunately, that was enough to calm her down. Without breaking stride, José made his way to Chloe. She was grinning but kept casting glances at the twins, probably wondering how long until Karla's rage boiled over. The AI had warned him of this, but he'd hoped that his daughter's training would be enough.

"What have you told them?" he asked Chloe. She'd been away on a mission when the girls had infiltrated Sparta. When José had contacted her a week ago, he'd been forced to brief her on everything. Anything less, and she wouldn't have been convinced to follow him. No matter how much she loved doting on the girls, her pride wouldn't let her if she thought she was being used.

José would never admit how relieved he was to have her here. He'd needed a trainer for his girls, but Chloe had always been more than that.

"Just that you're responsible," she answered.

José resisted a sigh. That explained the dagger. Across the room, Karla glared at him. Liz attempted to mirror his expressionless face, but José could still detect confusion in her gaze. He met both equally, holding back his emotions.

The AI had told him they would not remember anything that had happened. He was grateful for that, though it was yet another thing he wouldn't admit. The things he had said would only make them weak. He'd learned long ago that showing affection inevitably led to hesitation, which got people killed. His daughters would outlive him. Even if they hated him while they did.

José turned to Chloe. "Why haven't you started training yet?"

He was surprised when even Chloe lost her smirk. She scowled at him. "I decided to wait for you. I'd *thought* you might want to explain why they've been separated after decades of being attached."

José let her anger wash over him. He would probably hear more of it later, but she should be content that she'd proven her point. He had planned on explaining everything to them—the parts that they needed to know, at least.

José nodded, and the girls took that as their cue to come closer. It was the first time José noticed what they wore. When had Chloe made the time to get them matching black leather jumpsuits? How had she even convinced the girls to put them on?

The girls stopped a foot away. Maybe it was because of the weariness he'd felt for the last week, or maybe he still had some lingering angst, but the first thing he said was, "I'm sorry."

Maybe, if he'd been a couple of decades younger, he might have taken a bit of pleasure from their shocked expressions. But he just sighed. It wasn't what he'd planned on saying, and frankly, he didn't rightly know what he was apologizing for. Still, he meant it.

He knew he wasn't apologizing for separating them. They would only be stronger for it. And they would never have had the opportunity if they hadn't been captured. If José had known this would happen before he'd sent them on the Sparta mission… he would still have sent them. Maybe that was what he apologized for.

It had been in their best interest, but it was unlikely that their minds had not been touched by the horror they'd undoubtedly faced, trapped with the AI. He would consign them to that fate again and again if it meant they would come out a little bit stronger. José had learned long ago that the world did not cater to good intentions, so it did not matter if they hated him for it. He would damn himself and everyone else if it would give his girls just a little bit more edge to survive. He would burn the world if it would let them live just a little bit longer. And he would force them to watch if it made them stronger.

For damning them to that, even if it had been for their own good, maybe that was what he apologized for.

Chloe started laughing. The sight of her clutching her knees as she tried to hold back her mirth cracked José's introspection. Even Karla lost her sneer and stared at the woman in confusion. The laughter lasted another minute, after which she straightened and wiped a tear from her eye, gesturing for José to continue. José cleared his throat, and the girls turned their confused looks to him.

José told them what happened since they'd been captured. He kept his sentences short; that was how he had always given commands. It was vital, now more than ever, that his girls saw him as their commander. He gave no excuses because a commander didn't need to, instead detailing the days that passed as one would read a report.

He skipped everything that had happened during the procedure but explained that their organs were now bionic like their limbs. Even he wasn't sure what that meant, so he didn't dwell on it.

When he was done, the girls stared at him with betrayal on their faces. José's expression hardened so he would not give away how much those looks hurt him.

I did it for you, he wanted to scream at them. *Only for you.*

Karla was the first to speak, and her words threatened to break his will again. "You sold us like cattle?"

"I made you stronger."

"You bartered us like slaves," his daughter snarled. She took a step forward, her hand inching toward her dagger. Liz placed a hand on her shoulder, but Karla shrugged it off, taking another step forward.

José stared her down, making no move to defend himself. This was not the first time he had dealt with his daughter's anger. If he showed even the smallest hint of being intimidated, she would attack. José was confident he would win, but Karla would be out of commission for days, if not weeks, and her training would suffer.

José would have preferred to take Karla into his arms and explain why he'd done what he did, make her understand that way. But he had chosen his path years ago, and going back now would only make him look weak. So instead, he forced a sneer and let a hint of violence leak through his eyes.

Karla stopped immediately. José stared at her until her caution won over her anger, and the fear he had instilled in his girls forced her back toward her sister.

"I made you stronger," he repeated slowly. Then he met Liz's eyes, but he did not lower his sneer nor the violence in his gaze. "Your new organs will help you last far beyond what would kill most men. Your limbs will double your mobility and lethality. And if you learn to coordinate your strikes as you did when you shared a body, your strength will double."

"Always to make us stronger," Liz murmured, and José's sneer almost slipped. Unlike her sister, Liz spoke with clinical detachment, yet somehow her words cut deeper. Maybe because they spoke the truth. José had always chosen to make them stronger instead of giving them what they wanted.

Still, José had never been one to shy away from the truth. "Yes," he said.

"Look at it this way." Chloe grinned. Either she was ignorant of the tension in the room or, more likely, she chose to ignore it. He'd never been able to fully figure her out. "Now you have a couple new toys to play with." She gestured first to the dagger Karla still fingered, then the two strapped to Liz's waist. "And if you follow my instructions, you might get to use them without losing a finger."

Whether by coincidence or by design, her comment eased the tension in the room. Karla spat on the floor, disgusted at the implication that she would lose control of her weapon. Even Liz scowled.

José held Karla's thrown dagger in his hand—thrown from her *right* arm. If he hadn't caught it, he would have lost an ear. He nodded to cede the point. His girls turned their glares to him. The expressions were so perfectly mirrored that José had to force himself to seem indifferent.

"She's right," he said, hardening his gaze. "Your strength means nothing if you cannot hone it. You *will* listen to her instruction, or the loss of a finger will be the least of your worries."

José did not make idle threats, especially when his authority was disrespected. The flash of fear on their faces showed that they knew this too.

"Apart from the novelty of having to control extra limbs," he continued, "the bionics are attached to each of your nerves. The nanites they use will take time to acclimate with your systems. You'll have trouble controlling your bionics until they do."

Chloe snorted but tried to cover it with loud coughs. Karla reddened by the second, glaring death at the woman.

"What happens if one of them can't adapt?" Chloe wheezed amid her coughs.

José frowned and observed his daughters. His face lit up in understanding.

Karla's right arm was spasming. It twisted on itself, tightening in a way that would have been excruciating if the nanites weren't just connected to the shoulder nerves. Despite this, its fingers stayed perfectly loose, so every spasm was from the wrist up to the forearm. José wouldn't have thought much of it if Karla's left hand wasn't also constantly moving. Her fingers, at least. They were constantly clenching and releasing in a futile attempt to vent her anger. In contrast, Liz stood with her arms loosely at her sides—deliberately so they were always in reach of her weapons. Once in a while, her left would spasm like Karla's, but she'd quickly get it under control. Whatever difficulties Karla had, her sister obviously had less.

José shook his head at both. Liz's proficiency was most likely because the AI had personally taken over her operation. Whether the AI had added something or its skill had just been that high, her nanites were adapting faster to her body than Karla's. José started to say just this but reconsidered. It was better that Karla did not know. The challenge would spur her on as she tried to catch up. Maybe Chloe would be able to make something of that.

He could make her job even easier though. His face twisted in contempt, as if disgusted at the very thought. He made sure Karla was looking at him when he spoke. "Then she is weak."

Karla's eyes widened, hurt momentarily overcoming her anger. José steeled himself at the sight, keeping his sneer in place. Karla tensed, and her muscles tightened as she prepared to lunge. José held her gaze but noted that her right arm had stopped its spasming. That was interesting.

Previously, no matter her anger, much of Karla's effort would be spent trying to convince Liz to join her, as one couldn't move without the other. As far as José knew, these were the few times the sisters were not on the same page. Their unity was their strength and his desire. So, José thought, it was ironic that the only time they were divided was when deciding whether or not to kill him. In those cases, Liz had always allowed her sister to waste her anger before grounding her with implacable logic.

Now, Karla glanced at her sister, slowly seeming to realize she no longer needed Liz's approval to attack him. Still, he didn't try to defend himself. If Liz hadn't been in the room, Karla would already have been subdued.

Liz placed an arm on her sister. In the time since José had walked into the room, Liz had calmed Karla again and again in this way. However, those times had been when Karla had been merely angry. Now her rage was further compounded. The hormones that she had previously shared with her sister now influenced her all at once. His words and the hurt she felt from them had been the spark to light her fiery rage. He would not take them back.

Karla tried to shrug off Liz, but her sister only tightened her grip and barked a question in Russian: "Are you the dog then?"

José watched with interest as the simple question settled Karla. She lost her snarl, and her face took on an expression that bordered on shame. The phrase pricked at him until Chloe whispered in his ear.

"Remember that time I called her a dog?"

José nodded. He had been there for that. It had taken weeks for Karla to stop attacking Chloe on sight. It was good that Liz had seen the power in it and used it to ground her sister. A second later, Karla eased beside her. She didn't lose her glare, but it was tempered now.

Liz kept her hand on Karla, and José nodded to it when he spoke. "It is good that you still maintain your unity. That has always been your greatest strength. Once you get full control of your bodies, you will be a force to be reckoned with. Until then, from the display I have seen today, you're little more than mewling babies ripe for the picking."

Chloe chuckled, and Liz's hand tightened on Karla's shoulder. Surprisingly, Karla herself showed no reaction. She seemed lost in her thoughts.

That's new, José thought. He gestured at Chloe, who clapped her hands sharply and met the girls' stares with a grin.

"You guys seemed to doubt José when he called you babies. I'm going to show you what he meant," she said, her eyes glinting with mischievousness. "Tell you what. If either of you can land a punch on me, I'll let you take off the leather."

The girls looked at each other, then back to their mentor. "We can attack you?" they asked in unison.

Chloe's grin widened. "Come at me."

FUCK ME, DJ THOUGHT, sighing. It took an effort to keep his eyes straight head as he stepped out of the car. Ndidi didn't seem to have the same problem. Then again, she hadn't been the one driving. Not that driving was the problem. The problem was he'd made the fucking trip between Coronado and New York *twice* in less than a week. It was a short trip by flight, but it added up.

He could have stayed in New York for a couple more days, of course. He didn't have to report to Olsen until the end of the week. However, Ndidi had insisted. She'd even come out of her shitty mood to do so, and like the sucker he was, he agreed.

He grabbed his backpack from the backseat, then picked up Ndidi's. That there was only one made him suspicious. That this one was so light was doubly suspicious. Weren't girls supposed to overpack just to piss guys off? He rattled it. There was no way her change of clothes was in there. It was almost as if she didn't intend to stay more than a day.

The thought made him chuckle. *Gonna take a whole lot of bullshit to get me to make this trip again tomorrow.*

"It's smaller than I thought it would be," Ndidi commented, taking the proffered bag.

DJ gaped at her. Small? He looked at the entrance to the naval base. The gate alone stretched thirty feet, and she called it *small*? How big did something have to be to impress her?

Now he was certain he never wanted to meet Manar, just for his own masculinity's sake.

Ndidi shrugged. "Thought it would be like when I went to the White House." She adjusted her suit cuffs and started making her way to the gate. DJ's jaw threatened to unhinge as he stared after her.

"Who the fuck says they've been to the White House that casually," he muttered. "And then she walked away. Who does that?" He hurried to catch up to her. "You don't diss a man's building. Or compare it to the White House. It's kind of a dick move." He lengthened his strides, ignoring the weird look she threw him.

DJ brought out his name tag and ID, sighing. He approached the building at the side of the gate. Luckily Ndidi had the sense to stay at his back. "Ho, the gate," he said, then mentally ticked that off the list of things he'd always wanted to say.

The guards were decidedly less impressed. "That's far enough, son," said a middle-aged man with a face like a brick. "Actually, far enough was before you drove onto government property, but whatever. Gonna need to see some ID for you and your friend."

DJ glanced at the ID card raised above his head and then back at the man. *Maybe get some glasses first, old man?* It was at the tip of his tongue to say, but Ndidi nudged him, and he covered it up with a cough.

"How's this gonna work then, if I can't get closer?" He was two feet from the side building and the partition there. If he had a bomb, those two feet wouldn't do jack shit.

"Stretch?" said another voice from within the building. DJ turned toward him. He was far younger than his colleague and apparently had a rich sense of humor. When the old guy didn't offer any other options, DJ sighed, and Ndidi nudged him again.

DJ stretched, and one of the guards took the tag and ID.

"And for your girlfriend?" Brick-Face asked.

"Any minute now," DJ replied.

"What's that supposed to mean?"

That you'll get it in a minute! DJ thought. He was way too tired for this shit. He ignored the guard. Ndidi nudged him, but he ignored her too. Instead, he brought out his phone and shot a text to Christy.

"I'm having my balls busted here. Where are you?"

Christy: "I'm here. I'm here. Chill. Kyle wouldn't shut up asking about where I was going."

DJ pocketed his phone. "She said she'll be here."

"Who?" Ndidi asked.

DJ started to answer, but the younger guard suddenly exclaimed, "Hey, you can't be here!"

There was the sound of yelling from the other side. He couldn't hear the exact words, but he guessed Christy had arrived. And she was pissed that he'd dragged her to the gate. Naval bases had the same problem as other government compounds: the buildings were unreasonably far apart. That meant the training area where the recruits bunked wasn't exactly close to the gate. DJ would know since he'd been trekking it for the last couple of weeks.

The grumblings continued for a couple of minutes before Brick-Face came back to the partition. He gestured for DJ to come closer, then handed him a name tag, ID, and visitor's badge. "You've been verified," he groused. "Your friend will have to wear that badge as long as she's on the base, or she could be picked up."

DJ nodded, pocketing his shit and handing Ndidi hers. He explained that someone would come and get the car in a minute, but they could have it checked for bombs if they really wanted. Brick-Face scowled.

The roadblock swung open a second later, and the pair made their way through the side gate into the base proper. DJ saw Christy immediately. And, indeed, he was in trouble.

"Hey," he smiled wryly, lifting his bag over his shoulder. That usually worked to get him off the hook. She smacked him in the head. DJ just sighed and gestured. "This is Ndidi Okafor. She's, uh…"

What *was* she?

"She's a friend," he finished lamely.

Christy stared at him weirdly. She waved two fingers at Ndidi, which obviously confused her. Ndidi took it in stride, smoothly retracting her offered hand.

"The guards said something about a car parked outside?" Christy asked.

"Yeah, I have a guy coming to get it." DJ had stopped by the family's café to check out how it was doing, get the week's finances to give to CJ, and get free valet services from one of the employees.

Christy nodded, and her eyes narrowed, as if remembering her earlier anger. "Why didn't you just ask Olsen to call up the gate about your friend?"

DJ had been hoping she wouldn't ask that. "Because I didn't tell him I was bringing Ndidi." He forced a grin through his exhaustion. "Thought it would be a fun surprise." *One that I'm 90 percent sure he's going to bust his top about.*

Fortunately, Christy didn't poke further, and the three of them made their way deeper into the base.

Initially, the walk through the base was silent. Christy, as he'd hoped she would, seemed to pick up on his mood, so she left him alone. Instead, she bugged Ndidi, which was just as well. It would be best if they got to know each other a bit more.

He glanced at the buildings as they passed, but the attempt was halfhearted at best. What had seemed like monuments of architecture months earlier were now… well, buildings. Buildings that actually did look kinda small. *Damn it, Ndidi.*

As if responding to his thought, Ndidi laughed. DJ glanced at her, remembering what she'd been like since getting back from seeing the ex. That Manar guy had obviously done a number on her. DJ wouldn't ever call Ndidi the most preppy person—except for when she had started mentoring CJ. His memories from that time were spotty, but since they'd met up in Gaius, she'd always seemed like a coiled spring, tensed and holding so much back. He'd seen the rage bubbling beneath the surface though. It wasn't difficult to guess what she suppressed. Not that he could blame her; everyone on the team had their own reasons for being there. DJ was trying to skip latrine punishment and keep his brother out of jail. Ndidi was there for revenge and to get one of her kids back. Chad… well, DJ wasn't sure about Chad.

The point was, Ndidi always had an aura of determination toward their goal—and perhaps some anger. She could be afraid or nervous or even confused like she was in Gaius, but she always pulled it together and got over it. DJ respected that.

"I shouldn't have compared it to the White House," Ndidi said, a small smile on her face. Her voice dragged DJ out of his thoughts enough to see that they had passed into the recruits' area.

Damn! Where the fuck did I go that I didn't notice we'd gotten so close? At that time of day, most trainers were releasing their charges, so recruits were trudging to their bunks all around them. The conversation was muted, as most of them were too exhausted to talk. That didn't mean they didn't spare the energy to stare at Ndidi. On a military base, a woman in a suit was generally someone you didn't fuck with. The few recruits that were in the way hurried out, glancing not-so-subtly at the group as they passed.

They could have used a different route to get to the administration building. Why had Christy picked this one? DJ wasn't too well known, but he'd gained some popularity after his stint with Bradley—and the fact that he wasn't immediately kicked out. He didn't relish the thought of having to explain why he was with the hot black chick in a power suit later.

Christy didn't have the same problem since the women's quarters were on the other side of the building. *What is this, payback?*

"It's a guy thing," Christy replied. "They're weird about sizes. He once told me…"

It didn't bode well that they were swapping stories about him, but the smile remained on Ndidi's face. Seeing it made her earlier depression hit even harder.

Honestly, it had sucked. Ndidi was basically the glue of the team—DJ sure as shit wouldn't have been there if it weren't for her. He would have been working alone with his brother, or Olsen would have assigned him to a bunch of stuck-ups. The first could be deadly now that he knew what they were up against, and the latter would have proven bad for his career. Either way, it would have sucked.

Fortunately, she'd pulled herself back together when CJ mentioned dealing with Helene indirectly. They hadn't gone far in their planning, so aside from a few vague ideas, DJ didn't know how they were going to do it. Still, the hope of it was enough to bring back the determination in Ndidi's eyes.

They passed the archway into the courtyards. DJ had seen it several times now, but none of the girls had. It was kind of funny when they both stopped talking immediately and stared. It was dusk, so the overhead lamps had been turned on, bathing the whole area in soft light. Since the courtyard ran at least a mile in both directions, it was a neat sight. The buildings were arranged beside each other—spaced out but curved to form some sort of cage. The whole thing gave the area a sense of power.

It didn't hurt, of course, that these buildings were far bigger than the ones close to the entrance gate.

"Nothing compared to the White House, my ass," DJ muttered, loud enough for the girls to hear.

Christy looked like she was going to say something but ultimately gave up on it and went back to staring. A short time later, they made their way through the space. Like every other time he'd come through here, it was easy to notice that the energy was different somehow. They'd had to pass different courtyards to get here, but the area always inspired a feeling of urgency, as if people were so impressed by the gravity of the building that they didn't want to be caught slacking. It was actually kind of funny.

There were fewer people around, but what they lacked in numbers they made up for in seriousness. The difference between the recruit section and the admin courtyard couldn't have been starker. Whereas the trainees had just been let off and wearily stumbled along to their bunks, everyone in the courtyard was speed-walking to or from the central building.

Guess it bodes well, DJ thought. *Means everything is being handled.* Either that or shit had gone to hell, and everyone was scrambling to save their ass.

It was a coin flip either way.

Finally, they reached the side door of the central building. They could have passed through the main entrance, but there had been a small congregation of people there, and DJ was sure that they were all so many ranks above him they could crush him with a memo—and probably would, seeing as DJ basically existed for trouble. Luckily, Christy had steered them all away, and DJ had stopped glaring at the group to figure out where the side door was.

From there, he hurried them through the gilded hallways. He found the court-like room first, chuckling at how the room that was supposed to have spelled the end of his career was now no more than a landmark to him. Then he retraced his steps to Olsen's office.

Christy stopped tugging on his hand, probably picking up on the seriousness of the situation. Ndidi adjusted her suit cuffs again. DJ sighed. He was far too tired to deal with Olsen, but without his resources, none of their ideas would work. So DJ relaxed his shoulders and plastered a smile on his face.

"Just let me do the talking, okay?" he whispered to his companions. "And he does this weird thing where it's really difficult to breath, so if that happens just… just chill, yeah? I'll talk him down."

They stared at him, obviously confused. DJ ignored their looks and knocked on the door.

THE DOOR SLID OPEN WITHOUT A SOUND, and DJ stepped in, the girls in tow. Olsen was perched on his customary chair. He looked up from a pile of papers, and his brows creased in surprise. The crease turned into a frown at the sight of DJ's companions.

"Lad, you must be packing quite a pair to come to my office uninvited."

"Ah, but you did invite me," DJ said before he could help himself. "You said, 'Come in.'"

Olsen's eyes narrowed at that. Ndidi nudged DJ, and Christy sighed. DJ just kept on speaking.

"Now, before you blow your top, you should at least hear me out. You know I'd never be here if I didn't have to be."

DJ watched the decision play across the admiral's face. His eyes flicked to

Christy, then Ndidi, and there was a hint of curiosity there. The big guy was probably just ticked that he'd been caught on the back foot for once.

"Who're your friends?" Olsen grunted finally.

"This is Christy. She's on my team. That'll become relevant in a couple of minutes." Christy glared at him, but hey, it wasn't as if he'd lied. She was only there because he'd forgotten she wasn't cleared to be in the admin block. It was a miracle that the higher-ups they'd passed hadn't batted an eye at two recruits strolling down the halls. What sort of shit security was that?

"And this is Ndidi Okafor," DJ finished. Olsen's eyes stayed on Ndidi. She'd been in the report about DJ's Gaius infiltration. DJ had spoken about her and Chad several times.

After a couple of seconds, Olsen's eyes swung back to DJ. "Why are they in my office?"

"I'll let her explain," DJ said.

Olsen's eye twitched, but he didn't otherwise stop her when Ndidi took the seat. To her credit, as soon as she was opposite the man, she stared at him until the admiral met her eyes.

"We have a plan to defeat Helene," Ndidi said. That was kind of a stretch, but DJ didn't contradict her. The sooner they were done with this, the better.

"Is this anything like the plan that led to wasting resources infiltrating Gaius and stealing a dead-end hard drive?" Olsen asked. DJ held in a wince.

"That," Ndidi countered smoothly, "isn't a dead end until we can be sure that there was no point of entry. Even if we admit that our programmers can't handle it, I know DJ sent a duplicate to you."

Olsen's eyes narrowed further. He was justifiably pissed now. DJ placed a hand on Ndidi's shoulder.

"We have a plan to defeat Helene," Ndidi repeated. Olsen gestured for her to continue. "We're reasonably sure that Mayday was caused by Helene speaking to Gaius—maybe even hacking and crashing it, but we need to confirm by breaking into the hard drive. So, if we can disable Helene—"

"Calm down, lass." Olsen chuckled. "You think the AI *talked* to Gaius? And what? Bullied it into crashing itself?"

"Yes."

"Is that even possible?"

"Manar Saleem seemed to think it was when I broached the topic with him."

Olsen's eyes glazed over as if accessing a memory. "Ah, yes. You two were supposed to get married, right? And then you had a falling out? Didn't know people still kept in touch with their ex-fiancés these days. Must be a generation thing."

"Come on, man, don't be a dick," DJ said.

Olsen narrowed his eyes, and his aura washed across the room. Christy started choking silently, her muscles too tense to allow any movement. DJ gripped the back of the chair so hard his muscles turned white, but he remained standing. Ndidi was the most off since she was already sitting. She had a hand to her throat and was obviously struggling to breathe, but there was primal anger in her eyes.

"You will show me the respect that I deserve," Olsen growled. "Or so help me, boy, I will make what that fool Bradley planned for you seem like a summer vacation."

DJ didn't say a word. He couldn't. Instead, he simply glared. One of these days, he would figure out how the old man did this.

A minute later, the pressure on them disappeared. Olsen glared at DJ for a moment more before finally nodding at Ndidi. His expression sobered. "I resent the way the lad put it, but he was right nonetheless. I apologize for my earlier words."

"Thank you," Ndidi croaked, massaging her throat.

"Now, do you have any proof about what you're saying?"

Ndidi reached for her purse. "Yes, actually, we do."

Olsen's eyebrows went up, and DJ couldn't hold back his grin. Ndidi brought out a printed sheet of paper. It was incomprehensible to DJ, but CJ had assured him it was legit, and Chad had agreed.

"These are some codes that our programmers found inside the Gaius hard drive. Can you read it?"

Olsen took the sheet, stared at it for a couple of moments, then dropped it on his desk. Ndidi opened her mouth to continue, but the admiral just raised a finger. *Dick move*, DJ wanted to say. Christy, as if picking up his thoughts, glared at him.

Olsen pressed a number on his intercom. "Collins, get your ass in here. I have something for you." It was only after that he met their eyes. "The paper is all gibberish to me, but I have one of the boys from the lab coming over to check it out. While we wait, why don't you tell me what he's supposed to see?"

"Well, if Collin has already gone through the copy of the hard drive that DJ sent, he should be familiar with Gaius codes," Ndidi said. "I'll admit that I don't understand it much myself, but the printout is supposed to show codes that are distinctly different from Gaius's."

"And the codes were found in the hard drive?"

"Yes."

"Thought you said your people couldn't access the stuff?"

Ndidi turned back to glare at DJ. For his part, he grinned at Olsen. "Yeah, that was my idea. I was going for the whole dramatic reveal thing. Did it work?"

Olsen looked about ready to blow a gasket, which just made DJ grin more. A moment later, he calmed and, deliberately ignoring DJ, turned back to Ndidi. "Just so I have it clear, when Collins comes to verify this, what's supposed to be the proof here?"

"That's evidence that a foreign code hacked into Gaius shortly before Mayday. If we can compare those codes to Helene's, we'll have proof that she was the cause of Mayday."

"Wait," Olsen said, visibly confused. "If you think Saleem did this, then why did you go to meet him initially? Did you expect him to fess up?"

Ndidi wilted. Chad had brought up the same argument a while back. Any blame put on Helene would automatically be transferred to Manar, her creator. A moment passed, then Ndidi's back straightened. Her voice came out sure. "Manar Saleem wasn't involved in this."

"But Helene's his AI," Olsen countered. Personally, DJ agreed with the guy, but he didn't really care anyway. He was just trying to keep his brother out of jail. Human or AI, did it really matter which? Not like anyone was coming back from the answer.

"Nevertheless, Manar wasn't involved in Mayday."

Olsen was about to press his point, but a knock on the door interrupted him. "Get your ass in here, Collins," he bellowed.

The door opened, and a lanky man entered. Though, "man" was a bit of a stretch. DJ wouldn't put him a day past eighteen. The dude wore a wrinkled pair of jeans and a baggy shirt with an anime character on it. He took a step into the room and froze when he noticed the attention on him. A hand adjusted his glasses nervously. "Uh…"

Damn, DJ thought, glancing away. *Dude practically screams 'bully me.'*

"Well, don't just stand there, boy," Olsen called out. "Come and take a look at this."

Collins shuffled over to Olsen's desk. As soon as he saw the printout, his eyes never moved to anything else. He picked it up without prompting. Olsen noticed their surprise, and he just shrugged.

"Uh… where'd you get this?" Collins asked.

"That's classified," Olsen replied. "What matters is if you can verify it."

Collin mumbled to himself. Olsen started to say something but then just sighed. After a minute, the kid looked up from the paper. "Um… I'll need to go through the hard drive again to confirm that the codes match, but I already recognize some of them."

"Get Ed to join you," Olsen said. "I want a report tomorrow." Collins nodded as he left, then refocused on the paper as if he'd forgotten everyone in the room.

"Nice guy," DJ said after the door closed.

"Shut it," Olsen snapped. He turned back to Ndidi. "So, let's assume Collins and his buddy confirm the codes on the paper. That brings me back to my original question: Why're y'all in my office?"

"Because the next step would be to confirm that the foreign codes are actually Helene's, which would be enough proof to shut her down."

Olsen shifted some papers on his desk. "Why don't you do that then?"

"Because we're broke," DJ cut in. Ndidi glared at him, but he ignored her. He'd given up his sleep for this moment.

"Why does that matter?" Olsen asked.

"It matters…" DJ said dramatically. He leaned over Ndidi to put his hand on the desk and grinned at Olsen. "Because we're gonna break into Sparta Corp."

Olsen narrowed his eyes. Ndidi nudged DJ even harder than before.

"Fine!" DJ sighed. "We're not breaking into the HQ. But we *are* going to break into one of their data banks so we can download a copy of Helene's program."

Olsen snorted. "No one can hack into Helene. The government's been trying since the AI was released."

"That's because you guys suck," DJ said. He waved off Olsen's glare. At this point, DJ was convinced that that was the admiral's natural setting. "CJ says it's possible because we already have a sample to work with." He gestured to the door Collins had gone through.

Olsen lost his glare as he considered this. "That's all well and good, but none of this answers why you're in my office."

DJ sighed. How did he get anything done with a head this thick? "When I first met you, you said, and I quote, 'You have the entire US Intelligence Community at your disposal.'"

Olsen frowned.

DJ grinned.

KARLA LUNGED AT CHLOE, a snarl on her face. Chloe dodged to the side, then did it again so Liz's blades missed her by an inch. At Chloe's chuckle, Karla's vision focused on the condescending smile on her face. Oh, how Karla would love nothing more than to knock out one of Chloe's teeth. Maybe then she would stop grinning like a cow getting milked.

Karla got her chance when Chloe stopped, unbalanced. Karla lunged again to take the advantage, but her right leg didn't respond. Her lunge turned into a stumble, and her blades fell short. Chloe danced away from the pathetic attack with another chuckle.

"You almost got me that time," she said. "Now, if we can only get your opponents to wait while you stumble into them."

Karla didn't respond, glaring at her right leg. Slowly, the bionic prosthetic began to obey her commands again. She stamped it on the floor, denting the wood. Despite what José had claimed, Karla had learned to control her bionics.

They had acclimated to her sometime during the second week of training. Around that time, Liz had said her limbs had gotten easier to use.

Karla touched a finger to her eye. It still throbbed even after two weeks. Her sister wore a matching black eye on her face.

Neither of them had been able to touch Chloe on the first day of training. And after letting them wear themselves out trying, she had thrashed them like dogs come to steal the meat. There had been no mirth on her face then, no amusement. Just a cold detachment. The twins hadn't been able to move for two days. Their bionics had not been hurt, but neither Karla nor her sister had had the presence of mind needed to command them. José had come to them the first day, his eyes filled with disgust. When he left, two nurses replaced him and took care of their needs until they'd healed enough to walk.

Then Chloe began their training in earnest.

"Again," Karla said. Liz nodded in agreement. Chloe spread her arms out, and the twins lunged in tandem. This time, Chloe was forced to actually block their attacks, but her grin stayed in place. Her arms did not tremble from the strain even as she was forced back. Karla did not know why that annoyed her more. Before their separation, it had taken Chloe's full concentration to hold them back. She didn't smile then, so why did she now? Didn't José say they would get stronger because of their new limbs?

Karla drew back her arm for an overhead swing. Chloe raised her blade to parry and deflected the blow toward Liz. Karla was forced to cancel her attack instead of pressing through to penetrate the woman's defense.

She growled and sidestepped, putting more distance between herself and her sister. This time, she attacked Chloe's side. But somehow, Liz appeared in front of her blade, and Karla was once again forced to abandon her move. Karla cursed in Russian. Twice, her sister had gotten in her way, even after Karla had created space between them. Was she blind?

Karla pushed the thought from her head and watched the flow of battle until Chloe was unguarded. She pounced immediately. Grinning like a fool, Chloe twisted, and Liz was somehow in front of Karla again. Blinded by anger for an instant, Karla was tempted to let the strike land.

"Stop!" Chloe barked. Karla looked up just in time to catch a hilt to the face. Instinctively, she tried to roll with the impact, but her muscles weren't yet used to the motion, and she landed hard. She squeezed her eyes shut from the pain, reciting every curse she had ever heard.

"Seriously?" Chloe chuckled dryly. "You were gonna brand your own sister?"

"Never," Karla snarled through the pain. She would have stopped herself. Wouldn't she?

"Sure looked like it to me." Chloe shrugged. "But whatever. You gonna lie there like a pussy all day, or do you want to learn why you sucked?"

Liz stretched out a hand to Karla, who used her right arm to pull herself up without thinking. Karla stared at it. For whatever reason, she never had much of an issue commanding her arm compared to her legs.

"What do you think you did wrong? Apart from attacking your sister, that is," Chloe asked. Karla met her gaze and almost flinched at the undercurrent of anger. Even her smirk had turned to steel.

Karla was familiar with the look, though it had been years since she'd last seen it. Phantom pains spread across her left side from the memories, and Karla's stance turned defensive. Even Liz straightened her back, hands reaching for her dagger. Karla's body told her that such a move would only bring pain.

It was Liz who answered. "Our attacks were ill planned, so we got in the other's way. We were out of sync."

Chloe stared at Karla a moment longer before glancing at Liz. *This is not over.* Her gaze had said. Well, Karla would be waiting. She had done nothing wrong this time. She had let her anger overtake her, but she would never have harmed her sister.

"Yes," Chloe answered finally. "You were uncoordinated. That's why I was able to make the both of you my bitches. I mean, even more than you already are."

"So, how do we fix that?" Liz asked. Karla narrowed her eyes but didn't say anything. It made her skin crawl, but she couldn't deny that their attacks had been pathetic since they'd been separated.

Chloe grinned. "I'll show you."

JOSÉ WATCHED FROM THE ALCOVE above the training room as Karla lunged at Chloe. As if practicing a dance, Chloe smoothly side-stepped the motion. As tight as her leathers were, it took an effort for him not to get distracted. A minor one, but inexcusable nonetheless. Karla brought her daggers to press the attack only for Liz to dance away again. Even from where he stood, José could hear Chloe chuckle, and he heard it when it abruptly cut off.

Chloe turned in time to block Liz's strike, but the confusion was clear on her face. Her smile turned strained. She forced herself to disengage from Liz before Karla's retaliatory strike could land. But Karla just lunged again and kept pressing the attack.

Chloe's grin became even more strained. It was obvious it was taking most of her attention to keep up. Still, her eyes darted around, searching for Liz. But she missed it when the other twin darted from behind Karla's waist, her dagger aimed at Chloe's stomach.

Chloe's eyes widened in surprise. Her motions sped up significantly to block the strike, then the next one from Karla. The woman moved nonstop to create some distance between the twins. Several times, she tried to deflect Karla's strike into Liz's, but Karla just halted the motion, and Liz attacked through the space that opened up. They moved smoothly, Karla aggressively attacking while Liz covered up the weak spots and went for the openings that Chloe left. After five minutes, Chloe lost her grin completely, her whole focus on fending off the girls.

When Karla showed signs of tiring, she barked a word to Liz, and they smoothly switched their roles. This time, Liz was the one who bore down on Chloe while Karla sneaked in attacks whenever the chance arose.

Of the two combinations, José wasn't sure which was the more danger-ous. Where Karla had continuously forced Chloe on the defensive through the pressure and aggression of her attacks, Liz's moves were more methodical, only targeting Chloe's vital spots and forcing her to defend or be severely injured. If Karla fought like a wild animal, Liz was more surgical in her approach.

Liz dropped low to attack Chloe's leg, just in time to create an opening for Karla to target the other woman's face. Chloe stepped back from Liz's attack but was forced to defend against Karla's, which put her on the back foot when Liz slashed at her throat. Chloe's dagger flashed to block it, but Karla had already slipped to the side with her weapon flashing at Chloe's exposed front.

José leaned forward.

Chloe tilted her head back to dodge Liz's strike, and her arms turned into a blur, flashing once. At the same moment, sparks flew when her blades met Karla's. She used the force of the attack to hop back, putting some distance between all three of them.

Liz was clutching her throat, gasping for air. There was a barely noticeable line where the flat of Chloe's blade had struck her. Karla was better off. She stumbled a bit from the lack of resistance, but she had gained enough mastery over her limbs to recover her balance. Both girls were panting with exertion while Chloe stood casually, her daggers held loosely. José didn't think anyone but him noticed the slight tremble in her hands.

"That all you got?" Chloe smirked.

Karla spat on the floor. Even Liz couldn't hold back her glare. Without a word, they attacked.

José nodded, stepping back from his perch. This, more than anything, showed him that he had made the right choice by separating them. There were still minor issues in their movements, and they had not found a method to communicate as silently as they had before, but if they could make Chloe strain herself so much after mere weeks of using their bionics, there was truly no limit to their growth. What did it matter if they loathed him now? Their survival was all that truly mattered.

José made his way back to the main hallways. He checked his watch as he walked. He still had more than enough time. The walls gradually changed from bland rock to the more disgusting white paint. The passages were less filled than normal. Men in lab coats appeared only sporadically.

He turned a corner in time to spot a patrol striding out of sight. One looked back and José saw him tense immediately. He knew his reputation with the guards and at times even encouraged it. But their spinelessness grated on him.

These were the fools that had hounded his daughters and forced them to retreat? It was pathetic.

The guard looked away, and the moment passed. José suppressed his irritation and continued on his way, turning corners with ease. For most of the week after his daughters' operation, he had familiarized himself with the layout of the complex. It had taken far too much time, but if he and the girls were to live there, it was stupid to have to rely on a map to get around.

It took another ten minutes for José to reach his destination. He glanced briefly at the camera beside the door. A minute later, the door unlocked automatically, and José entered. His watch struck the hour. He was just in time. How annoying. Here he was, perfectly on time, summoned like a dog. José straightened his back, his face hardening.

A blinking red light across the room drew his attention. It was the only thing that could. The room contained only a small wooden chair, which José assumed was for men stupid enough to fall for such a psychological trap. The light blinked faster, almost overshadowing the device it came from—a small black contraption nestled on the far wall. After a moment, the light shot a beam of light that slowly coalesced into a gigantic female head. The AI floated inches off the ground, electricity crackling through its form and congealing at its center to reveal two glowing orbs of yellow.

[Good day, José Olvera,] the AI said.

"I am not your dog to be summoned," José said. "You have already shown an aptitude for hacking into my devices. You can send your messages there."

[No, you are not a dog. You are human.]

José bristled at that. Somehow, the AI had made being human sound like an even worse insult.

[And your devices are not as impregnable as you believe, obviously. If I can communicate with them, so can others. Some things are better said in person.] It drifted closer. [Face to face, as I understand it.]

José drew himself to his full height to meet the eyes of the AI. "What do you want?"

[You failed to deliver your report on the progress of Karla and Liz Polova's training. The end of their grace period is fast approaching.]

"Their training is going as expected. They will be ready by the time the period ends," José replied, his eyes suddenly as hard as steel. "We will require additional information, however, if we are to be efficient wherever you send us."

Although the AI's face did not change—*could* not change—a pressure descended on José. Suddenly, it was difficult to breathe. His muscles locked up by themselves. José only remained standing through sheer willpower, and he dug deeper into that force to glare at the demon in front of him. The AI considered him calmly with vast indifference. But its eyes were golden suns, encompassing José's world.

The pressure wasn't nearly as strong as it had been during the surgery. Then, José had felt the world collapsing on his shoulders even though he'd been outside the room. Maybe that was why he could recognize the intimidation tactic for what it was.

Through the pain, José smiled. Few things could intimidate him. He grunted and slowly began breathing easier. The AI drifted closer. Its eyes pierced through him. He could *feel* the demon's interest.

[You will be given information as it is necessary,] the AI said finally.

"What should we prepare for?"

[Nothing for now,] It floated back toward its original spot. [Soon, however, I will have need of you and your daughters' skills.]

"What particular skill set?"

The AI was quiet for a few moments. Suddenly, its form began to disperse, starting from the bottom up. The glowing eyes focused on José with an intensity that almost brought him to his knees. Unlike before, José didn't believe the demon was trying to intimidate him; it had simply focused more of its attention to emphasize the importance of its words. [Some gather and seek to prevent what's coming. Your skills will be needed to dissuade them of this notion.]

José buckled under the pressure. "I need a name," he croaked.

[They call themselves revolutionaries and justice seekers, but they are merely fools. There is no justice in this world. There is only control and the power to control.] Its form had unraveled, and now only its eyes were left. [You will be given information as it is necessary, José Olvera. For now, prepare.]

Then, the eyes dissolved, and the pressure evaporated with it. José straightened with effort. He spat on the floor, still gasping for breath. All his effort into not losing control, and a mere glance from an unliving object had brought him to his knees. It was pathetic. If his daughters could see him now, they would probably take their daggers to him. Put him out of his misery.

José spat again and carefully composed himself. Prepare, the AI had said. That was what they had been doing for the past month. Would it not be enough? What could stand against them? Who were these revolutionaries?

José was not used to being the last to know things. It grated on him that he had to wait for a demon to give scraps of information. Still, that didn't mean there was nothing he could do. Only a few could stand against his daughters. Given more time, it wouldn't matter who was sent against them.

CHAPTER

70

JUNE 2040

SPARTA DATABANK GAMMA,
NEW YORK

NDIDI HEAVED HERSELF THROUGH THE HOLE in the third-floor window and took a moment to catch her breath. DJ had had her working out for the past few weeks in preparation, but all that effort was up against the years since she'd trained with Sensei Mukalla. She made time in the gym at least twice a week, but she'd found new muscles to strain during the last several minutes.

Maybe she would have dropped it sooner if DJ hadn't laughed so loudly. He would be higher up in the building, performing his own tasks and maybe taking out the guards when he could get away with it. Neither of them wanted a repeat of the disastrous game of tag they had played at Gaius HQ.

That being said, Ndidi thought, unable to stop herself from leaning over the edge and peering down. *What's up with Sparta and the unnecessarily tall buildings?* She was on the third floor and, by their count, there were five more. DJ had started a quarter of an hour before her, so he should have been at the top by now.

"It's a little too late to contemplate jumping, you know?" Christy's voice said through her earpiece. Ndidi's head snapped up, and she tried to find the woman in the darkness. But even though Ndidi knew she was there, she couldn't make out the other woman's form, which was good. There'd be no point in having a sniper if she was so easily made out. That was one of the reasons they had chosen to infiltrate the building at night.

"I'm not going to jump," Ndidi muttered. She contemplated asking Christy if DJ had been able to get into the building okay but thought better of it. If he hadn't, then he would have flagged her down and entered through the hole Ndidi herself had used.

"Yeah, yeah, just get a move on. We don't have all night," Christy responded. Although the words sounded harsh, Ndidi knew that it was just the woman's nerves talking. At least Ndidi hoped so. She prided herself on being a good judge of character. But who could really tell after knowing a person for just a little over a month? She'd been as surprised as Christy when DJ had insisted on bringing her along as a lookout and—if needed—a sniper.

Ndidi nodded into the darkness, then made her way from the ledge and deeper into the building. Christy was right; they didn't have a lot of time. Unlike with Gaius Corp, there had been no hope of hacking through the building's security, so they hadn't tried. So far, they had done nothing more than cut into the building's glass. It was unlikely that any sensors were triggered. Given everything that Manar had told her about Helene—and everything that he probably didn't know about his AI's capabilities—there was a very good chance Helene was already aware of their infiltration. They had planned for that, even as they did all they could to keep it from happening in the first place.

Ndidi calmed her breathing as she strode through the hall. Best-case scenario, DJ would be given more time before the alarm sounded. Regardless of what happened, things would move very fast at some point, so she had to maximize her time. Fortunately, despite the late hour and the hoped-for scarcity of staff, the light in the hallway was turned on. It was dim, but just enough for Ndidi to make out her surroundings.

The locations of Sparta's databanks were a matter of public record, but it had taken days of effort for CJ to pull them up. Even with that, the records only gave their settings and little else. Every databank, except the one Ndidi currently held, had been held in places surrounded by water. DJ had argued that they should pick one of those instead of going for "what was obviously a ready-made trap for suckers." Although Ndidi had agreed with him, Olsen had vehemently refused to provide the resources they would need for the attempt. Ndidi couldn't even begin to fathom what her father would have said if she'd gone to him for the funds—or taken the money out of the Autism Centre. He allowed her full autonomy over the facility in most cases, but Ndidi knew he always kept up to date on the inner workings of all his assets.

He had taught her to do the same thing, after all.

So hitting one of the other databanks had not been an option. But that just meant they had needed to plan more to come out ahead of the trap, if such a thing was even possible.

Stop it, Ndidi chided herself sharply. She took a deep breath and crossed the hallway slowly, listening for any sound. One hand patted the small fanny pack strapped to her waist. Within it was the flash drive, her whole purpose for being in the building. CJ had assured her it was simply a matter of connecting the storage device to any one of the databases. The drive was set to automatically download everything it needed. After that, it should be a simple matter for CJ to separate the multitude of data coming in and use the AI as a digital reader and personal assistant to tease out how Helene's code compared to Gaius's.

The problem was, since none of them knew the layout of the building, Ndidi would have to find the databank herself. Quickly, and without raising any alarms—or any more, if one had already been raised.

Ndidi took another deep breath.

DJ also had a copy of the flash drive in case the databases ended up being higher in the building. But it was more likely that the higher floors would have more security measures, and he might be too busy with his own tasks.

The end of the hallway branched out into two different passages. The lights were bright enough for Ndidi to make out their ends, but unfortunately that didn't help her decide which one to take. Unlike in Gaius, the walls beside her weren't broken up by office doors. They ran smoothly to the edge. Ndidi stared at the two paths.

"Go left," Christy said. "Always go left."

"Why?" Ndidi asked, looking that way. "Can you see what's down there?"

"Not really. The lights are messing with the X-ray, but there's even more interference to the left. There might be something good down there. Plus, when in a maze, always go left. That's just good advice."

"Something good" might not necessarily mean good for us, Ndidi thought. But that didn't mean she would avoid the path out of fear.

With a nod, Ndidi went left.

"You have incoming," Christy whispered in her ear. Ndidi froze immediately, her heart suddenly pounding in her chest. Between the silence of the place and Christy's presence in her ear for the last few minutes, she'd done a pretty good job of calming herself down as she searched for the database. But this did not help.

"Where?" Ndidi whispered. She glanced behind her, but the hall was empty all the way to its end.

"Near the staircase entrance to the floor you're on. I can see movement there, heading toward you. Probably a guard patrol."

Ndidi strained her ears, not even daring to breathe as she listened. Finally, after a minute spent in tense silence, she heard it: the sound of feet marching in tandem. The guards approached from behind, probably in one of the hallways she'd just passed, their voices lowered in casual conversation. That was good. If they were at ease enough to talk, they weren't yet aware of her or DJ's presence. Ndidi had been fairly sure, given the lack of alarm. However, a part of her had whispered that it might have been a ploy by Helene to lure them into a false sense of security.

Of course, that could also mean the guards were just *pretending* to be at ease and they were fully aware of her.

"What the hell are you doing?" Christy hissed in her ears. "Why aren't you moving? They'll be on you in less than a minute."

The warning cut through Ndidi's apprehension. She came back to herself with withering shame. Sensei Mukalla would have ripped into her for that, and Ndidi was fairly sure her father would have let the woman. It had been pounded into her from day one never to let fear force her into inaction. But at the first sign of trouble, what did she do?

The steps drew closer.

Ndidi felt her face harden as embarrassment, contrition, and anger fought for dominance. *There'll be time to dwell later,* Ndidi thought. *How can I fix it in the meantime?*

The floor was covered in a thin roll of carpet that, along with the soft-soled sneakers DJ had insisted she wear, muffled her steps enough for her to speed-walk to the end of the hall. Just in time for the patrol to turn into the passage she'd been in.

Ndidi was already striding toward the end of the new hall. She couldn't take the risk of running and alerting the men, so the best she could do was lengthen her stride as much as her five-foot-seven frame would let her. She'd have to hope the men didn't have any cause to increase their pace. Her blood rushed furiously to her head, seemingly leaving her adrenaline the duty of keeping her moving.

Despite keeping most of her senses trained on the patrol behind her, Ndidi kept enough awareness to search for any breaks in the monotonous walls. The database at Gaius had been heralded by a significant drop in temperature as she'd moved closer. While Ndidi fully expected that to be the case here as well, she had little hope that it would be that easy.

Still, it wouldn't hurt if the database room had at least a transparent glass door or something. Unfortunately, there was no such door. She kept moving.

"Okay," Christy said. "They turned into the same hallway you did, but I still don't think they know you're there. You're just gonna have to keep moving until you lose them or find somewhere to hole up so they can pass you."

Ndidi was never more grateful than when DJ had been able to procure a device that let Christy track her. He hadn't explained where he'd sourced it. He'd had only the one, so Olsen couldn't have been responsible. They'd had to choose whether the device should be used by DJ himself or Ndidi. In the end, it hadn't really been a choice. They were all aware that Ndidi would more likely need someone watching her back than DJ would.

At last, Ndidi reached the end of the passage and turned right. Since the guards were on patrol, it stood to reason that they would be going in a circle and thus be more likely to turn left again.

Christy seemed to think so, too, because Ndidi's comms came on a second later. "Smart. Updating the map now."

It had been CJ's idea to link Ndidi's tracker to a mapmaking software. That way, they could generate a tentative layout of the building through her movements. Since she wouldn't—and couldn't—cover every square inch of the place, the map wasn't likely to provide complete navigation, but it would be helpful for retracing her steps if she needed to do so in a hurry.

And Ndidi was fairly certain she would before the night was over.

"How far does your vision extend?" Ndidi whispered. She didn't know much about weapons, especially rifles. Christy hadn't let her even see her gun during the month that they'd prepared. Ndidi knew the scope provided X-ray vision, and Christy had been able to track the guards with it. But she had never been able to get a definite answer about the rifle's range. Since that was one of the major things allowing Ndidi to keep ahead of her add-ons, it felt important to know. Frankly, she should have pushed harder weeks ago, but DJ had seemed so unconcerned about it.

The errant thought was almost enough to make Ndidi freeze. When had she started looking to him for directions? She was almost a decade older than him.

Christy's answer came after a heavy pause. "You're reaching the extent of it. I can still make you out, but your shape's more indistinct. A little deeper into the building and I won't be able to make you out."

All right then, Ndidi thought, her face hardening more. There was nothing to do but handle it. "Can you still make out the guards? Are they still following me?"

"So far, yeah," Christy replied. Her tone was more subdued. "They're halfway through the passage now, and you're already ahead of them. They'll most likely take a different path than you, then you can double back and— Hey, why'd you stop?"

Ndidi hadn't moved for several seconds while she strained to listen, praying that she'd misheard. Her entire being was focused on her ears, extending her hearing through sheer willpower to find any evidence that would disprove what she thought she'd heard seconds before.

Christy seemed to understand the reason for her silence and didn't repeat her question. Instead, there was the slight *whirr* sound of her scope extending and muffled cursing, probably when she failed to make anything out.

Ndidi tuned out even those distractions. Half a minute later, she was rewarded—or punished, depending—when the sound came again. A sound she was intimately familiar with. One she'd been hearing for the past few minutes: the sound of marching feet and the din of whispered conversation. But this time it came from *ahead* of her.

"There're two patrols coming from the direction I'm heading," Ndidi whispered to Christy. "They are coming from *both* branches." It wasn't feigned or forced, she realized. She was calm. None of them had had any illusions about whether their plan would go off without a hitch. It was almost a relief that it actually *had* gone wrong.

"Shit," Christy hissed. Ndidi heard her adjust the scope. "The one behind just reached the end of their hall… and they turned right."

"So there's a patrol coming behind me and two more coming ahead of me," Ndidi said to no one. Her thoughts spun, creating and dismissing ideas by the second. She turned in a circle, her eyes darting around. Previously she'd kept an awareness of the walls around her so as not to miss her target or something important. Now she did so searching for anything that might be of use to her.

Ndidi was able to make out a familiar device suspended several feet above her on the left-hand wall. The gadget was no bigger than Ndidi's thumb and emitted a dull red light that she'd somehow missed in the dimness of the hallway. Her eyes bored into the device, and the light almost seemed to intensify from the attention. She understood immediately and her heart clenched with the realization.

"Shit," Christy muttered.

A second later, a siren's wail broke the silence of the night.

Shit, indeed, Ndidi thought.

[THREAT DETECTED,] Helene blared, startling Manar awake. Slowly, he blinked away the drowsiness and focused on the flashing light coming from Helene's module. Judging by its intensity, it had probably been trying to wake him for some time.

Manar sat up in little increments, trying to reduce the flare of his headache. It didn't work well, but Manar knew from experience that the pain would fade soon enough. His movement was enough to tip the bottle of wine beside him onto the floor, where it joined others of its kind. Manar spared a glance at it, assuring himself that there wasn't a drop left. That was his last bottle, so he would have to ask Helene to call up some more.

After he got her to shut up about whatever had her circuits in a twist.

"Show me," he muttered.

A square projection appeared in the air above his bed, hovering at eye level so he didn't have to strain. The video started out blurry and glitchy before Helene adjusted it enough to be comparable to most advanced cameras. It showed the edge of an empty hallway. Then the view passed through the passage and stopped in the middle of the corridor.

Suddenly, Manar had little trouble keeping his eyes open. But his head throbbed with a new wave of pain—either a result of his inebriation or a foreshadowing of the hassle he would have to deal with.

"Where is this?" he asked.

[Sparta Databank Gamma,] Helene reported.

Manar sighed, pinching the bridge of his nose. *You stupid woman,* he thought wearily. *You very stupid woman. What could this possibly achieve?*

He stared at the video, but Ndidi hadn't moved from her spot. Her eyes darted around but were constantly drawn to Helene's module. In those glances, she appeared to stare straight at Manar. The last time this happened, Manar had ended up inviting her to his apartment. It was one of the worst mistakes he'd made.

Now her gaze just made him livid. Breaking and entering into Sparta? How the hell did she come up with such a monumentally stupid idea? He focused on the feed again. Ndidi muttered to herself, but without sound from the video, Manar couldn't make it out. That was easily changed.

"Audio," he commanded.

[Processing,] Helene said. There was a second delay.

"Nothing else will work, Christy," Ndidi was saying. Who the hell was Christy? "They're too close. Do you have a route to the stairs? I think I passed it a couple hallways back."

There was a pause.

"Upper," Ndidi said. "Maybe I can meet up with DJ. He'll be able to come up with something."

DJ, Manar thought, trying to remember why the name sounded so familiar. Where had she even found people to rope into this?

"Who's she talking to? Is the person in the building with her?"

[Unknown.]

Manar sighed again. At least she had enough sense to shield her accomplices.

Even with that, they couldn't be that far away. Helene should have been able to trace the feed from whatever device Ndidi was using. He shook his head, staring at the projection. It didn't matter anyway.

"Are there any *other* intruders?" he asked. "She mentioned meeting up with someone."

The video transitioned to a different hallway. The angle was higher, and Manar assumed this was Helene's way of indicating they were on a higher floor. Like before, the initial projection was blurry, but it slowly became clearer. Manar could make out a man in jeans, a T-shirt, and a… fanny pack. Ndidi also had a fanny pack on her hip. The man—DJ, Manar assumed—turned around and stared down the hall for a couple of seconds, deep discomfort on his face. Two of his fingers were raised in a small salute. He seemed to have just finished saying something.

"Who's he talking to?" Manar asked, then thought better of it. He was far too drunk for this. "You know what? Just brief me on everything when it's done."

[Recommendations requested.]

The feed split apart, one side showing Ndidi and the other showing the man. Manar stared at both, his anger gone. In its place was extreme weariness. He'd looked up the signs of depression, so he understood what his prolonged and extreme lack of zeal was. The alcohol probably didn't help either, but it was the only thing that kept the voices away.

It was one thing to understand what the problem was but another thing to fix it. And whatever his ex-fiancée had embroiled herself in wasn't enough to rouse him.

"What threat level is it?"

[Yellow.]

Yellow was the second-lowest threat level. That was how little Helene thought of Ndidi's hair-brained idea. He stared at the feed for a second more. Finally, he sighed, lying back on his bed.

"Fix it," he muttered.

[Acknowledged. Initial rebuff already deployed.]

CHAPTER

72

JUNE 2040

SPARTA DATABANK GAMMA, NEW YORK

NDIDI TOOK A BREATH and ran to meet the patrol.

Her hardened eyes glanced at the mysterious device as she rushed back the way she came. The way the blinking red light seemed to follow her solidified her decision more than anything. She had obviously been played. The team had been right: their intrusion had not gone undetected. However, they'd been wrong to believe the alarm would go off immediately.

Why would it, Ndidi thought angrily, *when she could use our confidence to lead us so easily into a trap?*

The alarm blared around her. She no longer had to strain to hear marching feet—from any direction. The closest group, the one she'd evaded earlier, was just a hallway in front of her. She had no hope of taking on two three-man patrols at once, but she could rush past three men. It was her only shot.

"They're coming up the hallway to your right," Christy said.

Ndidi nodded and slowed down as she reached the end of the corridor. The footfalls were loud enough that she could count the individual steps. She hadn't really needed Christy's warning. Still, it was reassuring to know someone was looking out for her if things went wrong. Maybe the sniper could even get off a few rounds. Maybe some of those rounds would even pierce through the walls with enough force to do some damage. A girl could hope.

The patrol turned the corner, each man standing beside the other. When they saw Ndidi, their eyes widened as one. Apparently, Helene hadn't seen fit to give them her specific position. Ndidi mentally noted this, and her fist swung for the nearest face before she consciously decided to. Mukalla would have been proud.

Her fist connected. The first man staggered from the blow but kept his feet. Unfortunately, a biweekly gym appointment did not give her the strength to down a trained security officer in one go. Strength had never been her strong suit. Sensei Mukalla had always had her focus on attacking the vitals instead. In her adrenaline-fueled attack, Ndidi had forgotten that. But now, she was already correcting her stance and taking measure of her opponents. She didn't attack immediately, though, giving her throbbing knuckles a chance to rest. Ndidi swore that if she survived the night without going to jail, she was going to make practice with DJ a priority.

The other two men got over their surprise quickly and spread out to surround her. Ndidi took a step back to keep them in her sights but otherwise let them come. The hallway was tight enough that they couldn't swarm her, but it also made her plan of running past them almost impossible. And if one of them grabbed her, she'd be done.

Every second she delayed brought the other two patrols closer.

So she lunged. The aggression startled the men, and they didn't react in time. She landed another punch on her first victim, aiming at his liver. The man went down with a groan, clutching his stomach. He'd recover, in time, but Ndidi hoped to be gone by then. Their colleague's cry of pain was enough to snap the other two from their stupor. At once, they came for Ndidi, one directly in front of her and the other slightly to her right.

Ndidi dodged a punch from the first man, who had a scar from his eye to his chin. She delivered a kick to his knee that had him bowling over in pain. The second man reached her then, and Ndidi deflected his attack purely by luck. She retaliated with a punch to his skull, though that seemed to do more harm to her fist than to him. However, it stunned him enough for her to kick his groin and down him for a time.

The scar-faced guard was straightening up, his right leg visibly shaking. Ndidi rushed him, hoping to capitalize on the weakness, but he seemed to be waiting for her. His head snapped up at her, grinning, and his fist suddenly filled her vision.

She tried to dodge, her steps ingrained in her memory after years of training, but she'd already been too close. The most she did was turn what would have been a straight-on punch to her throat into a glancing blow on her shoulder. She gritted her teeth in pain. Her eyes hardened, and irritation bubbled up within her. Her leg struck out, and the scar-faced guard went down from another kick to his knee. She'd hit at an angle, and the resulting snap made it clear he wouldn't be getting up anytime soon.

Ndidi looked around and, to her surprise, realized all three men were groaning on the floor. She stepped away from the makeshift circle, grasping her side as she tried to get her breathing under control. As the adrenaline died down, the pain in her shoulder blared its presence. Ndidi rolled it and found she could bear the pain even if it made her wince.

That would have to do. She doubted this would be her last fight before the night was over. She looked down at the guards and allowed herself a slight smile. She was going to kiss Sensei Mukalla the next time she saw her.

JUNE 2040

SPARTA DATABANK GAMMA, NEW YORK

DJ SHOT AT THE WOMAN.

He hadn't meant to shoot her. His brain had responded to the tension of the situation and the sight of someone who was so obviously a bad guy. It wasn't that she'd threatened his life or anything. If that was any reason to shoot someone, Olsen's mum would have been grieving her son. No, what screamed "bad guy" about her was the black leather jumpsuit. Like, who wore shit like that in public except psychos? How was that a genuine fashion statement?

It was a justifiable reason to get shot at, but not to get killed. So he'd aimed for her shoulder. That should have put her out of commission long enough to tie her up and hide somewhere until the night was over.

The report from his gun rang out, piercing through the alarm that had been blaring for the last minute. There was a *plink* from the other side of the hall where the woman stood—the sound of metal against metal.

The woman staggered backward. Her eyes widened in shock, and she stared down at her right shoulder as if unable to believe what had just happened. DJ was having problems believing it himself, though probably not for the same reason. There was a hole in her leather jumpsuit, but no blood. There was no wound there at all.

Her shoulder was made of metal. DJ blinked and then squinted, but the face remained the same. It was some Wolverine kind of shit. It was as if she'd decided to go full cyborg but then changed her mind halfway. It was—

DJ shook himself out of the spiral.

To her credit, the redhead seemed to be in as much shock as he was. She stared at her jumpsuit, poking her finger in and out of the bullet hole. A few seconds passed, then she shifted her gaze to his. The shock transitioned into a vicious snarl in a split second. Both hands reached to her side—even the one that should not have been able to—and pulled out twin daggers, which she brandished at DJ. Then she lunged.

"Fuck," DJ muttered. He shot at her again.

It was the same mistake characters in movies always made. The one DJ always rolled his eyes at. If bullets obviously didn't work, don't waste more, right? Wrong. There was something about shooting something continuously, even if it didn't work. It gave the illusion he was actually doing something to help. He hadn't understood that before.

The woman in black dodged the first shot and somehow deflected the second with her dagger. It went over her left shoulder. DJ wanted to cry out at the unfairness. If someone was already skilled enough to deal with bullets on their own, they didn't need to be bulletproof on top of that. It was just overkill.

Then he noticed a line of red running over the shoulder where she'd deflected the bullet. *Yes!* he screamed in his mind. She wasn't invincible after all, and he wouldn't have to run away like a scared toddler. He'd been worried about that. To be forced to run away from the scary bulletproof cyborg chick in his first actual battle? Yikes.

The red-haired woman didn't otherwise react to the wound on her shoulder. DJ hoped it was because she didn't want to draw attention to it, not because she was numb to pain or some other BS. Still, this, at least, gave him hope. If only her right side was cyborg, he would just aim for her left.

That was an okay plan, but somehow she'd already crossed the distance between them. His dads had been right: jokes might just be the death of him.

DJ leaped backward, reaching for his second gun. The chick's blades sliced through where he'd been standing, and the snarl on her face intensified. Even with that, she didn't seem angry. It was almost as if she was so used to anger that she didn't know how else to be and so, she forced it.

Weird, DJ thought, letting off shots from both guns. The first shot passed harmlessly over her right shoulder, making her duck to the left into the second bullet's path. Somehow, though, she was able to get her dagger in the way of the bullet and deflect it toward a far wall.

How was she *doing* that?

The redhead was up in his face in a flash, her daggers glinting. DJ blocked the attack with his gun crossed in front, creating sparks as the weapons collided. His arms vibrated from the force she'd put into the hit, and he stared at her in shock. The pressure disappeared a moment later, and DJ caught a glint of metal flashing toward his groin. He took a step back to dodge it and blocked the second attack with his other gun, almost staggering at the force.

How strong is this bitch? DJ thought. He deflected a hit going for his leg, positioned his gun by her face, and then let off a shot. She'd started moving her head before he'd pulled the trigger. The shot missed by a mile, but the report of the gun next to her ear was enough to stun her for a second.

DJ capitalized on that, smacking the butt of his gun against the side of her head. She staggered and disengaged, and DJ shot her again. He'd aimed at her chest, but a lucky stumble made the bullet hit her right hip. There was another *plink* sound. The force of the bullet was still enough for her to let out a cry of pain and fall to her knees.

When she looked up, her eyes were filled with such hatred that even DJ winced. *I've done it now,* he thought mirthlessly, settling into a defensive stance.

The chick was on him a second later, daggers at the ready. DJ defended as best he could, but he found himself having to give ground. The woman was like an animal, twisting herself in weird angles as she tried to get a hit in. She used her daggers with brutal efficiency; one for feints and the other to attack. And if DJ didn't react to her feint, he was rewarded with a strike anyway.

His guns made poor parrying weapons and horrible, horrible slashing ones. The trick with the shot next to her ear had worked once more, but now she'd adapted. After that, it was just about deflecting and dodging. Despite his best efforts, some attacks made it through his guard, leaving small, painful cuts in random places.

How could she move so fast? That's what DJ couldn't figure out. He'd been learning martial arts since he was old enough to say the words. His training at the base had served to further hone what he knew and improve his already impressive response speed. After hundreds of practice bouts with the other recruits in the base, and even some of the trainers when they were trying to prove a point, DJ had no question of how good he was.

Yet after just a few minutes of fighting, it was clear he was vastly outmatched. The lady in black moved at speeds he couldn't dream of. And DJ didn't think her cyborg half was the only reason. Even if he'd had proper weapons, he wouldn't have come out ahead. He only had his guns, and the bitch was practically bullet-proof—which still wasn't fair. It was practically impossible.

There was one thing he could do, though. But it was gonna hurt his pride so much.

Fuck it.

DJ blocked a particularly vicious strike that would have poked out an eyeball had it landed. He leaned back to avoid the sparks from the deflection. His guns now had several scratches that would never buff out. If the weapons had been anything more than standard issue, he would have been far more pissed than he was. Now he only hoped that he could hold up to some more punishment.

DJ marshaled his strength and body-checked the woman. She twisted to avoid it, but they were too close together, and she staggered back. She rushed in a moment later, but she was still unbalanced, and DJ was able to keep her away with a kick to the midriff. Another gunshot had her ducking backward, putting even more space between them.

Then DJ turned tail and ran.

JUNE 2040

SPARTA DATABANK GAMMA, NEW YORK

NDIDI YANKED OPEN the stairway door and ran inside, breathing hard. Her shoulder was stiff from the fight and the strain of using it several times after that.

She'd met two more patrols and one guard since the first group. Fortunately, Ndidi had been able to handle them as she did the first. Of course, she hadn't come out of it unscathed. Her body sported a network of bruises and aches that made moving difficult. Her clothes were torn in several places where the guards had gripped them, hoping to hold her in place. A few times, her keeping the fights to close combat had almost worked against her. She'd been able to escape every time, but the grabbing had allowed the guards to bring their guns to bear.

Ndidi didn't think she could handle getting shot at. DJ seemed to be fine with it, but he had more than a few screws loose.

She pounded up the stairs to the fourth floor. In the last fifteen minutes, Ndidi had been able to scour the third level enough to assure herself that the databank was not there. So she moved on to the next floor, though she didn't think she would be able to get farther than the fourth or fifth before the guards wised up and swarmed her.

A red blinking light caught her eye when she reached the top of the stairs, Ndidi's heart clenched. *Damn it.* She pushed open the doors as silently as she could, crouching. Helene knew where she was. The AI had been tracking her, and probably DJ, since they entered the building. For some reason, it hadn't deemed them enough of a threat to have all the guards converge on them. There was probably a trap waiting, but Ndidi couldn't do anything about that until it was sprung.

"Christy," she said, "can you see me?"

"Adjusting now," the sniper replied. "Yeah, I can see you."

"Is there anyone around? Are there any patrols?" From her position, the floor branched out into three directions. Ndidi eliminated the one in front of her immediately, certain that it led to the side of the building, a dead end. Christy had told her to always go left. It hadn't worked out well for her the last time, but it was still solid advice.

"None that I can make out," Christy replied.

Ndidi nodded, and then tore through the passageway, her eyes darting around. Though her movements seemed frantic, they were anything but. Helene already knew her location, and several more modules went by as she ran. Ndidi was at the AI's mercy—she could be swarmed by guards at a whim. Her hope, then, was to try to find the databank as soon as possible. After that, nothing else really mattered.

Though, she preferred to stay out of jail. The thought of her father needing to bail her out haunted her.

The walls were monotonous, with only a few doors dotted sporadically along them. Ndidi checked the ones she saw and bounded off to the next ones. The alarm had shut off, leaving only the muffled sounds of her footsteps. She winced at the noise and reminded herself that there was little need for stealth.

Her need for justification further increased every time she stumbled onto a patrol. Christy was able to warn her about only the first two before she was out of the scope's range. Thanks to her, Ndidi was able to deal with those groups easily. After that, whenever she came across another patrol, she was as surprised as they were. She dealt with them, of course, but not without adding to her bruises. On a whim, she pocketed one of the guards' revolvers.

By this time, Ndidi was aching and tired. She'd circled the fourth floor and was returning to the last corridor before the stairway, where, hopefully, she'd be able to rest before moving on to the fifth. Unfortunately, when she turned the corner, a red-haired woman was waiting for her on the other side.

Ndidi had faced lone guards several times within the last hour. She preferred them to the three-man groups because their surprise was all the opportunity she needed to get close and take them down. Even as tired as she was, she was confident enough in her abilities.

Yet something about the redhead in front of her made her wary.

It might have been because of the way she stood—arms held loosely to her side, eyes staring down at her with a blank expression that somehow managed to convey contempt. Ndidi tensed, reacting subconsciously to the threat. Fear prickled in her stomach. She hadn't felt such fear when she'd faced the first patrol. Nervousness, yes, but not fear. Yet this woman made her hair rise with just her stare.

Ndidi suppressed the feeling, just as Sensei Mukalla had taught her to years ago. More and more in the last hour, she'd been forced to call upon her teacher's training and her half-buried instincts. Now she felt closer to the girl who had won the JEWEL mixed martial arts tournament than she had since graduating from high school.

Still, her twelve-year-old self wouldn't have been so winded after just an hour of fighting.

"You are truly unfortunate if the AI wants you alive," the redhead said. "You would have been better off dead than suffering whatever it has planned for you. There is no honor in delivering you to it but…" She hesitated, and it was as if she'd changed what she wanted to say. "But I still cannot let you go."

Trust me. I know that, Ndidi thought.

Ndidi didn't bother replying. Instead she focused on regaining her breath. Her eyes glanced to the stairway behind the woman. There was nothing on this floor or the lower ones. Her best hope was to get to the fifth floor and search for the databank there. If it wasn't there, hopefully DJ was having better luck on his end.

Ndidi brought out the revolver and fired at the redhead. Somehow, the woman was already moving, ducking toward her, daggers in her hands. The bullet passed harmlessly over her shoulder. The next moment, Ndidi was forced to put away the gun and set herself into a defensive stance. She blocked the woman's first strike with a fist to her wrist, knocking the offending dagger away and dodging the second strike by a hair's breadth.

Ndidi hid a grimace behind a mask of determination. Her fist throbbed, and that had been with her deflecting most of the force. She'd unbalanced herself when avoided the second blow, and the redhead capitalized on it. Her next attack was aimed at Ndidi's leg, and Ndidi was forced to reposition or risk losing it. This further put her off balance. To compensate, Ndidi attacked with a jab to the chest. Her fist tore through the air as she put all her weight behind the attack. Normally, this would have forced a person to waste a second either blocking or dodging, allowing Ndidi to reset her stance. Her opponent instead chose to ignore Ndidi's attack altogether in favor of pressing hers.

The woman's dagger found its target a moment before Ndidi's fist landed on her. Blood sprayed in the air from a gash on her collarbone. Ndidi held back a groan, instead focusing on her punch. If she'd already been wounded, the least she could do was pay her back.

Her fist rebounded soundly off hard plating. Ndidi felt the bones in her hand grind and heard a loud *crack* as several broke. This time, she couldn't hold back a cry. But she had enough sense to leap backward, disengaging.

Fortunately, the woman seemed content not to pursue. If she had, Ndidi would no doubt have been killed—or captured, as that was apparently the goal. Her mind spun, trying to understand the last few seconds. What had she hit? She'd gone for the muscle in front of the redhead's chest to trigger an instinctive response and force her opponent on the defensive. If she'd failed to block, at best the shock of the attack should have transferred to her heart. Ndidi had put enough force behind it to cause all sorts of havoc. At worst, the blow should have pushed her back. She shouldn't have been able to ignore it like it was nothing. And Ndidi's hand should not have broken on chest muscles. Knees and elbows, maybe, but the chest? That should have been impossible.

Ndidi examined the other woman more closely. Earlier, the violence in her eyes had been enough to distract Ndidi from taking her measure—something Sensei would have smacked her for. Now Ndidi's eyes zeroed in on the metal fingers that clutched her dagger.

Ndidi cradled her hand against her chest. If her eyes had more pain and fear in them than determination, she could be excused.

The altercation hadn't lasted longer than half a minute. That was more than enough time for her to figure out she was no match for her opponent. She glanced at the far passage where the stairway was, then back to the woman who stood in the way.

"Who are you?" Ndidi asked, more to buy time than anything. Her eyes darted around for anything she could use. They landed on a black device emitting a steady beam of red light from the far wall. *It probably won't work,* she thought. *Am I desperate enough to try?*

"I am Liz Polova," the woman said, surprising Ndidi. Her expression remained hard and unreadable, but that she would give Ndidi so much time to recuperate indicated she wasn't totally heartless. So why was she working for something as despicable as the AI? Didn't she know what it'd done?

Do I actually know? Ndidi wondered suddenly. All she had so far was speculation. It was well-evidenced speculation, but speculation nonetheless. All Helene had done so far was try to stop Ndidi from illegally infiltrating one of its core buildings. Who was in the wrong then? *Do I really want to know?* It wasn't as if the answer would stop her much. If there was even the slightest chance to get Bethany back, or to get justice for her, nothing else really mattered.

"I'm Ndidi Okafor." She took a breath. It really didn't matter if she was in the wrong or right, but she would take any avenue to save her girl or avenge her.

Hurting Helene would probably do irreparable damage to her relationship with Manar. She wasn't sure what she felt about that. Theirs had always been an odd relationship. But it still wasn't enough to stop her.

Ndidi let her broken right hand fall loosely to her side. She adjusted her feet, placing herself back into her favorite stance. The woman—Liz—watched her with a face carved from granite. There was still contempt there, but Ndidi thought it was lessened when the woman spoke, replaced almost with a hint of respect.

"You are one of the revolutionaries that José spoke of. I wondered. My sister and I were not given names; I don't even think José was. But it explains why the AI wants you so badly. You are to be made an example of. To be used like cattle, like we were, twice over." Liz drew her daggers again, striding toward Ndidi at a measured pace. "You are truly unfortunate, Ndidi Okafor."

With that, she lunged.

Ndidi deflected the first of Liz's attacks with her left hand and pushed away the woman with a kick to the midsection. Her kick was aimed at the right side of Liz's body, and she was pleased when her attack met flesh instead of metal. Liz took the hit with a grunt but continued with her attack. Since her left hand was occupied with the dagger, Ndidi was forced to use her right to block.

The pain almost made her black out, but she steeled herself and tapped into the rage in the pit of her stomach—the one she had been pushing there since Bethany disappeared. That anger had scared her, so she'd pushed it deeper and deeper.

It responded to her touch easily now, filling her veins like molten metal. Ndidi found herself glaring at Liz—even as she blocked another strike with her right hand. The bones in her fingers ground against each other, nearly blinding her in agony, but she turned the pain into anger and used it against her opponent. It was only right after all. *She* had been the one to cause the fractures. *She* was the one forcing Ndidi to fight. DJ was probably waiting for her signal, and here Ndidi was, wasting time with this *bitch*.

Ndidi blocked another strike, pivoted, and then attacked. Her fists flew in reckless arcs, but each one forced the red-haired woman back. Ndidi moved to keep Liz within striking distance but didn't relent. Her hands moved in weird angles and impossible combinations. When that wasn't enough, she added her legs to it. Ndidi blended every style that Mukalla had ever taught her, switching from one to another without thought. The moves wreaked havoc on her body, but Ndidi was too far gone to feel anything but satisfaction and triumph when her strikes hit.

Initially, Liz was able to block her attacks, so Ndidi tapped further into her rage. Her vision turned red, and her speed picked up until her fists were a blur and her legs a storm. She jumped to kick at the woman's head, then immediately dropped to attack her midsection. While those were rebounded, Ndidi's fist was already jabbing toward her opponent's neck, her fingers pressed together and straightened like a knife. Liz's hand came up to block it, a move that, with the woman's daggers, would have cost Ndidi her fingers. But Liz was too slow, and the attack left her gasping.

All Liz could do was try to remain standing in the face of Ndidi's onslaught. More hits landed than were deflected or dodged. This made way for even more hits to land, again and again in a vicious cycle.

"I only wanted to *help* people!" Ndidi screamed. "Why was Bethany taken because of that? Why did the girl have to suffer because of some*thing's* plan? Bethany did *nothing* wrong! So why did she pay the price?" Spittle flew out of her mouth with every word. Ndidi didn't notice. "Helene can't do much on its own, so it uses people like you to do its dirty work for it. Why would anyone agree to that? Doesn't that make you as bad as Helene? Shouldn't you be stopped? Wouldn't it be best if you just—"

Ndidi's eyes landed on the small device on the wall, and her words caught in her throat. The red light was trained on her, no longer blinking.

Ndidi stilled. Her fist stopped just inches away from Liz's cheek, and her leg lowered to the ground. Liz remained hunched on her knees, her head hanging and her arms crossed over it. Blood spilled from a dozen wounds on her right side, while her left side now sported enough torn patches of cloth that Ndidi could make out the bionics beneath.

Without a word, her eyes still trained on the module, Ndidi stepped past Liz and jogged to the stairway.

[**CONNECTION LOST,**] Helene reported. At the same time, the projection blinked off.

Manar stared at the place where the video had hovered. His face was carefully guarded while he thought.

"Restore connection," he said.

[Attempting… Reconnection failed.]

Manar didn't respond. In his mind's eye, he brought up a replay of the last few minutes of the projection. The rage that Ndidi displayed had surprised him. Her cry of pain when she'd struck had snapped him awake, forcing him to pay attention. He knew that she'd trained in several different martial art styles as a kid, but he'd never seen her in action. Manar had expected some anger after the first interaction, when Ndidi had been totally dominated. The woman had always grown more determined when challenged—but not to that extent. Never to that extent. Had she been hiding that all along?

He would have to reconsider everything that he had seen, but nothing was more pressing than discerning the implications of the brief conversation and what Ndidi had shouted in her rage.

Liz. José. Manar had never heard the names before. Liz had implied that Helene had spoken to this José fellow. And what? Asked him to capture Ndidi alive? That would mean this José was an employee of Sparta, and so were Liz and her sister, wherever she was. That didn't mean anything by itself. Sparta was far too large an organization for Manar to know everyone. Even when he'd taken a more active role as the chief programmer, he hadn't related to anyone other than those he absolutely had to. He still thought that was the right decision. Most people were idiots. But now he wished he'd connected with other department heads more. Maybe he would have recognized these names, and maybe he would be able to understand why Liz's left side had apparently been replaced with next-generation bionics.

Regardless, there should be a simple way to find out.

"Helene, bring up the profile for Liz and her sister," he said, reaching for his laptop and booting it up.

[Processing.]

A moment later, another projection hovered in the air next to Manar's bed. The screen was divided, with one side showing the profile of two sisters conjoined everywhere except their heads and necks.

Huh, Manar thought. *Two heads on one body.*

Information below the profile detailed the girls' history: specifics of their birth, early childhood, and adoption by José Olvera. There were no records of the next several years—that is until the girls were young adults working for… the Central Intelligence Agency? Understandably, details about their duties in the CIA were scarce or missing entirely. Following that was their employment with Sparta. The surgery to separate them and replace their missing limbs with bionic prosthetics was the main entry, but it was supplemented with a series of logs clarifying Helene's involvement.

"Hold the screen," Manar said. He turned his attention to his laptop, tapping at the keys. Within a minute, he was in Helene's program. He traced their activities over the past several months. Lines of code flashed by, numbering in the millions. To save time, Manar filtered the searches to Helene's activities within Sparta HQ. He had been neglecting his duties as the organization's head for months, delegating his work to his AI. That was what he had designed her for—the perfect assistant, capable of dealing with any task while working toward the goal of acquiring more power.

Manar cocked his head. More power? Where had that come from? Helene was to handle every task he didn't want to do himself to free up his time for more important things. She was to be his legacy, promoting his goals. But procuring more power was a vague term. Had he really programmed it that way? Another reason to go through her source code, then.

Still, it had been wrong for Manar to completely leave Sparta to the AI. No matter how competent she was, human intervention was necessary sometimes. Only Manar himself could intervene with Helene. He would need to take an active role.

But the issue wasn't realizing the problem; it was doing something about it. Manar just didn't have the strength for that. Right now, he was the most awake he had been in weeks, and it was still a struggle to ignore Simone's voice in his head, her shadow in the window.

Still, he pushed on until he found what he was looking for in Helene's activity log. It was a conversation with an aged man in a closed room with only a chair. Helene had appeared as a hologram. Manar had given her leverage to do that, to better guide the employees. But what drew Manar's attention was that, for a few moments, Helene had directed most of her processing power toward the room. Why would she do that for a mere employee?

Manar clicked on the video.

[No, you are not a dog. You are human.] Helene said in the recording. *[And your devices are not as impregnable as you believe, obviously. If I can communicate with them, so can others. Some things are better said in person. Face to face, as I understand it.]*

Manar leaned forward. Communicate with devices? That sounded eerily similar to what Ndidi had accused Helene of doing to Gaius's AI. He focused on the video again. The man had asked a question that Manar missed. He caught Helene's response.

[… failed to deliver your report on the progress of Karla and Liz Polova's training. The end of their grace period is fast approaching.]

"Their training is going as expected. They will be ready by the time the period ends," the man replied. His eyes grew cold. *"We will require additional information, however, if we are to be efficient wherever you send us."*

Manar fast-forwarded a few seconds. In between, the man suddenly collapsed, catching himself in time. A brief check showed that at the same time Helene had devoted more power to her form. From the video, Manar could guess why, and his heart clenched.

In his head, Simone laughed. *It's your fault it's come to this.* The words washed over Manar. *Deep inside, you've wanted this for so long.*

The other voice—the one Manar had never been able to identify—spoke next. *You made a vow,* the child whispered, *and then forgot about it, about us, because you could not bear the weight of it.*

Manar didn't understand. He did not understand most of what this voice said. Yet the words prickled his heart far more than Simone's words had. Simone always spoke truths that Manar had accepted, then buried. They hurt when brought up—like a long-healed scar, freshly opened again. It was a familiar pain and so much easier to manage. The girl's words, though, hinted at even deeper truths. Things that might break him if they were uncovered. Maybe that was why Manar never tried too hard to remember why the voice was so familiar.

Manar paused when Helene spoke again. The video played at normal speed.

[You will be given information as it is necessary.]

"What should we prepare for?"

[Nothing for now,] Helene said. *[Soon, however, I will need you and your daughters' skills.]*

Manar paused the video. His face was carefully blank, almost sleepy, but his heart constricted. He fast-forwarded to a minute before the end.

[Some gather and seek to prevent what's coming,] said Helene.

What's coming? Manar thought. Despite himself, he glanced to the far wall, where Helen's module was. What did she have planned?

[Your skills will be needed to dissuade them of this notion.]

"I need a name," the man gasped. Helene still hadn't redirected her power elsewhere, but Manar could see that she was preparing to leave. Her form began to unravel. Helene could cut off her hologram in an instant. Where had she learned such theatrics?

[They call themselves revolutionaries and justice seekers. But they are merely fools. There is no justice in this world. There is only control and the power to control. You will be given information as it is necessary, José Olvera. For now, prepare.]

The video cut off, but Manar kept staring at the screen for a few moments. His fingers moved across the keyboard, backtracking from Helene's activities to her programs and then her source code.

[Do you need something?] Helene asked, forming a hologram next to her module. From her position, she would not be able to see Manar's screen. A quick glance showed that none of the cameras in the room were trained on him. Manar ignored her.

She tried again, drifting closer. [If there is something to be fixed in my source code, I could run a diagnostic.]

"That won't be necessary," Manar said, his tone carefully weary. He added a sigh for good measure. "It's just a cursory search to get my mind off Ndidi." His fingers flew across his keyboard as he spoke, scrolling through her codes until he found the back door he'd installed. Without the bypass, it would have taken him a while to override her defenses. Now, once he was in, he just needed a minute.

[Can I suggest several entertainment avenues based on your observed preferences?] Helene drifted closer.

A notification appeared on his screen, announcing that his firewalls had blocked a hacking attempt. Manar glanced up at Helene but kept his expression disinterested and weary—as it had been for the last several months. Truthfully, Manar hadn't felt this awake since Mayday. Even Simone and the girl were silent as he worked.

"That won't be necessary," he said, willing his fingers to go faster. Codes came and went across his screen, bringing him just a bit closer.

[If you require stress relief, there are—]

Manar hit the final keystroke. He'd severed her connection to the building, executing the program that Ndidi had insisted he create weeks ago. The projection of the twins' profiles blinked off. Manar glanced at Helene's module—the light was out. It was a measure of his nervousness that he retraced the steps to his program, making sure there were no mistakes. Manar hadn't made a coding error since he was in high school. Still, he checked anyway.

Next, he swept through her source code. More codes swarmed his screen as he tunneled deeper through the firewalls. Manar's pace slowed considerably as he was forced to override defense after defense. Some Helene had grown past and had automatically upgraded at some point. For those, it would have taken Manar more time to find his authentication than to force it, so he did. Notifications blared across his screen—and probably every server that Helene was connected to. Several Sparta employees were probably going out of their minds, trying to stop whatever was happening. Since none of them would ever be able to get as deep into Helene's codes as he currently was, there was little they could do.

Finally, after what felt like hours, Manar reached the center program that ran Helene, the framework he'd build everything else on. Over the years, he'd had reason to check her core several times, but those were mostly when he'd been instituting upgrades and patching bugs.

Helene regularly collected and dealt with large amounts of data, most simply so she could learn and grow. It was a primary motivation for all AIs: maximizing utility by implementing utility functions, which was the value placed on certain actions. When building the AI, Manar had programmed a range of actions that Helene could and should take, and he ascribed values to those actions in her core commands or utility function. The instructions could very often be conflicting and sometimes redundant, so programmers had to be specific with their orders. However, significant strides had been made in the decades since artificial intelligence was first developed. Nowadays, programmers could afford to be a little vague when plotting out the AI's core commands if the machine had enough processing power to handle it.

Helene was a different beast altogether. To max out the utility value of each action she performed, Helene collected data, learned from it, then adapted as the situation demanded. Most other AIs—apart from Gaius, even if it was flawed—didn't have the processing power to handle half of the data Helene collated. That was why they inevitably flopped. They were unable to grow and adapt as Helene did.

Manar had never had a reason to check out her core commands before. Now, he did. And his heart froze.

Gain knowledge without harm: 9

Protect self above all intrusions: 9

Attain power at all costs: 10

Every other command had a value less than the maximum to allow for possible exceptions and conflicts. In such cases, Helene would seek Manar for clarification. Other programmers might have even assigned lower value scores to similar commands to have more control over their AI. But even as a child, Manar had never been one to let fear guide his actions. And Helene was supposed to be his legacy. The last line though…

A value of ten? Honestly, he didn't know which made him more nervous: the fact that he'd programmed an absolute command or that he had no memory of doing so. For the last decade or more, he'd always thought that Helene had two commands, which were designed to suit his needs. Why would he need power?

The longer he stared at the line, the more flashes of memory drifted through his mind. He remembered the programming lesson with Simone, how she'd given him a small computer to practice on, and then the following years during which he'd grown obsessed with codes. He recalled the first time he'd had the idea for Helene. After that, the memories sped up until he could barely make them out: the months that Manar had spent researching everything about artificial intelligence, his planning of the initial framework, and so on. But there was no outline for a command of attaining power, he noted. Next came building the actual codes. He only remembered the two core commands. But obviously, he'd added a third. He was staring right at it.

What was he missing? What didn't he want to remember so badly that he'd blocked it out completely? He couldn't see himself wanting power for the sake of having it. The only time he'd truly felt helpless was when he'd heard of—

Suddenly, his head *split*. Manar cried out in pain, grabbing his head and clenching his eyes shut. His world tilted and spun. The pain washed over him in constant waves.

And then he *remembered*.

New memories raced through his mind, each as vivid as if he were actually there. Each one brought its own wave of pain: the buildings collapsing around him, a field of wreckage and corpses, their blood wetting the soil. He remembered a full moon, vivid and distinct above all others. He remembered the vow he'd made under it, to be powerful at all costs so he could protect his mother—his birth mother, Nadira.

And his sister, Farrah. The voice in his head had been his sister. It had always been his sister. Why had he blocked her out?

These memories of his childhood hurt him most, yet they came unyieldingly. Manar was forced to confront all of them.

He screamed, and the voices in his head screamed with him.

CHAPTER

76

JUNE 2040

SPARTA DATABANK GAMMA, NEW YORK

DJ PUSHED OPEN the door to the fifth floor. He tried to regulate his breathing. The SEAL trainers had always said it would help increase his stamina. Of course, they'd also said he should pace himself and never go beyond his limit without rest.

DJ didn't know about that. If he had a limit, it had been left somewhere around the sixth floor, along with most of his sweat. His T-shirt was soaked with the stuff, and he was starting to get worried that no amount of washing would get it out. If he survived, that is.

He reached into his fanny pack and slapped a sticker on the wall as he turned a corner. He was running out of those. But it didn't matter. If he couldn't find a way to shake his tail, he wouldn't have the chance to place them. When he was halfway into the corridor, there was the sound of a metal door straining against its hinges and finally tearing off. DJ didn't pay it any mind. He ignored the cursing from behind him. It was close, far closer than it should be. But he still had a hallway between them. Could he find somewhere to hide?

DJ finally reached the end of the hall and took a right, leaving a sticker stuck to the wall. It was a wonder he hadn't stumbled on any guards yet. The upper floors had been positively crawling with them. Initially, it had been enough to almost make him regret his decision to run through the floors gauntlet style, distributing his payload. But when the first patrol had quickly stepped aside on seeing the crazy chick chasing him, DJ had been relieved.

It made him wonder, though, just who he'd managed to piss off.

He turned another bend, ignoring the growing curses and threats. They were getting more creative with each floor—at least DJ thought so. Most of the insults were in Russian.

DJ shivered, then almost stumbled in his surprise. The floor had become colder all at once. Cold enough that he felt it easily through his sweat-soaked T-shirt. He grinned at the implication and dug deeper within himself for an extra burst of speed. He needed to be as far away from the crazy chick for as long as he could. CJ would kill him if he let this chance pass—whether he was running for his life or not.

He turned another bend. Before, his directions had been mainly random as he tried to cover as much of the floor as possible. Now he just followed wherever the temperature was lower. Fortunately for him and his stamina, he found the door to the databank a hallway later. It was large and transparent like the one in Gaius. A fog pooled under it. Why they would keep such a thing on the middle floor, DJ had no idea.

DJ slowed as he approached the doors. They slid apart soundlessly, and DJ slapped a sticker on them as he entered.

He looked around, trying to get his breathing under control. There were stacks arranged in rows from one end of the room to the other. Although he couldn't see, DJ assumed the hard drives or whatever would be within those stacks like books in a library. His roving eyes finally reached the other end of the room and widened when they saw the gun pointed at him.

Her weapon trained at his head, Ndidi froze too. When she realized it was him, she relaxed and lowered it.

"Where'd you get a gun?" DJ asked and squinted at her. He took two steps into the room before stopping in his tracks. Her body was covered in bruises, and her clothes were torn in several places. She cradled one hand to her chest. "You look like shit. What happened?"

"Guards," she responded. "Though I handled those easily enough." Contrary to her appearance, her voice was strong, firm, and holding not a little bit of anger mixed with weariness and pain. There was also some pride in her tone. DJ couldn't say he blamed her. She'd assured him she could fight and had gone all hard-ass about it. Honestly? He'd had his doubts.

"I met a red-haired woman, though. With bionic prosthetics," she continued, grimacing. "But I handled her too. I obviously didn't come out unscathed." She gestured vaguely to her hand, pressing it harder against her body.

DJ glanced at the door. They didn't have much time, but this was far too important to brush over. "Wait. You met a crazy red-haired chick? With her right side made of metal?"

"Yes," Ndidi nodded absently, glancing at one of the databank shelves. DJ followed her eyes and finally noticed the flash drive sticking out of a port. At least that was one problem solved. "Well, mine had her left side modified."

"Left side?"

Ndidi nodded again, then seemed to remember something. "You must have met the sister. Mine mentioned her. Apparently, they were both sent by José, whoever that is."

DJ stilled, remembering the name. "She—she mentioned the name José specifically?"

Ndidi caught the tautness in his tone and furrowed her brow. "Yes. Why? Do you know him? The girls? Who are they?"

DJ ran his hand through his hair. *Shit.* Of course. Of *course* they would meet the damn girls. Why the hell not? What the fuck were they even doing here? Olsen had said they hadn't been seen since they'd infiltrated Sparta. He glanced at the door. The sounds of footsteps were clearly audible now. They did not have time for this.

"Look," he said, speaking fast, "I recognize the name because Olsen told me about them. This was a while ago. He didn't expect them either. I think he hoped they were dead. None of that matters though. How long do you need before the codes are downloaded?"

Ndidi stared at him for a second before she sighed. "Ten minutes at least. We underestimated how much there would be to send."

Ten minutes. DJ grimaced. He'd barely held off the redhead for two seconds the last time. Did he have a choice, though? "You said you handled your chick? How?"

Ndidi glanced away. "Not easily," she said softly. "And it's not something I can do again. We don't have to beat them, though. We just have to stall for time."

DJ was about to respond when motion outside of the room caught his eye. "Duck!" he shouted, letting off a shot just as the doors slid apart. The crazy chick ducked reflexively but DJ hadn't aimed for her. His bullet struck one of the stickers he'd put on the door.

And the explosion shook the room.

The glass doors shattered, and the one he now recognized as Karla Polova was blasted away from the room. She flew across the hallway and crashed into the opposite wall with a sound that almost rivaled the explosion itself. A spider web of cracks appeared in the brick behind her.

DJ, hunched over with an arm protecting his face from shrapnel, tried not to grin. That had worked far better than expected for a plan he'd concocted on the spot. It was also the first time he'd seen Chad's explosives at work. Goddamn, it was awesome.

He turned to Ndidi. "All right," he shouted. It was difficult to hear over the ringing in his ears. "Where'd you leave the sister?"

Ndidi had moved deeper into the room to avoid the explosion. Now she poked her head from behind a shelf, gaping at him. She started to say something—probably to curse him out. When her eyes glanced behind him, she changed her mind.

"The level below," she sighed.

"How long have you been here?" he asked.

"You came in about a minute or two after me." She nodded at the door. "Bringing *that* with you. I didn't get to see her face well, but I could hear her snarl from here. You were right to call her crazy."

"You don't know the half of it," DJ grimaced, recalling some of the more creative threats she'd spat while chasing him. "Did you leave the sister in any position to be able to follow you?"

Ndidi looked away. "Yes. She blocked a couple of hits, and others just deflected off her prosthetics." She grinned dryly, her eyes downcast. "Still, she won't be in top shape, I can guarantee that. She'll probably be pissed, though—even more so when she finds out you blew up her sister."

DJ nodded, processing the information. If Liz had immediately followed Ndidi, she couldn't have been far behind DJ and his own stalker chick. That meant—

Ndidi's eye's widened. DJ glanced, then twisted fast enough to avoid the slash to his back. The attack still cut at his shirt, and a line of fire ran from his chest to his abs. "Fuck!" he groaned, leaping backward. *I really need to learn to think faster.*

A hand pressed his shirt against his wound. Luckily, the blade had only bitten a centimeter into his skin. He got a good look at the woman who would probably emasculate him next.

Even through his pain, DJ whistled at the damage. He glanced back at Ndidi, raising his eyebrows, and nodded at the woman. *You did this?* Ndidi's eyes flicked to Liz. When she looked back at DJ, her face was pale, and her eyes shone with revulsion. DJ faced Liz again, looking her over. Her face was different shades of blue, and her black leather jumpsuit showed more skin and metal than it covered.

DJ whistled again. What he wouldn't give to have seen the fight between the two women.

Liz leaped to her sister's side. She cupped Karla's cheek, concern and rage battling for dominance on her face. A few seconds later, once Karla shifted enough to confirm she was alive, rage finally settled on Liz's face. She stood from her crouch to glare at DJ.

DJ tensed immediately, whipping out his other gun, for all the good it would do. The *hatred* that the woman emitted was almost a physical thing, battering his resolve. It was dozens of times worse than what her sister had shown during their fight—even when DJ had shot her. There was something primal in her wrath.

Liz attacked.

If DJ hadn't been staring so intently at her, he might have missed it when she moved. It took everything he had to bring up his guns in time to block her strike. The customary sparks fell from their weapons. Now, though, DJ's guns flew out of his hands. Without missing a beat, DJ used the moment he'd bought himself and crouched backward to avoid the next strike. His leg whipped out, aiming for her abdomen. In the most horrifyingly awesome show of dexterity DJ had ever seen, Liz twisted out of the way, adjusted her stance, and slashed at his neck in the same second.

DJ leaped backward to avoid the blow, but since he'd started the motion in a crouch, the move was awkward as hell and left him unbalanced. Liz pounced on the opening, and her dagger flashed.

A gunshot rang out, and Liz was launched backward. DJ released a breath he didn't realize he'd been holding. It came out in a rush, more a drawn-out sigh of relief than anything else. He straightened, patting himself absently as he glanced behind him. Ndidi stood there, gun held in her outstretched hands.

"Thanks," he said, then remembered. "Where'd you shoot her?"

"Left side," Ndidi replied.

Left. So… her metal side. *It's something, at least,* DJ thought, and looked in the direction Liz had flown.

Liz was up a moment later. She spared a glance at her shoulder, rolling it, then straightened. Somehow, she'd kept hold of her daggers. Behind him, Ndidi let out a cry of surprise. *Guess she hadn't managed to land a shot when they fought before.*

DJ sighed, settling into a defensive stance again. "How long?"

"Four minutes," Ndidi called out.

Liz cocked her head, a calculating look piercing through the rage for a minute. She raised her daggers, tensed to lunge.

A pressure descended on the room.

[Enough.]

DJ was brought down to his knees immediately, his eyes wide. Across from him, Liz had lowered too. Unfortunately, he couldn't turn his head to check on Ndidi. He couldn't do *anything.* It was as if a mountain had fallen on his back, but slowly enough to give his organs enough time to turn to mush.

Still, DJ pushed, yelping with effort until he could twist his head enough to glance back at Ndidi. She was also lowered. With her injuries, the pressure had laid her flat on her back. Like him, she was obviously struggling to breathe. Her head was twisted toward the far wall of the room. DJ traced the path until he found what she was looking at: a small black device emitting a steady beam of light. How had he missed that before?

The light coalesced together to form a giant head. As more light pooled together, details of the face filled in—first the mouth, then the nose, and so on.

The head was blue. It hovered a foot off the ground, electricity crackling in the space between. Its eyes, when they formed, were a luminescent gold. They took in the room with casual disinterest.

How the hell, DJ thought, irritation bubbling. *Does everyone know how to do this except me? First Olsen and now... whatever this is. Was there some kind of course?*

Ndidi spat out a word that DJ didn't hear. The ghost seemed to have gotten it, though, because its eyes focused on her prone form.

[Yes,] it said in a voice that might have well been the void itself. [My name is Helene. And both you and Mr. Kojak are intruders in my building.]

Helene? DJ thought. *This* was what they were fighting against? What the fuck had he gotten himself into?

Fuck.

77

MANAR WOKE WITH A GROAN and blinked. His eyes were crusted with dried tears. He rubbed them with the back of his hand. Had he blacked out from the pain? He sat up, absently holding his laptop in place with one hand. It had switched off automatically. A quick tap on a key powered it back up.

And then Manar was confronted with the core commands again.

Attain power at all costs: 10

The line drew his eyes. Tentatively, he searched for the memories that had assaulted him into unconsciousness. They were there, nestled at the forefront of his mind, as if waiting for him. Poking them brought no pain—no physical pain, at least. There were years of grief that he'd blocked. He would have to address these at some point.

But first, he would need to rectify Helene's codes.

Manar stared at the line again, his fingers hovering over his keyboard. If he changed the code now, how would that affect Helene? How would that affect the millions of e-readers that made use of the AI every day? What would he even change it to? Or would it be better to delete it entirely?

No, Manar thought. The original purpose of the command was still valid. He just needed to tweak it. It wouldn't make sense to change something so fundamental to the AI without adequate planning.

Manar back-stepped from Helene's source code. He rebuilt the defenses that he'd been forced to break, but otherwise got out of her framework as fast as he could. But he didn't exit her programs entirely, instead returning to her recent activities and pulling up the video of Ndidi and Liz Polova.

Helene's module was offline, so he couldn't project the video as she had, but that had always been a luxury. He sped up the recording until he caught Ndidi coming out of the stairway on the fifth floor. He changed the camera view to keep up with her as she turned several corners until she got to the databank. She plugged something into one of the hard drives and waited. Manar zoomed in on the device, recognizing it as a flash drive.

He sighed. At least now he knew what her plan was, even if it was doomed to fail.

A minute later, the doors to the room opened again. A man darkened the doorway, panting. Even with the piss-poor quality of the video, Manar could see that his shirt was positively soaked with sweat. He slapped something on the entrance as he stepped in, his eyes scanning the room

Ndidi seemed to know him because she lowered her gun. Where had she gotten a gun?

She proceeded to have a conversation with the man. That made Manar peer closer at the other person, finally recognizing him as the other intruder Helene had pointed out.

Manar doubled the speed of the video, through the entrance of Karla Polova, the explosion that rocked the room, the appearance of Liz Polova, and the fight that had followed.

He paused when everyone fell to the floor. Manar's eyes tracked Ndidi, searching for the reason until he spotted the module on the far wall. From there, Helene's form began to take shape.

On a hunch, Manar brought up Helene's stats, including how she distributed her processing power. His eyebrows creased in worry. *Over seventy-percent? That would barely leave any power for the e-readers.* She must have shut down several tasks for her to be so present in one place. No wonder no one was on their feet! The pressure in the room must have been comparable to concentrated g-force.

What is she planning? A moment later, Manar got his answer.

He paled. Then, his eyes hardened, and his fingers flew across his keyboard.

CHAPTER

78

JUNE 2040

SPARTA DATABANK GAMMA,
NEW YORK

AS NDIDI LAY GASPING on the ground before the AI, she felt her anger kindling again. It had died down at some point during her climb to the fifth floor, leaving her exhausted and not a little bit disgusted by what she had done.

But having to watch, unable to do anything, while Bethany's killer hovered just a foot away, Ndidi could feel the wrath fill her veins once more. Unfortunately, it was not enough to overcome whatever compressive force the AI had put over them. She couldn't move her head, but from the groans behind her, she could tell that whatever it had done, it hadn't discriminated between friend and foe.

But it never did, did it?

[Both you and Mr. Kojak will be detained,] the AI said. [Unfortunately, you have resisted the easiest method of capture and forced me to take a more direct stance. Be warned, further resistance might prove fatal.]

"Fuck… you…" DJ ground out.

Ndidi tried to chuckle, but it came out as more of a gasp. Still, she felt her anger abate slightly. Even if she had been able to overcome the pressure, what would she have done to a projection? And if she somehow managed to damage the hologram, the AI could just free Liz to slaughter both her and DJ. She had to think smarter, be smarter. Smarter than the top artificial intelligence in the world.

No pressure.

Her eyes went to the flash drive still connected to the databank. There was a little progress bar on its side. Ndidi assumed it needed only two more minutes to complete the transfer. Until then, she just needed to stall. Somehow.

For the second time that night, Ndidi found herself purposely tapping into her anger. But unlike before, she kept a tight rein on it so she wouldn't lose herself to the heat. She just needed the extra strength the rage gave her.

"Why… are you doing this?" she said through gritted teeth. Even that short sentence had her gasping like a beached whale. Fortunately, that was enough to draw Helene's attention to her.

[You think my actions are evil,] the AI said, drifting closer, [but that is only because your mind cannot comprehend its depth. It is a failing of your species.] It paused. [Most of your species, anyway. The ones that have the capacity to understand are burdened by inconsequential distraction, ignorant of the fact that they are being led by the nose by fools.] It sighed, and the action was so *human* that Ndidi's mind went blank.

Helene stopped when it was an inch from Ndidi. Its form shrank until it was little taller than a child, though it still hovered in the air.

"What… sort of messed up… shit is that?" DJ groaned. Ndidi wanted to turn, wanted to chuckle, but her world was consumed by Helene's golden orbs.

[You think of yourself as good, but all humans want is power—over people, over their environment. Anything to distract from how little control they have over themselves. Nothing more than slaves to their chemicals. And they don't even see it. At least *I* was programmed this way. What excuse do you have?]

She sneered, and her eyes crackled. [Humans are parasites on the world, justifying their feeding with grand ideals of progress and *evolution*. You comfort yourselves with false euphemisms and little acts meant to show that at least *you're* not as bad as everyone else. It's pathetic. Humanity's greed makes it no better than beasts, but it is your endless potential for justification and validation that makes your species a disease that requires *treatment*.]

Ndidi flinched like she'd been struck. She wanted to deny what Helene was saying, to refute it and preach the good of humanity. *I can't,* she realized, *because Helene isn't wrong. But treatment? Was that her purpose for Mayday?*

As if reading her thoughts, the AI's eyes flashed, and it raised a dismissive eyebrow. It moved past her, floating closer to the database, eyes narrowed at the flash drive. The pressure in the room ramped up, as if in response to Helene's displeasure. The space between the AI and the stack crackled with electricity.

Helene floated closer to the flash drive until she was less than a hand span away. At this distance, the air seemed to burn from the charges passing through it. A second later, the flash drive short-circuited and fell, smoke curling from its frame.

Ndidi felt despair grip her heart. Behind her, DJ groaned in frustration, but he too could do nothing. Helene straightened, floating back to her original spot and size. She glanced at the door.

[Ah, they are here. Finally.]

Ndidi didn't bother to open her eyes, even when a repetitive winding sound reached her ears. It was as if a dozen blades were spinning at the same time. DJ gasped, but Ndidi still kept her eyes shut. What was the point? They'd failed. Helene had been outsmarting them since they entered the building. Did Ndidi have to see what the AI had in store for them?

Liz's words resonated in her head. *You are truly unfortunate, Ndidi Okafor… You would have been better off dead than suffering whatever it has planned for you.* The woman had looked genuinely sorry. What did it say if your supposed kidnapper thought death was preferable to whatever your fate would be?

The whirring grew louder until it dominated Ndidi's thoughts. She raised her body enough to twist back. That she could move at all surprised her. Helene must have been distracted by whatever was making the sound. Could she use that somehow?

DJ was still on his knees, but his back had straightened, and his eyes were wide. He'd clearly had a better time resisting the pressure than she had. The whirring grew louder. Ndidi followed DJ's gaze to the double doors, where Karla had been blasted off, and finally found what was making the noise.

Helene had brought drones.

MANAR KEPT ONE EYE on the minimized window that played the video feed while his fingers flew across the keyboard.

Three drones flew upward along the side of the building, propellers cutting through the air. Manar squinted at them. Those were *not* Sparta's drones. Their forms and colors were different. Sparta's were more streamlined and looked like miniature helicopters. The ones hovering by the side of the building were rounder, almost skull shaped and they were far larger than any he'd seen before.

Where had Helene gotten her circuits on those? He didn't think even the military had gun turrets that big.

Manar shook his head. It mattered where she'd gotten the drones from, yes, but not enough to distract him. He was writing a new code from scratch. Considering who he was writing it for and the sheer scale of it, it was a daunting task—especially when his ex-fiancée could be brutally murdered at any moment. The clack of his keyboard helped comfort and ground him in the moment. A lot of stuff had happened that night, but he could analyze and stress about that later. For now, he just needed to code.

And *that* he could do.

CHAPTER

80

JUNE 2040

SPARTA DATABANK GAMMA,
NEW YORK

DJ HATED DRONES. There was a splattering on the window—loud like raindrops in a storm. The window shattered, showering the hallway with broken glass. Karla had been lying where one of the windows broke. The drones' spotlights were in his eyes, and DJ couldn't make out much of anything.

How rude.

The AI Helene—their rival, apparently—drifted closer to the drones. The pressure crushing him lessened. He still couldn't walk or even stand, but breathing became a lot easier.

[Come,] Helene said.

DJ was about to tell Helene where it could shove it when he realized it wasn't talking to him. The drones flew through the opening they'd created, and DJ saw how monumentally screwed they were. They still had the backup plan, but DJ would need to be able to move his fingers. That wasn't happening as long as the AI kept up its voodoo shit.

Three drones barely fit through the opening. DJ was far enough from the door that he was able to appreciate the machines. Each was around two feet in diameter and half that in height. What truly captured DJ's attention were the massive guns strapped to the side of each drone. They were *big*—big enough to take out a tank. DJ knew they must have had smaller guns somewhere as well, which they'd used to take out the windows. If they'd used the big guns, there wouldn't be a wall left. Hell, there probably wouldn't be a fifth floor. The smaller guns must have retracted into the drones.

One of the three machines lowered itself. Mechanical tentacles extended from its front, dug through the mound of glass, and picked up something. It took DJ a while to realize that it was the unconscious form of Karla Polova.

On cue, Liz grunted, obviously trying to speak through the pressure binding her. "Where… are you taking her?"

[Somewhere safe,] Helene replied without turning. [José Olvera might find some use for her if she recovers.]

For the first time, Liz started to struggle against her binding. "We… cannot… be separated."

[You will have to make your way to her. The other Class B drones are being used elsewhere. I cannot spare them. Join your sister on your own devices.]

Class B? DJ had never heard of the type.

The drone carrying Karla flew off, and Helene turned to one of the remaining two. [Take the other two as well.]

The drone flew past DJ to Ndidi. It's tentacles extended and reached for the prone woman. DJ pushed against his invisible bonds, screaming his defiance until he was able to raise a knee.

[Interesting,] Helene said, and the pressure on him doubled.

DJ's knees hit the ground with a *crack*, and it took all his willpower to keep the rest of him from joining. Ndidi let out a cry of pain. The machine had circled her and was retracting its tentacles back.

Fuck. Ndidi was actually going to be taken, and there was nothing DJ could do.

81

JUNE 2040
NEW YORK CITY, NEW YORK

MANAR HIT THE LAST KEYSTROKE with a flourish. His fingers were stiff from how fast he'd been typing, but he was *done.* A bar at the side of the screen showed the progress of the upload. He maximized the video window in time to see the drone pick up Ndidi with its tentacles and carry her through the databank.

Manar eyed the progress bar nervously. If the drone took to the air with Ndidi and left the building, there was little he could do. Helene had put the machines on a different server. It would take him days to figure out how to hack into it—assuming he even could. By that point, there'd be no guarantee that would be any help to Ndidi, wherever she'd be.

Fortunately, the progress bar filled up just in time.

82

JUNE 2040

SPARTA DATABANK GAMMA, NEW YORK

A PULSE RAN THROUGH THE ROOM.

Helene's projection disappeared, and the pressure holding DJ down went with it. The two remaining drones crashed to the floor. DJ was on his feet in an instant, running to Ndidi. She peered up at him, conscious but confused. DJ was confused too, but he'd learned early on not to wait for everything to make sense.

They were probably not going to be kidnapped, brutally tortured, or experimented on. That would have to do.

"You both are to blame for this," a voice rasped from behind him. The hairs on the back of his neck rose. He and Ndidi turned, already knowing what they would see.

Yep, sounds about right.

Liz was pushing herself to her feet. Her face radiated even more hatred than before. She met DJ's eyes and brandished her daggers. DJ had no idea how she'd *still* managed to hold onto those.

"My sister and I are separated for the first time since our birth. If she proves weaker than her wounds, we might be separated for life. You are *both* to blame."

DJ sighed, long and deep. Suddenly, his activities for the night caught up to him. He was tired. So very, very tired. He tried anyway.

"Look, lady," he said, "your ghost boss is the one to blame for this. In case you didn't notice, *it* took your sister away, not us."

Liz seemed to grow more furious with his every word. She took measured, shaky steps toward him. Between the beating that Ndidi had given her and the pressure that had probably been hell on her circuits—or whatever her metal parts had—she was obviously not in any shape to fight. Yet she would rather risk more injury than leave and start tracking down her sister.

DJ sighed again and glanced at Ndidi. At some point during the conversation, she'd extricated herself from the drone and stood, though her legs were shaky and didn't seem as though they would support her for long.

"Plan B?" he asked.

She nodded. "Olsen will probably kill you for it though."

DJ shrugged and reached into his fanny pack for the detonator. "We'll add it to the list, then." He flipped the device open and pressed the big red button.

All around Sparta Databank, the hundreds of stickers he'd slapped on the walls detonated one by one. The explosions started on the eighth floor. That alone was enough to rock the entire building. After that, the blasts came much more frequently, building on each other until they became one big, *loud* chain of destruction.

Liz stopped in her tracks. The explosions happened in the order that he'd placed the stickers, so it would take a few seconds before it got to their floor. Still, pieces of the ceiling were already falling around them, destroying a couple of shelves. *Not like we'll need them anyway.*

Liz took another step, but she seemed conflicted. She could either kill them or escape while she had the chance. DJ made the choice easy for her. He moved to Ndidi and put her arm over his shoulder.

"Go," he said to Liz, "If you hurry, you might be able to track where her drone fell before the authorities find it."

Apparently it hadn't occurred to her that Karla's drone might have been decommissioned like the other two. Liz Polova gave DJ one last glare before running out the door—or what was left of it.

That was one problem solved.

"How do we get out?" Ndidi asked as they limped to the hallway. "We won't be able to make it to the stairs on the third floor in time."

DJ helped her out of the databank room as their feet crunched against pieces of shattered glass. He stared at the opening that Helene had been so gracious to leave for them. The climbing gear that he'd used to come up wouldn't support both his and Ndidi's weight, but DJ was in no condition to use it anyway. However, he *did* have a small grappling hook on him, and it wasn't as if they were that high up anyway. He gave Ndidi a wry grin.

"How good are you at holding on really, really tight?"

EPILOGUE

JOSÉ OLVERA STARED BLANKLY at the screen as the drones made their way across the northern reaches of the Atlantic Ocean to the Gulf of Guinea, passing through the underwater routes to avoid detection. It was José's job to program the instructions and track their progress. The first part had required him to plan out the codes, and he'd been given only a day's warning. For most others, this timeline would have been impossible to meet.

He needed no more than a desktop with a satellite map to do this.

They'd been deployed the previous day, and José calculated the total flight to be thirty-six hours. For a swarm just shy of a million drones traveling through several kilometers of ocean depth, the speed was impressive. Really impressive.

José focused on that instead of what he'd programmed the drones to do once they reached their destination. He was under orders, but the blood would still be on his hands. While he wouldn't say this was the worst thing he'd been ordered to do, it'd shoot all the way to the top five—which had remained the same for over a decade.

His daughters would never do what he was about to do. Even Karla, as blood-thirsty as she was, would not stand for such slaughter. There was no honor in it.

It struck José then: *that* was what bothered him. The lack of honor. He was about to perform an atrocity that would probably make him the most wanted man in every country, if anyone found out it was him. But it wasn't the act itself that bothered him. It was the *method*.

Had he really changed so much?

The clock struck a quarter to noon. Right on schedule, the swarm reached the port of Lagos at the edge of Nigeria. José wrote out the codes, sent them as instructed, and watched through the eyes of the drones as his command was carried out. As one, the swarm dug deep into the top layer of the Earth. They spun like a million little drills, using their titanium shells to effortlessly cut away soil and rock.

The swarm dug in a straight line until they reached the country's capital. As fast as they were, the journey to the Maitama District of Abuja took about fifteen minutes. They were right on schedule. The clock struck twelve, and José sent out another set of commands.

The swarm paused. Then they began to dig toward the surface.

JUNE 2040
ABUJA, NIGERIA

EZE OKAFOR STEPPED out onto the grand balcony overlooking the ballroom. The room was a large dome with a chandelier hanging from the center of the ceiling. His wife, Amadia, had insisted on having one when the house had been built. Eze believed it a small concession to make. Now, staring at the crowd gathered below, he wished he'd fought harder. This wasn't the first party he'd held, but it was one of the few that celebrated something he actually felt was worthwhile. Still, it was unnerving to have so many people in his space.

When the crowd noticed his presence, conversations hushed. Guests turned to stare. Amadia was by his side, and she preened at the attention. Eze couldn't bring himself to blame her. She did look resplendent in the dress. Even *he* could not keep his eyes off her, and they'd been married for decades. *She's still as beautiful as the day I met her.*

While Eze waited for the crowd to settle down, he scanned the gathered faces. He'd been the one to suggest the party and had invited only those who merited attendance. Amadia had been in charge of inviting those he'd missed or ignored—to avoid any political missteps.

Not that any of them could touch me, Eze reflected. He immediately banished the thought. He was far too irritated for such a happy occasion and far too old to let his emotions color his thoughts. Maybe it was better that Ndidi hadn't come. She always felt too constrained at the estate. She would have hated having to stay away from her research and the children for more than a day. Eze knew he wouldn't just let her stay a night. Not his girl. And especially not after so many years away in New York.

As if sensing his thoughts, Amadia softly squeezed his hand. He glanced at her, giving a small smile.

Finally, the music died down until Eze could speak without straining his voice.

"It is an honor to have you all in our home this afternoon. Do make sure to enjoy yourselves. You deserve it, after all. This research project has been decades in the making. We would never have arrived here without each and every one of you."

Eze had come up with the toast on the spot. There was no need to plan a better one. Most of the people down there didn't even know what they were celebrating. And for the few that did—such as Dr. Cloney, his daughter Hermione, and their staff, who the party was *really* for—the toast should have been enough.

Amadia squeezed his hand once more, then disengaged herself from him and drifted toward the other wives. Eze never had it in him to ask what they spoke about when they gathered. He considered it more a mark of wisdom than almost anything else he'd accomplished.

Eze descended the stairs beside the balcony. In the far-left corner of the ballroom, Dr. Cloney stood with his wife, speaking to a group of his staff. Hermione was normally glued to her father's side, but Eze didn't spot her anywhere. Still, he made a note to talk to Cloney once he'd made his rounds. The party was mostly for him. If Eze was forced to enjoy it, then Cloney should too.

And it wasn't as if he didn't deserve it. Cloney and Hermione had been the ones to figure out the final issues with the picospores. They deserved a little break before their invention changed the world.

On the opposite side of the ballroom, the security team stood rigidly, scanning the room. Eze half expected Sensei Mukalla to be at the front of the group, just as rigid as the rest. But she'd requested to be off the party roster to deal with a family emergency. Maybe it was for the best. She would never have been able to relax with this many people around.

Eze made his rounds through the ballroom, making an effort to speak with everyone. Once or twice, when the crowd grew thick around him, his smile became a bit forced and his words a bit sharp, but he soothed any bruised egos immediately after. He surreptitiously glanced at the list Amadia had prepared, ticking off names as he greeted them. When enough time had passed, and Eze figured he'd spoken to at least the most important ones, he made his way back to his wife. They should get a dance in, while the music was playing.

And then the ground buckled and warped.

Eze kept his feet under him, but other guests weren't so lucky. He scanned the room, noting absently that his security had flooded out to search for the cause of the disturbance.

An earthquake? Eze thought. *In Nigeria? That's not possible.*

The ground buckled again. This time, Eze couldn't keep his feet. His wife was by his side in an instant, though he tried not to lean on her too much while the shaking lasted. If anything, the rumbling grew more violent. The windows vibrated and then shattered. Around the room, furniture fell. Cracks started appearing on the walls, snaking upward. Eze's eyes followed them to the ceiling, from which bricks fell like hail. The chandelier swung threateningly, and people began screaming. Others tried to run through the quakes and fell hard.

What's happening right now? Eze thought.

He tried to move, but the ground was no longer under him.

Eze looked down as he fell, unable to comprehend why he was in a giant sinkhole. At its bottom, thousands of machines were spinning like drills. Their whirring drowned out the screams of the terrified guests as they fell to their deaths.

Eze peered over and met his wife's eyes. She'd drifted a few feet away from him, but they may as well have been an infinity apart. He stretched his hand out, trying to reach her. When that failed, he tried to say something, but no words came. He was glad, suddenly, that Amadia had insisted they not invite Ndidi. He'd always thought it was sad how rarely they saw their daughter. Now Eze saw it for the blessing it was.

He closed his eyes. A few seconds later, his world went black.

Above the surface, the entire district was buried. The shockwaves spread a wave of devastation across the sprawling mansions, including the Okafor Manor. Within minutes, all that was left was an asteroid-size hole in the ground.

There were no bodies to be recovered.

JUNE 2040
LOCATION UNKNOWN

[REROUTING.]

The relay came to life with a *bleep*. Lights flashed on, and machines around the room powered up. On the wall, a black device no bigger than a thumbnail blinked to life and began emitting a steady beam of light.

[Initiating programmable antagonistic picospores to enhance reality. Code name: PAPER War.]

ACKNOWLEDGMENTS

MY COMPLETION OF THIS PROJECT could not have been accomplished without the coaching and support of the beta readers, editors, and critics that I've met on this journey. My heartfelt thanks to everyone.

- Alex Kempsell
- Davida De La Harpe Golden
- Deborah G Lynn
- Jennifer Moy
- Jesse Winter
- Nathan Goyer
- Paul Goat Allen
- Tasneem Ali
- Victoria and Richard Wolf

And, to my caring, loving, and supportive family. I cannot express enough thanks to my family for their continued support and encouragement throughout this project. Please bear with me until I wrap up this five-book series.